and the previous HAMMETT and
HERODOTUS Awards-winning novels
featuring Maj. Abel Jones

OWEN PARRY

REBELS OF BABYLON

HarperTorch
An Imprint of HarperCollins*Publishers*

HARPERTORCH
An Imprint of HarperCollins*Publishers*
10 East 53rd Street
New York, New York 10022-5299

Copyright © 2005 by Ralph Peters
ISBN-13: 978-0-06-051393-1
ISBN-10: 0-06-051393-4

First HarperTorch paperback printing: March 2006
First William Morrow hardcover printing: March 2005

10 9 8 7 6 5 4 3 2 1

To my sister, Annie,
who turned up unexpectedly on the levee,
waiting for the Robert E. Lee

The spirit of the master is abating,
that of the slave rising from the dust. . . .

—THOMAS JEFFERSON

REBELS OF
BABYLON

I CHASED THE NEGRESS with the snake through the door of the Ursuline convent. We plunged into the courtyard and the cold, accompanied by the shrieks of girls and young women. Nuns converged from distant parts, fluttering and furious, calling upon the Lord and a host of angels. Their outrage called to mind the Afghanee disturbed at his depredations, and I hoped they understood that the negress, not myself, had committed trespass against them.

The place was Bedlam, pure.

I should have thought nuns fearful of a serpent, but every one showed plucky as a mongoose. They hiked up their skirts and rushed toward the two of us, baring their teeth.

Perhaps they sought revenge for all that apple business.

Well, if the snake failed to frighten the nuns, I must say it worried me. Hissing over the shoulder of the negress, it feinted and jabbed, bead eyes fixed on my face. A veritable accomplice, that serpent was, yellow and brown and anxious to keep me off.

I hoped it was not poisonous.

Had I been able to close the distance between myself and the negress—not two yards as we ran—I would have given that snake a whack with my cane.

Abundant of girth and short of leg, the woman barely

eluded me. But my bothered bones do not let me go as fast as a fellow likes.

Girls in demure uniforms fled our path, screaming with such abandon that I began to suspect at least a few were enjoying themselves. Nuns charged, with crosses swinging over their bosoms. A large dog added his barking to the confusion, but stood unsure of which leg deserved his bite.

Just ahead of the negress and myself, a black fellow old as Methusaleh stood with his hand on the gate. He looked thrice as befuddled as the dog.

"Shut the gate!" I called in a tone I had used in my sergeanting days. "Shut the bloody gate, man!"

The negress waved a stubby arm, making some queer sign. The old fellow looked as frightened as a child.

"Shut the gate!" I pleaded.

I fear my own figure was not as imposing as that of my corpulent quarry.

A nun placed herself astride the snake-woman's path, clutching her cross and beads as she extended a delicate hand to interdict us.

The collision did not even slow the pace of the negress. The nun flew into the gatekeeper's arms, as if she had been struck by a runaway omnibus.

I nearly grasped the fugitive, just before she burst into the street.

"Halt!" I shouted. "Stop in the name of the federal government, you!"

She did not heed me. Or give a backward glance. She was all forward motion, like a locomotive got up to speed along its tracks.

Now, Chartres Street is not the city's busiest, at least not at the end where the convent sits, but traffic enough there was in that dirty lane. Along the walks, women in vast crinolines formed moving ramparts courtesy dared not breach.

The snake undid them.

A tumult erupted the likes of which have seldom been seen or heard upon this earth. The uproar may have been equaled at Babel, or, perhaps, at Jericho, when Joshua's clarion notes collapsed the walls. The cries surpassed those heard in our sack of Delhi.

But let that bide. The damage done to New Orleans that noontide threatened to surpass a cannonade. You might have thought the devil himself, and not a snake-charming negress, come plowing through the throng.

Women fumbled and tumbled, bellowed and wailed, swinging their nicety bags until they battered each other to swooning. Market baskets flew skyward, defying Mr. Newton, and bottles and sacks of every sort fell underfoot. The *marchandes,* as they call the negresses who peddle goods from baskets perched on their heads, were most of them quick to secure their wares and fade into a courtyard. But one poor coffee-colored lass, who balanced a great pyramid of popped-corn balls, was struck from behind and flattened. A swarm of boys and beggars—of both there was a plenty, in every hue—scrambled to snatch her treats, cramming them into their snouts without remorse. In the midst of it all, one grizzled pilgrim found himself run over by a dog cart.

A navvy leapt to intercept a tender young lady's faint, harboring her in his burly embrace in a manner I thought suspect. As if surrounded by robbers, an elderly gentleman thrashed about with his walking stick. And a barber rushed out, armed with a razor and towel.

Not one of them managed to slow the she-devil's progress.

Cold it was, although I had ever been told that New Orleans burns torrid. Bitter and raw, with smoke creeping down, not upward, from the chimneys, it might have been a January in Wales. Yet, I was in a sweat, that I will tell you.

"Stop her!" I bellowed at the wide world, in all its embarrassed confusion. "Stop that woman!" But the wide world paid no attention.

When a witless troop of damsels threatened to block her flight, the negress lofted the serpent from her shoulder, unraveled it from her neck, and dangled its startling length in front of herself. The snake curled and whipped, sweeping womankind before it.

Ladies and their lessers fled into the mucky street, clawing and clambering over each other, treading on hems and tearing at seams, while slapping their slower sisters out of the way. Those who were not cursing and spitting like veteran fusiliers, wailed as we must believe their Sabine sisters did at fortune's ebb.

Horses reared and carts collided, wheels interlocked and harnesses got in a tangle. A buckboard of fish on slabs and oysters in barrels embraced a lamp-post, feeding the street with slime. Two drivers went at each other with their fists, encouraged by men and ladies alike, and a rough-looking lad swung a board at the warring pair. I regret to say harsh language was employed.

The negress carried all the field before her. Pumping along on short, determined legs, she threw off so much sweat it seemed to be raining.

I spotted a pair of our Union boys ahead of us, guarding a doorway with bayonets fixed and ready.

"Stop that woman, stop her!" I commanded. "You there, private! Stop her!"

As she approached, the negress howled at the soldiers, offering them a generous hint of snake. One of the lads leapt back with so much vigor he drove his comrade through a milliner's window.

"Stop her! *Stop her!*"

Queer it was. No man was man enough to interfere with her. And ladies were unlikely to be enlisted in my support. The negress might have been Leviathan, the way she split the waves of mankind before her.

They all seemed oddly afraid, not just surprised. As if there were more dangerous matters at hand than just a snake.

A pair of grimy sailors—ever worthless sorts—leaned at a corner and watched us. As my quarry rushed past, trailed by my Christian self, one of the tars remarked, "Now don't that just beat all, great God Almighty?"

The negress dashed between converging vehicles, a fancy brougham and a wagon piled with cotton bales. How she did it I cannot say, but the creature confounded the teams and their harnesses, blocking my path with a wall of horseflesh and leather.

Bales began to spill into the thoroughfare.

"Stop . . . that . . . woman!" I shouted, although I could not even see her now, with the vehicles barring me like a stockade wall.

I rushed behind the lacquered brougham, which to my wonderment bore a couple whose race looked as suspect as their riding-out garments were elegant. Searching for the broad back of the negress amid the chaos, I slipped on a pile of equine slop and nearly took a pratfall for my trouble.

I fear intemperate words escaped my lips.

Just as I righted myself from my stumble, I glimpsed the woman a pistol shot ahead.

The nature of the street began to change as we charged along, with ever more shops in evidence beneath the curlicued galleries. The crowds on the sidewalks thickened,

Frenchy-looking the lot of them, with a sort of dandified shabbiness to the men and a gadabout air to the ladies. If ladies they were. Negroes mingled freely among the fair, along with others of origin indeterminate. Boys whistled and dogs pestered.

The fugitive's progress transformed the scene. Man and beast flew out of the woman's way.

A sensible man might have quit the chase, considering the damage already done. But Abel Jones is not a quitting man.

The negress plunged through the multitude. I followed as swiftly as my thankless leg allowed, struggling to hurry along in her wake before it closed up again.

Frenchy protestations let me know that I was far less welcome than the snake. "Creoles" do not care for Union blue, see. And we had neared the ramshackle heart of their quarter, an ancient town around which the city had grown.

Perhaps they would have respected a Punjab cobra, a nice twelve-footer.

Little boys made fun of me as I went. Although most were more intrigued by the disquiet of the horses and the inventive curses of teamsters yanking on reins.

A gussied-up fellow gave me a wicked look, brushing off his dove-gray topper after it paid a visit to the gutter. He jabbed a finger toward me as I passed, complaining about a "shappo" or some such matter.

I saw the woman turn from the pavings and flee beneath an archway. With her serpent back on her shoulder, on the look-out. I hastened along, certain that I had marked her course precisely.

She had fled down a narrow passageway, a corridor of brick walls beneath low vaulting. It stank of convenient usage by the multitude.

I tapped and crabbed my way along, avoiding the clots of

waste as best I could. The tunnel was so narrow I could hardly imagine my quarry, who was a woman of some abundance, fitting herself through it. Twas so close overhead even I had to crouch as I went.

The passage opened into a barren rectangle about the size of our parlor back in Pottsville. The new, larger parlor, I mean. In Mr. Evans's house, which had come down to us.

And I found myself flummoxed.

The negress and her snake could not be seen.

Yet, there wasn't a single door.

Nor a window. Nor a stairway.

Not a ladder and not a rope.

Not even a cellar chute.

I marked where openings once had been. All were filled up with brick so old it crumbled.

There wasn't so much as a drain in that little yard.

Now, women do not simply disappear. Not even negresses intimate with snakes. And well I recalled the hidden doors of the Maharanee's palace, behind which Jimmy Molloy played peek-a-boo until he nearly fell in a pit of spikes.

I tested the walls for hidden levers or catches, but nothing gave or moved. Next, I rapped along the bricks with the hilt of my new sword-cane, listening for cavities. When that failed to produce any hint of a gap, I tapped at every flagstone in the courtyard.

Twas queer as a barking cow, her simply vanishing.

Look you. I am not often wrong about such matters. And certain I was that the negress had fled down that particular passage. I will admit to suffering a toothache. But that does not affect a fellow's eyes.

It made me short-tempered, though.

I looked up yet again, in anger and frustration. The height of the yard was two stories at the rear and three on each of the other sides, with the outline of a cistern visible over the lip of a pediment. Had I spotted so much as a piece of string, you might have convinced me, at that point, that the woman had climbed it assisted by her serpent—before making her escape by dancing over the rooftops. But all I could see were parapets of brick, a few trails of smoke, and the gray clouds overhead.

It made no sense, not the woman's disappearance nor the purpose of a courtyard without so much as a kitchen door or a window. The place was as blank as the deserts of Baloochistan.

Half an hour before, I had possessed no inkling that the negress and her serpent were part of this world. Events had converged with great suddenness. I had applied for an interview with the senior officer of the Ursulines, who I believe is called the "mother superior," in response to a note slipped under my hotel door. Encouraged I was to visit the convent to ask about a servant who disappeared. Now, the provost marshal had reports in plenty of negroes unaccounted for. Twas almost an epidemic. The judgement of the authorities was that most had simply absconded, for the colored races are most of them unsteady. But the note submitted to me tied the missing servant girl to Miss Susan Peabody, late of Albany, New York, whose murder had provoked my trip to New Orleans.

I had been admitted, grudgingly, to the little room at the front of the convent that serves as a receiving room for gentlemen. The mother superior's greeting had lacked enthusiasm as decidedly as her English lacked vocabulary. I was sitting there and trying to make out her meaning, prodding my rebellious tooth with my tongue and doing no harm to man nor beast nor Catholic, when I heard a great rumpus behind me.

Those nuns talk French, which I do not. But when I heard that screeching and shrieking rolling through the halls, I knew things were not square in any tongue. It sounded like Mr. Milton's Pandaemonium. If not worse.

Just as I rose to investigate matters—relying rather more on my cane than I liked—the negress rushed past the open door, a one-woman swarm, trailing an imposing length of snake.

"La femme diabolique! Marie Venin!" the old nun gasped, lifting both sleeves Heavenward and revealing withered forearms. She shouted that I should "arrety" the intruder.

Well, I did not understand her Frenchy jabber, and the English with which she had greeted me was quits. But plain enough things seemed. The trespasser was a thief, or something worse. So off I went, knocking over a chair and a coatrack, leaving my greatcoat and cap behind, chasing a black woman wider than she was tall, who was garbed as an African gypsy and wielding a snake.

The commotion inspired thereafter would require an explanation to our authorities.

All my bother had gained me was that courtyard, bleak and featureless, with one way in and out. The snake-charming negress had disappeared like a wraith.

I gave up all hope of solving the riddle immediately. Covered in sweat I was, yet chilled to shivering, and nagged again by toothache. And the courtyard reeked to a puking, forgive my frankness.

Never one to shilly-shally, I turned back to the passageway to leave. And heard metal slam against masonry.

I wheeled about, expecting to see a ghostly door yawn before me. But nothing had changed in the yard.

Twas then I got the old shiver down my spine. The one that warns of danger before it strikes.

I realized what had happened, of course.

Still, I had to look.

At the streetward end of the passageway, someone had shut a solid metal door. I did not need to test it to understand that I had been locked in the courtyard.

I was now the quarry, not the hunter.

I DID NOT know that I had foes in New Orleans, yet in hardly a week of residence I had excited enemies in plenty. As I would learn. It is a town where nothing is as it seems, where smiles devour.

I spent an hour alternately banging on the metal door, bellowing for my release by any passerby, and stamping about in the courtyard, hugging my sodden shirt and tunic against me. It took that long for my enemies to gather, see.

I never even heard them. They dropped the net from a rooftop as I strode about complaining to myself. Its weight made me stagger as its meshes covered me.

Before I could respond in any manner, someone played artfully on the ropes and I found myself on my back, caught like a fish.

Next, I was hanging upside down, unable even to stretch out my arms to shield myself if dropped.

Laughing at the ease of their catch, they began to haul me upward. My well-being failed to concern them. I bounced off the bricks like a ball of India rubber.

Before I could get my bearing, a crew of rough-handed fellows pulled me over the parapet and dropped me onto a flat expanse of roof. Glimpsed through the mesh, my captors were black and white and every shade in between. But one among them drew my especial attention. He was a giant. With a pattern of scars on his broad, flat, caramel face.

There was no sign of the snake-woman.

"Give 'im the whiff, just give 'im a whiff right quick," a bearded white fellow cried.

In a moment, I smelled ether.

I wriggled most ferociously. It would have been wisest of them to give me a crack on the head with a club, as they might have done a flounder. But they seemed determined to put me out with fumes.

The mesh held me so tightly I could not defend myself. Still, I twitched about as if having a fit.

I had one hope, see. I needed them to release me from the net. For when they harvested me, they caught my cane, which contained a lovely blade within its shaft. Properly armed and on my feet, I was ready to take on all the rogues in the world.

"Get 'im, Pie! Jes' conk that there dwarf-man over his haid."

"Watch he don't bite, now."

A son of Africa tried to wrestle me flat. Larger than me by half, he still could not quite fix me. And no one helped him. Look you. At times it is a blessing, being made small. For those of greater stature underestimate you.

"He jes' ain't got no give-up in him, Tiny," my wrestling partner grunted. "He slippy as a cottonmouf."

Each time the drug soaked rag approached my face, I forced the netting away from me, twisting and turning.

"Just get him out of that damned fish-trap," someone said. "You can't get at his muzzle like that. He got you all foxed. Get that net off him, Pie."

"Jes' help me hold him on down," my assailant demanded. "I can't do bofe things to once."

"Laissez! Laissez!" the giant snapped. "You make yourself a fool."

Miraculously, they began to loosen the meshes.

When he knows you have come close enough, the cobra does not hesitate to strike. Nor does a veteran soldier, given a chance to survive.

Before they realized themselves how loose the net had become—and while it still veiled my face—I discarded the sheath of my sword-cane and jabbed the nearest fellow in the groin. Not deeply, you understand. I did not want the blade getting stuck when I needed it. And two or three inches of steel will take your enemy from the battle, if the tip is properly placed.

My victim howled to wake the dead. My blade had come as such a surprise that the lot of them stopped their doings and wasted a moment looking from one to the other.

By the time they bore down again I was on my feet and free of the net's restraint. I slashed the bearded fellow across the face, meaning to splash as much gore as I could. Only the boldest soldier can ignore the copious flow of his own blood. Then I pierced a yellow man's belly. Low, where it gives the most pain.

I had no wish to kill them, see. Not unless they insisted. But I could not afford to be gentle with my kidnappers.

Twas then I made a mistake. I should have kept on cutting human meat. Instead, I took time to kick over the bottle of ether. I booted it back toward an open hatch in the roof. It struck wood and shattered.

The three brutes who remained untouched by my blade produced a collection of weapons that lowered my hopes. Two of them—the giant called "Tiny" and a bald, brown fellow with a glass jewel in his ear—drew cutlasses they had concealed on their persons. In defiance of the provost marshal's regulations, I must add. The third produced a billy as long as a bayonet.

They attempted to encircle me. Employing needless profanity all the while.

I had to avoid the three men already down, in case one might regain sufficient possession of himself to trip me up or take a knife to my legs. Nor did I wish to entangle a foot in that net.

Jimmy Molloy would have laughed to see me jigging about that roof.

I backed toward the parapet over which they had hauled me in. It promised a three-story fall.

The fellow with the glass earring charged me first. Bullies they were, not trained to fight as partners. This lad was the sort who swings a blade wildly, pressing the attack with all his vigor, but with little strategy, expecting simply to overwhelm his opponent. We clashed our steel but twice before I hopped aside, bad leg or no. As he stumbled past, I swept my blade across the small of his back.

He tripped and fell forward. Smashing his jaw on the parapet.

Bad though his situation looked at the moment, he seemed the sort to get back up for another go. I would have liked to give him a proper sticking, but his comrades did not mean to spare me the time.

I lunged for the fellow with the club, forcing him backward with the tip of my blade, then wheeled about on my good leg. Just in time to parry the giant's cutlass.

He had real might in those arms, that big mulatto did. The force of his blow near astonished me. Glad I was that my blade did not simply snap in two, thin as it was and so light compared to the cutlass.

He had more skill than his underlings. Wise enough he was to know that a small man's blade can kill as easily as the lance of the tallest Johnny Seekh in the regiment. He chopped at me as if cutting cane, forcing me backward without exposing his flesh.

He was giving the fellow with the club the chance to maneuver behind me.

"Oh, Jeezis Gawd," a supine figure called. Twas a stunned cry. An instant later, flames rose at the giant's heels.

The fellow whose groin I had pierced had struck a lucifer match. I do not know whether he meant to burn his pain away, or to attempt to close the wound or to purify it. But the match had ignited the ether or some other substance dormant upon the roof.

The poor, black bugger rose, a man of fire, clothes and hair as vivid as the sunrise.

I nearly lost my poise, remembering another figure, a woman, who had become a creature of flames not long before, back home in Pennsylvania. But that has naught to do with the tale I must tell you.

Twas another woman entirely who had brought me here. A sad, young lass who had washed up dead and embarrassed on a levee.

The burning man hurled himself from the roof, as if he expected cooling waters to greet him. He screamed until we heard his body strike. After which we shared an instant's silence.

The roof was afire, burning like thatch. My enemies regrouped. The kidnapper with the slashed back and smashed jaw had got up on his hind legs again, while the belly-stuck devil produced a Bowie knife, clamoring for my blood between his groans. Staggering toward me, full of spunk. Only the fellow whose face I had slashed, half-blinded by his own blood, failed to rally. He merely tried to crawl away from the flames, struggling to gain the hatch in the roof and escape.

Four of the devils stood arrayed against me, although I might have claimed a fifth to honor the giant's size. Each and every one in a terrible temper, they pressed me toward the rear of the roof. What lay beyond, I knew not.

The fire urged them on, and they urged me.

The scars on the giant's face formed the oddest pattern. As if his skin had been carved up with a purpose.

I eyed that hatch in the roof. Twas bothered by flames and behind the big fellow's back. But it was the only way off the roof that did not promise broken bones or worse.

My best chance was to surge into the attack, to dart past the mighty mulatto, slashing as I went, then hurl myself through the opening and take my chances.

The fire's appetite grew. My assailants crowded me.

My plan come to naught. They rushed me, four at once, before I could charge them. I parried madly, retreating toward the horizon.

From the middle distance, a woman's voice cried "Fire!" Another voice at once took up the warning. Still others joined in, shouting, bellowing, screaming.

As I stepped back toward the edge of the roof, a feminine shriek rose behind me, seconded by a chorus of terrified wails.

The fellow with the club made the error of looking toward the voices for an instant. And got his nose slashed open for his folly.

He dropped his weapon, staggering backward into the fire's embrace.

Male voices called out *"Fire!"* now and church bells rang to summon up the water carts. Indeed, the old cathedral's towers were in plain view above the flames and smoke.

The giant aimed straight for me, brushing aside my blade with the ease of a drill instructor tutoring a private.

I had to step me back to avoid his cutlass. And I took a step too far.

The women's screams redoubled as I fell.

I dropped hard, but not far. I landed on a sloping roof and immediately slid downward. Still clinging to my blade, I struggled to dig the fingers of my free hand into the roof. Rotted through, the shingles broke into bits.

I believe that, at such moments, we are supposed to review our lives. And I had much to review. But all I could think of was how foolish I had been to leave my Colt revolver in my room at the St. Charles Hotel, all because I had not wished to offend the Ursuline sisters with a firearm.

Well, that is the reward of proper manners, I told myself, as I went over that second ledge on my way to the earth below.

I bellowed.

Abandoning my blade, I grabbed at the roof and gutter for dear life. But the roof was as weak as putty, the gutter was rusted through, and everything I touched seemed to disintegrate.

Now, I believe that those blessed to own property have a Christian responsibility to keep things in good order. But that afternoon I had reason enough to be grateful for the disrepair of our Southland.

Just as I was about to spill into space again, the gallery collapsed, dropping me onto a railing just below.

The railing gave way in turn.

Now, I am a Welshman and made robust by nature, but I took a nasty bruising, all the same. Still conscious, I found myself with the wind knocked from my lungs and with just enough of my torso sprawled on a porch to inhibit my continued fall.

A dismayed negress stood over me, wiping her hands on an apron as broad as a sail.

"Y'all done growed yo'self a whole *pas*sel of troubles, white folks," she observed. "Bustin' up Cap'n Dev'ro's back-porch roof . . ."

I meant to advise her of the fire above us, which seemed to me a matter of greater concern, but the giant mulatto swung down from a beam before I could speak.

With a howl, he raised his cutlass.

The servant granted us privacy.

I had no choice but to drop again, with a blade slashing at my forearms.

My cascade ended in a delirious instant. I crashed through the weak upper branches of a tree and stopped, nearly impaled, on the limbs below

My old bones were unhappy, that I will tell you. The age of thirty-four is too advanced for such a fuss.

The giant leapt into the tree behind me. Swinging his cutlass and calling me names—not a few of which sounded French and nasty—he might have been Goliath in his prime. Branches split beneath his weight, but the limb below mine caught him.

He roared as he yearned toward me with his blade. The fellow seemed determined to hack off a limb or two, preferring mine to the tree's.

I struggled and twisted to free myself from the grip of branches grown fond of my trousers. Increasing the confusion, a host of female voices, close at hand, screamed their delight and dread. They seemed to be choosing favorites, like Mr. Gibbon's Romans at a spectacle.

Church bells pealed across the quarter. For all the din about me, I heard cracking whips, galloping horses and mad shouts in the distance.

Scrambling onto one of those fancy galleries, all iron-work and ornamentation, I found myself surrounded.

A bouquet of women pressed against me, as distinguished by their various scents as by their many complexions. Their stems were uniformly the white of undergarments.

Twas not an abode of virtue.

Ruder than I am wont to be to the gentler sex, I pushed my way through the pack of them, limping the worse without my cane and angry at the the world for all its contrariness.

Mr. Seward had gotten me into a pickle this time. With his habit of doing favors for the rich men of New York.

A burst of screams just at my back announced the giant's arrival on the gallery.

I hurried through a warren of rooms whose daytime shabbiness longed for evening's shadows. Hurling myself down the first flight of stairs I saw, I found my path blocked by a missy and her gent.

They were on their way up to a randy-voo, but I had an even more pressing need to go down.

I plowed right through them. With some violence.

But look you: That fellow was white of hair and beard and should not have been there at all, corrupting those girls. And he certainly should not have been there in the daytime. He was old enough to know better and should have been home reading sacred texts, while pondering the journey that loomed ahead.

His enchantress gave me a slap as I plunged past.

Steps thumped just above me. The lass I had just out-brazened screamed for dear life.

Still, I was close to safety. I had the front door in sight. And I did not think our battle would be continued in the street before the public.

The giant hurled himself over the banister, landing square in my path.

In the moment it cost him to regain his footing, I wheeled about and fled into a parlor.

Fear swept through me the instant I crossed the threshold. I thought I had been ambushed. Two heavy figures loomed, one to either side of my path. In the amber twilight of a large receiving room, with heavy drapes drawn and no lamps lit in welcome.

But the figures did not move to intercept me. They were ancient suits of armor, of the sort preferred for general wear in the works of Mr. Scott. Guarding the interior of a fancy house.

I tore a pole-axe from the mitt of the figure on my right, toppling the clattering hollowness in my haste. When the giant burst into the room, eyes bulging as a dog's will in its fury, I stood there waiting with a proper weapon.

As a once-respected instructor of the bayonet, I felt my confidence renewed.

The huge mulatto roared and seized a halberd from the other knight.

We two went at each other, neither in the mood for taking prisoners. My opponent was not unskilled and possessed the advantage of height and weight. But I had relearned my footing after my misfortune at Bull Run. Give me a weapon whose length resembles that of a musket with bayonet fixed, and I will give a proper account of myself.

For all of our clanging and thrusting and banging, neither of us got our blade-end on the other. Although I gave his fingers a nasty whack.

But I must not claim that the parlor was left undamaged. He swung at me and gutted a massive grandfather's clock. In drawing his blade out again, he toppled the device over a table decked with plate.

I missed a few attempts on his life, but slew a long couch draped in Turkey carpet.

As we were cracking and clanging and baiting each other amid the wreckage of springs, split wood and slaughtered china dogs, a woman appeared in an archway at the rear of the room. She had hellish-red hair upon her head and an old, single-shot dragoon pistol in her right hand.

She lifted the weapon and fired in our general direction.

"Damn-yankee sumbitch worthless nigger no-good two of yuz," she explained.

Yet, our interview in that "sporting" house was polite and calm compared to the uproar in the street without.

"Ya git jus' git damn yuz all and stay git goin' to be hell to pay Champ Boulez sees this mess kill yuz both an' spit on your no-good graves," our hostess elaborated.

She then produced a second pistol and fired that one, too.

By George, she winged the giant well enough to spin him about and spill him over a chair.

I moved to take my leave, discarding the pole-axe with as much gentility as the press of events allowed.

"Ya just come back here damn-yankee sumbitch worse'n Spoons Butler who said ya'll could leave worthless blue-belly who's to pay for all this mess not that no-good nigger, hear?"

Good manners are ever of value. Had I paused to excuse myself, as a gentleman should have done, I might have fared far better.

Instead, I took myself off like a guilty boy, dashing for the front door.

They awaited me in the hallway, just beyond the parlor.

Two grim survivors of our rooftop clash. Seizing me with greater respect than they had paid me previously, they slammed me against the wall and plastered the rag over my mouth before I could rally.

The ether finished me.

two

WERE I A BETTER Christian, I would have found solace in prayer as death approached. Instead, I kicked against the masonry, shouting to bloody, blue blazes.

The first thing I did when I woke was smack my head. Erupting from ether dreams, I nearly knocked myself unconscious again. My only salvation, if such it was, lay in the meager distance between my prickly bed and the ceiling of my prison. Twas hardly a pair of inches, as my forehead learned.

The stink come to me next. Twas gagging ripe. I would have twisted onto my side to keep myself from choking, but when I tried to roll over I found myself shut in so snugly I could not shift my person. I was caught between old bones and the roof of a tomb.

That is where I regained my senses: inside a burial vault. When I turned my head to the slight degree I could manage, my lips met a skull. With shreds of leathery flesh still clinging to it. I could not see in the blackness. Twas darker than the Maharanee's cellars where we slaughtered her bodyguards after their surrender. But a man knows a skull when he meets it, tooth to tooth.

I had been buried alive. Shut in with bones and rot and rags, piled up so high they pressed me against the roof of the narrow crypt. My arms had but a few inches of freedom.

My final breaths would be fumes off rotting corpses. The thought put my lingering toothache in its place.

Were I a dishonest fellow—which I trust that I am not—I would tell you that I thought of my wife and son, of the child due to us soon and of Fanny, my ward. And, perhaps, of one last person, lost irreparably.

The truth is that I thought of Abel Jones. Of myself and of none other.

I was afraid. I am not certain I had ever known such fear as that terror of suffocation among the dead. My pride and manliness quit me and I wailed. Kicking as best I could with good leg and bad, I hurt myself but did the tomb no damage.

As I struggled, desperate and incapable, ancient bones gone brittle snapped beneath me. Splinters poked through my clothes like impatient fingers.

Cornered by death, I was a maddened animal. Our greed for life is stronger than we know.

I began to gasp.

The tomb was air-tight as a cholera coffin. My tantrum, which had accomplished nothing else, robbed me of dear minutes of breathable air.

Forcing my body to calm, I lay as still as a living man could do. Even amid decay and bones, each instant of life remained precious. I hoped, although there was no hope. And I raged against my weakness and the world.

The truth is that I even failed to pray. I did not think of it.

It shames me now to think how unready I would have been to go before my God. After such a graceless end. I did not ponder that sweet Beyond, but only thought of here and now, of living.

I am unworthy to call myself a Methodist.

The air thinned further still. My lungs began to rule my body, trying to lift my torso, contorting me in their famished quest for sustenance. I banged my head again and bruised my limbs. Using up still more of that reeking necessity.

I wanted to *live*.

The only prayers I said were spoken with fists and feet against the masonry walls.

Twas my comeuppance for the sin of pride, for thinking myself a steady, courageous fellow, firmer than others. The hunter of tigers fears the lowly worm, as a *fakir* once told me.

Choking, dying, with lungs in disbelief, I imagined that I heard voices. Dreaming that I felt blows at the wall of the crypt.

Twas then that I began to pray at last. I had failed to call upon Our Lord to save my soul when I was doomed to perish. But now I called upon Him to save my life.

I tried to cry out, but could hardly muster a voice.

I felt as if I were collapsing inward and exploding at the same moment. My lungs burned. Gulping nothing. Rot. Stench. Gagging down the filth of my companions.

I began to twitch madly, yearning for air, that cheapest of commodities.

Then I began to die.

I DID NOT understand what had happened at first. I felt the rush of cold air before I realized I was breathing. Gulping life.

A voice said, "God amighty, drag him out of there."

Hands began to tug me by the ankles. A great mess of bones chased after me as they drew me free of the tomb.

"Peeeee-*yooo*!" a soldier complained as he embraced my falling body. I had been sealed into a vault set high and we tumbled earthward together.

A muddle come over the lot of us. We found ourselves

sprawling, adorned with death's forget-me-nots. In a landscape of granite and marble, of whitewash and brick.

Twas the queerest place this side of a heathen temple. Lit by the lanterns of the rescue party, a jumble of tombs crowded round. Their architecture ranged from the humble and low to masoleums so elaborate they must have annoyed our Savior's sense of propriety. My intended deathbed had not been among that warren of crypts, however, but in a space built into a wall as thick as a Punjab battlement. A taller man would not have fit without first being dismembered.

Now, when he has been buried alive, a fellow requires a moment or two to collect himself. I was at sixes and sevens, and beg no pardon for it. Much of the world remained disordered, as if devils were playing a parlor game with time, mixing up the counters to confuse me. I trust that I mumbled my gratitude to those who had saved my life and I saw full well that their uniforms were of the same hue as mine own. I even recognized the necropolis for what it was, although twas of a different order than the one in Glasgow where we had a fuss.

But I am not certain I knew what I was about. The queerest thing it was. I grasped that I sat upon the earth of New Orleans, yet I hardly understood how I had gotten there and seemed to have but the weakest grip on the moment. Memories that had eluded me in the tomb swept over me now. I did not know if I was a child in Wales, or a fusilier putting paid to Johnny Seekh, or a broken-hearted fellow in Lahore.

And then I did something I am not wont to do. I turned over and retched. As some fellows do in battle's lulls, although I was never that sort.

Perhaps my organs were purging themselves of bits of

death breathed in, of particles of the sort described by that Greek fellow, Mr. Aristotle, whose estimable works I had read on my voyage down from Baltimore.

The soldiers rose and cleansed themselves of the debris as best they could. One succumbed to panic, slapping at himself and leaping about, anxious to separate his person from death's adhesions.

The officer in charge of the party, a captain with an unfamiliar face, bent toward me.

"You all right, Major? God amighty, I swear. You were yelling like Hettie with her skirt on fire. God amighty."

"Captain . . . you have me at a disadvantage."

My attempt at good manners baffled him, for he was from Iowa, as I come to learn. And Iowa is a wild place, fit only for the undemanding Swede and dull Norwegian. As for myself, I had been studying the formal ways of a gentleman since my recent increase in fortune.

"Who are you?" I asked directly.

I remained a bit short of wind, seated still in the slop and wreckage of death.

"Simon Peter Cincinnatus Bolt," the fellow told me. His air of recitation conjured schoolrooms. He had a sturdy, presentable face that bore no special burden of intelligence. "Captain Sim Bolt, mostways to folks. Pleased to make your acquaintance."

He half-saluted, tipped his hat and extended a hand to draw me to my feet.

Having lost my latest purchase while tumbling from that roof, I was again without a stick to help me. The loss angered me, that I will tell you, and not only because I found a sword-cane useful. I had spent a painful amount— so much I am ashamed of it—to replace my first such implement, which had been given to me by a curious fellow in Scotland. I had left that blade in an old madwoman's bowels.

But that is another tale.

In furnishing myself with another stick, I had indulged my vanity in Philadelphia's second-best shop for gentlemen, a luxury I never should have allowed myself.

Funds should never be squandered on pride, as any Welshman in his senses will tell you.

"God amighty, you're one lucky man, Major. One lucky man. Swear to God, I really do. You just don't know how close you came there." Of a sudden, his face pruned with doubt. "You *are* Major Abel Jones, aren't you?"

He underwent a moment of discomfiture. As if he might have rescued the wrong major entirely. As if the cemetery were positively thick with majors buried alive and he might have wasted his efforts by saving the wrong one.

I began to suspect that his candle did not burn quite so brightly as an officer's should. Yet, he seemed a good-enough fellow. And in John Company's regiments in India, a drop of noble blood in the youngest son of a bankrupt country squire was thought a more useful quality than intelligence. Twas especially so in the lancers, where every sort of thinking was discouraged.

"I am Major Abel Jones," I assured him. "Now if —"

"Well, thank God for that much, just thank God down on your bended knees, Major, that's all I can say. I never heard of such a thing in my life. Swear to God. Never once in my life. Had to make the men here do all the breaking in and busting up after those darkies ran off. Just threw down their shovels. Darnedest thing I ever saw or heard. Don't know what goes on in their heads half the time."

He grimaced at mankind's deficiencies. "Pulled up in the wagon and half of them took one sniff and started talking loony about some Marie Venison or somebody. Two blinks, and they're gone, quick as a nickel at the county fair. Just plain gone, the half of them, without a wave goodbye. I got the rest inside here, complaining every step. After that, I was all busy trying to figure out how this place is organized, working my way down to where they had you sealed up. And God amighty, if the rest of them didn't start hollering and run off, like they just saw Kingdom coming their way and didn't much like the look of it."

He shook his head. "Grabbed one by the arm. Swear to God, I never seen a man so afraid. Not even at Gaines' Mill. No, sir. When I asked him what the dickens, he started jabbering about some brown gal floating in the air and clawing at the tomb they got you shut up in. He was scared half white." The captain grimaced. "They're *all* crazy down here, black *and* white. And every shade in-between. All of them. Swear to God. Every useless one."

I owed him gratitude as my benefactor. But I found his language wanton. The name of Our Lord is not mere punctuation.

"How on earth did you even know to look for me? Or where?" I asked.

The events of the day swirled about me and my legs opposed my desire to remain upright. My toothache, having fled at the prospect of death, returned to haunt the living. Although I was glad to be alive, I was not at my best.

"Who sent you to rescue me?" I demanded. I had grown a bit cranky, now that I was safe. "Who told you where I was?"

The captain nodded to himself, recalling his own excitements.

"The fat man," he said.

* * *

THE BULLET MISSED me and spared Captain Bolt. But a soldier just behind us tossed up his hands at the sound of the shot. He called for his mother as he fell, then sprawled on the ground as only the dead can manage.

It was the lad who had been so anxious to dust off the scraps of death.

"Stay here!" I commanded. A hint of battle brings me to myself, see. I snatched a rifle and cartridge belt from the stacked arms of the detail, collapsing the rest. "Put out those lanterns," I called over my shoulder. For I was already off at a run, bad leg or no, scuttling down the lanes between the tombs.

First, I had to get me deep in the darkness, into a realm where the marksman and I would be even. I have a good sense of direction and sought to work my way toward the killer. Perhaps he had already fled, if other gates there were in the boneyard walls. Wise snipers do not linger. But if he had been fool enough to stay, I meant to bag him.

The moon had not come out to flirt, so the lonesome dark embraced me. Treacherous the going was, for some of the tombs were cordoned by low rails with cast-iron spikes. A fellow saw the paleness of the crypt, but not its shadowy guardians. Such reverence for the dead was hard on my shins and I took a nasty spill that near impaled me.

Still, I know how to make my way in the night far better than most. I learned my skills from Johnny Seekh, then polished my talents in the Afghan hills. A man whose feet cannot find their way in silence does not live long in the East.

A wilderness of stone it was, dense and disordered. But I was certain that I had my bearings. I lowered myself as close to the earth as I could without crawling on my hands and knees. Dragging my disloyal leg behind me.

And I listened.

The rustle of a city late in the evening reported life beyond the boneyard walls. I heard the crack of a whip, then whinnies and creaking wheels. Struggling to fix my ears on closer matters, I found that I was panting like a beast.

And then I heard a boot scrape over gravel.

I stood to fire over a low vault. The world exploded with light.

My quarry had lit a torch. Hurling it from behind a tomb, he meant to spoil my vision in the darkness. To allow himself the next shot.

I dropped back to the earth with one eye shut. A bullet nicked the crypt where I had stood.

The shot had not come from my enemy. One of the soldiers behind me had fired the round.

Twas my own fault and I should have known better. They were not proper veterans. Nor could I trust the quality of their leadership. I had told them to remain behind. But I failed to tell them to let me do the shooting.

The torch crackled on the earth. Just beyond the vault where I was kneeling. If I stood up, I would show myself to both the sniper and my fellow soldiers. And likely earn a crossfire for the risk.

Whispering stronger language than is my habit, I crawled away from the sputtering torchlight, embracing the ground like a native scout in the Khyber.

I heard footsteps. Fleeing.

The gunman would have his back to me. I took a chance and rose, rifle locked back tight against my shoulder.

I saw his shadow in the dying light. But before I could aim, another bullet bit the marble wall behind my head.

Again, it issued from my fellow soldiers, not from mine enemy.

I could not call out to tell them to hold their fire. That

would only give me away to my quarry. Instead, I scuttled along like a seashore crab, dropping the hammer on the rifle so I might use it as a stick to help me.

I was unwilling to give up the chase, although my own comrades, having rescued me earlier, now seemed anxious to send me to my reward. Lucky it was they were not better marksmen. I do not think that Jimmy Molloy or I would have missed our target at that range.

My heel crunched broken pottery. Loud as gunfire.

Another bullet struck nearby. Close enough for worry.

Now, that was queer. Whoever had confused me with the gunman could not hit me with the help of a torch, yet had the skill to hunt by the sound of a footstep.

Had I not seen the haplessness of those soldiers with my own eyes, I would have thought at least one of them meant to hamper me.

I had no time to ponder matters further. Another scamper of steps teased me, farther away than the last.

The assassin meant to escape us now, although he had delayed doing so at first. Why might that be? Had my pursuit surprised him? Or had he paused to make good on his kill? If so, why did he fail to fire again?

I did not doubt that his shot had wanted my life, not that poor soldier's. But why on earth would a killer have been lurking to take my life, when I had already been sealed inside a tomb? Had I been fated for release from my live burial all along? If that was the meat of the matter, why go to the trouble to cook it up so grandly? Only to have an assassin kill me anyway?

And what did this have to do with the late Miss Peabody?

My mind was running much too fast and without sound direction. Time there would be to think such matters through. I had to concentrate upon the chase.

The gunman was seeking a gate in the boneyard wall. I felt it with every awakened instinct soldiering had given me. My only chance of taking him was to guess where the gate might be and cut him off.

I moved in measured dashes, as we did whenever my old regiment cornered Afghanees. Going back to ground before the enemy risked his powder. Or, in this case, before my fellow soldiers could shoot me.

I sneaked around a crypt and saw the gate a pistol shot distant. Twas hanging open. Lamps shone in the street beyond.

But I had revealed myself in silhouette. A shot punched the air at my shoulder.

I did not drop to the earth that time. For it seemed to me that the shooting was being done by a single marksman to my rear. Who always missed me by about the same distance.

My fellow soldier would need time to reload. And that time was mine.

I ran for the gate, rifle at my waist, as I had charged on the field of Chillianwala. My scarlet coat was gone to the moths and I had a bit of a limp. But the spirit of a fight bids a man to wonders.

I closed on the gate and wheeled about to welcome my would-be assassin. His form loomed up the same instant. Running for dear life along the wall.

For a fatal second, he stopped. Surprised to meet me.

And he did the oddest thing. Instead of trying to shoot me dead, he raised his rifle to wield it as a club.

I shot him. Amidships, as they say. Twas done by training and instinct, not by choice.

Down he dropped. A shadow tumbling backward. When a man falls thus, the bullet has met his spine. His weapon clattered upon the gravel path.

"Over here!" I shouted. "Don't shoot! I've got him! Lads! Over here, by the gate! Bring the lanterns!"

I kicked the rifle farther from the fallen man. Holding my weapon ready to crush his skull, should his fingers hint rebellion.

"Vodu!" the fellow moaned in terror.

He sounded like a dying man. And he was.

I knew not if his speech was French or something even worse. But his tone was plaintive, begging. You might have thought him a dying Christian begging the Lord's attention.

"Vodu . . ." he repeated, weakened by the expulsion of the syllables.

"Water, is it?" I tried. "Do you want water, man?"

The humility in his voice declared him no more threat to me.

"Vodu . . . li Grand Zombi . . ." he whispered, with sweet life quitting him.

The soldiers clattered up. Their lanterns fought the darkness.

At last, I saw the fellow whose life I had shortened. Twas a negro with skin the hue of a well-cooked sausage. Terror ruled his eyes.

As the lads closed round, I saw him ever more clearly. His face was tattooed with swirls and dots and hachures. He much resembled the giant with whom I had enjoyed a tiff that afternoon. Although this poor fellow was smaller.

A lantern shifted. And the negro saw me.

His dying eyes swelled. Struggling to raise his shoulders, he yearned to flee, as if he had met the devil face to face. But his body was quits with him. Its final vigor was spent pumping blood from his torso.

"Book sand corn!" he cried. His eyes were horrid, locked in a stare with mine own. *"Book sand corn!"*

Then he died.

"You got him, all right," Captain Bolt informed me.

I resisted the urge to give him and his men a lecture on firing by night when unsure of their target. It would have been ungracious, under the circumstances. After all, they had freed me from a tomb. And no harm had been done. Except to the negro.

"Wouldn't want to be on your bad side, no, I wouldn't. Swear to God," the captain told me. "Let's us get out of here, all right? Get you back to where you can get rid of them stinking clothes. Boys can take care of the nigger. Shooting at white men like that. And us wearing Union blue, down here to save 'em. Swear to God, they're every one of them crazy."

He moved toward the gate. But I did not follow him. There remained an aspect of matters that made no sense.

Unless he is a mighty fool, a fellow with a rifle fires it before he uses the weapon as a club.

"Bring the lantern closer, you," I told one of the privates.

"He still alive?" Captain Bolt asked, turning back to the pack of us, impatient. He lacked the dutiful nature an officer must display and doubtless longed to return to his cakes and ale. For all I owed the fellow, I could not like him. But plenty such there were in the Union Army. Men whom war had overtaken as they counted sacks of flour or curried mules. Men who lacked the urgency for soldiering. They filled our ranks, but barely filled their uniforms.

"No, Captain. Dead he is. As dead as a salted cod. Still, he may have something left to tell me."

First, I inspected his weapon. It was a proper rifle, one of our own, manufactured in Springfield, Massachusetts. But it was, as I had suspected, empty of ball and innocent of a cap.

Yet, the fellow had only fired once. All of the other rounds had come from behind me.

"Hold the lantern just there," I pointed.

The dead man's pockets were sopping with gore, but I found what I thought likely: Nothing at all. Unless I count a pair of copper coins and a queer sort of charm.

"Guess he's not going to tell you much, after all," Captain Bolt said.

I nearly contradicted the fellow, but caught myself in time. There is often a good deal to be said for not saying a good deal. And I had learned a curious thing, indeed. The negro assassin had only possessed a single round for his rifle. Nor had he carried additional powder or caps.

I did not believe his poverty was the reason. The rifle was fine and new. Someone had given it to him. But they had not seen fit to arm him with more than one bullet.

It made no sense. Unless his employers believed that his marksmanship rivaled a tiger-hunter's. And why on earth had he failed to run away after that first shot? He must have been given lunatic orders without the power to refuse them.

Of course, that happens in armies all the time. But one expects better judgement of assassins.

What had his employers meant to achieve? If they wanted me dead, why not give the fellow more bullets? Or why not leave me buried in that vault and be done with the matter? Why seal me up, then send our soldiers a message likely to save me?

I use the word "employers" because I could not see why such a fellow would bear me a grudge that spurred him to a killing. Nor should he have known about my living burial. He had been sent by master puppeteers who knew more than I had the wit to ask.

I felt as baffled as Lazarus must have been when he rose from the dead.

All such matters would have to wait. The captain was correct that my clothes were stinking. And my tooth was nagging again.

"No," I agreed with Captain Bolt, "the fellow had nothing to say to me. It is right you were. And now I think I might do with a proper wash."

three

MIRACLE OF THE modern age, the baths in the cellar of the St. Charles Hotel welcomed a fellow with roiling, boiling water straight from the tap. The mighty edifice shook from top to bottom when the engine ran below and the rumbling might have been mistaken for gunners at their trade on the field of battle. But the water ran hot and not too brown, and the St. Charles baths were as lovely as Heaven on Sunday.

I would have been content to lie in that tub for an hour complete, had a hand not reached through the curtain.

A snake dropped into my bathwater. Rather a large one.

I cannot say who was the more discomfited, the serpent or myself, but when that writhing creature splashed between my legs, I leapt like an Irish girl at the sound of a fiddle.

Perhaps the water's temperature confused the snake. Whatever the cause, its brief addlement saved me. My leg just cleared the bath as the serpent attacked.

Its fangs struck metal, which must have been disappointing.

Now, I will tell you: I have seen the cobra flare its hood and did not like it, but I never saw such a creature as that snake. When it opened its jaws to strike, its maw puffed up like a dirty gunner's swab. You might have thought it was puking a ball of cotton.

Its hiss was nasty, too.

I hastened to put some distance between the two of us, but the curtain I opened concealed a solid brick wall. My entrance had been accomplished on the other side and the snake, which I judged a proper seven-footer, had taken possession of the tub in between.

My state of undress was conducive to neither courage nor ingenuity.

The serpent reared its muscular body. Dripping bathwater, it fixed black eyes on mine.

I did not even have a towel to hurl at it.

Twas one of the rare times in my life when I knew not what to do. And that made twice in a day. The cabin was barren of places to hide and the snake commanded each avenue of escape.

It was about to strike.

Behind the serpent's head, the curtain parted again. I looked at the new intruder in amazement. So startled I was I near forgot the snake.

The serpent winced at the commotion, delaying its strike by a second. In that blessed interval, a derringer pistol appeared between sausage-like fingers and shot it dead.

Exiting the creature's skull, the ball nearly caught my leg.

The snake collapsed with a splash. A portion of its body draped over the lip of the tub, slowly withdrawing into the spoiled water.

I hardly glanced at the serpent's final twitches. My attention was devoted to my rescuer, whose rotundity paused halfway inside the curtain.

"Mr. Barnaby!" I said, astonished.

"Begging your pardon, Major Jones," the gentle fellow answered, "begging your pardon most terrible. I doesn't like to intrude on a gentlemen at his ablutions, I don't. It ain't quite the thing. But I 'eard you cursing like a jockey in a race what ain't been fixed and wondered at the commotion."

"Mr. Barnaby," I said firmly, "it is grateful I am, see . . . but I do not think I cursed."

Surprised I was by his presence in the city. I had not seen him since the previous spring.

Embarrassed by his error, my acquaintance looked away. "All's one, sir, all's one. My 'earing ain't what it was and I admits it." He gave the snake another glance. "The St. Charles 'as 'ad a comedown since the war began, sir. Standards ain't what they was."

As for my Christian self, I had begun to wonder whether the citizens of the "Crescent City" kept snakes as pets, the way decent folk keep dogs. The creatures seemed ever-present. Then I recalled the condition in which I stood before my acquaintance, reminiscent of Adam before the Fall—another business that involved a serpent. There was greater cause for Mr. Barnaby's embarrassment than his misapprehension of my speech.

The snake was dead, but my rescuer looked agitated.

"Pardon me, Mr. Barnaby," I said, "but might there be a towel out there?"

His remarkable physiognomy quit my sight.

I must remind you of Mr. Barnaby's history. He had been a gentleman's haberdasher in the very city where we stood that night. Until the Yellow Fever took his family. Thereafter, he lost his spunk and lost his business. When first we met, in the shocked weeks after Shiloh, the fellow was a gentleman's gentleman in service to a Confederate of good family.

An excellent doer at table, Mr. Barnaby was confident at the hip. Shaped like a ripened pear, he was not slovenly fat, but stout and strong. His beef rode high in front. It looked as if a cannonball were about to explode upward through his waistcoat. Bald but for a fringe of chestnut hair and long of face with a plump nose misattached, his person made no proper sense, but seemed randomly collected, if abundant. He was a good-natured fellow who killed without dismay, when events required.

English-born though he was, we had grown fond in the days we rode together, pursuing killers who claimed to act for God. But that is another tale. When last I saw him, Mr. Barnaby had enjoyed a wound to his posterior, which invalided him from the field for uncertain months.

As I heard his footsteps returning, I recalled that Captain Bolt had said "the fat man" had been responsible for my rescue.

Had Mr. Barnaby saved me twice in the course of a single day? That was a heavy debt.

He had retrieved not only a towel, but also the clean uniform I had left with the bath attendant.

Averting his eyes as a gentleman should do, Mr. Barnaby tossed me the cloth then looked over my uniform, inspecting the stitching and trim. He did seem in a state of some anxiety.

"Lovely work!" he declared. "Fit for a very general! Why, when I 'ad my establishment on Canal Street, I 'adn't no more than two tailors I could call upon to do such sewing as this 'ere."

"It is my own wife's work," I told him proudly. "My Mary is become the proprietress of a grand dressmaking establishment."

Now, you will say: "Since when is your wife's dressmaking shop so grand? We thought it was a small affair in Pottsville." But I will tell you: Grand enough it seemed to me, and a fellow must not insult his dear wife's efforts. And truth be told, who among us does not like to put the best face on matters?

"Lovely work, just lovely! And, bless me, not a single drop of blood on any inch of it!"

"Why," I asked, as I rubbed myself down and the serpent gave a jerk, "should there be blood, Mr. Barnaby?"

His eyebrows lifted as if to say the matter was self-evident. "Well, the fellow who 'ad the night duty was brushing down your kit when they cut 'is throat. Gashed as wide as a melon carved with a butcher's knife, 'e is. They must've been wicked quick, sir, for I didn't see nobody as I stepped in myself." He looked at me, disregarding my condition of immodesty. "I must say, begging your pardon, Major Jones, that you does seem to leave an unreasonable number of corpses behind when you visit us."

"Mr. Barnaby . . . I must ask you a thing. Did you report to the authorities that I had been buried alive?"

He shook his head. Bewildered. "No such thing, sir! No such thing at all!"

I was befuddled. "But . . ."

"All I told 'em," Mr. Barnaby said, "was that you 'ad been kidnapped from a 'ouse in the *Vieux Carré*. Couldn't 'ardly believe my eyes, when I seen 'em dragging you out of Miss Ruby's salon, as we likes to call it. Couldn't 'ardly believe it." He shook his long head until his belly trembled. "At first, I thought you might 'ave 'ad a few sips too many and made a bit of trouble for the ladies, requiring a certain amount of physical restraint. But then I remembered 'ow you was always going on about John Wesley and Methodism and other such dreadful matters, and I began to suspect that something wasn't quite right between Brighton and Bristol. After I saw Petit Jean come down the steps, 'im bleeding like an Irishman's 'eart at the sight of an empty bottle, I knew you 'adn't found New Orleans welcoming."

I wished to inquire as to the identity of "Petit Jean," who I supposed must be the giant negro. But Mr. Barnaby had grown extraordinarily agitated. He searched my uniform as if two hands were inadequate.

"Something wrong, is it?" I asked him.

He raised a worried face. "I can't find it," he told me. "What 'as you done with it, sir? Begging your pardon, but tell me where you put it . . ."

His demeanour was transformed. A fellow of aplomb in the midst of battle, he had grown as nervous as a lass who cannot find the slippers she meant to wear to her first ball.

"What *are* you—"

Staring at me, the fellow seemed pushed toward madness.

"For God's sake," he cried, "where *is* it, sir? We 'ave no time to waste!"

"Whatever are you on about? Surely, we—"

"The charm, the charm . . . where is it?" He did seem terribly anxious. "Petit Jean always sneaks one onto 'is victims, for good measure. Did they put anything in your pocket? Around your neck?"

"You mean that stinking little bag?"

"That's it, that's it! What 'as you done with it, sir?"

"I threw it away. It was oozing powder and—"

The poor fellow took such alarm I feared he would swoon.

"Dear God!" he bellowed. "We 'as to find it. Quick, sir."

"It was just a filthy, little sack and—"

"Where is it, sir? I begs you. If you wants to wake up in the morning!"

"It's in the dustbin in the changing room. Just down the hall. As soon as I—"

He hurled my uniform at me, launching himself back

through the curtains so fiercely I thought he would tear them from the railing.

"Dress!" he shouted behind himself. "For the love of God, get dressed, sir!"

It all seemed rather a fuss.

As I was pulling my trousers high and snapping up my braces, my rescuer reappeared between the curtains.

His face was pale as fresh milk in the bucket. He held out a little satchel, just the size and shape of a human finger. Holding it at his arm's full length, as if it were a thing he feared to touch.

His voice was quieter now, cut to a whisper. "We 'as to go. 'Urry up, sir."

"Mr. Barnaby," I began, "you *must* calm yourself. You said a fellow has been murdered. And someone made an attempt on my life with that snake. There are matters I must attend—"

Twas the queerest thing. When I tried to draw my right brace onto my shoulder, my arm refused to obey me.

Mr. Barnaby watched as I struggled to make my limb behave.

"Dear God," he whispered. "It's already begun."

MY REBELLIOUS HANDS were fussing with my buttons as he pulled me from the hotel's lower entrance, straight out between the shut-up shops and beneath the pillars that aped a Roman temple.

He did not so much select a cab as seize one. Forcing me inside, he followed after, depressing the carriage's springs by at least six inches. He slapped shut the door, then thrust his head back out through the window leathers.

"Bayou John!" he cried, "By the shell road, past the race course. I'll tell you when to turn off."

"Twice the fare for them parts," the driver said. "Night-time, too."

"Go!" Mr. Barnaby ordered. "Drive, man! *Go!*"

The coachman whistled. "Hoo, she must be sumpin', yes, sir!" He gee-upped his horse and the cab rocked into motion.

Returning his attentions to my person, Mr. Barnaby said, "This ain't good at all."

"Mr. Barnaby," I began, "while I appreciate your concern for my well-being, I assure you that my arms are simply cramped. I've been through more than is sensible today, with falling off roofs and and buryings and such like. I will be fine in the morning, when I am rested."

"You doesn't understand!" he cried. "If you ain't dead when the sun comes up, you'll be paralyzed and worse!"

"My dear Mr. Barnaby—"

It was the queerest thing. My tongue had begun to swell. And my throat tightened. Forming words grew difficult, which is a hard fate for a Welshman.

A realization struck me like a cannonball.

"Poison . . ." I managed to say, with a new and terrible fear sweeping all through me. I had seen it turn men cholera-black in India.

Mr. Barnaby pitied me by the flicker of the cab lamp. "It's worse than that, it is. If only it was poison alone, we might put things right with a call on the apothecary."

I wished to tell him I would not believe any nonsense about spells or charms or spooks. But my powers of speech were disarmed.

The cab rattled and banged along streets that declined in quality. Sentinels at a guardpost made us halt, but when they glimpsed my rank, they let us pass. It seemed to me a lax defense for a city.

The road grew so rough I feared the cab would break its

springs or even shatter a wheel. Yet, Mr. Barnaby urged the driver to greater speed. We rocked through the darkness, unhelped by the moon, and only Providence spared us a frightful accident.

My companion leaned out of the window almost constantly, tilting the carriage.

"There, there!" he cried of a sudden. "Turn into that yard!"

The cab jounced to a halt, with the driver cursing.

"I ain't going in there," he told Mr. Barnaby. "And I ain't going any closer. That's one of them nigger hant-woman houses. Ain't it? Anyways, it's too sumpy."

Mr. Barnaby did not waste time on argument, but dragged me from the vehicle. My good leg had begun to behave as meanly as the bothered one. I gasped for breath and my arms were utterly useless.

Royally frightened I was by then. At the thought of poison seeping through my veins.

"Oh, dear, dear!" my friend remarked.

"That's fifty cents," the cabbie hollered. "Not including the—"

"Wait there! " Mr. Barnaby snapped without breaking his stride.

He moved with such haste that he almost seemed to carry me. I saw the outlines of a shack and the hint of a glow behind some window rags.

"Don't let on that you 'as any reservations," Mr. Barnaby whispered. "Don't say a word what might be taken ill . . ."

He had no cause for worry. My mouth was sealed as if I had the lockjaw.

"Madame Bette! " he called toward the shanty. *"Madame Bette! C'est moi, Barnaby! "*

Now, that was French, a language I don't trust. I did not like the way things were developing.

"Can't you walk any faster?" the fellow begged me.

I grunted in the negative. I could hardly walk at all.

A woman appeared in a doorway, lofting a lantern. A negress she was, of the sort they call a "mammy." Wearing a ragged dress and a turban dishevelled.

With a great sigh of effort, Mr. Barnaby lifted me onto the porch and set me down before her.

Her eyes widened. *"Perdu!"* she muttered. *"Il est perdu . . ."*

"Nothing of the sort," Mr. Barnaby said, in a voice that had changed utterly. He sounded as confident as a banker's banker. "You can put 'im right, Madame Bette. I says to myself, I was saying, 'There's only one woman in all Loosy-anne can put this one to rights, and that's Madame Bette.' I've been telling 'im all the way 'ere not to worry."

The woman's features gathered toward her nose in consternation.

"Been crossed good, eh?" she asked me. I believe I detected the faintest hint of a laugh. "You been crossed *terrible, monsieur.* Cost you gol' money, not just jingle-silver, lif' that crossing off you."

"Spare no effort!" Mr. Barnaby told her. "Spare no effort, spare no cost, Madame Bette!"

Now that is the sort of thing no sensible Welshman would ever say, poisoned or not. A fair price for all must be agreed in advance of any undertaking. But my ability to interject myself was limited.

Mr. Barnaby held out the stinking bag my abductors had tied round my neck.

The woman's eyes showed their whites again.

"Marie Venin," she muttered. "That's her work, how you been crossed." She grew excited, like Mick Tyrone, my doctor friend, at the sight of a challenging patient. *"Allez, allez!"* she called, rushing into the shanty.

I blush to tell you what I next experienced. The woman's abode might have been the lair of one of those *fakirs* who haunt the lanes of Lahore. Stinking it was, with smells ineffable to our Christian noses. By the lantern's cast, I saw the skins of every sort of reptile, dangling from the ceiling to dry or nailed to the walls in bunches. Jars and pots of every shape competed for space on tabletop and floor, along with plaster statues not a few of which had strayed from a Catholic church. An advertisement for a steamboat line hung beside a cloth stained red with symbols recalling the village mosques of the Punjab. A newly skinned cat lay over a bench, its black pelt drying beside it.

Without warning, the woman tossed a handful of dust in my face. Then she began to chant:

> "Walk on needles, walk on pins,
> Papa Limba, wash our sins . . .
> *li Grand Zombi, li Zombi Grand,*
> *vaincre, vaincre, Marie Venin . . .*
> *l'homme perdu, l'homme perdu . . .*
> he walk on gilded splinters to you . . ."

That did not resemble anything Charles Wesley wrote.

Hardly had she finished her singing than Mr. Barnaby laid seven gold coins on the planks, forming an arrow that pointed toward a back door.

To my mortification, the two of them undressed me.

"Begging your pardon," Mr. Barnaby said, "there ain't time to be modest."

I might have interfered. But my every limb had stiffened and my tongue was beyond speech.

A devil of a time the two of them had, though. For I had grown stiff as a musket barrel. They had to sweep the dead

cat from the bench and lay me down to draw off my shoes
and trousers. Impatient with all niceties, Mr. Barnaby took a
knife to my underclothing. That was a terrible waste. The
garments were almost new.

The queerest thing it was, though. I seemed literally of
two minds. The right and proper part of me dreaded the
coursing poison, yet clung to some last instinct of propriety.
A darker side hushed every fear, seduced by a peculiar
warmth sweeping my body. Twas almost like dreaming, although I remained awake. I began to feel that dying might
not be unpleasant.

My state was rude and shameful, but it mattered less and
less. I could no longer summon much embarrassment, although my parts had grown remarkably stiff.

"Alors!" the mammy said, after considering me.

They ferried my rigid form over the gold pieces. After
that, Mr. Barnaby tilted me backward while the woman
forced a potion into my mouth. Grim enough that was. But
she was not finished. She had Mr. Barnaby turn me over so
that she might introduce the cure elsewhere.

"Papa Limba, lif' the cross," the woman called ecstati-
cally, "man be saved, the gol' be lost . . ."

Together, they hustled me to the rear door. Then Mr. Barnaby dragged me into the darkness.

He tied a rope around my naked waist.

"You've really 'ad the finest luck," he told me. "Couldn't
'ave picked a better time of year for it. The mocassins is all
tucked up—your bath-mate, notwithstanding—and the alligators move wonderful slow in the cold. You'll be in and out
before any 'arm can come to you . . ."

At that, the fellow heaved me over his shoulder, carried
me down a reedy slope and hurled me into a watercourse.

I sank.

The thing of it is, I am not much of a swimmer. Even when my limbs do not dissent.

Icy water closed over me. I seemed to descend forever. Yet, it cannot have been more than a few, crushed seconds. I stopped face down in heavy mud and grasses. With no air in my lungs.

Something happened. Twas like the slap across the recruit's face that calls him back to duty on his first battlefield. My arms and legs thrashed back to life. The frenzy was almost miraculous. I fought and splashed and thrust and found my footing.

Mick Tyrone could doubtless have explained it all, how the shock of the freezing water vanquished my lethargy, how the mammy's potion had conquered the poison through some knack of chemistry. Spells and such like had nothing at all to do with it.

The water was not deep. In moments, I was drinking the cold night air, feet planted solidly near the "bayou's" shore.

Mr. Barnaby tugged on the rope, nearly spilling me over.

"I can extricate myself now, thank you," I called toward the bank.

"Lovely, sir, that's lovely," he said. "But you might wish to 'urry a bit. The alligators ain't so slow as all that."

Hurry I did.

As I climbed onto the cold mud of the bank, dripping and shivering, I sought to hide my shame from the mammy's lantern. But she cackled, "You cain't cover no big ol' thing like that with one little stubby hand."

I turned about to free myself of the rope. Twas wet and stiff and slimed.

Mr. Barnaby assisted me. Still, we took some time undoing the knot.

"It hardly seems to have been necessary," I observed as the rope fell away.

Mr. Barnaby shook his head and whispered in my ear, "Madame Bette's skills ain't always that reliable."

WE DROVE TOWARD the city, with the driver grumbling so loudly we could hear him within the cab. He complained of being delayed and of being hurried, of the tendency of our guards to shoot before issuing a challenge to night-time travelers, then of the poor security provided to honest men of business such as himself. He complained to his horse of wicked practices so various I doubted a single city could contain them all—even New Orleans—and he condemned our Yankee prudery.

We passed the sentinels again. For a second time, my uniform went our bond. As the city's humbler lights appeared, I turned to Mr. Barnaby.

"Surely," I said, "you don't believe in that sort of thing. Voodoo, or hoodoo, or whatever it may be called. Science can explain everything. It was all a matter of nervous electricity, of chemical transactions and the like."

The slackness of his jowls betrayed the hour, which had slithered past midnight. Truth be told, the fellow had undergone some exertion on my behalf. Dubious though his methods may have been. I was not ungrateful, but troubled.

"It ain't so much a matter of what I believes," he told me, "but only of what works, begging your pardon. I wouldn't say as I *believes* in any of it, not yours truly, Barnaby B. Barnaby. But it always seems to me a fellow should keep 'imself alert to possibilities." He sighed, wishing to give me satisfaction. "I looks on life as a business proposition. Not in your mercenary sense of the word, Major Jones. But as a system of trading back and forth, of going to one shop for a certain good as one requires, but to another for something entirely different. One for bottles, one for boots. You might just say I took us to the right shop, that's 'ow I'd put it."

Glad of my recovered powers of speech, but nagged again by my dull, insistent toothache, I said, "You seem to know a good deal about such matters." My tone was not as nice as I would have liked.

He shrugged. Even widened by his coat, his shoulders were markedly narrower than his waist. "Oh, I does and I don't, sir. I learned a good deal from my little Marie, bless 'er. Never was finer woman born to man. I miss 'er still, I does."

"You mean that . . . you allowed your wife . . ."

"All's one, sir, all's one. Marie was . . . oh, I'm not ashamed to say it, I ain't. 'Er background was mixed, if I was to put it politely. Not that you'd of knowed it, sir. Not that anyone made a fuss. Looks is what matters in our fair city, looks, not facts and other trivialities. French she looked, so French she was, and mum's the word hereafter. But she 'ad a wild streak in 'er, sir, and I wouldn't of 'ad 'er different by an inch." He sighed again and slumped. "Oh, she kept me 'appy, sir! 'Er and the little ones. And if a man's kept 'appy, what more can 'e ask?"

That was a lax philosophy. Though not without its point, that I will give you. For happiness is rare enough among us.

"Lucky you was, though, sir," he continued. "That spell was put upon you by no less than Marie Venin 'erself, who is second only to Marie Laveau the Elder. The Widow Paris, as some calls 'er. It's a blessing that Madame Bette was 'ome and not drunk to an excess."

"Mr. Barnaby, I realize that conditions are . . . somewhat different here. The French influence, no doubt. But was that woman worshipping the devil? Who did she call on? 'Papa Limber?' Is that Satan?"

"Oh, no, sir! Not the devil at all, sir, not at all! I wouldn't 'ave nothing to do with that sort of thing, at least under general circumstances. Papa Limba's only St. Peter. You must 'ave seen the statues. They prays to 'em just like us regular folks."

"Well, since you have a degree of expertise, Mr. Barnaby, perhaps you can help me understand some matters."

"I should be glad of it, sir. Indeed, I would."

"This evening . . . after I was rescued from the tomb . . . there was a violent affair. A darky spoke to me as he lay dying. I recall it clearly, astonishingly so. He said 'Vodu.' Thrice. His mother's name, perhaps?"

"Oh, no, sir. Not at all. Vodu's their snake-god. Out of Africa, 'e comes. That's why they've always got a snake somewheres about, the women who take up as priestesses. A *voudouienne* can't do 'er work without 'er snake to 'elp 'er." He rolled his stomach forward. "Vodu, 'e's the god, although there's others. Voodoo's the practice of worshipping 'im. And a few other things besides that don't bear mentioning."

"You said there was no devil worship."

"There ain't. Not exactly."

"But . . . a snake-god? What could such practices have to do with St. Peter?"

He rolled his head to one side, then the other. "It all becomes a merry bit of a muddle down 'ere, Major Jones. Folks ain't particular that way. They take what suits, in life and things thereafter. An altar rail's fine for the morning, but they don't mind a bit of voodoo after dark."

"That's paganism!"

"No, sir. That's New Orleans."

"All right, Mr. Barnaby. I will not argue. Not now. But back to the dying fellow, the negro. After he called upon this . . . this false god . . . he gazed at me by the lantern light. Just before life left him. And he said the queerest thing. He looked at me and said, 'Book sand corn.' Now, what do you make of that? Their religion, too, is it?"

My companion was mystified. By the inconstant light of the carriage lamp, his face took on an expression of thought unrewarded.

"Book sand corn," he repeated, testing and tasting the words.

"Exactly."

". . . book . . . sand . . . corn . . . I must say, I've never 'eard the—"

The fellow sat up. Straight as a grenadier. Although the light was untrustworthy, I do believe his face paled beyond white.

"You said . . . you said 'e looked at you, sir . . . then 'e said, 'Book sand corn.' That's what you said?"

"Exactly. What's the matter, Mr. Barnaby?"

"Le bouc sans cornes . . ." he whispered. You would have thought he was staring down the devil and starting to falter.

"But what does it mean?"

"Le bouc sans cornes . . . oh, dear." He leaned toward me, belly preceding the advance of his arms and head. "It's French, sir, that is. It means 'the goat without horns.' "

"A goat without horns? You mean a sheep, perhaps?"

The poor fellow shook his head gravely. "No, sir. That ain't it. It's a human being. Usually, it's a babe they takes. But on special occasions they chooses themselves a man. As a sacrifice to the snake-god." He leaned closer still. "And you said the fellow was looking right at you?"

four

*M*R. BARNABY SHOUTED NEW instructions to the driver. We clattered over cobblestones, making a frightful ruckus, but I heard him speak of the "Roo" St. Philip, by way of the "Roo" Dauphine.

As my companion dressed the bench with his abundance again, I said, "You told the fellow to drive us to the French Quarter. My hotel is on the American side."

"Right you are, sir, right you are. No time to be wasted."

"Mr. Barnaby . . . I have had a tiring day and must report to General Banks in the morning. Grateful I am for all you have done, but—"

He shook his head. "Won't wait, sir. We've got to visit *Père* Champlain this hour, and not a breath wasted! They won't stop trying to kill you and otherwise acting unfriendly, begging your pardon. Only *Père* Champlain can 'elp us now."

All I wished was a bit of rest and a proper shave come morning.

"And who," I asked, "is Pear Champlain?"

"*Père* Champlain, sir? The Americans . . . those what lives on the other side of Canal, I mean, calls 'im 'Papa Champ.' But it's Père Champlain what's 'is proper name, and so 'e's called by them what admires and respects 'im."

"But who *is* the fellow? It must be two in the morning. Why on earth must we—"

"*Père* Champlain's neither this nor that. 'E's a little bit of everything. But if anyone knows what's going on, it's 'im. I'm counting on 'is mercies, sir, since 'e's always taken a most peculiar liking to me. Of course, I *was* the one supplier of gentlemen's articles and conveniences what come up to 'is needs and standards." Mr. Barnaby succumbed to a moment's revery. "Such times we 'ad, before the Yellow Jack spoiled 'em . . ."

"He's not another of these voodoo fellows, is he?"

"*Père* Champlain? Not a bit of it, sir, not a bit of it! I do believe 'is brother was a Jesuit. Although there's them what might not see the difference. *Père* Champlain's a splendid fellow, known to all what knows. A secret's not a secret in New Orleans until *Père* Champlain's 'eard it twice."

We turned into the old city. The smells grew worse and the look of the creatures haunting the shadows turned grimmer.

"Won't the fellow be sleeping at this hour?"

"*Père* Champlain?" Mr. Barnaby looked at me in surprise. "Not at all, sir, not in the least! I doubt 'e's even sat 'imself down to dinner." Registering my confusion, he explained, "'E don't much like the sunshine anymore, sir. Says it's bad for the digestion, at 'is age. I dare say 'e likes the quiet after midnight. The better to 'ear things what doesn't wish to be 'eard."

Twas clear that Mr. Barnaby would not be discouraged from helping me and I hardly had the energy to resist. I sat back and tried to put my thoughts in order, coddling my tooth with my tongue. It had been an unruly day and I must say that I did not like New Orleans. Even after the sack of

Delhi, the natives were kinder disposed to us than the creoles were to soldiers in blue coats.

We passed into a curious street of cottages packed together. In one doorway, a colored lassie stood thoughtlessly in her nightdress, holding a candlestick, as a white fellow kissed her farewell.

Mr. Barnaby noted my dismay. "Begging your pardon, sir, but it ain't what you're thinking. It's true love that, true love! The gentlemen keep their darlings 'ere, them as custom forbids a lad to marry, thanks to certain indiscretions what 'appened at birth. The situation's good for one and all, sir. Oh, many's the marriage been saved by a wife's blind eye. And vicey-versey."

I did not comment, but thought, instead and unwillingly, of India.

We pulled up before a well-lit house that seemed to have strayed into that forlorn street. Old it was. Although I was unfamiliar with the architecture, it hinted at a colony's early days, in the second generation, when a founding family begins to distinguish itself and spends more on appearances than is sensible. Of two stories, the establishment was not great in size, yet wore a telling grandeur of intent. Two curling staircases, one at either end of a high verandah, reached down to the street like arms stretched out in welcome. Upstairs, lamps shone brightly through the shutters. Yet, a second glance warned that the house would not look so fine by the light of day, but wanted paint and a nail or two.

Remarkably agile for his bulk, Mr. Barnaby leapt down from the conveyance. As I followed after, a hand caught me by the arm. I nearly gave its owner a lick of my fist.

Twas a negro, black as a cat and graven with service. He wore an antique livery so faded even the darkness paid it no compliments. Guiding me down, as if he knew me well, he might have been helping a matron in a ballgown.

As soon as my two feet were in the muck, the fellow released my arm, stepping back politely. His eyes evaded mine, just as the servants in India showed us humility. Whether they felt it or not.

We caused more than a creak as we climbed to the porch. Planks begged to be retired. If the proprietor of the house had not been awake, our arrival would have roused him.

We might have been expected all along, the way the double doors flew open to greet us. A pair of negro servants— ancient twins they looked—stood to either side in Regency liveries. They even wore gray wigs tied back, although the mops looked overdue for replacement.

The instant I got a look inside, I stopped myself in wonder.

Never had I seen a man so fat. Not that I wish to speak rudely of any Christian, but a wonder it was that any device for sitting could support him. Or that the floor did not collapse at once. But sit he did, beneath a chandelier, in the center of the room beyond the entry hall. He was so wide the archway barely framed him.

Broad as a young man's hopes he was, with a jolly face whose plumpness masked his age. He wore old-fashioned breeches and a smoking coat whose fabric might have rigged a Yankee clipper. Chuckling in delight at our appearance, he let his tongue's tip peek between his teeth. An antique excess of white hair, suited to the fashion of our grandfathers, waved as his body jiggled.

He consumed a good deal of the room he sat in, hardly leaving space for a scatter of chairs and a pair of service tables. The pictures on the walls showed well by candlelight, as portraits and women will.

"Mr. B!" he cried fervently, "I hardly recognized you,

skinny as y'all done got! You're wastin' away, *cher*. Folks going to think you've taken the consumption. Where you feeding these days?"

Mr. Barnaby bowed with the grace of a dancing master. Our host tilted his head and as much of his body as agreed to follow, peering around the bulk of my companion to gain himself a better look at me.

"Brought us a new visitor, I see." Mirthful, he shivered like a splendid jelly. "And if I don't mistake me, it's that spite-the-devil Yankee I been hearing talk about. The one sent down to ask us about that New York gal who washed up dead on Louis Fortune's levee." He favored me with a grin as wide as the New Orleans waterfront. "Major Abel Jones, if I'm not misinformed?"

I was nonplussed. Our authorities had assured me that the fate of Miss Susan Peabody remained a secret from the general public. Nor had my mission been broadcast on the exchange.

"Come right on in here now!" the fellow insisted. "You look like you just found out your daddy was in the circus. Don't be so surprised, *cher*. If *I* didn't know who you were, I'd swear off sugar-coffee for a week." He canted his head, reducing his laugh to a smile. "Mr. B, just bring that dashing Yankee right on in here and we'll have ourselves a brandy with our macaroons."

I declined the brandy, of course. In its place, I was provided with coffee so delicious it partly appeased my alarm at learning that my purpose was common knowledge. Nor did our host restrict himself to brandy. He took his own coffee in a cup the size of a chamberpot.

Sly and wicked, my toothache sneaked into hiding. As if it knew I would indulge myself, after which it might ambush me without mercy.

"Yes, sir, yes, *sir*!" Our host smacked his lips. "Heresy it may be to some, but I myself have been more than content to sacrifice the romance of our glorious cause for a good cup of coffee. Never saw this city so glum, as when your blockade cut down on our coffee supply. No, sir. Our dear General Beauregard hadn't reckoned on that."

Tutting over the breadth of mankind's foibles, he told us, "Young man, now, he likes a little excitement before he settles down. And a war tends to sound like just the thing to those who haven't been in one. That's all it's about, tell the truth. High spirits and stupidity. The rest is just pompous bluster. One cause'll do as well as another, for a young man, Major Jones. They were all just looking for a scrap. And now they've got more of a scrap than they reckoned on. Yes, sir. My family's seen the French and the Spanish come and go, then come and go again. Then the Americans came courting, and they wouldn't take no for an answer. But one master's good as another. Hardly matters, say what people will."

He laughed. "All this fuss over whether it's folks up in Washington or over in Richmond who pretend they're governing us. Or in Paris, for that matter. Doesn't make a spit of difference, except in the quality of the provisions. No, sir. *I* measure the success of a government by the quality of the coffee beans on offer."

The entire room seemed to vibrate along with his jollity. "Tell you a little secret, Major Jones. Tiny picayune of a secret. Folks in this city never were happier than while your General Butler was strutting amongst us last year, favoring us with his follies. Especially our ladies. Oh, I don't doubt that you've heard to the contrary. You'll hear more. But the fact is that nothing makes a denizen of this lovely city happier, more positively *joy*ous, than having somebody they can hate with an unrestrained passion. No, *cher*. Spoons Butler gave us somebody to blame for the sunshine or the rain in equal parts. He'll be missed for years to come."

I began to see that our host's merriment had inflections, that it changed like the light on a field of rye on a cloudy, windswept day. A bit of shadow crept upon us now.

"But your General Banks, *cher. He* has been a terrible disappointment. Too much of a gentleman. We're having trouble finding something we can hate about him and make stick. We like our Yankees rude and larcenous, thank you. But my fellow *citoyens* feel as if they ought to almost *like* General Banks. I dread to think what's to become of us, if he doesn't hurry up and excite our outrage. It's been building up inside us, ever since General Butler's recall. I fear to think of the explosion that's on the way."

He gobbled a biscuit of the sort they call a macaroon, a confection of sugar and coconut. Tasty affairs, those served to us were of a quality that would not have disgraced my dear wife's kitchen. I fear I ate too many, which was rude. And foolish, too. The sweetness would carry a penalty, as the many forms of sweetness often do.

"I have to wonder, Major Jones," our host resumed, as he licked the crumbs from the landscape surrounding his mouth, "why you didn't come to call on me before this? Most folks passing through come on by to say hello. You've been a guest among us how long now? Week? Two? Almost unfriendly, I'm inclined to judge it. But I suppose you've been busy with your Miss Peabody." As he spoke, one eyebrow had been rising, while the flesh around the other eye congealed. "Water downriver now. Consider yourself forgiven. But there's one thing I have to ask you, pardon my forwardness."

I was just draining my coffee cup and had not time to reply before he continued.

"Why on this here earth of ours did you go chasing Marie

Venin halfway down Chartres Street, only to get yourself
shut up in an old slave pen? Starting a fire, too. My system
of intelligence must be failing me, *cher.* I didn't know you
and Madame Venin were acquainted. Or you and Petit Jean,
for that matter."

During the conversation, Mr. Barnaby had been as silent
and respectful as a son, but he alerted when he heard our
host speak of my chasing this Mrs. Venin. Twas clear that he
knew little of events, for he looked at me as if I had just
emerged from Fingal's Cave.

He even clattered his cup on his saucer, which my Mary
Myfanwy has taught me is bad manners.

"The woman with the snake?" I asked.

The old man nodded. "So I hear tell. What on earth set
you running after our second most accomplished *vouduoi-
enne,* Major Jones? And you waving your stick at her?"

"She violated the Ursuline convent," I told him. "And appeared up to no good."

My host smiled mildly. "I suppose there might be something in that. Always suspected there was a bit more violat-
ing among the good sisters than a fellow's intended to
believe. I take it, then, your action was . . . spontaneous?
That you didn't know who you were chasing?"

Looked at through another's eyes, the vigor of my pursuit
did seem excessive. But, then, I was a sergeant for some
years, in my John Company days, and such always suspect
that others are guilty of something.

I shook my head in admission of my ignorance.

"Well, well, *well,*" Mr. Champlain said. "Mr. B here could
tell you that your course of action . . . may not have been
well advised. I do not know, Major Jones, how deeply you
are acquainted with the language of civilization and the arts,
but in my family's native tongue, *'venin,'* as in Marie Venin,

means 'venom.' Madame Venin made her reputation through her knowledge of various poisons. Concoctions even more dangerous than those forced down our throats by our doctors of medicine." He tutted. "It's said she can stir up a potion to make a man do most anything she wishes." He looked at me, one eyebrow up, the other eye narrowed again. "Now . . . what do you think Madame Venin might wish to do to you? After your . . . escapade?"

I thought of the hours that I had spent unconscious in the power of mine enemies. Time enough there had been to force a concoction down my throat, or to apply some devious lotion to my flesh.

Encouraged, I asked, "So you would say that this woman's abilities lie in her chemical skills? And not in the power of Satan?"

The old fellow laughed heartily. "At my age, *cher,* I would find it a great inconvenience to believe in Satan, given his reputation for excessive hospitality toward sinners. On the other hand, I'm wary enough of our human vanity not to assume that I know all there is to know. I'm content to sit right here and let the world entertain me. Without feeling compelled to sit in judgment on its morals or its meanings. As for voodoo . . . I never was drawn to such things myself. But I *do* wonder if somebody with a different temperament than mine . . . might not be able to make a superstition at least halfway real just by believing in it hard enough."

He grinned, then cupped a hand around one of his body's folds. "I'm inclined to wonder just how much of a person is this sullied flesh . . . and how much is the mind's talent for believing. I suspect that some of the things folks come to believe grow more real to 'em than anything you're likely to see on the corner of Bourbon and Toulouse. No, sir, if mankind has any one talent that distinguishes us from the beasts of the field, it's not our over-advertised sense of morality—which always strikes me as particular, rather than general—but our ability to believe in things we can't see. Whether we take God, Satan or our Glorious Southern Cause as an example."

He refreshed his smile, but did not force it to fullness. "Of course, I'm speaking in hypothetical terms, not as a Christian who already hears uninvited footsteps in his bedchamber. Not, sad to say, those of a pleasant-minded young woman . . ."

"Do you believe this creature wants to kill me?" I asked bluntly.

He shook his head decisively, without dropping his smile. "Not in the least, *cher*. At least, not in this particular instance. See here, now. From what I hear of the past day's events, you might have been killed a half-dozen times, then three more for good measure, if anybody really wanted you dead."

His voice grew almost serious. "If I may presume, Major Jones, I'll put myself in your place—although I fear I wouldn't fit in my entirety. If I were you, *cher ami,* I likely would be asking myself just why it is I'm sitting here, gay as can be, drinking sugar-coffee and eating macaroons, as alive as ever I was. Look at things that way, it strikes me that folks wanted to give you a right-good scaring. Nothing more. If they wanted you dead . . . well, opportunities were not lacking."

"But then . . ."

"Why frighten you half to death, then leave you alive to help yourself to another one of Auntie Ottilie's macaroons? Do help yourself, please. I should be insulted, otherwise. See here, now. You can figure out the answer yourself in another swallow or two. If your reputation is to be believed."

Twas Mr. Barnaby, not myself, who blurted out the solution. "Dear me," he said, "they know who Major Jones is and why 'e's come amongst us! And they 'ave something to 'ide, they does, something 'e's been sent 'ere to find out. But it's better for them to 'ave Major Jones in plain view, but made careful of 'is actions, than to 'ave another secret agent sent, or maybe 'alf a dozen, and them not knowing where to look for the next one. You might say 'e's the devil they already know . . ."

"Mr. Barnaby," our host declared, "you have the penetrating mind of a scholar within that emaciated frame."

It is not the most appealing situation for a confidential agent to find himself in conditions where everyone around him knows more about his lot than he does himself.

The only thing that saved me from a black-dog sorrow was the arrival of a tray of hot, sugared buns. I did not wish to spurn my host by refusing to eat my share. And the truth is that I was hungry, since I had not taken a bite since the forenoon.

Still, I did not let our host's generosity deflect me from my purpose.

"Mr. Champlain—"

" 'Papa,' please. Just suits my ears better."

How on earth could I call such a fellow "Papa"?

"Yes, sir," I said. "Now, given the extent of your knowledge of local doings . . . I must ask what else you have heard about Miss Peabody's murder."

"*Was* it murder?" he asked quickly. Resurrecting his smile, he reached one hand behind himself—not without some exertion—to scratch unseen parts. "Oh, I expect so. In one form or another. Even if a plain woman—you'll forgive me that honesty, in regard to Miss Peabody—if a plain woman were to drown herself . . . over an unrequited love, say . . . I suppose even that might be murder in a sense. With the guilt accruing to her beloved for his failure to appreciate the depth of her emotions . . ."

He paused for a sip of sugar-coffee, which he drank nearly without cease.

"Of course, the way I hear tell," he resumed, "love of that nature was not the most evident of Miss Peabody's emotions. Although still waters run deep, as they say. But let us assume that Miss Peabody's final immersion wasn't the result of an *affaire d'amour* of the sort that leads young ladies to threaten to drown themselves—though few actually do so, since it spoils the complexion. I still have to wonder if her tragic fate didn't have something to do with desire, if not with love. Understand, *cher,* I don't cast even the tiniest stone at Miss Peabody's reputation. Indeed, I hear tell the young woman was virtuous with a fury. In that sense."

I had to wait for him to consume a hot fluff of dough crowned with a snow of sugar.

"Man requires a *beignet* or two this time of the evening," our host said, "to save his stomach unnecessary suffering before dinner. Now, I don't pretend to be a philosopher, Major Jones. Although I do spend a fair amount of time sitting and thinking these days—at least sitting. But I tend to see the entirety of human actions explained by our desires. Whether we're speaking of your own desire for another of those little delicacies of ours—do have one while they're still hot—or the desire to reform the world. You'll forgive me, but I never can quite see the difference, in quality or merit, between one desire and another. They all seem to me to come from the same source, from that merciless—*merciless*—hunger within our poor souls. One man desires a fair woman, another desires gold. A third desires to be worthy of whatever deity he's chosen to scare himself with. Although I do suspect the latter of being the least worthy. Nuzzling up to God the way a dog

licks his master, no pride at all. But be that as it may. Desire
for the object of a great passion, or for earthly renown . . . or
for a new malacca cane . . . I just don't see how folks tell one
form of desire apart from another."

He lubricated his throat with a gulp of brandy. "See here,
now. Only difference between one desire and the next is
whether it's opportune. Strikes me that most folks who get
themselves murdered, here or in China, probably were the
victims of inopportune desires. Whether on the part of the
murderer or the poor unfortunate." His sugar-dusted lips
pursed to mock the world. "Tell me what a dead man or
woman truly desired, and I'll lay you better than riverboat
odds the desire's what killed them."

He recalled his welcoming smile. "But I'm monopolizing
the conversation, which Aunt Calpurnia taught me a gentleman must not do. So I'll make an end to all my speechifying
by summing things up. Young woman washes up dead—and
in *deshabille*—on a levee. It's either a case of her being the
object of an inopportune desire on the part of the killer—
which I'm led to believe may not apply in this affair—or a
case of her own desires having become inopportune to the
person or persons who took her life. Lord, I do believe this
is the first time my guests and I ever have exhausted the
household supply of fresh *beignets* at one sitting. You will
accuse me of inadequate hospitality. But *entre nous, cher,* I
believe that all you have to do is to discover—or uncover—
what it is your Miss Peabody desired above all else. The rest
will be clear as a transaction in the front room of a bank."

His gaze pierced the swollen mounds of his cheeks. "Find
out what she wanted and couldn't have. And you'll find out
who wanted her death, Major Jones. But I do hope you and
Mr. B will be kind enough to join me over dinner? Although
I fear we aren't as well prepared as—"

"Why," I demanded, surprising myself with my insolence, "would you tell me any of this, Mr. Champlain? Why should I believe you want to help me find Miss Peabody's killer? Among your own people?"

I was tired and cranky, of course. Most likely, he understood. No trace of anger appeared in his face. Instead, he smiled handsomely.

"Why," he said, "I believe it would entertain me, *cher*. It's not the most exciting of fates to sit here night after night, no matter the quality of the board or the amusing nature of my callers. But how is it you're certain the killer is one of 'my' people? Whoever they may be? Fact is, I'm the one sitting here wondering why this Miss Peabody, a young woman of notoriously uninspiring virtues, matters so much to your own people in the midst of a bloody war? I'm simply amusing myself. But what about you? Why does she matter to you?"

TWAS NOT A pleasant question to answer. And I did not attempt to answer it for my host. Disappointing Mr. Barnaby near mortally, I insisted on returning to my hotel.

Why did Miss Susan Peabody, late of Albany, New York, matter so much in the midst of a great rebellion? Only because her father was a wealthy man, and wealth bought power. I had been sent—ordered—to New Orleans as a personal favor to a rich fellow whose daughter got herself drowned in the Mississippi. It was a matter for a common policeman, not for a major in our Union Army. But the power of democracy does not rest unencumbered upon the ballot.

I did not like the business one least bit.

I had resolved to resign my commission and return to our dear Pottsville. I had not only had enough of war, but had seen more than enough of the crime war breeds. I wanted no more to do with corruption and murder, whether on a campaign or down an alley. I had almost reached the age of thirty-five, at which a man had better settle down.

There was much else, as well. My darling was with child and soon to be delivered of her burden. For all I knew, at my remove from home, a second son or a daughter might already have been born to us—God grant the best of health to mother and child.

And then there was our new fortune, to be frank. My darling and I had come up rich in the wake of a death in the family. And wealth wants attention. It will not mind itself. There was a fuss at the colliery over our coal lands. Even though Mr. Matthew Cawber himself gave matters his attention, he had far more to tend to than mining anthracite. Philadelphia claimed his first allegiance. I worried that my wife would be overwhelmed with the cares of business. Nor would she give up her dressmaking shop, but kept at that work, as well.

I had tried to refuse the journey to New Orleans. You will think me hard, but in the midst of so much death I cared little for Miss Peabody, who was unknown to me. I wanted only to live my life, surrounded by those I loved, and to be loved in return. To go to work and to chapel, all steady and sound. I felt that I had given our Union enough.

Mr. Seward went to work. Before he was done, Mr. Lincoln himself had ordered me South, with a smile that covered steel. He would not accept my resignation, but flattered me. Promising that, once the matter of Miss Peabody was settled, I might resign, if I still wished to do so.

What did I know of Miss Peabody even now? Little more than Mr. Champlain did. Yes, she was plain. On that, all were agreed. Except, perhaps, her father, with whom I had an interview in Washington. He told me that his daughter had been an abolitionist since childhood. She had insisted, against his advice, on removing herself to New Orleans in the wake of its occupation. She meant to improve the condition of the negro, an intention her father thought giddy.

"She was always a good girl," he told me. "But headstrong, Major Jones. With all sorts of addled notions about the nigger. For which, I suppose, we have Mrs. Stowe to thank."

I made the voyage down on a Navy ship. The crew watched for blockade runners and I moped. I suspected that Miss Peabody's abolitionist sentiments, once publicly displayed, had provoked some local no-good. And nothing more to it. Grumbling at the great waste of my time, I had already determined that her murder was so simple an affair a lieutenant could have unraveled it.

My assumption did not survive my first day in New Orleans. I went to the boardinghouse that had sheltered Miss Peabody. It was a dour establishment, without the enticing kitchen smells or even the cleanliness of *Frau* Schutzengel's house. Once her sympathies had become known, no genteel boardinghouse could accept Miss Peabody. And, of course, a woman traveling alone cannot seek a hotel.

The matron of the house was a native of Newcastle-on-Tyne and no Confederate. As soon as I pronounced Miss Peabody's name, she exploded my notions.

"I shouldn't wonder if the niggers done 'er in," Mrs. Crawley told me. "I shouldn't wonder at all. I never in my life met a lady nor even a gentleman what hated them so bad as Miss Peabody done."

DURING OUR RIDE back to the St. Charles Hotel, I was harsh to Mr. Barnaby.

My brain was swirling, see. And my temper had grown imperious, fueled by the mean reappearance of my toothache. The sweets had told, and my spirit had grown sour.

My thoughts careened. If Mr. Barnaby had not informed our authorities of my burial in that vault, who had? How many factions had interests in my business? Had Mr. Champlain's extraordinary propositions been right? Even in part? Or was I being led astray, by one voice then another? What had changed Miss Peabody's mind about the negro? If her mind truly had been changed? What *had* she desired, in her last days? Or in her final hours?

My suspicions began to turn nasty.

Precisely what, I asked myself, had Mr. Barnaby to do with my affairs? Why had he been helpful to an excess? If, indeed, he had been helpful. The truth was that I did not know him well, although I had liked what I knew of him. Had he abused my trust for his own ends? Was he involved in the Peabody affair? What did the fellow want from me, after all was said and done? I had seen him on his best behavior, serving his young master. But there was no sign of his master now. Why was Mr. Barnaby in New Orleans?

I began to fear I had misjudged his character.

"Mr. Barnaby?" I said.

Our cab passed the muddy meridian that separates the squalor of the *Vieux Carré* from the broader streets and cleaner habits beyond.

My companion had been drowsing. He sat up at the sound of his name.

"Yes, sir? What is it, then, sir? I was only resting my eyelids, begging your pardon."

"*Why* have you been helping me?" I asked him straight out and no nonsense. "I don't believe it's simply out of friendship."

I could not see much of his face, but I had the unmistakable sense that the fellow blushed.

"What are you after, Mr. Barnaby?" I pressed him. "What do you want from me? Why should I believe you want to help me?"

Mr. Shakespeare understood the nastiness of suspicion. He warns us of false fears, again and again.

"I'm sorry," Mr. Barnaby began, in a pathetic, pleading voice, "if I been misleading you as to my purpose, Major Jones. I meant to tell you, I did. Only there ain't 'ardly been a chance the evening through."

"The truth now, Mr. Barnaby. The truth is always best."

"Oh, yes, sir. No doubt of it, sir. As my father always said, God rest 'is soul. And 'is own father before 'im, what stood on this very ground, so to speak, with Pakenham, until they all run off together. 'The truth's always for the best,' is what 'e said to me, 'except where the ladies are concerned, in which case a man must use 'is common sense.' But that's neither 'ere nor there, sir. About the ladies, I mean. They don't 'ardly figure in the matter, as I can see."

"Just *say* it, Mr. Barnaby. Admit what you're about!"

"It's a terrible thing, sir."

"Out with it, man! Just say the words and have them off your conscience."

Of a sudden, he changed. I could feel the atmosphere shift in the cab, as if a cold wind had blown down from the Khyber, when all the winds before had blown warm from the Indus.

"It ain't nothing to be ashamed of, I didn't mean. I didn't mean that at all, sir. It's only that I needs your 'elp, and needs it terrible badly. I couldn't believe my good fortune when I seen you, sir, all trussed up like a pig for the knife and bundled into a dust-wagon. I likes to think I would've 'elped in any case, I do . . . but when I seen you packed away, I said to myself, 'Mr. B, it's your lucky day, this is! Major Jones is the very man to 'elp you!' "

"And what, Mr. Barnaby, is the nature of the help you require?"

"It's Master Francis, sir," he said despairingly. "Got 'imself captured, 'e did. While I was convalescing. Oh, I shall never forgive myself, I won't. So I come down to New Orleans through the lines. 'Oping to find a means of communicating among your Yankees, sir. Some way to 'elp the poor lad, before 'e's beyond 'elp. We've 'ad one letter telling us 'e's shut in a prison camp in Elmira, New York, and that conditions ain't fit for the lowest beast."

The big fellow reached out through the dark and laid his hand on my wrist.

"I thought per'aps, if I was a genuine 'elp to you, you might 'elp Master Francis in return. With all your 'igh connections up in Washington, of which you told us when we was riding together. I doesn't want 'im to die up in Elmira, sir. Nor anyplace else. I'd sooner die myself, than see 'im buried."

He was in tears. "I'll do anything you asks me to, if you'll only do what you can for Master Francis. You'll never figure New Orleans out on your own, sir, upon my father's honor, and that of 'is father before 'im, rest 'em both. It's like peeling a onion what's growing layers faster than you can strip 'em. You needs a fellow like me to be your guide, sir. And all I ask is that you 'elp Master Francis, once you're finished with all your murdering business."

five

SORRY I WAS TO hear of the young fellow's capture. Even though he had worn the enemy's gray. Lieutenant Raines, whom I had met in the course of a foul affair in Mississippi, was a splendid lad confounded by the times. Educated at Harvard College he was, and unlucky in love. A softly handsome boy, his charm was the sort that wins the girl, but loses the woman. Francis Drake Raines was an innocent—although he had killed other men in battle—and, truth be told, the ladies like a leavening of danger in their sweethearts. Although we think them made up of spun sugar, women have less fear in their hearts than men. Anyway, the boy was brave and silly. He fought because his fighting was expected, not least by his father, but the lad was not the sort who finds a taste for it. Perhaps his capture held a hidden blessing. He was the sort of lad that war devours, a student of theology who strayed.

"It must be 'orrible up there in the snows," Mr. Barnaby told me. "With 'ardly a blanket betwixt the sorry lot of them. And think of the terrible lonesomeness of their victuals . . ." At this, he patted his belly as if it were wounded. "I doesn't think I'd last a week myself."

"Mr. Barnaby . . . I would like to help young Raines, but—"

"Oh, would you, sir?" he cried with delight. "I calls that the act of a gentleman!"

"—I must tell you a thing. And you must listen, see. I have it in mind to resign my commission upon my return to Washington. And that will not endear me to the powerful. I can but promise to put in an honest word. It may not—"

"Oh, would you, sir? That's all I asks. That's all a gent could ask, sir, nothing more. I'll take it as a bargain at the price, a capital bargain!"

He shot his hand through the darkness and found mine.

We rolled up to the St. Charles Hotel, where gas lamps burned through the bitter morning hours. The establishment quartered a number of our officers and a scattering of soldiers affected to guard it. But the lads only wanted relief from the sullen cold. They sheltered in doorways, clutching themselves, and would not have scared off a child with a wooden sword.

I said goodnight and took me up the steps to the hotel, which looked a Roman temple in its glory. Great columns it had, and a face of solid granite. Its size might have housed a regiment, with room left over for a troop of horse. Only the Customs House, where our headquarters had been posted, outshone the place in grandeur of scale and pride.

Still, times were hard in the city of New Orleans. It did not take experience to see it. In the pre-dawn hours the lobby looked forlorn as a looted village. It smelled of old cigars and wretched feet. Two guards drowsed in high-backed chairs, their rifles tipped to the wall, while the night clerk snored to fright Beelzebub.

I was sour. My toothache had returned, like Banquo's ghost.

I do not like a toothache and would sooner consult a cobra than a dentist. The least thing makes me scold when a tooth annoys me.

I gave those sleeping guards what for, warning that better

men had been shot for less. Nor when I gathered my key from the clerk did I pretend to admire his lack of diligence.

He passed me a letter from the provost marshal, expressing dismay at the trouble I had caused, along with a note from General Banks reminding me of our appointment.

I owed our officials a proper explanation. But little there was I could do at four in the morning.

I limped upstairs, with a hand on my jaw and no cane to aid my progress. Unarmed, I inspected every shadow and hang of drapery with an eye alert to assassins. I hesitated to enter my own room.

But mine enemies had paused to rest themselves. No sign of danger hampered me in my approach to the bed I had been allotted. At a reasonable rate, I should add, with the prices watched by our military government.

My Colt was still in its own bed, deep in my bag. I inspected the chambers, then set it near my pillow. After hurrying through my ablutions, I did not forget my prayers, although I will admit they were perfunctory. Except when I asked the Lord to stop my toothache, at which point I copied the bluntness of St. Paul.

Given the hour, I did not pursue my nightly habit of writing to my darling, but only laid me down for a bit of a nap. Even my toothache could not keep me awake. Nor did I dream of devils or snakes, of violent struggles or even, God help me, of India. Morpheus swallowed all life's fears and miseries.

I *slept*.

Now, I am an old bayonet and a veteran of John Company's fusses. Schooled by creeping enemies, I rise before the dawn. I am as punctual as the Great Western Railway, as dependable as the Bank of England, and did not fear missing my appointment with General Banks, who commanded all of our forces in New Orleans. Twas fixed for eight o'clock, in the Customs House, but I rise well before that hour. Even after marching half the night.

I did not rise with the lark that day. Nor with the sun or even with the city, which is Frenchified and slow to leave its bed.

I woke to a pounding on my door that might have been a barrage from a dozen batteries. Leaping up, I reached for a ghostly musket, thinking myself in India again.

Ripe, the light recalled me to the present. My spirit shriveled. I rushed to the door and undid the lock, with no regard for my rude state of undress.

General Nathaniel P. Banks stood at my door. His glare might have slain the Basilisk and stopped Medusa cold.

Now, General Banks is a fine-looking fellow, with blade-point eyes, a full mustache and a little goaty beard. Gallant of aspect he is, and pleasing to ladies. But he did not offer me a winning countenance.

"You sorry, little bastard." He pushed halfway into the room. "You sleeping one off? What the devil do you think you're—"

He stopped. Staring past my shoulder.

"Who's *she*?" he demanded.

That was a question to which I had no answer. Even after I wheeled about and forced my eyes open wide enough to take in the brown lass cowering in the corner. All balled up she was, like a beaten child.

Still, you saw at once that she was a woman.

"You no-good bastard," General Banks said in a quiet growl far harsher than a shout. "You were supposed to report an hour ago. And I find you bedded down with a high-yellow whore."

I was not "bedded down" with any creature. Nor did I believe the general had sufficient evidence to slander the young woman, who was fully, if simply, dressed.

Nonetheless, I wondered what the lass was about myself. My face must have gone as red as a grenadier's sleeves.

"I've had enough of your tomfoolery, Jones," General Banks informed me. "You had half the damned city in an uproar yesterday. More than half. Place looked like a damned battlefield. Undid half the good I've done since I got here."

His eyebrows rippled like two ranks in the attack. "I don't care *whose* authority you have behind you, I won't tolerate this. I won't have it. I'm writing to Stanton today. *And* Seward. To Abe Lincoln himself, damn you. I'll have you court-martialed, before I'm done with you."

He slapped a pair of gloves from one hand into the other, glanced at the lass again, grunted unpleasantly and stalked off down the hall.

"Have that gimp-leg bastard in my office in thirty minutes," he told his subordinates, one of whom was Captain Bolt from the boneyard.

Bolt was the one who stepped forward to put a point on things.

"I was you, Major," he said. "I'd get dressed about now."

GET DRESSED I DID. In a hurry that would have suited a camp overrun by Pushtoons. And as I dressed, with the door shut on the soldiers, I turned to my uninvited, unwelcome guest.

"Who are *you*, then?" I demanded. "What are you up to, Missy?"

Along with a certain urgency in the kidneys, my toothache robbed my manners of civility.

In response to my tone, the woman began to weep. Which I found unhelpful.

I could not say who the creature was, or how she entered my room, or what she sought. And she, apparently, could not say it, either.

She wept and made noises and cowered.

I picked up the Colt to return it to its holster. The sight of the revolver made her shriek.

God knows what the lads in the hall imagined. I have a gentle manner with the ladies, and keep my doings proper in every regard. But the soldiers beyond the door must have thought me nasty.

Only one good thing come of her howl. Her jabber began to resemble human speech. Although the words had a worrisome, Frenchy sound.

Yet, French is light, like a rapier. It sneaks and stabs. The young woman's tone had a weight to suit a cutlass. Twas French and not French. I could not grasp a word.

"I do not understand you," I told her, with a hand on my sore cheek. *"Nix verstehen,"* I added, although that is German and did not help us much.

Of a sudden, the young woman rose from her crouch. Just long enough to hurl herself at my feet. A gold cross on a chain slipped from her bodice, brushing my toes. She clutched at my ankles, then at my calves, and finally at my knees. Staring up with a tear-swept face no man would accuse of beauty.

She looked to have colored blood, but was no African. Her face put me in mind of India's servant girls, the sort a wise mother chooses to avoid tempting her sons. But for the tawny color of her skin, she might have been a mill-girl in the North, hoping to marry him that would have her soonest. Young she was, but without the bloom of youth. Her eyes were green and she smelled of worn clothes.

As a Methodist I must admit that I am a man no better

than the others. Had she been a beauty, I might have conducted myself with greater kindness, toothache or no. The
handsome face asks handsome manners, while plain meets a
plain response. It is not fair, this world of ours. We see the
golden hair and miss the golden heart.

She raved in opaque words, her terror impenetrable.

A fist addressed the door. Captain Bolt's voice, dull even
when excited, called, "Major Jones? You coming along now?"

He shouted to be heard through the wood, drawing the
world's attention to my predicament.

I could not employ the chamberpot in the presence of a
woman, no matter her color or plainness. My loins seemed
about to burst with the past night's coffee. My tooth raged.
And General Banks was furious. All the while, yesterday's
troubles perched upon my shoulders.

I fear that calm reflection was beyond me.

"I do not understand you," I repeated to the lass. "I do not
know what you are saying."

Clearly, there was a service the young woman wished of
me. She seemed to have made no mistake in her choice of
rooms. Although she never hinted at my name.

I could only assume the lass wanted protection. But why,
then, come to me? I had barely managed to keep myself
alive.

How did she intend to share her story?

My curiosity had to be shelved. General Banks was waiting. I did not even have time to scrape my whiskers.

"Wait here," I told her, which was silly of me. I could not
think of another thing to say. Not that she would have understood me, anyway. "Wait here. I will come back."

I freed myself, not easily, from her grip.

The best for which I might hope would be the appearance
of Mr. Barnaby, who seemed to have an ear for the local di-

alects. Perhaps he could translate the woman's pleas and make some sense of her presence.

I left the lass with dread upon her face.

"IF I HAD the authority," General Banks said, "I'd rip those boards off your shoulders, Jones. You're the kind of officer who disgusts me."

Too furious to look at me, he glared out through the window. The wharves below were crowded with steamers and barks, with high-masted schooners and gunboats.

"A damned whoremonger," he continued. "Destroying public property. Brawling in the streets." He folded his arms across the chest of his neatly fitted uniform. "And wrecking a fancy cathouse." He grimaced. "You make me want to puke in a bucket."

"General Banks, I—"

"Shut your mouth. Unless I ask you a question." He thought for a moment. "Are you *sober* enough to answer questions?"

"I never even—"

"Why were you chasing a colored mammy through the streets?"

"I did not realize—"

"You didn't *realize*? Who were the men you were fighting on that roof?"

"I cannot say exactly, but—"

"Why did you start that fire?"

"I did not—"

"What were you doing in a whorehouse in the middle of the afternoon?"

"I was—"

"And who pulled that prank of walling you up in a crypt? Not that you didn't deserve it."

"I cannot say, but—"

His face narrowed in accusation. "What about the murder of that bath attendant?"

"If I could—"

"Who's that nigger trollop in your room?" He looked on the verge of spitting. "You can't even pick whores, Jones."

"I do not know her, sir."

"Don't lie to me, you insolent little bastard. I don't care how many letters you have from Lincoln. This city's under martial law. *I*'m in command here." He pulled a face, as if smelling an unpleasantness. "Who are you, anyway? You bribe your way into a commission? Or was it political pull? I've never seen anyone look less like an officer in all my—"

I had taken advantage of a communal water closet before leaving the hotel, so my temper was not as brittle as it might have been. But my tooth remained confounding. Nor had General Banks, of all people, grounds to question my aptitude as a soldier. He was a Massachusetts politican, made a general for unmilitary reasons. He had been trounced in Virginia, with many a lad's life lost. And I am vain about my soldiering past. May the Lord forgive me.

Inspired by pride and my toothache, I turned on the fellow.

"General Banks," I said, favoring my better leg and the easier side of my mouth, "you are *wrong*, sir. And you are unfair. And you are ignorant. And you are ungentlemanly. You may draw a fool's conclusions if you will, but you will *not* blame your foolishness on me. Look you. I have no more wish to be in your city than Moses had love of Egypt. But I have been ordered to see to a task, and see to it I will. No, sir. *You* will listen now. And you may talk of courts-martial when I am done. But you do not know the half of what has happened under your nose. Nor will you find out by shouting at the heavens."

I drew out the letter Mr. Nicolay had given to me in Washington. General Banks had scanned it upon my arrival, but needed reminding.

"You are to give me *every* assistance," I told him. "Mr. Lincoln's signature grants me the authority to call on you for troops, or to call on the Navy for a vessel, or to imprison any man, in uniform or not, who interferes with me. You may write your letters to Nebuchadnezzar, Zachariah and Absalom, but until the president's order is countermanded, *you* are in mutiny, General Banks."

My reaction startled him. He stood behind his desk, hand in mid-air and mouth open, staring at me. So it is with the powerful. They grow so used to treating the rest of us as their pack of hounds that they do not know what to do when a dog barks back.

"What is more," I continued, "I am a Christian man and have taken the Pledge. No drop of liquor has passed my lips in this city. Nor will it. Nor do I break the vows of holy wedlock. And I have done *my* soldiering in the field. Not behind a politician's desk. So I will have no more of your insults, General Banks. I suggest you go about your proper business, and let me go about mine. Or we can *both* write letters to President Lincoln. Whom I have served on more than one occasion," I added all too proudly. "And I will tell him that you do not know what goes on in this city a hundred yards from the comfort of your office. And that you do not wish to know."

"You insolent little bastard. I'll lock you up."

"That you will not do. For you are pleased that you have relieved General Butler. But General Butler is not without great friends. And I hear that he would like to return to New Orleans. If my sense of Washington holds true, he would be glad to learn that you had prevented the president's agent from investigating a Union citizen's murder. *And* General Butler brings the president as many votes as you do, I believe. Not to speak of the father of Miss Peabody, who delivers Albany. Along with Mr. Seward, of course. Who I believe stood godparent to the dead lass. Sorry that would be, General Banks, to have your reputation damaged by your enemies . . . while you are serving our flag in Louisiana."

His face abandoned shock in favor of outrage. "You're blackmailing me!"

"No, General Banks, I am advising you. Against taking a decision before you are in possession of the facts. I hope you will maintain the best credit in Washington. Where every general wishes a good account."

He cast aside his haughtiness with a smirk. He was, after all, a successful politician and was not deeply troubled by convictions. His military service was but an interlude.

"Listen," he said, reducing the distance between us. "The last thing any good Union man should want is for Ben Butler to get his greedy paws on this city again. He's done more damage with his corruption and caprice than any twenty—"

"I did not say I wished General Butler's return. Only that *he* wishes it. And there are those in the North who think of him highly. For his advocacy of raising negro regiments. And he is favored by the press, who believed his sternness proper."

"Oh, that's enough, damn it. You can stop your cant now, Jones." He rolled his handsome head back over his shoulders, exhaling dramatically. "Don't you *see,* man? I'm trying to fix the damage Butler did. And he did plenty. I can't have the local population stirred up again." He tossed up his hands. "I'm not saying Ben Butler did no good, either. He cleaned up their streets, for one thing. He brought a certain measure of law and order. I'll credit him with that much. But the man didn't obey the law himself. And his brother . . . that man lived up to every charge of scandalous behavior the Rebels ever leveled against us. Look here, Jones. All we want the people of this city to do is to be quiet and go about their business. So we can get on with the war. So I can push upriver. While that drunkard Grant sits in Memphis, doing nothing. And that lunatic Sherman throws his men away." He shook his head in disgust. "They'll never take Vicksburg. Or anything else worth taking. West Point men are worthless. You must know that. It's up to men like us to win this war."

"Well," I said, with my voice gentled, "I do not wish to interfere with matters of strategy."

"I won't have trouble in the streets. I *can't* have it."

"And I will not hunt trouble. In the streets, or elsewhere. But I cannot promise that trouble will not hunt me. For I will tell you: More there is to the murder of Miss Peabody than any of us thought. What it is about, I cannot say. I have more questions than you have, General Banks. But there is a rottenness I can smell from here." I touched my cheek unwillingly, yearning to calm my tooth. The flesh was hot. "Parties I do not know have tried to discourage me. But they have done the opposite . . ."

He did not look at me, but inspected the floor. Which wanted a proper cleaning. Past visitors had sometimes missed the cuspidor.

"Just go," he said, in a voice that established a truce between the two of us. "Get out of here. And try to do as little damage as possible."

I WENT OUT through the hill of blue ants the Customs House had become, holding my palm to my jaw and scowling helplessly. The day before, my toothache had been an annoyance. Now it was a misery, thanks to my indulgence at

Mr. Champlain's house. But I *like* a sweet. And virtue must have *some* reward.

Positioned to the rear of my mouth, the offending tooth seemed to swell in all directions. It wanted a remedy soon. But even the thought of dentists makes me squeamish, for they are cruel. A battle is but half the trial we face in the dentist's chair.

Nor would I apply whisky, which some fellows do.

On my way down the last corridor of our headquarters, I overheard a captain complain that he had been sent to run the city workhouse, but could not keep the inmates at their labors for lack of material. What was he to do? A plump civilian promised a colonel a lovely supper at Galpin's, while a clerk worried over a troop of negro laborers. The darkies had disappeared with a ditch unfinished, leaving a cesspit fouled at Jackson Barracks. Before his host could contain him, a cotton factor bellowed that he would not pay the same bribe twice.

That, too, was war, but not the sort we chronicle.

A better Christian than myself would have rushed back to the hotel and that frightened young woman. But I wandered the city, searching for a dentist. Even as I tried to avoid finding one. My walk was a crooked scuttle, for I had not had a chance to replace my cane. From head to toe, my person was awry. Nor would my thoughts come straight, for all my trying. I walked the pavements and crossed the mucky streets, with my ears as cold as they would have been back home. Imagining my face the size of a melon.

The city was in a queer state that January. Our occupation had opened the port to trade again and the shops were overflowing. But the men and women who crowded the streets could not afford to buy. They are as proud as peacocks, the creoles, but you saw at a glance that last year's wardrobe had not been refreshed and a lady's skirts had been hemmed with mismatched ribbon.

Just off Customhouse Street, in the Rue Chartres, Madame Olympe announced new Paris fashions. Her windows drew a crowd, but the shop stayed empty. On the corner of Canal and Royal, S. N. Moody's advertised the finest in Gentlemen's Furnishing Goods. Idle clerks minded the counters, while fellows afraid to try their credit strolled by. Men of fifty years looked sad as children as they passed the merchant's door in their frayed cuffs. Hardly a fellow went by that shop without tugging down his coat sleeves or sneaking a glance at his shoes. New Orleans was a fancy ball that woke to a threadbare morning.

And then I saw a fearsome sight before me. I had made a circle, coming back toward the Customs House again. I never will forget the least detail. The address was 194 Canal Street. His name was Dr. Fielding. The sign, well worn, promised PAINLESS TOOTH EXTRACTION.

Indeed.

I told myself that I had no choice but to enter those awful premises. The pain was such that I could not eat, and that would never do. I hoped the fellow might offer a simple solution, allaying my fears that pulling had become necessary. But my hackles went up as I climbed the narrow staircase. It should have told me something that the fellow's office was one flight above a woodworker's shop that sold coffins.

And it should have warned me off that the fellow's office was empty and dark. The door stood open, revealing an antechamber furnished with a church pew and two chairs. A bright-smiled beauty, recorded in a posture of innocent joy, advertised Groton's Perfect Tooth Powder, which was GOOD FOR THE GUMS, AS WELL.

"Hello?" I tried.

That got me no reply. Twas almost excuse enough to take me right back down those stairs. But I am stubborn, if not always wise.

"Hello? Dr. Fielding?"

Again, I got no answer.

Turning to flee, I heard a response at last, from another room. Twas a groan that might have swelled from the lair of a beast disturbed in its slumbers.

A moment later, an inner door creaked open. A fellow too large for the premises, with a blacksmith's shoulders and several days' growth of beard, revealed himself in the foul light of the waiting room. He rubbed his eyes, yawned mightily, then fixed his eyes on my uniform, not my face.

"Hmmmph," he said, blowing his nose in a rag that wanted a wash.

"Dr. Fielding?" I asked doubtfully. His dress evoked a bankrupt gambler, not a medical man. And his waistcoat was undone.

Yet, he had a look of strength, which is a dentist's most important quality.

"Tooth?" he muttered.

I lowered my hand from my rebellious jaw. "It has become a bother. Mayhaps it is nothing at all."

"Have a look," he said. Gesturing with his thumb toward the room where he had been lurking.

I do not cut and run. I refuse to play the coward. Advancing slowly and cautiously, as if looking out for an ambush, I followed the fellow back into his surgery.

The light within was dreary. It hardly seemed sufficient for his trade.

"Sit," he told me.

There was but a single chair in the room, of the sort employed by barbers, although this example had straps for the patient's forearms.

I took my place and told him, "No need of belts, Dr. Fielding. I can hold my position, see."

Oh, pride of man!

His surgical tools did not look especially clean. But Mick Tyrone's concern with sanitary effects is not widespread in the medical professions.

"Really," I told him, as he fixed a strap over my forearm, "that is not needful."

"Hmmmph," he said, pulling the belt tight. He moved to the other wrist.

"Really, I—"

"Leverage," he grunted. As he cinched the straps I smelled him rather more closely than I wished.

"Open," he said.

The instant I parted my lips, he shoved my head backward. Lowering his bewhiskered face as if he meant to fit it into my mouth.

"Bad," he told me.

I wished to request some further detail, but a fat thumb jammed down my tongue and approached my windpipe.

Of a sudden, he grew loquacious. "Ought to take 'em all out. Get it over with."

"Juth un, juth un," I insisted.

"Take 'em all out and your breath won't stink so bad. Get yourself a nice new set made up."

"Juth un," I pleaded.

"Well, which one?"

"Bat un."

"Which one of the bad ones?"

"Bat un."

He shoved a metal instrument into my maw. Its tip collided noisily with a tooth.

I fear I made a sound that was unmanly.

"That one?" He stabbed the appliance into a crevice. Twas then I understood the need of those belts.

"Unh," I assured him.

"All right. But you're a damn fool not to take 'em all out and be done with it."

He removed his thumb and fiddled with his tools. Then he bent to a cabinet and produced a nearly empty bottle of whisky. He held it up to the bit of light that seeped through the dirty window.

"I have taken the Pledge, sir," I told him, not without a certain regret.

He fortified himself with a swig from the bottle. Then took a second one.

"Open," he said again, bending over my person. The smell of sweat and whisky was a punishment.

I opened.

He inserted yet another tool and tapped it on my tooth. Had I not been restrained, I might have leapt from the window.

"That one?" he asked, as if he had forgotten.

"Unh," I agreed.

"Hold on." He chose a tool that might have done for a blacksmith's shop. It stretched my cheeks when he forced it into my mouth. I tasted metal. And rust.

He leaned his bulk against my chest, grinding my ribs with his elbow. One paw held my jaw open, while the other applied the tool.

Fastened down, the chair creaked under our weight.

"Think about something happy," Dr. Fielding said.

Then he yanked.

Now, I am small, but strong in the chest and shoulders. I am no weakling. It remains an amazement to me that I did not topple the fellow over and rip the chair from its moorings.

He turned away to grab a rag, which he held under my mouth. Then he picked up a spittoon from the unswept floor.

"Spit out the blood," he told me.

"Ith it out?" I gasped. I felt as though a navvy were going at my skull with a ten-pound hammer.

"Part. It broke off. Rotten through. Spit out that blood. I have to dig out the roots."

"Tomollow," I told him. "Do it tomollow."

"Can't wait. You'll get blood poisoning, I leave that in there. Maybe gangrene."

I tried to think of happy things. But my concentration failed me.

"Open," he commanded. He raised a pair of implements that might as well have been a pick and a shovel.

I did my best to be manly, but did not meet success. I have been shot and stabbed and sliced. My bones have been broken and I have been burned, as well. But I do not think I ever knew such misery as I met in that dentist's chair.

There is a place in Mr. Shakespeare's Scottish play where the murderess says, "Yet who would have thought the old man to have had so much blood in him?" She might have been speaking of Abel Jones, not her victim.

od exploded over my clean uniform. Twas the last I had in reserve. Blood splashed over the dentist himself. Blood splashed across the floor.

"Almost done," he assured me.

I began to feel sick and faint.

"Cut a little deeper," he said. "Then we'll have it."

He did some work down deep that made me wail.

"Thought you didn't mind pain?" he said disdainfully. "Just another minute. I need to trim away the extra meat."

"Pleath," I begged. Tears blurred my eyes. Cold though it was in his rooms, I was soaked with sweat.

He peered into my mouth again. Twisting my neck to find the light from the window.

"Deepest roots I ever saw," he said.

He bent to his labors. To my shame, I bawled like a baby.

"There now," the fellow said at last, flicking bone and flesh into a bowl. "That wasn't so bad, was it?"

"Ith all out?"

"Have to charge you double. Complicated operation." He looked at me thoughtfully. "Sure you don't want to take the rest of 'em out? While you're here?"

Speech pained me. So I shook my head. Extravagantly.

"Well, all right," he said. "If your mind's made up. Just sit there and rest while I put in a few stitches."

I STAGGERED BACK toward the hotel, drenched with sweat and blood. I must have appeared as wild-eyed as a recruit after his first battle. People stared, but I barely registered their alarm. I was stunned by pain, both present and remembered. My head seemed the size of an observation balloon.

A patrol stopped me, afraid that I had been a victim of crime. It cost me painful speech to assure them that I had merely visited a dentist. The guards at the hotel stared.

But the most alarmed of them all was Mr. Barnaby, who awaited me in an armchair in the lobby. He jumped to his feet and rushed between the loiterers to assist me.

"Dear me!" he cried. "I knew I should have come earlier! Who was it this time?"

"Toof," I explained. "Dentith."

At first, he looked relieved. Then his expression darkened. "*Which* dentist?" he asked quietly, as if fearing the answer.

"Fielthink."

He winced in sympathy. "Oh, dear. I wished you'd consulted me, I do. You needed to go to Dr. Dostle, on St. Joseph's Street. 'E's the Union dentist, Dr. Dostle is. Dr. Fielding's a terrible Confederate, sir. 'E don't like Union blue even when 'e's sober. . . ."

six

I DID NOT FOREWARN Mr. Barnaby of the woman who had slipped into my room. My jaw hurt too much when I tried to speak and the side of my face was nearly immobile with swelling. Were the lass still present, the fact would be self-evident and Mr. Barnaby could help me solve her riddle. Had she deserted the premises, report of her could await my jaw's recovery.

I was not thinking clearly, if at all. That is the truth of it. Pain empties the mind of all that is not immediate. The voodoo devils fled my thoughts, along with the serpents and killers. I hardly cared a fig for the late Miss Peabody. Or even for Mr. Lincoln and the war. I only wanted the misery to stop.

It hurt worse than the cutting I got in the Khyber.

As I dragged myself up the stairs to my room, Mr. Barnaby prattled. "Dr. Fielding's known as a famous prankster, sir. Especially when we comes up to the Marty Graw. Which ain't to be this year, it ain't to be! Oh, 'e's bound to be in a wicked mood, after your Yankees 'as banned outdoor assemblies. It's the same as forbidding the carnival itself! Not that there's money or spirits to do it proper. It wants a certain outlay, for balls and such. But that's all by the by, sir, by the by. Spilt milk. It's a glum year, robbed of merriment. But what can a body expect, sir, with more bankrupts than beaver hats between the New Canal and the *Place d'Armes*?"

When I opened the door to my room, the chamber was empty, the young woman gone. But the queerest thing occurred.

Mr. Barnaby lifted his nose like a hound catching a scent. His expression of anxious cheer grew perplexed and wary.

I will report my speech as I intended it, not as it sounded with my mouth all ravaged.

"What is it, Mr. Barnaby?"

He shook his head and said nothing. His eyes stared through the walls as he sniffed and snuffled.

"Smell something, do you?"

He lowered his face and spoke in a tone of bewilderment. "It's nothing, sir, nothing at all. Only . . . I thought I detected a fragrance." He took a last, wistful sniff. "A scent as I ain't smelled these many years . . ."

Tucking away his interest in the matter, his face resumed its usual affability. "All's one, sir, all's one. But would you like a shave? I'm quite the barber and ain't ashamed to say it. I used to scrape Master Francis and the senator. I could parse your whiskers in such a way as your poor jaw wouldn't feel it."

It was his polite way of saying that I did not look my best. But when I touched my fingers to my cheek, I decided to elude the snares of vanity.

"I will do without shaving, thank you."

The grand fellow understood me, though I lisped and lagged and slurred like an Irish drunkard.

"Better part of valor, sir, the better part of valor. But I suspects you'll wish to change your uniform? Before we goes out, sir?"

"Out?"

"To the Garden Disrict," he told me, "on the American side. To see Mrs. Aubrey, sir. Who don't take time for just anyone."

"I do not have another uniform, Mr. Barnaby. This was the last, see. Anyway," I snarled, having just suffered a knockabout wave of hurt, "I do not recollect asking to be taken anywhere this afternoon. Who, pray tell, is this Mrs. Aubrey of yours?"

"Rich as Croesus!" he exclaimed. "Or Mrs. Croesus, to put a feminine point on it. Even now, sir, even with the war. She could buy and sell us all like a slab of bacon. Oh, they're clever sorts, them Aubreys. Never put their faith in Secession banknotes, if the world's report is true. Pounds sterling and Yankee dollars. Golden guineas and London shares, all listed on the 'Change. I believe 'er 'usband made 'is fortune at sea. With the Royal Navy, sir, the politest pirates what ever sailed the waves! But that's all by the by, sir, by the by. She's old as the 'ills and rich as a duchess and won't even offer us tea." He looked at me pityingly. "Not that you'd be in quite the mood to drink it, sir."

"But who *is* she, man? Why would I want to squander my time in her company? There's work to be done!"

My grump was much too harsh. The poor fellow looked crushed.

"I only meant to 'elp, and nothing more, sir. Sorry if I overstepped my bounds. Know better next time, I will. It's only that I asked about and made inquiries, begging your pardon. Mrs. Aubrey's said to be the last person in New Orleans to see your poor Miss Peabody alive . . ."

WE DID NOT go directly to Mrs. Aubrey's manse, which lay on the far side of the American town, where things were done proper and only the servants spoke French. First, Mr. Barnaby conducted me to a shop where he oversaw my outfitting as a gentleman. With his background in haberdashery and such matters, the fellow was particular about fit and fabric to a degree that would have done credit to my darling wife's establishment. Although she would have been mortified by the sums Mr. Barnaby challenged me to spend.

"You 'as to *look* a gentleman, sir, or no one in New Orleans will acknowledge you," he explained. "It don't 'ardly matter 'ow black your crimes, as long as you looks a gent from top to bottom."

Now, do not think that the new-gained wealth of my Mary Myfanwy's inheritance had led me to corruption of the spirit. Parting with such a sum to a clothier pained my pocket almost as cruelly as dentistry wounded my jaw. But I must admit that after Mr. Barnaby was done fussing and criticizing and generally terrorizing half a dozen anxious clerks and tailors, I was fond of what I saw in the shopkeeper's mirror. Despite the gross distortion of my cheek.

I will never pass for Edwin Booth, whose visage so impresses all our ladies. But properly fitted out and viewed from a winning angle, I believe that I am a most presentable man.

"It's all in the cut, sir, all in the cut and the pattern! Vertical stripes on a waistcoat is most lengthening. As is the stripes in the trousers. You almost looks the normal height of a fellow! And there's nothing like a black frock coat to bring it all together into a parcel. While lessening the disproportion of the chest. Begging your pardon, Major Jones, you looks less like a runty bull and more like a regular person." He stepped back to admire the result. "You doesn't look 'alf so queer now. A fellow might think you was president of a bank," he told me. "And an honest-run bank, at that."

Mr. Barnaby arranged for my uniform to be cleaned up proper and sent back to the hotel—where my greatcoat, left with the Ursulines, had been delivered. So off we went, with me garbed in my finery and the fellows who had attended us fawning like Mrs. Mickles before the Queen. Yet, for all the crackling green dollars we left behind, I believe the clerks were glad to see us go. For Mr. Barnaby knew their trade too well. A clerk prefers to find himself more knowledgeable than his customer, which guarantees the riddance of poor merchandise, along with a tidy profit.

As we sauntered down Canal Street toward a rank of cabs, Mr. Barnaby sighed and said, "A lovely thing it was to 'ave my own shop, sir. We only carried the best, and nothing less. That's what I offered the gentlemen, the *crème de la crème* of cloth and cut and finishings! They used to come from Natchez, even Memphis. That's 'ow I come to know Senator Raines and Master Francis. Before the fever took Marie and the children." A tear crowded his eye. "You would've 'ad better quality of me, sir, than anything you see in the shops these days. Things ain't what they used to be, and sometimes I thinks the world's going to the dogs . . ."

"Mr. Barnaby," I said, or tried to say, for my mouth remained recalcitrant, "before we go on I need to replace my cane."

"But you didn't want none back there, sir. Not that the quality offered was quite, quite. Although that one with the silver 'ead of a duck—"

"That is not it, Mr. Barnaby. I did not wish to speak before the tailors. But I have learned the advantages of a sword-cane. I thought you might know of a shop where such might be found."

"I did think you was being particular mindful," he admitted. "Now I understands it, sir." He thought for a moment.

"We'll 'ave to walk into the Quarter. But I knows just the place." He glanced at my bothered leg. "But would you kindly step out a bit? If you can, sir? We mustn't keep Mrs. Aubrey waiting too long. . . ."

We hastened across the boulevard and followed Royal Street. The complexions and the characters grew darker—I do not mean they were negroes, only Frenchies—and passersby showed more suspicion of strangers. Even without my uniform, I did not feel much welcome. But many a man tipped his hat to Mr. Barnaby, who seemed to enjoy a fine report in the city.

"I 'as to warn you, Major Jones . . . don't try to drive a bargain with *Monsieur* Beyle. He don't even sell to a fellow 'e don't take to, 'e's that particular. If you likes 'is wares, just pay 'is price and let 'im know you're grateful."

Easy for an Englishman to say. A Welshman is born with a sense of his pounds and pennies.

"I'll tell you this, I will," Mr. Barnaby continued, lifting his hat and bowing to a withered lady in a worn-out carriage. "You'll find 'is goods better than anything sold by those riff-raff Yankees on Poydras Street. Begging your pardon."

"Mr. Barnaby," I said, or tried to say, "won't your friends judge you harshly? If they see you associating with a Union man?"

He brushed the thought from the lapel of his coat, as if it were a crumb. "Not at all, sir, not at all! 'Aven't the least cause for worry, we doesn't. Business is business, that's 'ow they sees things in New Orleans, sir. They'll calculate as I'm making a tidy profit through our association. And where profit starts, the convictions of the best sorts doesn't mind resting. The creole adores a proper return on investments, almost as much as 'e loves 'is neighbor's secrets. Which is almost as much again as 'e loves 'is own. Oh, the lack of funds restricts their pleasures awful, sir. And a creole's pleasures count more to 'im than most anything in the world. They won't assume I *likes* you, Major Jones. Only that your acquaintance is a benefit."

"That . . . does not sound high-minded."

"Right you are, sir! And the world's a better place for it, begging your pardon. Call it 'ypocrisy if you likes, down 'ere we calls it manners." He nodded approvingly into his double chin. "A beautiful girl tears friends asunder, that's what Barnaby B. Barnaby always says. Just as 'is father and grandfather said before 'im. But a profit shared makes friends where none was expected. Why, if you—"

He stopped so abruptly he almost tripped up a delivery boy. With a swiftness that would not have disgraced a practitioner of Thuggee, my companion presented me with a fancy handkerchief, handsomely worked but frayed.

"You're bleeding at the mouth again," he told me. "And you doesn't want to spoil your lovely new garments."

MR. BARNABY STOPPED AT a narrow lane. Twas worrisomely like the one down which I had been lured the day before. By Marie Venin.

He began to grant me precedence, then thought better of it and squeezed into the passageway ahead of me.

"Begging your pardon, sir," he said, as he led me between brick walls. A faded sign read:

H. BEYLE
LUXURIES AND CURIOSITIES

We passed through a courtyard strewn with broken effects and cast-off furnishings. Beyond a litter of potted plants that would not wake with April, a windowfront bore the same advertisement as the sign at the alley's mouth.

"Be so kind as to remember, sir," Mr. Barnaby begged. "You musn't even think of bargaining, don't even think of it! You either wants what *Monsieur* Beyle 'as to offer, or you doesn't. And none's the worse thereafter."

Stepping into the shop itself, twas hard to imagine why I would wish to buy anything. No bigger than a proper Pottsville parlor, the room was cluttered wall to wall and floor to ceiling with gilt furniture, gilt frames and gilt-limned pots and vases. Gilt shone in every variety, from mottled orange and gold rubbed smooth to decayed yellows struggling to hide an underlying blackness, reminiscent of a harlot's hair. If you will excuse the comparison. Angles, curves and planes, the legs of chairs and tables and fancy cabinets gleamed and glittered, noisy to the eye. Such merchandise could only appeal to libertines or Catholics.

An oil lamp sputtered on a desk beyond the gaudy tumult, protesting weakly against the gloom of the day. But the shop made its own false sunlight, despite an impressive accumulation of dust. I found the place repulsive, yet compelling, like a morally unkempt beauty in repose.

Behind the desk that bore the lamp an ancient fellow watched us make our way. He did not rise an inch until we closed on him. And when he rose his height hardly increased.

Lean as famine, the proprietor's figure assumed the shape of a question mark, curved from mid-spine to the bottom of his skull. His face, sharp as a chevron, hunted upward from his body's ruin, hardly rising enough for his eyes to find us. Yet, framed by white hair falling to his collar, those eyes held steady as the finest marksman's. Blue they were, and impenetrable.

"But *Monsieur* Barnaby! Welcome!" he rasped in tainted English.

"*Monsieur* Beyle, your servant, sir, your servant! How many months and years, how many years . . . but may I present Major Abel Jones? Of the Federal persuasion? Pardon 'im if 'e don't do a great deal of speaking, but 'e's been through a terrible slaughter with Dr. Fielding."

The proprietor turned uncanny eyes on me. Examining my person the way a Jew looks at a gemstone, revealing nothing of his swift assessment.

"A mirror for your wife, perhaps?" His voice had been scraped by time and beaten low. "A genuine Louis XV bedframe, *Monsieur le Major*? Perhaps the cloth-of-gold bedcover made expressly for the niece of the great Pompadour? A set of chairs that belonged to no less a man than the Bishop of Autun?"

"Major Jones is after something different," Mr. Barnaby corrected him. "'E's not at all the usual sort of Yankee and ain't involved in selling cotton or contraband. 'E's looking for a sword-cane, *Monsieur* Beyle. To replace one what 'e lost in a to-do." My companion paused, then added, "The major's to be trusted, sir. As certain as I'm Barnaby B. Barnaby."

The old man nodded, shifting his humped back. His entire form turned round at once, as if it lacked an adequate number of joints. Trailing a scent of personal untidiness, he made the slightest gesture with his fingers, bidding us follow.

"The front room's only for Yankees," Mr. Barnaby explained, "or for them what 'asn't got the sense to know what they wants exactly, but who 'opes to make a great display back 'ome."

Watching the old fellow scuttle along, I thought, unreasonably, of my darling wife. Who is beautiful, and whose spine has but the faintest hint of a curve.

Behind an innocent-looking door that might have led to a

broom closet, a darkened hall awaited. I had the queerest sense of traveling underground, of penetrating deep into a cave. Although we were but a room away from the court-yard, the temperature seemed to fall with every step.

The old fellow struck a lucifer match. I could not see the lamp he lit with his person interposed, but the flame rose to reveal not gilt but gold. And silver. Educated by the loot of India, my eye told me twas solid goods, not plate. Extrava-gant as Babylon, fancy services glittered on shelves and counters, their stillness nursing stories of fallen families, of wastrel sons and ill-judged matrimonials.

"Voilà," the old fellow declared, summoning me from be-dazzlement. "In the corner. The finest selection for *Monsieur le Major.*"

Two cylinders wide as the muzzles of old Seekh guns of-fered up a fine selection of sticks. I had not seen such a grand display in the second-best shop in all of Philadelphia.

Yet, I was disappointed soon enough. His wares included more than a dozen sword-canes. Each was handsome and several had been worked to the level of jewelry. But when I drew the blades, not one had proper balance or trustworthy steel. That is the thing, see. Soldiering teaches you quickly that not all weapons are equally made. It is not enough to be armed. A fellow must be well armed to survive. The pretty canes he offered me were meant to make a gentleman feel secure as he strolled the streets. But they had not been forged for a fight.

Studying my frustration, the shopkeeper said, "Ah, *Monsieur le Major* . . . I see you are a fighting man." His eyes shifted to the scar on my swollen cheek, left by a blade in Scotland. "You wish a weapon that fights as well as you do. A partner, let us say."

The way the fellow looked at me would have given a

statue the shivers. I am not certain any other man has ever looked into my face so intently. Unless it was our regimental colonel, after India broke my will.

I tried to think of a gentle way to tell him his wares were inadequate. With my jaw rebelling. "It is only . . . these are . . ."

"They are only for the decoration," he said helpfully. "For the display, the pomp. The vanity. Of course! But you do not care about the display, I think?"

"A good blade," I told him, struggling to be understood. "I need one with a fighting blade."

He held up his forefinger, telling me to be patient a trifle longer. And he shuffled over to a battered chest, an item as poorly suited to the room as I felt myself to be. After unlocking its highest drawer, the old man fell into a stillness. As if unwilling to open it, after all. He took on a most peculiar air of intimacy, almost of sorrow.

Gesturing for me to approach, he seemed to have forgotten Mr. Barnaby.

"I would call this . . . a private collection," the proprietor said, beckoning me closer still. "Or perhaps I should say, 'Only for the finest of connoisseurs, for the *gentilhomme* with the unusual need . . .' "

He opened the drawer slowly, half an inch at a time, as if he feared its contents lived and longed to escape their prison.

It would not be the least exaggeration to say that I was stunned. Three sword-canes slept upon a bed of velvet. Each was beautiful—if we may claim beauty for such implements— yet each was as different one from the other as the three Graces themselves. Those girls the Greeks went on about, I mean, the ones who scampered about in their linens, pretending they were goddesses.

But beauty was not the thing of it. Not at all. I was no

young Paris torn between choices. My selection had been made for me, as soon as the drawer opened. I did not even need to try the weapon.

Truth be told, the other two canes were more finely worked than the one that held my eye. One was sleeker, another weightier. A man impartial might not have favored my choice. But there was no doubt in my mind.

So enchanted I was that my discomfort fled, as if warned off by the power of the blade. I gasped when I saw it.

The thing of it was this: Before me lay the perfect twin of the weapon given to me by the Earl of Thretford, a man who meant me good and ill at once. I left that blade in the bowels of a leprous witch. Fire had consumed it, along with the horrid shack in which I slew her.

But that is another tale.

"How much for that one?" My voice was impatient, which makes for unsound business.

"But you must try it, *monsieur*!" the old fellow said. "You must feel it, give it the test!"

I fit my palm to the sword-cane's hilt. Even before I unleashed the blade, the familiar weight made me ask again, "How much?"

The old man said, "But I have never fixed the price of that one, you see. Only the rarest connoisseur would have an interest. Only the most remarkable man . . ."

I did not like the sound of that at all. Of course, I had been too eager, which was foolish. Now he wished to raise the price as high as he possibly could.

I was about to tell the old fellow that I wished to know his price and no more dithering, when he laid the tips of his fingers upon my forearm.

The skin on the back of his hand was so thin you seemed to see not only bones but marrow.

"You must try the blade . . . to understand . . ."

"I *have* tried it," I told him. "I had one exactly like it, see. I lost it in a fuss."

His fingers slipped around my wrist, gripping me with all his remaining strength.

"You must be mistaken," he said. His eyes cut into me.

"No. I am certain of it. Look you. I do not pretend to know many things, but I know my weapons. It is not only the look, but the feel of the thing. Three months ago, I possessed a blade identical to this one."

"But that is not possible!" he declared. He seemed uncertain whether to be angry with me or astonished. And his voice held the slightest undertone of fear. "That is . . . it is so unlikely I must think it impossible. There were only five . . . only five were made so. Two are in royal collections, a third is said to have found its way to Persia . . . I say, 'found its way,' *monsieur,* because the blades choose who may carry them for a time. But do you know the story . . . the terrible story? I think you do not . . ."

Now, I had not imagined the Earl of Thretford's gift as anything special, beyond its obvious handsomeness. And as a fellow sensible of his purse, I had reason to be wary of any proprietor who spoke of royal collections and Persian wonders.

The old man inched closer, until I seemed to catch a whiff of mortality. "But you say that one is lost? One of the blades has been lost?"

"Destroyed," I said, struggling to pronounce my words correctly. "It was a nasty business."

Seen close, the skin on his face was so thin I seemed to see thoughts at work. I laid the weapon back down on its bed. Reluctantly. I did not wish him to think me quite so anxious as I had let myself appear.

"Then . . ." he said, ". . . there are four now. Only four left." He looked at me as earnestly as a parson stares at sin. "But if the legend is true . . . what is said . . . then let us hope that the blade that has been destroyed was the accursed one."

Now, all of this was beginning to sound like a fisherman's tale to me. Some sort of Frenchified method of haggling to squeeze out every penny from the customer.

He turned to my companion. "Ah, *Monsieur* Barnaby . . . please . . . in the bottom drawer of my desk . . . the armagnac. There are glasses, you will see them . . ."

Mr. Barnaby's concern with a late arrival at Mrs. Aubrey's appeared to have vanished. But then he always liked to hear a tale. He was a great reader, as I had discovered one night in Mississippi, although he always read in the same book. Twas a matter I intended to discuss with him. Once my mouth forgave me for its sufferings.

"But we must sit!" the old fellow said. "No, no. First . . . take up the blade again. Take it up! It wishes to be touched, I think. Unsheathe it. Let it feel the light of the lamp, the warmth . . ."

I took it into my hand once more, drawing the slender blade. Feather-light and substantial at the same time, it was instantly familiar, unmistakable. When I lifted it up to the light, the blade seemed to come to life in my hand, to grip me in return.

"Now put it down, *monsieur* . . . let it rest, it has been surprised. Let it listen to its own history . . . perhaps it will have something to tell us in return?"

Mr. Barnaby stepped back in, bearing a bottle that looked all too suspicious. But the good fellow, bless him, only carried two glasses.

"The major don't take liquors and such," he explained to *Monsieur* Beyle.

The old Frenchy gave me a glance that was less than approving. But his disappointment passed. As soon as Mr. Barnaby had poured the glasses a quarter full, the old fellow knocked his back and smacked his lips.

"Perhaps," he said, "I should begin with the old Saracen . . . or should I start with the young Englishman and his dreams?" He tutted. "They are both dead now, of course. God rest their souls . . ."

As he spoke I found it difficult to stop myself from staring at the sword-cane. I coveted the weapon. And covetous thoughts of any sort are un-Christian.

"But I am a foolish old man. It is only right to start with the Englishman." The old fellow's eyes, sharp and immediate until then, seemed to drift, to lose their interest in myself and Mr. Barnaby. "Yes, to start with the Englishman." *Monsieur* Beyle raised an eyebrow. "He was not . . . as it has been told to me . . . the sort of Englishman to which one objects. Not at all! He was a romantic young man, quite handsome *et très gentil* . . . an aristocrat of deeper lineage than pockets, who had fallen under the spell of the famous Lord Byron. In the matters of the poetry, I would say, not in the misuse of ladies and the bad behavior. It is said the young man was present when this wild English poet expires of the sickness while fighting the Turks. And that the young man is intoxicated with the poet's notions of freedom and *la guerre pour la liberté* . . . the fighting for the liberty. The famous Lord Byron has said to him *en passant* that five men of good heart can bring down a tyrant."

The old fellow frumped his chin and let his eyes roll gently. "Ah, but the Lord Byron's life proved otherwise, I think. Still, the young Englishman is romantic, he sees the dream, not the reality. For him, such ideas are like the first great passion for a woman, the love one never forgets. He resolves that he will be like the—I think it is 'knight-errant,' *non*? And he is like other Englishmen in one regard. He loves Italy, where reality is not important to him, only the dream of what he thinks Italy must be. It is, I believe, more than thirty years ago. Some years more, I think. The Bourbons have returned to the Sicilies, to Napoli, as if Bonaparte has never been. And this Englishman does not see the Naples that is real before him, no, *monsieur,* but the romantic dream of this city and its people, who are in truth no better than people in every city. Oh, they have tasted some freedom in the years of Napoleon, but it is all gone now. And not so much missed, I think, for freedom is not an affair of the poor, who have other interests. But the Englishman resolves to liberate the people of this kingdom. With only himself and four others."

The old man sighed. "But how is he to find the four others? That must wait, because he is not in Naples when he decides it must be free to become a republic. No, he is not there where he can see this city or smell it or hear its cries. He is in a place faraway, in Damascus, because the Englishman always goes where he is not asked, where he is not desired. He is in Damascus, which is ruled by the Turk, but he is an Englishman with a pass and maybe a little lost in the soul when he wakes in the night and decides he will save Naples from the House of Bourbon. He is in Damascus and he decides he will have five swords made of Damascene steel, secret blades that will be concealed in the canes of gentlemen, each one identical, each to be carried by a member of his brotherhood of five."

The old man nodded faintly to Mr. Barnaby, who poured him another quarter glass of liquor. But the fellow began to speak again before drinking. "Until then, I think, he is only the mad Englishman. But somehow, I cannot say, he becomes acquainted with an old Saracen." He smiled lightly, showing amber teeth. "Even older than I am, perhaps? I cannot say this, either. But he is old, the Saracen who will make the blades. And perhaps he is not even a Mohammedan? He may be a secret Jew, whose family brought the secrets of forging steel from Toledo. Or perhaps he is a disguised Christian, one of those whose faith is so select and so contrary it has been persecuted by all? One who passes down the secret knowledge the churches slaughter thousands to destroy? But perhaps he is only a Sufi, after all. One of the lesser sort, not even descended from the Assassins. Still, one whose ways are never what they seem. But this is too much to tell to you. You do not care for such details."

He took up his glass and sniffed the liquor. You might have thought him a young man enjoying the scent of his sweetheart. He sipped daintily now, licking his lips with a slow, gray tongue.

"But the five blades are forged! They are fitted to five identical canes, as the Englishman wishes. He admires the steel and is glad to pay the little price asked, but he does not perhaps see how the old Saracen looks at him, how his eyes are so strong. The Englishman is not serious when the old Arab tells him that he has put a special quality into the blades, that he has whispered to them in the fire, saying protected words, and that each blade will take the character of the man who first uses it to draw blood. The Englishman thinks this is only the foolishness and superstition of the East. And we must declare him to be correct, *n'est-ce pas*? But of course, he is right!"

The old man drank again. This time he closed his eyes, perhaps to savor, mayhaps to remember.

"But here it is! He returns, by which route I do not know, to Naples. There he has one friend among the Italians, a handsome, young, foolish man with whom he dreams of the brotherhood in the way that is so English and amiable in the young, so repellent in the old! And this Italian, who is a count—but there are so many counts in Italy!—he has a sister who is not beautiful, but more than that—she is the woman whose attraction does not engage the eye, but the soul. Oh, I do not mean that she is ugly, *monsieur*! *Au contraire, au contraire!* Only that her beauty does not fit the beauty of which we think, that she slips past the eye to the deep place in a man. She is good, not bad. She loves this Englishman who loves her brother. But the English are so stupid! They know nothing of women, nothing, *mon cher Major!* He does not feel her love at all, but loves only his fantastic revolution . . . and the Italian friend who is like a brother, who brings to him two other young Italians, two who are truly brothers and who are perhaps the cousins of this young Italian count. It is Italy, who can say? There are four young men. Four of the sword-canes are distributed. Childish oaths are sworn, with great seriousness, with the seriousness of which only young men are capable, the *faux* seriousness of words that intoxicates the heart in the moment, but cannot last as long as the oath demands. Four to topple a dynasty supported by all the powers of Europe! Four! And who will be the fifth? That is the question!"

Closing his eyes as if he had drunk, he did not touch the glass. On its velvet bed, the blade gleamed. The sheath glistened beside it.

The old man cleared his throat. "But who will be the fifth man? To make the revolution? Who can be trusted among these . . . these inconstant Italians? Already things have become unhappy, because the two brothers who are cousins of the count are both stupidly in love with the sister who loves the Englishman only. I think it makes an opera for *Signor* Bellini, only it is far sadder, you will see."

He tapped his knee. Four times. Then a fifth. "Who will be this *Monsieur Cinq*? Ah, there is a Frenchman. There is always a Frenchman in such stories. He is not yet old, but no longer young. Perhaps of forty years. He is, I am told, the youngest son of a good, but minor family. After Waterloo, their lands are restored to them, but not their wealth. But this son is not lazy. He is not like the others who inherit titles and mortgages. He is not ashamed to work. He leaves his commission in the cavalry because it is foolish to him. He cannot afford the fine uniforms that are so important, and there is no war to fight. He makes business instead, which his family thinks is shameful. But he believes they are the fools to imagine that blood and pride will fill the belly. He works hard. In Paris, in this lovely Paris that is so sad now, where all the life is gone with the little Corsican. But he has the name and is not ugly in the face, he has the fine manners. He is even honest, I think. So he makes the success. He marries. He loves. He loves too much. When the cholera comes and his wife is robbed from him, his wife and the little boy . . . all his success is nothing."

The old man smiled. "I think he is like our poor *Monsieur Barnaby*, no? He has loved like a gambler, staking all. And he has lost. The croupier is death, and he has lost everything. The love is everything, the rest nothing. All *perdu, perdu* . . . Still, he has money. Not so much. A little. Enough. He wanders. He goes to Spain, but there is nothing. Backwardness only, everything is of the past. He thinks he will go to the Americas. But the coach takes him to Avignon instead, then to Genoa, perhaps, or Pisa. In Italy, it is always like the gravity. Pulling him southward. He does not decide, he just goes. Firenze is too dark, too sad. It has too many ghosts of its own. Siena is a mortuary. In Roma, there are too many churches. They only make him think again of death. The society is decayed, it repels him. It is all false sweetness and a skeletal hand in the pocket. The women do not please him, though they wish to. Then he comes at last to Napoli, to Naples. The harbor is full, but his days remain empty. So he thinks that he will sail away. To Egypt, perhaps. The Orient. But he does not go."

The old fellow closed his eyes for a moment, rallying the strength to continue his tale. "He does not go. Instead, he meets a young Englishman in contemplation of a *désolé* painting of Caravaggio. How do they become friends? Who can say? Perhaps the Frenchman finds the passion of the Englishman for this dirty city and its hopeless people *amusant,* a good entertainment? Or perhaps he needs to believe again? In anything. Perhaps the object does not matter, only the belief."

He consumed a younger man's gulp of liquor. His eyes cleared again, but in a troubling way.

"And the Englishman? What does *he* wish? Only for a fifth conspirator. The Frenchman sees at once that the younger man is a fool, if a charming one. Perhaps the Frenchman thinks it is all folly, that the folly will soon pass. But he is given his cane with great ceremony, he is sworn to make the revolution and free the people. And the truth is that he will fight, if it comes to blows, because he hardly cares for the life he is leading. He will fight, if only to be alive for a little time again."

The old man shook his head mournfully. "But there is no revolution. It is Italy. There is only jealousy and betrayal. One of the brothers who are also cousins is stupidly in love. Perhaps both of them are in love. But one tells his love to the magnificent young woman who is not beautiful as we think of such things. He cannot live without her, he will die, she is more important than the revolution, than all things that exist! But she scorns him, she is annoyed. She tells him that her heart is given elsewhere, that there is no hope for him. He goes then to her brother, who does not think, who speaks before he thinks, who smiles and says that Marcella is in love with the Englishman, of course, only and always with the foolish, pretty Englishman, but perhaps things will be different after the revolution. Such a mad thing to say! And to laugh! The boy who has confessed his love is angry, he is furious. He goes at once to the Englishman, to challenge him! But the Englishman understands nothing of this matter of love. So the Italian who is in love thinks he is mocked, he draws his secret blade from the cane. The Englishman fights only to defend himself, he does not kill the Italian, but wounds him and the boy is carried off. His wound is not, perhaps, serious. Still, he confesses all, he tells everything to his brother. To his brother who is also in love with this *sirène*. And this second brother, who loves so much that he wishes them all dead, even his own flesh and blood, if only he will have this young woman for himself, this brother goes to the authorities and betrays the plot, even though it is hardly a plot at all, but only the foolishness of young men who have no power and no sense."

The proprietor sat as still as the wares that slumbered on his shelves, his white hair damp and limp. "They were, I am told, terrible times. With the secret police, secret prisons, torture still in use, as if the clock has gone backward. Instead of being rewarded, the brother who has informed is put in the prison, too, where he will die, I think. When the soldiers come to his bed of convalescence, the brother who is wounded attempts to fight. From his pillows. He swings his sword. The soldiers use their bayonets. The Italian count who is the Englishman's first friend is surprised in the garden of his palazzo. He has with him only his conspirator's sword-cane. But he, too, fights. With thirty, perhaps forty soldiers. They do not want to kill him, because they are only poor soldiers and his family is very old. They do not want trouble with anyone, only to do what they must. But he fights madly. In front of his sister, his mother. So they must kill him, too."

His eyes grew moist with the effort of his tale. "It is terrible. The sister who breaks so many hearts must watch her brother die. It is all miserable, useless. But she knows, she understands many things, even though she is a woman. She hurries to warn the Englishman, who is not at home. He has been sailing with the Frenchman, who does not think there will be so much seriousness, but who does not fear it. Perhaps he is glad when the young woman who is greater than beauty is waiting on the shore for her Englishman who even now understands nothing of love, whose only romance is the dream of his own republic. She weeps. She warns him, both of them. They must flee. But of course she has been followed. The authorities are no fools, the secret police are angry that they themselves have detected nothing, even though the plot is not a serious one. But they make a mistake. They come with too few. There are six of them, I think. Only six. And the Englishman and the Frenchman have their sword-canes, which they must always carry, it is in the silly oath. Oh, there are pistols in the hands of the authorities. But the Frenchman has been an officer of the cavalry, not a mere policeman. He cuts the pistols from their hands, one-two! He cries to the Englishman to take the girl and flee. But the English must be gentlemen always! The foolish young man draws his own blade and attempts to fight. He kills one, wounds another, but is shot through his brain, making the young woman scream and fall to her knees. The foolish policeman reaches for her. But she picks up the conspirator's blade herself. The Frenchman cries that she must not do this and he himself is wounded, only lightly, because he has let his eyes stray. But the young woman grasps the hilt with one hand, the blade itself with another, and thrusts it up into the policeman's belly. She is like a tiger, so fierce. The secret policeman, he shoots her in the throat before he falls."

The old fellow stopped for a moment. Perhaps his age was telling and he had to labor to recall the fable's details.

"The Frenchman becomes a mad animal! He kills them all, even those who are wounded and cannot fight again. He kills them like a beast. Because he has a secret in his heart, a secret he himself has only learned that day upon the jetty. He, too, has loved the woman! In his soul he has known always that he was to receive her . . . her . . . how must it be said? Her *authentic* love. Somehow that I cannot say, he has known that her love for the Englishman was—will I call it a rehearsal? Now he sees before him this future that has been murdered for nothing. She dies with her dark eyes open to Heaven and her black hair cast over the stones. He knows then that she was the only woman who could have surpassed the wife he had loved so dearly, the only possibility left for him in all the world. But she is dead. Of this stupidity."

The old man smiled, exposing ruined teeth. "*C'est la vie*, eh? The Frenchman escapes, of course. The men who do not care about life often escape, I think. And where does he go, this only survivor of so great a folly? This man who has indulged in the games of children, only to see the children murdered before his eyes? He goes to Damascus. Not fast, he does not go. He wanders. Slowly. I will not say he goes like a man in a dream, because his life is emptier than any dream. But this wandering takes him to Damascus. It is not to be avoided, why he cannot say. And he stays many months. That is how long it takes to find the old man of whom the Englishman has spoken with his little English laugh. He finds the old man, who looks fragile and mad, standing by his tiny forge at the back of a stinking lane. The Frenchman has been there so long he understands some of the Arab tongue, more than a little. So he understands when the old man looks at the cane, then at his face, and nods. 'I knew you would come,' the old Saracen says to him. 'Did the English *giaour* die well?' "

The proprietor touched my knee. Just once. "He told the Frenchmen many things as they sat in his filthy den, of how the blade that had been possessed by the betrayer would always be cursed. The other swords would be worthy of heroes, they would find their way to men who deserved to carry them. All this seemed almost magical, intoxicating to the Frenchman, who had been ill with one of the many sicknesses of the East. Then the old Arab told him other tales. Complicated stories. Perhaps the Frenchman could understand only part of all this, because the language of the Arab twists and turns, it is not straight like the blade, and he did not know so much of their tongue as that. But he gathered in scraps of the tales, bits about secret societies and hidden fortresses, about dungeons full of joy and the happiness that devours the soul like leprosy, of journeys to places still unknown to maps, of voyages and secrets destroyed in the telling. As the afternoon passed, the Frenchman began to see that the old Saracen was a madman, demented. He spoke of great wealth buried in the desert, of heresies and wars, of the twilight of the Arabs. Then, just when the Frenchman longed for an excuse to bid him goodbye, the old swordsmith smiled in a way that was the opposite of happiness. He told the Frenchman that he would live to a great age, but that his true life was over, that all of his happinesses would be small happinesses, and that he would never marry again. He told him that he would one day pass his sword-cane to another who would wield it more wisely than he had done, who would use it in the cause of justice. He would give it to someone who had killed many men, yet who loved the good. Of course, the Frenchman knew it was all madness. Perhaps the old Arab saw that and was insulted. Anyway, he told him, 'Go now. Go away. Go far. And await your destiny.' "

Using the edge of a cabinet for leverage, the old fellow hoisted himself to his feet. "But I think that was a long story, *non*? Too long for these times that go so fast. Too long for you."

But it had not been too long. Even if it was all made up to raise the price of the sword-cane, I admit I had been caught.

"What became of the Frenchman?" I demanded. I never had thought to feel such concern for a Frenchy, not even in a made-up tale.

The old fellow shrugged. "Who knows? Perhaps it is only a pretty story."

"But . . . the cane. How did you get it? Who sold it to you? The Frenchman?"

"Oh, *monsieur*! I am an old man! I cannot remember such things clearly, you understand. It came into my possession long ago."

"But you said that two of the other sticks were in royal collections . . . that one might be in Persia . . ."

"I will be honest, *Monsieur le Major*. In my business, many things are said, for many purposes. When I tell you I have heard that one cane lies in St. Petersburg in the private collection of the czar, that another is in the collection of the King of Prussia . . . or that one may have gone to Persia . . . I am honest in what I tell to you, but do not know the honesty of those who have told these things to me." He smiled oddly, but then old men have quirks. "Perhaps there never were five of the blades? I like to believe the story, you see. But I cannot prove a thing."

The queer thing was that I wished to believe the tale. And I realized, with a shock, that the telling had even drawn my thoughts from my jaw.

I braced for the inevitable. High time it was to move along and return to my proper doings. I wanted that sword-cane dearly. Yet, I promised myself that I would not be extravagant. I had already spent money like a rogue on my clothing. If his price was mad, I would simply walk back through the shop's front door.

"How much?" I asked.

The old fellow liked to draw things out, like a cat toying with a mouse.

"It has been with me many years, *Monsieur le Major*. Do you think I should part with it now? At any price?"

I did not like the sound of his last three words.

"Look you, Mr. Beyle. It should be in use. It does no good to anyone in a drawer."

"But such a weapon . . . might do harm, as well as good. Perhaps it is safest left in the cabinet?"

"I would not use it to do harm." I felt like a naughty child being questioned.

"But would you use it to do good? What if this was the blade that belonged to that Frenchman in his *tristesse*?"

"Then," I said, "that old Arab's pronouncement has proven false. He said it was to be passed to someone deserving. But it found its way to you and lay in a drawer."

"Well, then," the shopkeeper said with a smile, "perhaps this is not the blade that belonged to that Frenchman. But at least I do not think it belonged to the betrayer. No, I do not think it is the cursed blade, the bad one."

"How much, then?"

"Nothing. You may take it for no money."

I was nonplussed.

"Take it," he continued. "I could not set a price. There is no reference. I am so old . . . there is wealth enough. Take the blade. And we will have a bargain between us. Before you leave this city, you will return to visit me, *monsieur*. Or perhaps I will come to you? If the blade has been unhappy, if things have not gone well, you will return it. As if it has only gone on an outing. For the fresh air, let us say. But if we find that it must belong to you, I will ask you a favor. Oh, do not be alarmed. It will be nothing against your laws. Nor against God's laws, I assure you. I do not yet know what the favor will be. But it will come to me. We will meet again and I will ask a single favor, nothing too grand. Something virtuous, let us say. If any man may presume to call his whims virtuous."

The old fellow yawned, tapping his mouth with translucent fingers. "*Je suis fatigué!* How the years take their toll! To be a man of forty again! But I must rest, you must go. *Monsieur* Barnaby looks at me as if you have already stayed too long! Go now. Go along. The blade is like a prisoner. Locked away these many years. It longs for the fresh air, for the clear sky . . ."

It sounded like some Frenchy trick to me. Nor was the city's air fresh in the least. Drab and smoky it was. And the "Quarter," as they call it, stank to Hades.

Yet, I took the sword-cane with me. My covetousness would not let me do otherwise.

I left the shop with a sense of intoxication, despite the wicked sensation in my jaw. We passed a thousand people, but their faces remained vague. White, brown, maroon and pitch-black smears they were. I marked no details beyond those I needed to navigate my way beside Mr. Barnaby.

I wondered if any part of the tale were true. An old fellow like that must get frightfully bored sitting there day after day. Perhaps he had composed stories about every item he offered for sale? Perhaps he was no better than a novelist?

I veered between suspicion and a childish delight that the cane was in my hand.

What if the old fellow had meant his gesture well? What if it was not a business trick, but a heartfelt act on the part of a lonely, old man? The truth is that I rather liked the merchant. And not just because he had not demanded cash. Twas the first time I ever suspected myself of fondness for a Frenchman, Lord forgive me.

seven

"ONE FOUND MISS PEABODY'S attitude as unwholesome as her behavior was unfortunate," Mrs. Aubrey announced in her immaculate voice. The years had not annoyed her pipes, but burnished them like silver. Splendid in her widow's weeds and weepers, our hostess seemed as unlike that withered Frenchy shopkeeper as a duchess is from a dairymaid. Sitting straight-backed in a parlor that would have sparked the envy of my Mary, she maintained the impassive look with which the wealthy adorn themselves. "Indeed, one found it necessary to ask her to leave this house."

"And why might that be, mum?" I asked as clearly as my jaw allowed.

Had she not received us immediately, I would have liked to have a poke about the place. Twas a child's delight, with models of clipper ships proud on the mantle and nautical paintings hung high on the walls. Brass shone in the lamplight and a tall clock ticked the time. Hung with brocade, the room was upholstered in velvet. My son would have found it a lovely place to play hide-and-go-seek.

Mr. Barnaby had been right. We were not offered so much as a cup of tea. That is how the rich stay rich, I fancy.

Mrs. Aubrey paused before answering my question, seeking words to suit a lady's modesty. Although the hair was white beneath her widow's cap, her face was free of wrinkles and unblemished by those nasty spots that serve as mortality's freckles. Pale and neat of feature, she doubtless had been striking in her youth. I well could imagine the bygone romance between her and some braided sailor.

Slowly, almost warily, she spoke again. "Miss Peabody was . . . how might one best express it? She was . . . to put things gently . . . indiscreet."

"How so, mum? How was she indiscreet?"

The widow lowered her eyes. The gesture made me expect a blush, but her face remained white as powder. Although I do not think the lady painted.

"Really, Major Jones, this is all so . . . so terribly uncomfortable. One doesn't speak about such matters. From a lady to a gentleman." She cast a moment's glance at Mr. Barnaby, as if to dismiss him from our nobler society. Indeed, she was the first resident of New Orleans who did not seem to think him worth attention.

I found the taste of blood in my mouth again. My stitches had not been done snugly, that was certain. I spoke as cautiously as I could and as clearly as I could manage.

"Look you, mum . . . I do not wish to offend. It is only that this is a Federal matter, a high investigation. I must know all the facts that you can offer. In service to the law, not idle prying."

She shuddered like a curtain faintly stirred. "The details are mortifying."

"Your words will not become a public matter," I assured her. "But the law requires the truth, see."

"One should think so poorly of oneself. One doesn't wish to be cruel, you understand."

"No, mum." As daintily as I could, I patted the corner of my mouth with the handkerchief Mr. Barnaby had loaned me.

Staring into the field of her Brussels carpet, she inhaled from an invisible bottle of salts. "Miss Peabody was . . . indiscreet . . ." she whispered. "With negroes. One had to receive her initially, of course. You do know of our family relationship? A marriage between lesser cousins. Still, one has responsibilities. When her father wrote, asking that Miss Peabody be provided a measure of social guidance, one was obliged. And I must allow Mr. Peabody his honesty. He warned us the girl was headstrong. With her notions regarding the negro—I suppose they're quite the fashion in New York?"

The widow returned her eyes to mine. They were not as soft as her speech. "Pray do not mistake us, Major Jones. One needn't champion the views of our firebrands to grasp the insurmountable nature of the negro's inferiority. One needn't condone the whip to acknowledge the creature's anxiety for humane regimentation. One may see well-behaved sorts in this very city, yet one recognizes that the morally aware negro is an exception—a rare exception, sir—and hardly representative of its race." She lowered her voice again. "Should you pry a quarter of an inch behind its pretense of civilization, you will find that even the most developed negro remains best fitted to servitude, to a program of merciful supervision. Left to its own devices, the negro succumbs to indolence and viciousness. It apes our manners, but cannot fathom the essence. You understand me, of course."

"How was Miss Peabody indiscreet, mum? What did she do?"

"One doesn't discuss such matters in society."

"I must ask you to be forthright, mum."

Her expression hardened. "Where should one begin? Miss Peabody had as little control of her tongue as she did of her temperament. She was socially impossible and had not been a week among us before she made herself unacceptable to all of the better families. After *two* weeks, the wives of shop-keepers would not receive her. In addition to her mad no-tions about the equality of the races and 'universal ballots,' she allowed herself to be swept away by rumors. To the ef-fect that negroes were being spirited off. One couldn't per-suade her that it was simply a matter of runaway slaves disappointed in their new liberties, returning home as swiftly as their monkey's legs could carry them. Nor was she content with publicizing her philosophy. She associated with actual negroes. In the public realm, sir. Her antics even dis-tressed your fellow officers."

"Begging your pardon, mum, but it seems to me there's a good deal of associating with negroes here in New Orleans."

Her voice grew tart as gooseberries. "One speaks of re-spectable society. One knows nothing of what may occur among those who have faltered. A lady does not inquire."

Now you will think me ill-tempered, and I will admit to an unaccustomed surliness, thanks to the needling pain nag-ging my jaw, but I almost replied that a lady does not lie, ei-ther. I could not believe that one such as Mrs. Aubrey knew nothing of the wicked goings-on in her city, where color seemed no barrier to sin. She was a woman of business, and such are never fooled, whether they stand at a counter or sit in a carriage. Yet, I held my tongue, for the devilish truth is that society could not exist if the truth were told at every twist and turn. And to the ladies of our South, lying seems a form of mental exercise. Like draughts played between Welshmen.

I only hoped she would not lie about the things that mattered.

"Could you be plainer, mum? About her indiscretions?"

"Need one be?"

"I'm afraid so, mum."

"Surely . . . as a gentleman . . . you would not press a lady to continue? If it distressed her?"

"No one intends to distress you, see. But the girl is dead. And someone has to answer."

She winced at my indelicacy. Or, perhaps, at a memory of Miss Peabody.

"One wasn't especially surprised," she said, "to learn the consequence of her misbehavior. Her father must be heartbroken, of course. But whatever *can* the man have thought, allowing such an unsteady girl so much freedom? To be enjoyed safely, Major Jones, a young woman's freedom must be circumscribed. The wild rose is much over-praised. A gentleman prefers the hothouse orchid."

"Yes, mum. Why weren't you surprised?"

Mr. Barnaby stirred in his chair, leaning forward as far as his belly would let him.

"Because of the negroes. One cannot consort with them. Except as mistress of the house, speaking to one's servants, of course. Their inclinations are . . . brute." Again I expected to see a blush, but her smooth cheek never colored. "One dreads to ask . . . is it . . . true . . . that her person was found in disarray?"

"You believe that she was murdered by negroes, then?"

"Murdered," she whispered. "Such a horrid word. Yet . . . one fears it may be too gentle for her suffering." She wafted her fine-cut face from side to side, trailing her weepers. "If only she had listened to one's advice . . ."

"And what advice did you give her, mum?"

The widow straightened her ever-straight back until she sat like a mortified sergeant-major. "To begin, one told her to rid herself of that . . . that hussy of a maid she took up. A creature from one of those islands. The thing couldn't even

speak French. Or a word of English. And she bore the unmistakable countenance of dishonesty." The widow leaned a
split of an inch toward me. "One learns to read servants at a
glance. Susan . . . that is, Miss Peabody . . . would not be
warned. She told me she pitied the creature."

Mrs. Aubrey's features tightened, as if she had found a
dead mouse in her porridge. "One doesn't *pity* servants,
Major Jones. One *trains* them. Anything more or less is a
disservice to all concerned. Yet, Miss Peabody embraced
this wanton girl, as if we all were characters in a romance."

"You believe, then, that this maidservant had something
to do with her death?"

"One cannot draw a firm conclusion. One does not wish
to be unjust. But one would not be surprised if the little creature were complicit in Miss Peabody's misfortune."

Of course, I thought of the queer girl in my room. Who
could not speak to make herself understood. The girl who
was so afraid of the Lord she knew what that she threw herself
down and all but kissed my boots.

"And what, if I may ask, mum, did this servant girl look
like? Did she have a name, then?"

My ignorance disappointed Mrs. Aubrey. "Major
Jones . . . colored servants do not *have* names. They are
given names. As to the creature's appearance, she was as
unfortunate in that regard as Susan herself—oh, that was
unkind."

"You mean she was plain?"

"Yes. She was plain."

"Small or large, would you say?"

"Small. The small ones are the thieves. But there you have
it. Truly, Major Jones . . . one wishes to assist our government. Now that it has been returned to us. But one has
appointments."

"Begging your pardon, mum . . . you said you had to turn her away from your door. Would that have been the night you saw her last? Was it the night of her murder?"

She looked as disgusted as a princess forced to scrub a latrine.

"It was late afternoon. Not yet evening. She called in broad daylight, with a fancy darky in tow. She actually took the beast's arm, after the houseboy turned her away. How could she ever have imagined that one would receive her? The child had thrown away her last shred of reputation. Parading down the street with a nigger *beau*." She shut her eyes, reliving the horror. "People know there was a family tie, however distant. Even with one's standing in society, one shall never quite live down the shame."

"This negro with her . . . did you learn his name?"

She blushed at last. "The party was not admitted. The matter has been explained."

"What did he look like, then?"

The fury of Jeremiah claimed her eyes.

"He looked," she said, "like a preening animal."

WE RODE TOWARD the heart of the city in darkness thickened by mist off the swamps and river. Our driver took a different course from the one that had delivered us to Mrs. Aubrey and for a time we traded gaslamps for torches by the wayside. Twas an Irish slum by the shipping channel, whose residents did not regard us happily. I noted that the provost marshal's guards were nowhere evident. The very air seemed truculent, and all the world unhappy.

I am a man whose disdain for the Irish has softened over time, not least after the valor they showed at Fredericksburg. But I would not have liked to go for a stroll among the ragged Hibernians of New Orleans.

"She's rich as the Duke of Westminster on the day the rents are collected," Mr. Barnaby said as our cab creaked on. "They say she didn't lose a single riverboat, not even a bale of cotton, to confiscations after the city fell. Rumor 'as it that General Butler's brother and 'er was thicker together than mash on a shepherd's pie. Nobody knows 'ow many ships she 'as to 'er name, but they claims she 'as a better business 'ead than old Aubrey ever did, rest 'is soul."

"I do not think she told us all the truth," I said idly. Queer it was. I had not meant to say such a thing aloud. I had been toying with my new cane and musing between jolts of pain. I was not certain my words were understood, but once a Welshman begins to speak he is apt to continue. "What she said about that servant girl, I mean. About the lass being 'from one of those islands.' Look you. If Mrs. Aubrey had a nautical husband and is herself in the business of ships and cargoes, she would recall the island's name. It is a name she did not wish to say."

"Oh, you mustn't let that trouble you, sir, you mustn't let that trouble you at all!" Mr. Barnaby answered. "I wouldn't trust a lady who told the truth the first time you asked 'er for it. Not 'ere in New Orleans, sir. It just ain't done. There's nothing so distasteful to a lady—whether in the Quarter or on the American side—as telling the truth right out. They sees it as unbecoming."

I heard the driver's lazy whip and a desultory whinny. Earnestly desiring to help me understand matters, Mr. Barnaby leaned close enough for me to smell a staleness.

"It's this way, sir: If you was to ask a New Orleans lady if she 'ad been to a shop, right after you seen 'er going in and coming out of one, she'd reply 'ow she'd been to the 'ouse of a friend or off for a promenade. On principle, sir, on principle." The fellow snugged his coat against the evening chill.

"A gentleman about town would never expect a lady to tell 'im the truth for the asking. And 'e'd be terrible disappointed if she did." He thought for a moment. "Although I suspect there was bits of truth to be picked from all she said. There usually is. It's 'ow they likes to tease us, bless my soul."

"Lying is immoral. And improper. And she is an Englishwoman by birth. That ought to count for something."

"All's one, all's one, sir. Englishwoman or China girl with an opium pipe, once they comes to New Orleans and spies out the lie of the land, it's like they woke up and found themselves in 'Eaven, begging your pardon. There's no place makes a lady as 'appy to be a woman as our New Orleans, sir. 'Igh or low, they takes to lying quicker than a spaniel to a duck pond. Comes natural to 'em, it does." The poor, benighted fellow even smiled. "I doesn't say as it would do anywhere else, sir. But a pleasant lie or two just suits our ladies. They puts 'em on and takes 'em off like gloves."

"And if the lies are not pleasant? The things Mrs. Aubrey suggested were not pretty ones."

Our cab drew up at a row of commercial buildings that bore no slightest resemblance to my hotel.

"All the easier then, sir, all the easier! You just separates out anything nice she might 'ave said, which would never be true when spoke of another woman, and the wicked things are likely to be 'alf right. It's all a formula, sir, like mathematics, and they're just born knowing it some'ow. A lady knows 'ow much of a lie she can mix in with the truth and get away with it. I suspects you'll figure it out, clever as you been. But 'ere we are, sir, 'ere we are at last!"

"And where, exactly, is it that we are?"

He looked at me with incomparable pity. "At the dentist's, sir. At a proper dentist's, is what I mean. At Dr. Dostle's, sir, right 'ere on St. Joseph's Street. Dr. Dostle's a Union man. 'E'll put your mouth to rights."

Dread seized me. I must have gone as white as Mrs. Aubrey. I would have preferred to plunge into a pit of unhappy serpents, rather than have to do with another dentist.

Mr. Barnaby took me by the arm. Firmly.

"You 'as to come along now, Major Jones. You 'as me worried as to all what's been done to you. And you're bleeding again. Be careful of your coat, sir, careful does it."

"GREAT GOD ALMIGHTY!" Dr. Dostle exclaimed, "a drunkard butchering a hog would've done a cleaner job. If you don't die of gas gangrene, you'll be the lucky man out of a hundred."

The fellow inspected my mouth with the aid of a mirrored lamp. His office was as clean and bright as a Welsh wife's parlor on Sunday and, although he was almost as short as I am myself, his grip was strong and confident. Even his clothing was of quality and neat, except for a few spots of blood upon his shirtfront. I should have felt myself in good hands. But all I felt was terror.

"We'll have to rip those stitches out," he told me, "and do the job properly."

Mr. Barnaby shook his head, just at the edge of my vision. "'E went to Dr. Fielding, sir. I didn't 'ave time to stop 'im."

Dr. Dostle shook his head. "That man should be incarcerated. For the quality of his dentistry, as well as for his political convictions. A born traitor. And a born botch. If that man's a real dentist, he's a dentist I wouldn't let near my horse. Pass me that implement just behind you there, Mr. B. The one with the hook on it. The sharp one. No, the bigger one. It's the craziest thing—I can't get my Ulysses to leave that shack of his to help me. After all the training I've given him, all the time I've spent. He's so afraid he won't come out in the daytime. Sometimes I wonder if there's any hope for them, after all."

He looked into my mouth again, then straightened in disgust. Lofting an ominous tool.

At least it was not rusted like Dr. Fielding's appliances.

"I can put you out with ether," he told me. "Otherwise, it's going to hurt a parcel."

I shook my head. Given my recent experiences, I felt an even greater fear of unconsciousness than I did of the dental profession.

"Well," Dr. Dostle said wistfully, "I can't force a man to see what's good for him, can I? Open wide."

He bent to his work, smelling of cologne water and, faintly but unmistakably, of blood.

Speaking to my companion again, Dr. Dostle returned to his own concerns. "Ulysses has become a disappointment. Hiding under his bed like that. Leaving me without any help in the office."

I groaned.

"What are we going to do with them now, I wonder?" the dentist asked. "If Uly's any indication of what to expect? The poor devil's got the windows barred with planks and his shades drawn tight. Didn't even want to let *me* in. He said he had to be certain I hadn't been transformed into some kind of spook. 'Fixed,' he called it. Like he was talking about a gelding. Rambling on about how that Marie Venin has loosed the 'Grand Zombi' to drag them all off to his kingdom under the earth. They ought to lock that woman up, too. Along with Doc Fielding. Although I'm not sure her voodoo nonsense is any worse than his dentistry."

I shrieked.

Permitting me a moment's respite, the dentist said, "Just

calm down, now. Great God almighty, man. Jumping up and down only makes it worse." He shifted his voice, though not his face, back to Mr. Barnaby. "Old Uly's so scared you'd think he was a drunk dying of the trembles. Swears the Grand Zombi's going to grab him in the dark and carry him off. Hold still now! That thread's going to rot your jaw off, if I don't get it all out. Mr. B., hand me that rag, will you? No. The one with the blood on it."

The mopping and slopping did not interrupt the fellow's narration. "It's the funniest thing you ever heard, listening to that poor, old darky talk. Me thinking I had him half civilized and nearly trained to be a dentist himself. At least one good enough to work on his own people. Hold still, we're almost done. He swears that Yankee girl started it all and forced Marie Venin to turn the spirits loose. That girl who wanted to say her piece at the Union meeting, the one the boys shouted down. The one who washed up buck naked on the levee."

The dentist sighed. "That's what happens when white women fiddle with voodoo."

eight

J WAS NOT AT the top of my form when we returned to the St. Charles Hotel. Indeed, I felt I had been through a battle and was not confident that my side had won. My head seemed heavier than a stone and, to my shame, I staggered across the lobby like a man debauched by liquor. Stunned by pain I was, and most unhappy.

There was blood on my new clothing, after all, although I hoped a scrub would draw it out.

Mr. Barnaby promptly got the better of Captain Bolt, who was full of questions regarding my activities. A brisk account of my dental adventures, retailed by Mr. Barnaby, soothed the fellow. As long as I was miserable, the captain seemed content. His mental artillery was not of impressive calibre.

Pain wearies a man profoundly. Had I less faith and discipline, I might have indulged in whisky.

Mr. Barnaby led me to my room, only to pause unexpectedly on the threshold. Just for a moment, he stiffened like a dog catching a scent. I bumped into the broad expanse of his coat.

An oath leapt to my lips, although I do not think it was intelligible.

Murmuring excuses for his awkwardness, Mr. Barnaby hastened to the gas fixture and turned up the flame. It shed a merry light that worsened my mood.

I shut the door with needless force. And turned to find my companion weeping bitterly. With his shoulders slumped and his long face hanging down.

It astonished me to see tears stream into his whiskers. Pain makes us selfish, see. When we hurt, we imagine that we are not merely the center, but all the circumference of the world. We do not spare a thought for our brother's misery. His agony elicits, at most, a grunt.

Something had disarmed poor Mr. Barnaby. Ever a great one for manners and doing things properly, he did not stand on ceremony now. He plumped his bottom down on the bed and the whole contraption creaked. His countenance shimmered with sorrow. An explosion of tears it was. He hid his eyes behind a hand, sobbing like a broken-hearted Samson.

"What's wrong?" I asked.

The big fellow shook his head. Weeping so hard that teardrops spotted his waistcoat. He wanted to talk, to explain, for he was ever an obliging sort of man. But his suffering drove his power of speech to mutiny.

He lowered his head still further, straining his shoulders down over his girth, and pressed his face into his fleshy palms.

"I smells her, I does," he said at last. "I smells my little Marie . . ."

"IT'S THE SCENT," he told me between sobs, "the verbena what the *señoritas* wears in old Havana. I took a fondness for it in the days when I lingered amongst 'em. In the wild days of my youth that was, my salad days when I was young and green. Oh, I was an awful rogue, sir, and I doesn't try to excuse it." He wiped his big nose with a finger, then dried an eye with the backside of his thumb. "The passionate ladies likes a full-figured man in all 'is vigor, for they knows what's what, and I doesn't mind telling it, quiet like. And not only the *señoritas,* but the fair *señoras,* as well, with eyes as dark as chestnuts on the fire."

He brightened as he wept. "I'm wealthy as a lord in fond remembrance, sir. Almost tarried amongst 'em forever, I did. For I likes a dark girl better than a light one, and a Spanish lady knows 'ow to make things lively. But something pulled me onward to New Orleans." He lifted his face, revealing eyes aglow. "Fate is what it was, sir, fate and nothing less. I was destined to meet my little Marie and find my terrible 'appiness with 'er and our little ones." He clasped his hands together, as if praying. "Do you 'ave any idea, sir, what it means to love so much you feel you'll perish? That was 'ow I was with my Marie." He almost smiled, then recalled his sorrow. "Bought 'er that perfume, I did. 'Ad it brought in from Havana. She wore it to break your 'eart, sir. As if it was concocted just for 'er."

He shook his head, then sniffed the air and shook his head again. "May'aps I'm going mad, though I'd 'ate to think it. But twice today I thought I smelled that scent. In this very room. As if 'er very ghost 'ad passed before me."

He dropped his eyes and slumped until he seemed hardly more than a jelly. "I'm so lonely, Major Jones. It ain't the sort of thing a fellow says. But I'm so lonely I sometimes thinks I could fall down and die on the pavings, as if loneliness killed a man deader than the Yellow Jack. Oh, I knows I shouldn't pest you with my troubles, sir, with all the bothers upon you, left and right." Tears marched down his cheeks again, but at a slower cadence. "Life takes it all away, don't it? First Marie and our little ones. Now Master Francis. Who I loves like my own son. It breaks my 'eart to think of the poor lad suffering."

He managed half a smile. It rendered his features forlorn.

"We puts up a good front, sir, and tries our best to be affable. For we likes to seem a jolly sort with our fellows. They
expects nothing less of a gent with a generous figure. Like
poor, old Mr. Pickwick, may God bless 'im." He drew a
palm across his reddened face. "I'm lonely, sir, and I'll say
it this last time. But I'll never say it again to trouble your
kindness."

Despite my own discomfort, which did not relent for an
instant, I felt for the good fellow. It is our common feeling,
see. The loneliness that breaks the bones of the soul. I am
most happy in my marriage, blessed with a healthy son and
another child coming. There is Fanny, my ward, who has an
angel's voice but a better heart. Yet, I know loneliness. Or
knew it, I should say. Perhaps it is the one form of knowledge that comes to us all in time. Even in our rapturous
hours, it lurks.

Placing a hand on the big fellow's shoulder, I found it sur-
prisingly bony. As if his flesh had been tugged down by
gravity.

"It will be all right," I told him.

That is the commonest lie we tell each other.

The good man raised a tear-slopped hand and laid it over
mine own. He did not look at me. He could not. He only held
onto my hand. As far too many young soldiers have done
while dying far from home.

Odd it is how we esteem appearance and think so little of
the soul within. The beauty's sorrow moves our hearts, while
the spinster's despair eludes us. We think a fat fellow merry
down to his marrow and cannot imagine that pain cuts
through his cushioning. We think he wants his dinner, when
he wants a loving heart.

We claim that we are Christians, but we are as hard as
Moabites on a Monday.

"I'd give the rest of my life and give it gladly," Mr. Barnaby said, "to hold my Marie in my arms for a quarter hour."

Up he jumped, near knocking me off my feet.

In a blink he had his derringer in his paw, with one of the hammers cocked back. Ever remarkably deft for a bulky fellow, he prowled toward the blankness of a wall.

Moving as softly as a mischievous cat, he paused but a second to hush me, then moved on. It was a marvelous skill he had, the gift of stealth. He used it to kill men in Mississippi. But that is another tale.

Halting just before the wall, he sniffed the air again.

His great bulk floated across the planks. At the corner of the wall he began to tap, with the derringer ready.

Easing along the woodwork, rapping high and low, he listened to the uniform responses. He passed the spot where I stood, palm cradling my jaw, and knocked on the next panel.

He got a different answer. There was a hollow spot behind the wall.

Agile as a dancer, he jumped aside and waved me off, as well. In case a concealed person opened fire. I eased away from the false spot in the wall, even as Mr. Barnaby inched back toward it.

Pistol lowered but ready, he tapped again, outlining the dimensions of the hideaway.

I heard no sign of life and wondered if war had battered my hearing as badly as it had my hope of Heaven.

Mr. Barnaby glanced about impatiently. I understood what he sought. There had to be a hidden release in the room to unlock the panel.

Handsomely fitted the woodwork was. The innocent eye would never have thought it dishonest.

Mr. Barnaby shook his head, more to himself than to me. Then he positioned his figure before the hiding spot, aimed

his derringer into the wood at the height of a fellow's heart
and said, "Begging your pardon, we'd like you to come out,
sir. For otherwise I shall 'ave to shoot through the wood,
which would be upsetting to all of us."

He repeated his polite demand in a language that was unmistakably French. Then he said his piece again in a tongue
I could not label.

None of his little speeches had an effect. The wall remained the wall. As silent as the tomb in which mine enemies had sealed me.

He tried again, in a sing-song speech that raised the hairs
on my neck. I knew the sound, although I could not place it.
Twas both familiar and strange, an incomprehensible blood-
relation, as Irish is to Welsh.

A scratching sound arose behind the woodwork. As if the
mice were doing acrobatics.

A moment later, the panel began to open. Carefully.

Mr. Barnaby stepped aside, pistol fixed on the opening.

The segment of wall flew wide. A bundle of rags tumbled
out to land at my feet.

Twas the tawny lass who had visited that morning. Her
tongue it was that I recalled when I heard Mr. Barnaby speak.

She clutched my calf—through my trousers, of course—
and let go a stream of gibberish.

Mr. Barnaby lowered his weapon, staring as if witnessing
a marvel. His mouth opened like the maw of a fish, but no
speech followed after.

"What on earth is she saying?" I demanded. Something
beyond my jaw had made me angry. I sounded like a sergeant after his soldiers let him down on dress parade.

My companion ignored me. Shaking his whiskers and
dumb as a Delhi beggar-boy.

The girl raised her voice, as soldiers do when the vendors of India fail to grasp their desires. She knew that one of us spoke her tongue and she wanted recognition of her complaints.

I sometimes think the Lord's punishment upon us for the vanities of Babel was too harsh. I do not mean that disrespectfully, of course. But if we all spoke English like good Christians, the world would be a less confounding place.

I knew not what to do. And Mr. Barnaby seemed inclined to do nothing. But no female should be left in such humility. I bent me down and did my best to raise her, careful to shield my jaw from her flailing arms.

Moving like a sonambulist, Mr. Barnaby glanced inside the compartment. Looking was all the fellow could do. He was too broad of beam to think of entering.

Turning his gaze on my efforts to lift the lass, he made no move to help, but only watched, like a spectator at a puppet show.

When she come up to my level, smelling of sweat and scent, the girl got her first good look at my swollen face. She had not seen me since my collisions with dentistry.

"It's all right, missy," I assured her. Although she could not understand a word.

The lass was frantic. I looked to Mr. Barnaby in despair.

"I can't bleeding believe it," he said at last.

"What, for God's sake?"

"I bloody well can't believe it," he repeated.

"What's she *saying,* man?"

Of a sudden, he woke from his trance.

"Oh," he said, "begging your pardon, sir. She's says if we don't go to rescue 'im right now, the Grand Zombi's going to murder the fellow who tried to save Miss Peabody from the pirates what killed her dead." He wrinkled his brow. "I believe she's speaking of a colored fellow, although my

Spanish creole's wicked lazy. She claims this fellow what ain't dead yet knows all the secrets everyone's trying to 'ide. She says we still might save 'im, if we 'urries."

"NOTHING UNUSUAL, SIR, nothing untoward," Mr. Barnaby said as we raced down the darkened streets.

Captain Bolt and the girl jounced along with us in the cab. A quartet of soldiers followed in a second vehicle. Although there would be some expense involved, I had decided not to wait on government wagons. As for Captain Bolt, he had been perfectly willing to support our rescue attempt, as long as no funds were required from his own pocket. He did not even ask us for details.

"Really, sir," Mr. Barnaby said, "such things ain't unexpected."

When he wasn't calling directions to the driver, he explained the hidden door.

"Every decent 'otel in New Orleans 'as rooms with secret entrances," he assured me. "Although I doubt the St. Charles 'as a quarter so many as the dear, old St. Louis. That's where things gets bubbling in the Quarter, sir, and bubble up they do. Secret doors and passageways are commonplace as chicory in your coffee. It's a matter of convenience, sir, of convenience and propriety."

He leaned from the window and shouted, "Left at the corner," then resumed. "To keep things all polite like, let's say that it's a gentleman in question. What 'as taken 'imself a room for 'is own purposes. And the gentleman may wish to entertain a certain lady with which 'e ain't legally tangled, and I'll say no more 'ereafter. As a proper gent, 'e wants a quiet way to introduce 'is ladyfriend into 'is circumstances. Without the eyes of the world upon their doings. Out of consideration, sir, out of consideration! So a narrow staircase in the walls and a proper bit of deception in the woodwork saves all from unwanted embarrassments. Although it can go 'ard on a lady's crinolines."

Recovered admirably from his despond, the good man seemed near feverish with excitement. Of course, we fellows like a bit of a chase.

"There you 'ave it, sir!" he said. "The 'otel's 'appy, the guest is 'appy, and I'll say no more about the lady in question. Not that I suggests a lady guest would make use of such devices the way a gentleman might, but I wouldn't be an honest man if I told you straight out they doesn't. And mum's the word 'ereafter, mum's the word. I'll not say another word on the matter, since I knows you're dreadful Christian."

Had my jaw not been annoyed, I would have expressed my disapproval of such disgraceful arrangements in language that would have scorched the entire city. To succumb to illicit passion is sin enough, but to make its facilitation a matter for architects plumbs the moral depths of Sodom and Babylon.

Captain Bolt sat listening, although I was not certain he understood a great deal. The figure he cut was not one of capability. He chewed tobacco without sealing his lips, a brace of sins that would have appalled my Mary.

The lass sat in the coach's corner, small as a worried child, thin as the smoke from a poor man's chimney, and plain as a potato. Nervous of the very air, she seemed to be counting the seconds to our destination.

She startled me, jumping from her seat to point at a passing façade. She babbled again.

"Stop, stop!" Mr. Barnaby called to the driver, who brought the horses up.

Turning to me, my comrade said, "Begging your pardon,

sir, but I'm 'aving a bit of trouble understanding 'er. I gets most of it, I does. But she's a corker."

The girl leapt from the cab, crying, "Francisco!"

I TRIED TO explain to Captain Bolt that two of his men should rush to the rear of the house, in case anyone tried to flee. But neither he nor his soldiers grasped my meaning. Between the distortion of my speech, our haste and their mental indolence, they merely followed after me like orphans.

They were big lads, though, with the look of farmers about them. When knocking on the door brought no response, one broke it open easily with his rifle's butt.

"You're responsible for any damaged property," Captain Bolt warned me.

The girl shot through the door as it gave way. The interior was darker than the world without. Twas almost as black as Mr. Barnaby's mood when he returned with a lamp he had borrowed of our cabman.

"I doesn't like the ways of this," he whispered. "The colored sorts gather round when there's an excitement." He looked from side to side, but the street remained empty. "They knows something we doesn't, Major Jones."

I took the lamp from his hand, but nearly dropped it. Who would have thought that such a frail lass could scream to fright the horses?

Pushing the soldiers aside, I plunged down the hallway, lantern swinging. The dwelling was no shanty, but a proper home with engravings on the walls. You would have thought it fit for any white man.

The parlor was furnished with sensible horsehair chairs and a settee. There was a bookcase, too, and a handsome Bible stand. But I had no time to make a further inspection. The lass screamed again, close at hand.

A pair of curtained doors led to the dining room. Within was a sight to see.

The lass had flattened herself against the wall, agape and trembling. With good reason. The table had been employed for a devilish surgery. A well-muscled man lay upon it. You knew at a glance that he was well muscled, see. He had been skinned like an animal.

A guttering candle stood beside the corpse, perfectly placed to light the scene for visitors. The butchers had known that we—or someone—would come. They had splashed the walls and even the ceiling with blood as a form of greeting.

Twas worse than the regimental parade after we blew the sepoys from our guns.

The lass began to convulse.

"See to her, man!" I ordered Mr. Barnaby, who had stepped in just behind me. The fury the spectacle summoned lent me the power to spit clear words.

He peeled the girl from the wall. She resisted for a moment, then threw herself against him, casting her arms about his waistcoat, reaching as far around him as she could and hiding her face. He did not know how to respond at first. Then he embraced her. As a parent would a child pursued by nightmares. Holding her closely against his chest and patting her with one hand.

Twas then I saw what the lass had seen, just behind the candlelight. Dangling in an archway.

It was a sort of doll. The size of a man. Lumpish and awkward.

My gorge rose and I tasted my stomach's foulness.

The doll was made of the dead man's skin. Stuffed and sewn closed again.

"Good Lord!" Mr. Barnaby said.

Captain Bolt, who had followed us when there seemed to

be no danger, took one look at the scene and declared, "I'll be out in the street, if you want me for anything."

Nor did his soldiers tarry, though one disbursed his supper in the parlor.

It is as cruel a fate as men can devise, skinning a fellow. In India, they douse the fellow's meat with salt to enhance his suffering.

Mr. Barnaby's stomach shared the impulse haunting mine own. He began to gag and lost his grip on the girl.

She stumbled back against the wall. I saw a flash of eyes.

She screamed again, more fiercely than before. Locking her hands across her mouth, she slid down the blood-smeared wall. Gaze fixed on the table.

The raw muscles *moved*. Slightly. Enough to turn the head a quarter inch.

Lidless eyes sought any hope of comfort.

I forced myself forward, until I stood beside him with my lamp. May I be spared such a sight as that for the rest of my living days and after death.

A man is a thing of great and horrid complexity, once his flesh is stripped away.

Lipless teeth parted. I saw that they had let him keep his tongue.

Tormented, his eyes could not settle. The girl's shriek seemed to have wakened him from a daze. Which hardly seemed a mercy. He should have been dead, for life meant hopeless agony.

Demented eyes found mine.

I fought to keep my gaze on his, imagining stupidly that it might be a comfort to him to know he was not alone.

Exposed muscles and ligaments struggled. The poor man wanted to speak, perhaps to pray.

I did what any Christian man would do. Setting the

lantern on the table, I folded my hands and recited, "Yea, though I walk through the Valley of the Shadow . . ."

He growled. There is no other word for it. The sound of it shocked me into silence. Looking back, I think that is what he wanted. For whether or not he believed in Our Savior Jesus Christ and the power of prayer to redeem us, he wanted to speak his last words to mortal ears.

"Fishers of men," he muttered, mad eyes begging attention, "the fishers of men . . ."

His voice was worse distorted than mine own. But I understood him.

"Yes, yes!" I said excitedly. "That's right! Think on Christian things, think on Our Lord and Savior Je—"

He growled again, more fiercely. There was such desperation in the sound that no words I have learned can tell its intensity.

"Beware . . . fishers of men," he said, and died.

nine

$\mathcal{M}_Y$ DESIRE TO LEAVE the victim's house disappointed Mr. Barnaby. He rather liked the rumpus of detective work and seemed to think I should upend the furniture and turn over the carpets. But life is hardly a novel from Mr. Collins. The murderers would have purged the rooms, leaving behind false items to tease and mislead me. If hints of guilt there were, they would have required an eye more diligent and a mind less worn than mine.

I found a few sheets of paper in a secretary, along with a pair of nicely sharpened pencils. To rest my jaw, I scribbled out some questions for Mr. Barnaby. All the while, the lass cowered in the hall.

I will give you our conversation as if I spoke my part, although I only scrawled it.

"The lass will need a place to sleep. Can you see to her?"

He looked at the girl, then looked at me, then looked down at his shoes. Blushing. Having been a gentleman's gentleman, his sense of shame ran deeper than a lord's. He could not bring his eyes back up to mine.

"I fears it wouldn't do, sir. The truth is . . . things ain't rosy. We're poor, these days, sir, poor, though proud as ever. There's no work to be 'ad, not even temp'ree. I've been 'dining out,' as they say, and surviving on the mercies of my friends. Oh, friends is a glorious thing, sir, and I'm proud to say I 'ave some. But I sleeps in a sort of closet, at the moment. I 'ardly fits in it myself. It's in a low sort of place, where I wouldn't like to take you. To say nothing of a cultured lady's maid. It wouldn't be safe nor proper. Begging your pardon." He briefly lifted his eyes, but they failed him again. "I'd be ashamed, sir. Terrible ashamed."

"She cannot stay in the hotel."

He brightened a bit at that, for he knew his city. "Oh, that she could, sir, that she could! Without no improprieties considered. They'll make a face or two, sir, and pretend that it ain't done. But all they wants is a little tip to put a bit of beefsteak under their salt."

He looked at me and it was queer, but all at once I saw the fellow differently. Older he seemed than ever I thought, and worn through like the elbow of a jacket. He had an India-rubber face that fooled you. As long as his body was wide, that face seemed made for mortal man's amusement. You saw the merry mask and not the soul.

An hour before, he had wept over his loneliness. Now he smiled and only looked the lonelier.

I *always* looked at his face, that was the thing of it. Or at his general bulk. Despite his girth, his clothing was ever of a flawless order that tricked the eye into paying it no attention. I looked, but failed to see. Now, by cruel lamplight, with the smell of death pungent as India, I noted that his lapels were worn to a shine and his cuffs were frayed.

"You 'as to understand New Orleans," he assured me. "When all is said and done, a good many things is done what ain't to be said. We'll get 'er a nice servant's room in the 'otel, if nothing better. And you'll 'ave one of your own without secret passages."

I looked at that great, fat, diligent man and remembered

that he had not eaten his dinner. Myself, I had not taken a bite since those sweets the night before. Even though I am fond of my victuals as a rule, the nastiness in my jaw forbid the eating.

Mr. Barnaby was due for a feeding, though. And the lass was thin as a Hindoo.

I wrote instructions to Captain Bolt to post guards on the house, then took the lass and Mr. Barnaby off in our cab. Now, you will think me wasteful and extravagant, but I invited Mr. Barnaby to take a hotel room at my expense. I presented it as a practical matter of business, since I might discover an urgent need of his services.

The good fellow declined. "All's one, sir, all's one. Though it's a gentleman you are for thinking so kindly. A pallet's as good as a palace, if not better. Discipline and 'ardship builds the character! That's what my father before me always said. I was a soldier myself, if you recalls, sir. Although I ate my way out of the profession. No, sir, no. Charity won't do, and I won't 'ave it. All I wants of you, sir, is to see what can be done for Master Francis. Once your affairs in New Orleans is concluded. 'Ave no worries about old Barnaby B. Barnaby, sir. Barnaby always comes right, 'e does, as sure as the Queen loves Scotland." He hesitated a moment, then said, "But do what you can for the lass, sir. If I'm a judge of persons, as I likes to think I am, she ain't a bad one."

The fellow had his pride, if in his humble way. Even though his habits were irregular, I must admit I was ever disposed to like him.

He smiled and mastered a tear. "But 'ere we are, sir, 'ere we are! Back at your 'otel, where you can gather yourself."

The truth is that I dearly wanted sleep. The past two days had been a pageant of miseries. I wished to quit my companion and the girl, to flee to a darkened room and coddle my jaw. To forget all that had been done and wanted doing.

But a man who turns from duty has no worth.

I had to see to the lass's comfort and to Mr. Barnaby's feeding. And my duty it was to pry out her tale before I took me to bed. The truth is that the city was so wicked the poor girl might not live to see the dawn.

HER NAME WAS Magdalena, and she had a tale to tell.

Born a slave she was, on one of those bedeviled islands still possessed by Spain in freedom's hemisphere. Her father was a grandee and a drunkard, her mother a lady's slave with whom the gentleman interfered. Her plainness had been evident in childhood and so had her resemblance to her father, who sold her off at a loss to see her gone. Twas thus she left Santiago and sailed to San Juan with a *señora* who found her price notably more attractive than her person. An unexpected blessing it was that the lass had nimble fingers and could sew as finely as a Seville lacemaker. She had proved deft at other things, as well, clever at grasping the point of social rituals and reading the desires of her mistress before they come quite clear to the lady herself.

She never heard again of her captive mother and found no happy welcome in the household where a deed of sale had placed her. Yet, smiles, not sulks, win favor, and she knew it. She made herself of use at every turn and even learned to read—alas, not through the Bible, which the Spaniard imprisons in Latin. She created a world within herself, as slaves must do if they will not go mad, and grew so accustomed to believing that all her mistress's possessions were her own that it shocked her to be reminded now and then that she was a prisoner, owning little more than a change of linens.

She learned, of course, of voodoo, of Candomblé and the myriad cults of Africa that promise special succor to the slave. Such doctrines were ever present among the tormented. But she was won for Christ through the Roman church and never wavered. Although denied the Gospels on the page, the passion of Our Lord adorned her thoughts. Instead of celebrating heathen rites, she prayed she might be freed to become a nun.

She sewed and dressed her mistress and served coffee. She was not often beaten.

Can you and I imagine what it means to be enslaved? To go for a soldier is hard enough, taking orders from dullards and madcap lieutenants, yet even a soldier has his joys and his precious hours of freedom. But to be born a slave and live thereafter in subservience and unrelenting bondage . . . even for a negro that must be hard. For who does not yearn to do as he himself wants, instead of as another wants him to do? Who could bear to love, only to have his family torn asunder because the master's son lost much at cards and a slave sold off brought less pain than pawning a brooch?

Freedom is a wondrous thing. I do not suggest that the negro is, in general, of the white man's practical worth or high intelligence. Yet, think on what Mr. Shakespeare has old Shylock say, then set the tortured darky in his place. Hath not a negro eyes, hath not a negro hands, organs, dimensions, senses, affections, passions, fed with the same food, hurt with the same weapons?

I have observed a number of negroes myself. They felt the same emotions as a duke.

Shall we believe God damns us at our birth, by darkening our skin and curling our hair? The man who subscribes to such beliefs might as well be a Presbyterian.

This war of ours has led me to conclude that slavery is not

merely ruinous to the slave, but to his master, as well. For when we chain our brother, we chain ourselves. Think of Joseph and his wayward brothers, think on Pharaoh. How will we ever save our souls if we enslave the meek who shall inherit?

A man who is master to a slave will never be full master of himself.

I did not care a fig for the nigger when this war began, but I have come to see him as a man. I would not glorify the colored fellow, as our abolitionists do, but merely wish him free to make his choices. Some such will fail, as the Southron folk insist. But if one black man of a million rises, it justifies the freedom of them all.

But let that bide.

The girl had accepted her life, or so she said. Twas hard to steer our discussion, given that I had to scribble out questions, while Mr. Barnaby interpreted back and forth, thrusting his own curiosity into matters. I had stood them a proper feed at the hotel, although the lass had to eat with the downstairs help, and a good meal always inspired Mr. Barnaby's tongue. Following the repast, I had invited them, not without reluctance, to join me in the privacy of my room. No one in the hallways took any notice, and I excused the impropriety by reasoning that Mr. Barnaby served as chaperone. Nor did he mind. His spirits, real or affected, defied the grim events of the earlier evening.

When I forced the conversation back to serious matters, the girl explained how she had come to our shores.

Her mistress had been visiting relations, for many Spaniards lurked about New Orleans, relics of the city's benighted past. Our blockade had shut her mistress in, with dwindling funds and relatives left impecunious. When our gunboats and ships appeared above the levee, returning our flag to the town, the only wealth remaining to the *señora* was her slave.

The lady found herself in a proper pickle. Whatever sins General Butler may have committed, he put an end to slave auctions in New Orleans. Then Mr. Lincoln proclaimed that the slaves within the borders of the Confederacy would be free upon the New Year. New Orleans was no longer in rebellion, at least not officially, so the status of its darkies remained unclear. But General Butler leaned toward the negroes.

Nonetheless, the lass was not to be freed. Whether or not the slaves of New Orleans had shed their chains once and for all, Magdalena was the property of a citizen of Spain. And the Spanish consul, a dreadful friend of the Rebels, instructed our authorities that the seizure of Spanish property would be viewed as an act of war. Which would not have pleased Mr. Seward or Mr. Lincoln.

Democracy has confusions enough. Diplomacy compounds them.

Magdalena's mistress faced a conundrum. She possessed the capital of a well-trained slave girl, but could not sell her to raise the cost of a passage.

At last, the *señora* discovered a Portuguese captain willing to carry them to San Juan on a promise of doubled fees paid on arrival.

Magdalena did not wish to go.

The notion of freedom, sudden and fresh, possessed her with the force of revelation. She ran away, was found, and her mistress beat her. She slipped away again and was beaten worse. She was not hard to recapture, given her lack of any local tongue. Helpless as a babe she was, despite her many talents. And slavecatchers abounded, despite the presence of our Union lads.

Miss Peabody rescued her. Hearing of the poor girl's situation, Miss Peabody offered the *señora* one thousand greenback dollars, which was more than a young Mandingo lad commanded before the war. Of course, she did not "buy" Magdalena, but offered "compensation" for the *señora*'s willingness to abandon the lass.

Twas all a muddle. But the girl was free.

To Magdalena, Miss Peabody was a godsend. She spoke not only French, but Spanish, too, although it sounded odd to the creole ear. She offered the girl a salary to serve as her maid and companion, and Magdalena felt obliged to accept. But Miss Peabody was very different from the *señora* and did not care for lace and elegant dresses, for perfumes and "morning visits" made in the afternoon. She reminded the lass of a slave at harvest time, driven not by the master's whip but by a pride and purpose all his own.

"How did Miss Peabody learn of your plight?" I scribbled.

"Francisco," she replied through Mr. Barnaby. "François Pelletier." New tears followed the old.

I wrote: "The man who was murdered?"

She nodded, resisting her sorrow. "He was a very good man! A fine man. A noble man. He was a great friend to Miss Peabody. He told her about me. She had very much money. But he did not take it for himself, never," she said adamantly. "It was to help the negroes return to Africa. That was his dream, the dream of François Pelletier."

An oddity struck me. Even though her talk come filtered, twas clear the girl did not see herself as a negress. I give you that she might have passed for a gypsy or an Italian. But the lass had negro blood, and that was that. It would not take Mr. Darwin to explain it. But all these creatures have a most peculiar sense of hierarchies, of quadroons and octaroons and such, all in search of illusory distinctions.

I wondered what she thought herself to be? The truth is that we are as others see us. "To thine own self be true" is well and good, but a sound report among our fellows matters.

"Was he handsome?" I asked. "François Pelletier?" I was thinking, almost against my will, of Mrs. Aubrey's remarks about Miss Peabody. About the charge of unsuitable affections.

"Yes," she said, after a wary pause. "He was a very handsome man. Very strong. And pretty."

Next, I had to write an ugly question: "Was Miss Peabody fond of him?"

She nodded the moment the words left Mr. Barnaby. "Oh, yes! She thinks he is as good a man as any. A better man. She says he is a man who will do great things."

Twas not my meaning. Reluctantly, I scrawled: "Fond of him romantically?" I underscored the last word.

She shook her head ferociously. And yet, she chose to think a little further. Her face, for all its lack of charm, possessed a great expressiveness. Emotions warred on her brow.

"I do not think there is romance. No, I do not think it. I think for Miss Peabody the great romance is to make the negro free and even rich. She does not agree with François, who wishes to take the negro back to Africa. Not in the beginning, she does not agree. She wishes him to stay here, to grow powerful." The lass smiled wistfully, indulgently, as a woman far older might. "She believes the negro will be better than the white man, but I tell her that she must not hope for too much, that men are only men, the color does not matter. But she does not listen. She listens to François, but does not agree with him, either. Not at first."

She sat up quite primly. "I do not believe there is romance. I do not believe it, but I do not know truly. Sometimes Miss Peabody sends me away for this thing and that, for some hours. She says it is because I must not listen, that it is dangerous for me to know too many things. I think she tells the truth. But who can say?" The lass looked me straight in the eye. For the first time in our acquaintance. "Who can know what is kept in the other's heart?"

"Corazon" is the word she used. I cannot tell you why, but I remember it.

"Were you," I wrote, "fond of Mr. Pelletier yourself?"

She blushed when Mr. Barnaby put the question to her. She blushed and looked away.

"Such a man as that," she said, "would never look at me."

CAPTAIN BOLT BANGED on the door. He was an awkward fellow, hardly civilized. He wished to report that the body had been taken to the morgue. Along with the doll made of skin.

Had I not suffered the loss of speech because of my battered jaw, I would have told the fellow off, and properly I gave no instructions to move the body, only to guard it well.

Of course, a fellow like Bolt was bound to do the wrong thing, if not given detailed orders. Which I had not been in a state to give. Twas more my fault than his.

I had wanted to have a gander in the daylight. With my mouth less pained and a rested, sharpened mind. To see what I might have missed in my haste and the gore.

Well, done was done, and that was that. Bolt was like a child. Our soldiers may be glad that he had been harnessed in the rear and not sent forward to lead them to their deaths. He had no sense of where he was wanted and seemed inclined to join us. The fellow had a touch of the old maid about him, ever hungry for gossip that did not concern him. I had to drive him off with a push, grunting to express what speech could not.

He stirred me up so badly that I bled again. But he left us.

During my frustrations with the captain, Mr. Barnaby calmed the lass with his chatter. She did not much like uniforms, not even blue ones, and kept a wary eye on our intruder. Mr. Barnaby tried to cheer her up. Beaten down and destitute himself, he always had a jolly word for others.

What better could we ask of a companion?

The lass wore a look just short of a smile when I sat back down between them. Although I am not great of stature, I believe that I possess a manly dignity. My gravity made the girl grow somber again.

"Do you know of a Mrs. Aubrey?" I wrote.

The instant she heard the name from Mr. Barnaby, the girl snapped like a terrier. A torrent of words poured from her lips, and the words did not sound gentle.

"The *Señora* Aubrey? She is the bad one! She is not a woman of sincerity! I think she does not like Miss Peabody, although she pretends to love her with much pleasure. I do not like her, I do not like her at all . . . she has only the money, not the heart."

Corazon. That word.

Abruptly, the lass fell quiet again. Shrinking into her garments. I understood that she feared she had spoken unwisely, that I might be a friend of the Widow Aubrey.

"Do not worry," I scratched on the paper. "Only tell the truth. The truth will not hurt you."

When Mr. Barnaby translated that, the girl replied, "The truth hurts everyone. Always. That is the law of the earth. Only sometimes the truth does not hurt so bad as the lie. The lie is like the young lover, I think, and the truth is like a husband. The lover is good for the short time, but the husband is best for the long time."

As a proper Methodist, I found her comparison doubtful.

I wrote: "Mrs. Aubrey and Miss Peabody argued? Before Miss Peabody's murder? About Mr. Pelletier, perhaps?"

"But that is not true!" she said, thrusting forward her shoulders. "They are in the relationship of the family. Although I do not trust this *Señora* Aubrey, there is not any quarrelling. No, I do not think there is the argument between them. Never the argument. *Señora* Aubrey was to be helpful. For a price." She drew thin brows toward her deepset eyes. "Why would they argue about François? That I do not understand at all."

"Because Miss Peabody tried to introduce him to Mrs. Aubrey's abode," I wrote.

The proposition baffled the girl. "But how can this be so? François is many times in the house of the *señora*. Many times. I have seen him. Sometimes he is meeting Miss Peabody there, sometimes they arrive together. But François and *Señora* Aubrey . . . they know each other for more time, I think. It is the *señora* who tells François about me." The lass gave her head a snap. "I do not know why she asks François to inform Miss Peabody of this. I cannot say why she does not tell Miss Peabody herself. The *señora* knows my mistress well, there is old business between the families. There is no secret that I am to be sold to your Miss Peabody. It is a favor, an arrangement. But the *señora* is a woman of strangenesses."

Now, this was a bit contradictory to what I had been told. My impulse was to suspect the lass of lying. After all, she was recently a slave, while Mrs. Aubrey held a social position.

Still, I remembered Mrs. Fowler, of the Philadelphia Fowlers, who had been crueler than Bloody Mary.

I wrote: "You say François Pelletier visited Mrs. Aubrey many times?"

"Verdad," she said. I remember that word, too. *Verdad* and *corazon.* "It is true! Of course, it is true! Many times he has sat there, speaking of the price of hiring the ships to take the negroes to Africa. They speak of every detail. Of the price of hiring the ships, of the insurance of the voyage. Of the cost of the food and the dangers of the passage. Of many things they speak. Miss Peabody only listens. I think she cannot decide what is the best. But she has the good heart, the very good heart. Always you must believe that she has the good heart."

Corazon.

I wrote: "So Mrs. Aubrey did not believe there was an improper relationship between Miss Peabody and Mr. Pelletier?"

"Why is she to believe such a thing?" The girl went up like a mine under a redoubt. "And why will she care if there is, this old woman who has had so many lovers, who is famous for such things?"

Twas clear the lass was not fond of the widow. And hate is not an honest judge of character.

I wrote: "How could you know such things, Missy? Do not lie to me."

"Ask anyone!" she said. "The whole city speaks of it. In whispers. But they speak. The *señora* is a beast that devours. They say she has made the voodoo."

"Who told you that?"

"Francisco. François."

"Why would he tell you and not Miss Peabody?"

"Perhaps he tells her, too. I cannot say."

"But why did he tell you?"

"He was afraid."

"Why would he tell you even that?"

She caught a breath, then said, "We are lovers together."

There. She *had* lied. Not half an hour before. And one lie begets another.

"You said that such a man would not even look at you."

A single tear broke from her eye. "He does not look at me. He puts out the lamp and cries for Susan."

"But you just said they shared no affections."

"He is loving her, but she is not loving him. She loves only her ambition for the negro."

"But Miss Peabody was plain as a mackerel."

She looked at me mockingly, with an expression of majestic superiority. "You do not know the woman. It is only the little boys who die for the famous beauty. The men who are always only the little boys and nothing more. But Susan is the one who wounds the life of the man. He does not understand how she cannot love him. It amazes him. He burns."

"Why do you hate Mrs. Aubrey?"

"Because she hated Susan. Because I fear her."

"Why do you fear her?"

"Because she knows that I know, that I listen, that I see. That I do not believe her. She sees many things. She follows the voodoo."

"But you're a Christan. You don't believe in voodoo. What harm can it do you?"

She smirked. As though I were the greatest fool on earth. "What harm did it do Francisco?"

"That was not voodoo. It was murder."

"It was murder for voodoo. Of the goat without horns."

I had heard that expression before. And had not forgotten it.

"And you are afraid of being murdered? For voodoo?"

"No. For wishing that Susan is not forgotten."

"And is Mrs. Aubrey the one you are afraid of?"

"One of many. But I have more fear of the others. Not so much of the *Señora* Aubrey. Not now. Not yet. But of the others."

"Why?"

"Because," the lass told us, "*Señora* Aubrey knows that I am dead."

"IT IS BECAUSE of Susan that I am dead," she told us. "She has many worries. Now I understand such things. But she does not tell me of them then. She only returns from a visit that is not to Mrs. Aubrey and orders me to gather up my clothing. There are not many things that I have, but I go slowly, because I feel the wound. She speaks to me like the grand *señora* to the slave. She has never done this before. 'Pack! Now!' she says to me. I do not understand. Before this visit, she is so happy. Many negroes will go to Africa, she has agreed to this. She will pay, all is arranged. Then she is gone from me for two hours, perhaps three. And she returns in much anger. She is angry with me that I go slowly, she tells me that I am stupid. She is never like this before. Then she takes me in the carriage and pulls down the covers of the window, the way they take away the lepers from good families in the night. When the carriage stops, we are at the *convento*."

She smiled wistfully. "Susan has been many times in the company of the nuns, although poor Susan is a heretic who follows *El Rey* Henrique of England, who worships the Great Sinner of Canterbury. Susan gives the money to help the negroes who are very poor. For this, perhaps, she will not burn so long in the flames, I cannot say. But all has been arranged. I will stay with the sisters. Always, I have wanted to be a nun. But not now. Now I wish to be with Susan, who is my friend. And with François. But she leaves me with the nuns, and the *madre* tells me I must not go out even into the square. I must not look out of the window."

"Where did Miss Peabody go? That made her fearful?"

The lass shook her head. "I cannot know this. Many things she does not tell me. She visits many people, many places, for the good of the negro. The *Señora* Aubrey. The newspaper office where François makes his work. The Yankee soldiers, who do not like her because she disturbs so much. The homes of *los abajos*. But I cannot say where she goes that day to become so angry."

I had already pieced some bits together, but wished to hear the matter from her lips.

"Did Marie Venin go to the convent to find you?"

When Mr. Barnaby spoke that name, Magdalena made a cross over her breast as the Catholics do. If she had no current fear of Mrs. Aubrey, she had fear in plenty of the voodoo witch.

"Yes. But I am not there. François has come, he has taken me away, because you are too slow. At first, he believes that you will find me and protect me, but you are too slow. All things had been arranged, but he could not make you go fast. He spoke of the little soldier who limps, who is *el hombre sincero*, but who is slow. And then Marie Venin is coming first, so François must hurry to take me away from the *convento*. And I am glad to go with him, you understand."

Her features lessened into sorrow. "But he is different now. He is fearful and speaks only of the disappeared ones, of things I do not understand. Only then do I learn that Susan is dead, that she has been dead so long. I am like a prisoner in the *convento*, you understand. I know nothing. I wait. I think Susan has abandoned me. I weep. Then there is François, who tells me that Susan is dead. I begin to understand that she has protected me, not left me. It tears at my heart."

Corazon. Mi corazon.

"What did François fear? Who had disappeared?"

"He never fears before. But now he fears everything. Always he is strong and very brave. But now he fears. Perhaps he fears that he will disappear, too. I cannot say this. He does not tell me. He tells me only that I am dead, that he has told the *Señora* Aubrey this."

"Why did he tell Mrs. Aubrey you were dead?"

She found new tears. "Everyone is protecting me, only to die. Everyone I am loving. I do not understand, he will not tell me. But *Señora* Aubrey must think that I am dead. He says it is important." Unexpectedly, she smiled. "It is so funny, how he speaks Spanish like a Frenchman! But why François makes so much difficulty to help me, I cannot say. Perhaps it is for Susan, for her memory. Because she has wished to protect me. But he has told this *Señora* Aubrey that he has murdered me himself. Mother of God! Such a thing to tell her!"

The lass made the sign of the Cross again.

"Why would he tell her *he* killed you?"

"I cannot say."

"He would make himself guilty on the charge of murder. If she went to the provost marshal."

"I do not know. But I think she will not go to the Yankees. François knows this."

"So Mrs. Aubrey and Marie Venin both want you dead? Why?"

Again, the Cross. Then she patted herself below her throat, where that small gold cross was hidden.

"I cannot say."

"Did François or Miss Peabody speak of 'fishers of men'?"

She shook her head. Mystified. "I think they have not so much religion, those two."

"Does 'fishers of men' mean anything at all to you?"

"Of course! This is in the Gospel, it is spoken by Jesus."

"You did not answer earlier. Who were the 'disappeared ones'?"

"Perhaps the negroes. Many are going from the city. No one knows where."

"Perhaps they went to Africa? In Mrs. Aubrey's ships?"

"No. This is not yet. Some money is paid, I think. Susan receives money from New York, this I know. It is very much money. But there is no ship, not yet."

"Who are the 'pirates'? Did they kill François? Or Susan?"

"François speaks of pirates when he is frightened. Before he sends me to you in the hotel. He says that the pirates are going to kill him. But at other times he speaks of the voodoo that will be his death."

Mr. Barnaby, who had been translating with a wonderful lack of grammar, interjected, "Begging your pardon, Major Jones, but it don't sound right to me. Per'aps the fellow was raving. There ain't been pirates downriver in forty years. They're all gone with Lafitte, the times 'as changed. All we 'as nowadays is wharf rats and common robbers."

I decided to let the pirate business be. For the present. I had another question for the lass.

"You said that François sent you to my room. Did he arrange for the special room with the passageway?"

"The negroes in the hotel do this for him. The ones you do not see, who do the low work. They have more power than the *blancos* know. It is not a problem. François is much loved. He brings me to the hotel in the darkness so I can enter the secret way. By one of the secret ways that the white men have forgotten, there are so many. That is how I come to you. But you sleep, I do not wake you. Then these men make the hammering on the door and you are leaving me."

"How did Mr. Pelletier expect you to communicate? You cannot speak English."

She looked distraught. "He lies to me. François. Poor François. He tells me you speak Spanish better than the King of Spain."

"Well, I do not speak Spanish," I scribbled.

"*Verdad,*" she said.

I LET HER chatter nonsense with Mr. Barnaby for a bit. We all required a pause. Weary I was, and half sick. I could hardly tie the bits of her tale together.

According to her version of events, François Pelletier, now deceased, and Susan Peabody, likewise deceased, had been thick as thieves with the Widow Aubrey, arranging to transport negroes back to Africa. Miss Peabody paid someone a visit and returned an angry woman. Then she hid the lass in the Ursuline convent. Shortly thereafter, Miss Peabody's corpse washed up on a levee, with her garments embarrassed. After something more than a month, this Pelletier, who had used Magdalena for shameful purposes without the grace of wedlock, and who was himself enamored of Miss Peabody, suddenly appeared at the convent to spirit the lass away. Not long thereafter, I paid my call on the Mother Superior to discuss a "missing girl." And Marie Venin come racing past, frustrated that the girl was gone and unhappy with her reception.

A thought provoked me. Had Marie Venin, the voodoo witch, really gone to the convent to find the girl? Or to lure me to follow her? Certainly, much had been staged for my reception.

Yet, Mr. Champlain had pointed out the obvious. Had mine enemies wished to kill me, they had enjoyed opportunities in plenty. I had been kidnapped, then spared. Why?

Because, as Mr. Champlain and Mr. Barnaby both supposed, they wanted to put a scare into me to slow my investigation?

Or was there more to the fuss?

Why did François Pelletier, afraid for his own life, send as his envoy a lass who could not speak any language I understood?

Who of the whole bloody lot was telling the truth? If anyone?

Could Mrs. Aubrey have believed that I would not learn that conditions of amity had prevailed between her and Susan Peabody? And François Pelletier? Was she merely defending her reputation, or was there something more?

Was the girl treacherous? All those who could confirm her tale were dead. Was she enmeshed in the schemes of Marie Venin? Or even in the schemes of Mrs. Aubrey? Why had that dying man muttered, "Fishers of men?" Who were the "disappeared ones?" Mere negroes?

I roused myself and turned to Mr. Barnaby. Chattering with the lass, he looked happy as the baker's boy on Christmas. Rarely had I seen a man so changed.

I believed that I had spotted an obvious thing. Something far simpler might lie behind these deaths than voodoo and "fishers of men" and pirates. Something as timeless as mankind. Simple greed.

I wrote: "You spoke of a large amount of money Miss Peabody received. Was it paid out to anyone?"

"I cannot say," Magdalena told me. "Perhaps some is paid to *Señora* Aubrey for the ships. Not all, I do not think." She shrugged.

"Might it have been stolen?"

She shook her head decisively.

"Oh, no. This is not possible. The money has been given to your soldiers. For the protection, until it is needed."

ten

J WANTED TO SLEEP. Instead, I packed myself and Mr. Barnaby into a cab, fleeing Captain Bolt's offer to accompany us and leaving the lass locked safely in my room. Time pressed and I promised to see to her own accommodations upon my return. Twas all more complicated than I liked. The world should learn to behave itself.

Magdalena did not wish to stay behind, in my room or any other. But I tutted her.

I wished to speak with the provost marshal, and with General Banks. About Miss Peabody's money. But that had to wait until morning.

Meanwhile, I could speak with Mr. Champlain. My questions of the night before had been parried as much as answered. The fellow was a lovely host, but he played hide-and-go-seek with facts. As Mr. Barnaby put it, he did not lie but did not tell you all. Convinced I was that he knew more than he had troubled to tell me.

As we crossed into the Quarter, I noted only white men on the streets. The negroes were in hiding. From the Grand Zombi or certain "fishers of men." Or perhaps from the rancor of paler flesh unhappy with defeat.

Unable to scrawl my questions in the darkness of the cab, I struggled to speak clearly. I did not wish to bleed more.

"Is the girl lying?" I asked. At my second attempt, Mr. Barnaby understood me.

"Oh, no, sir! Not at all, I doesn't think. At least not 'ow the local ladies do. She ain't been 'ere near long enough and ain't yet been persuaded to dissemble. Ain't she a wonder, though?"

"A wonder" hardly seemed an apt description.

"Why," I asked, enunciating painfully, "did Pelletier send her to me?" It made no sense at all, given that the lass did not speak English. Or even French. He had not even given her a letter of explanation.

Mr. Barnaby tutted. "Clear as day, sir, clear as day! It's a wonder you doesn't see it, clever as you almost always seems. The fellow was in love with 'er, that's all. Smitten 'e was, as smitten as the lad what pecked at the chambermaid. 'E didn't care about 'imself so much as 'e did about 'er. 'E sent 'er to your room in 'opes of saving 'er."

That was absurd. François Pelletier, by evidence and report, had cut a splendid figure. The girl was a mouse.

"How," I battled my reluctant jaw, "could the fellow be smitten with *her*, man? He cried out for Susan Peabody!"

I touched the corners of my mouth to feel if blood had risen.

My skepticism astonished Mr. Barnaby. "Begging your pardon, Major Jones, but I fear you lacks an eye for feminine beauty. Oh, I doesn't say the bloke weren't set upon Miss Peabody in the beginning. Forbidden fruit, as they say, and who knows what all was in the petunias? But angels win upon the plains of 'Eaven, and she's an angel if I ever seen one." He rolled his generous person toward me, striving for intimacy. "Ain't she a marvel, though, that Magdalena? Fair as Dolly Dobbins in the May-time! And clever as they come, and terrible learned. I ain't seen such a prize since . . . since . . ."

And then the grand fellow went silent.

I was astonished. For truth be told, the creature was no beauty, but plain as Indus mud. Of course, not every woman can rival my Mary. But the lass was a negress, in any case. Mr. Barnaby was white as boiled cod.

Now, you will say: "Oh, hypocrite, Abel Jones! We know about your tawny love in India." But I will tell you: That was India, see. Where such things happen. This was in America, even if the locale was New Orleans. What might be done by dark and hid away would not find much acceptance in the daylight.

I worried about Mr. Barnaby. Broken-hearted fellows are prone to errors of the heart. I wished him well and did not want him ruined.

We halted in front of Mr. Champlain's manse, a structure neither big nor small, but laden with generations of inheritance, not all of it fortunate. I moved to leave the cab, but Mr. Barnaby held me back with a hand upon my shoulder.

"I 'as to say a word or two, forgive me, sir. But you'll want to be cautious about yourself from now on. Oh, I doesn't mean with *Père* Champlain, who wouldn't hurt a fly what wasn't stinging 'im. But generally speaking, like."

I wished to assure him that I am ever careful. But it was not worth the pain of further speech.

"It's just that business what keeps coming up," he continued, unwilling to release me. "*Le bouc sans cornes*. 'The goat without 'orns,' sir. What they done to that poor Mr. Pelletier is exactly what they mean to do to you, if you missteps."

"Skin me alive?" I asked in my crippled voice.

"It ain't even done with a knife," he added. "The Grand Zombi 'imself does it with 'is teeth. Mostly, they only skins a black cat for their ceremonies. But when they gets perturbed, they skins a man."

* * *

MR. CHAMPLAIN DID NOT stand on ceremony. In fact, he did not stand at all, but sat behind an enormous plate of victuals. The repast lay braced in front of his mighty belly with the help of an apparatus resembling a scaffold. He wore a bib like a mammoth babe and laughed like a child to see us.

"Welcome, welcome, all!" he cried, waving a half-et sausage in one paw and a great spoon in the other. He looked as jolly as John Bull over a beefsteak, although his line was French as soiled linens. "Mr. B., you're just in time! Sit right down there, sit right down. Have yourself a nice feed up, keep me company, *cher.* Constantine, get my skinny friend there some breakfast, something that'll put some meat back on those bones. And fetch up that paste Mama Delarue mixed up for *Monsieur le Major.*"

Restraining himself from biting into a sausage that longed for his mouth, he smiled at me, teeth florid with his meal.

"Honored, sir, to have the privilege of another visit after so short an interval. Honored! Thought you'd come on over tonight, I allowed myself that presumption. You and that poor fellow there who's starving himself straight to death, Lord knows why. Sure, now. Been expecting you, to tell the truth. That is, we hoped our hospitality would lead you back to our humble door. Terrible swelling you have there. Must hurt worse than a man's irrigation system a few weeks after a visit to Madame Pettibon's. But don't you worry, just set yourself down. Sit down, sir. I took the liberty of ordering up a salve, having heard something of your tribulations with the dental profession."

He glanced about himself in exasperation, then called out loudly, but amiably, "Constantine! Bring another fix-up of those *saucissons,* bring 'em right on up here now! I'm getting skinny as a young girl with consumption. Major Jones,

I assure you, from personal experience, that not half an hour from now you'll be a different man. Then we'll get some hominy mash poured down you, so you don't starve to death and embarrass our fair city. But sit down, *cher*! Be at home!"

I sat, drawing out my pencil and my dwindling supply of paper. I wrote: "This salve? Is it voodoo?"

I rose again to lay the note beside the grand fellow's plate, which was disorderly.

Mr. Champlain cackled so uproariously that a bit of half-chewed sausage struck my brow. "Voodoo? Mama Delarue? She'd be unhappy to hear it, most unhappy. See her over at St. Louis's every morning, on her knees without a cushion. That is, I'd see her if I ever got an urge to get up again and stroll over to the cathedral. Which I judge unlikely. But that's no never-mind. Mama Delarue's a better Christian than the *abbesse* herself. Just knows how to mix up a salve or toddy for when the apothecaries run out of patience trying to kill a man. Can't say where she learned it. Never ask about a lady's past or the ingredients of a sausage."

He held up a glistening specimen of the latter and devoured it with hardly a pause in his speech. "Relied on her myself. Many's the time. Why, if I had to stop enjoying my *petit déjeuner* just because of a little toothache, I'd shrivel up and die in twenty-four hours. Man has to keep up his health with a proper diet."

He shook with glee and the frame of the house shook with him.

The colored lackey, Constantine, reappeared. He balanced so many trays and plates and bowls that a Delhi juggler would have fled in terror. His antique dress seemed even more worn, his wig the sort of thing kept for remembrance, not for use. But whatever economies else the household practiced, food did not seem to be in short supply. After serving Mr. Barnaby without stint, the fellow placed a jolly plate of sausages—some gray, some brown, some almost black—before our impatient host. A regiment of the line could have dined on the bounty.

The servant stepped toward me, bearing a little crock and a swab on a stick.

"You just open up there," Mr. Champlain commanded. "Let old Constantine fix you on up. You won't regret it, *cher.*"

Now, you will think me foolish, but I opened my mouth as instructed. True it is that I knew not what might be mixed into that concoction. But my misery was such that the risk seemed minor.

The servant had fingers as deft as a London tailor. He daubed and swabbed and painted me up until I felt a tingle, almost a burning. The taste was not appealing, that I will tell you.

I did not interfere with the process, but only wondered at Mr. Champlain's system of intelligence, at his ability to sit within his parlor, as immobile as the mountain that declined to come to Mahomet, and still learn all the secrets of New Orleans.

When Constantine, who looked older than the sages of Benares, finished spackling the wound inside my mouth, he made a little bow and slipped away. The finest servants are like the best of women, silent and accommodating.

"Candle-inch from now," Mr. Champlain called after him, "you bring the major up a bowl of buttered grits. I know an eatin' man when I encounter one."

Although he could not be accused of daintiness as he supped, my host took such delight in moving morsels of food from his plate to his gullet that it seemed almost cruel

to interrupt his pleasure. But I had many a question. And not
an excess of time.

I wrote: "How did you know about my jaw?"

The question pleased the fellow better than the gift of a
ribbon pleases a country lass. He granted himself a dripping
bite of pancake, then said, "See here, now. Nothing dark and
mysterious, *vous savez*? Simple as chicory coffee, *cher*. Horatio over there could tell you better than I can. If he had a
mind to. Truth is, the folks who really know what happened,
what's going to happen, and what should've happened but
didn't here in New Orleans are the household staff. The stable hands, the yard boys. And those among the free coloreds
who aren't trying too hard to be free of their color. Nothing
but one big spy-on organization. They see all and tell all. But
they don't tell all *to* all. The important things have a price.
But the common coin of affairs, they spend that freely. A
white man can't sneeze in the *Faubourg* Marigny without
some *dame blanche* out on Washington Avenue asking her
lady's maid whether *monsieur* has the pneumonia or just
snuffed up some pepper."

He chuckled. "It's their great power over us, Major Jones.
That Marie Venin you had some confusion with? Or Marie
Laveaux, for that matter. The mother or the daughter,
doesn't matter. Voodoo-hoodoo, poodle-tootle. All slops for
grandmère's pet *cochon*. They don't read minds or fortunes,
our *voudouiennes*. They just know when to slip a picayune
into Auntie 'Phelia's pocket, or when to threaten some
sprightly, high-yalla gal with everlasting heartache, she
doesn't tell every last thing going on in that house where
she's serving with two fingers and listening with two ears.
No, sir. Goes for all their womenfolk, to some degree. That
ability to pry. *Madame Noir* may not be a born queen. But
she has the power to drag a queen down from her high-

society throne, she takes a mind to. Sure, now. No self-respecting white woman in New Orleans believes a single word her sister tells her. But they all believe what their colored hairdresser has to say. How's that jaw?"

The truth, strange though it seem, is that my mouth felt remarkably improved—so much so that I had not even noticed. Present pain demands our attention, but when pain creeps away, it slips our minds.

I nodded to signify my improvement and my gratitude.

Unable to contain his delight in the victuals any longer, Mr. Barnaby cried out, "Capital! Absolutely capital! A body's never disappointed, when 'e calls at *Maison* Champlain."

"You ain't half fed up, Mr. B.," our host insisted. "Horatio? You go tell that worthless Constantine we're missing half our meal up here. Tell him to see if he can't find us the other half."

The vast fellow chortled. "Dear me, Major Jones! Almost forgot to ask you about poor François Pelletier. I hear there's been a misfortune. Fact is, I hear he's dead and done up voodoo-style. That true?"

I nodded. Touching my jaw to see if the skin remained feverish. Warm it was still, but not hot to the touch as it had been earlier. Even the swelling seemed to have decreased.

"To be expected, I suppose," Mr. Champlain decided. "If the voodoo folks hadn't come after him for one thing, I suspect some of our less amiable white citizens might have paid him a call over another. Does sound needlessly unpleasant, though, what the whispers claim was done to him. Almost enough to make a body wonder whether things might not be a touch more complicated than they seem. Acourse, plenty of folks resented François Pelletier, whether for good reasons or bad. So very many. Some just thought he was too pretty, I suppose. And the Pelletiers aren't native to the city. From Haiti, originally. Rich folk at one time. Talk is they crossed Henri Christophe, had to leave quicker than a man likes to go. Anyway, not even the less-than-white felt much affection for his ideas. Founding a newspaper, calling for the vote, talking about running for office, things like that. Plenty of coloreds have done mighty well among us, *cher*. Owned slaves themselves, and they're going to miss 'em. So they weren't all that happy with François. Said mean things, hard things about him. I don't know how much of the talk a man should believe, in the end. *Par example,* I heard it said he planned to set himself up an African kingdom, stocked up with liberated slaves. Though I personally believe his ambitions were somewhat milder."

He lowered his head down into the folds of his neck, watching me with one brow raised above a flesh-packed eye. "Now, I don't have your skills of investigative thought, Major Jones. Wouldn't pretend to. I'm just a fat, old man who sits and thinks things over. You're the great Descartes. I'm simply *un petit* Pascal. *Très petit.* At least in that regard. But I do have my *pensées.* And it does seem to me that, if someone felt an irresistible desire to kill young Pelletier and do it all tidy, so no blame would fall on the actual killer, that someone would be happy to create the appearance of a voodoo ceremony to misdirect the authorities. Might even hire himself—or herself—a *voudouienne.* Have her followers do it, make it look sincere. Might hire her for any number of other things, for that matter. And everyone in this *bonne ville* would simply accept that Pelletier had crossed his fellow negroes and paid the price. That Constantine gets slower by the hour. Horatio? I swear, I've been deserted by those boys for the last time. Probably downstairs eating themselves into a delirium."

Our host enjoyed the heel of a loaf of bread, lathered so richly in butter that I could smell it.

"Take your Miss Peabody," he resumed, although he had not finished the task of chewing. "To my head-hanging-down shame, I was indecorous in my remarks last evening. When I mentioned a certain lack of physical grandeur. Can't think what came over me. Ungentlemanly. And I never did finish my thought, only told you the half of it, as I recall. But, then, I'm an old man, easily distracted. Times I don't even remember what meal I'm eating on. But Miss Peabody, now. Would've liked to meet that young woman. Half broke my heart that she never had the courtesy to call. Had to rely on the eyes of others to form my picture of her. And the problem with the eyes of others, *cher,* is that they're only eyes."

His expression grew as winsome as a cat's. "See here, now. I don't have the flair of the cavalier like our mutual friend, Mr. Barnaby. Oh, I had my *amours,* when I was young. But look at me now! Ha! Only thing I'm going to romance is a roast chicken. But a man learns a thing or two, if he pays attention. A man who lives long enough appreciates that the sweetest meat is in close to the bone, not that perfect-looking cut on the outside. A man learns to prefer the oyster to the gumdrop, Racine over Molière. And if a man's fortunate . . . or terribly unfortunate, you might say . . . once in his life he meets a woman who just doesn't make any sense to him. First look at her, he thinks she's an embarrassment to the eyes, beneath his notice. Yet his eyes never quite look away completely, because they can't. He just can't help continuing to notice her. Can't explain why. He never can say what it is about her. He'll look for reasons. Drive himself crazy trying to figure out what's happening to him. It's her 'charm,' he'll tell himself. Or maybe her eyes.

Or how she sings and plays the piano. But the truth is that it isn't any of those things. It's just her. The woman-magic in its highest degree."

He laughed, but not happily this time. "It's a thing far beyond *voudou,* the power certain women have over us. First time we meet 'em, we think we'd be embarrassed to be seen with 'em on our arm. Next thing, we're on our knees. Or all the way down on our bellies. Begging. Helpless as infants. So deeply in love and lust and passion and desire and any other names you can think of for it that we don't know whether to shoot her through the heart or shoot ourselves through the head. Sure, now. I'd bet a case of Leoville-Lafitte that Cleopatra was that sort of woman. Maybe even la Pompadour." He smiled. "Or Eve."

I wrote: "You mean Miss Peabody?"

"Couldn't rightly say. Never met the poor mam'selle. I'm merely speculating. The way old men like to do." I caught a glimpse of his collar, but his chins quickly hid it again. "Even if she *was* one of those sirens, one of those unexpected vixens, not every man would've seen it. Some men do, some don't. The appeal of the flaxen-haired *demoiselle* is universal, Major Jones. Or almost so. But these other women, the deadly sorts . . . their appeal seems tailored for certain men. For the unsuspecting connoisseur. Such women sacrifice the casual desire of the masses for the all-consuming passion of the few. Who knows if Miss Peabody had that sort of appeal? Or whether she just managed to confuse a poor, pretty-face buck-nigger. Like our Mr. Pelletier."

His smile twisted like the rope in a hangman's hands. "Come to think on it a little more, I'm afraid I might be leading you astray, *cher.* And it would shame me to frustrate the noble cause of justice. I didn't mean to suggest that Pelletier might've killed Miss Peabody in an outburst of passion.

Though I suppose that, too, is a possibility a man like you would consider all on your own." Small eyes gleamed behind barricades of flesh. "Fact is, I'm not suggesting anything at all. Though I've known cases, here in this city, where just the right nudge turned an impassioned lover into a brutal murderer. Say, if he was torn between his unquenchable desire for one of those inexplicable sirens . . . and a good woman who just loved him and meant well by him. Say, if he was a poor man. With ambitions. And he saw that the seductress with the lopsided face and the brown mole would only ruin him, saw it plain as day. God forbid that any question of funds entered into the matter. Between the confusions of love and the lust for money . . . *cher,* I'm afraid that anything could happen. Anything at all. Although I doubt that any of this applies in the instance of which we speak. But here's Constantine, delivering your much-needed sustenance!"

BUTTER ALONE FLAVORED the lukewarm mash, but I devoured it greedily. All the while, my host and Mr. Barnaby chattered about society, speaking of friends and enemies, then of friends who had become enemies, and finally of enemies who had begun to appear in a friendly light. Two hopeless gossips they were, and you never heard the like between two men, except in a barracks. Only their gentler bearing toward sin distinguished their conversation from that of two ladies.

When I looked up from my bowl at last, Mr. Champlain smiled. "Grits taste a sight better if you salt and pepper 'em, but I figured that might not suit your grave condition. Terrible thing, when a man can't even chew. Though it strikes me you've been chewing over a couple of other things. Weren't wondering how to ask my opinion of the Widow Aubrey, were you? Sure, now. I do hope you enjoyed your visit with her. Not many folks do. Sitting in that woman's parlor is akin to standing before a judge who makes up the law as it suits him. Or running afoul of a banker who holds your paper. Hard woman. *Hard*. But a woman who runs a shipping concern has to show a certain mettle, I suppose. Not much more I'd choose to say about her."

I decided to take a risk and wrote: "She was dishonest with me. She denied a close relationship with Miss Peabody and Pelletier. There seems to have been much familiarity."

Papa Champlain shrugged when he read my scribble. Roiling the skirts of his coat and disturbing his cutlery.

"Could be any number of reasons for that, I suppose. Not least her embarrassment at the end to which her distant, but undeniable, relative had come. I suspect most any lady in this city would be inclined to revise her memories of intimacy with the victim. Myself, I'm never surprised when a lady amends the truth . . . although there are times when I'd like to know why she repaired the facts exactly the way she did."

He brushed a few crumbs from his breast, ignoring a hundred others. "As for the late Mr. Pelletier, we must assume she knew nothing about his recent decline in health. But it strikes me she might have no end of *other* reasons for wishing to disavow any contact with a figure who has excited such controversy. All sorts of reasons for a fine, high lady like our Mrs. Aubrey to shy away from acknowledging any business she might've carried on quietly with François Pelletier. Acourse, you could *only* be suggesting a business arrangement. Not a social relation."

I pressed ahead, although it was poor manners, and wrote: "There have been suggestions of indecencies."

Papa Champlain read that and laughed. "Sure, now. You wouldn't want to corrupt your investigation with idle gossip, *cher.* Anyway, not a man or woman I know doesn't have *some*thing worth hiding. This town'd be duller than a Saturday night in Boston, if they didn't. But I don't recall hearing anything much about the Widow Aubrey's private affairs. Nothing much that would have any bearing on the matter you've undertaken to resolve. Truth is that we mustn't be ungentlemanly. And when all is said and done, a good deal more is said than done."

He paused to gaze down the long slope of his waistcoat, past knees that had not touched each other in years. "Greedy woman, though. Terribly greedy woman. I'll allow that much. Wouldn't want to do business with her. If squeezing a profit out of every poor soul she touches is indecent, then I suppose there've been indecencies aplenty in that woman's life. But that's the worst I'd choose to say of Jane Aubrey."

Disappointed I was. I had hoped to hear lurid tales. Such nastiness of temperament is shaming to me as a Christian, but the truth is that I wished to hear of sins.

How is it that we like to think ill of our brothers? Our Savior told us to let the sinless fellow cast the first stone. Yet, it is words, not stones, he should have warned us against. Rocks are hurled openly. We see the damage by the light of day. But wicked words are daggers in the night.

The truth is that I had not liked Mrs. Aubrey, who seemed as dry as a water bottle after a summer march. But how small of me it was to wish to hear Magdalena's charges of sin confirmed, to be told that Mrs. Aubrey's past was sordid.

I wish I were a better man than I am.

Well, I was worn and weary. I will allow myself that. And tiredness troubles our judgement. The calming salve and then the bowl of mash might as well have been opium for the sleepiness they brought me. And I had heard so much that day, so many contradictions, that I could barely keep my questions straight.

I managed to remember two last questions I needed to put. I wrote: "Do the words 'fishers of men' mean anything unusual to you?"

Mr. Champlain lifted a shoulder in a half-hearted shrug. "The words of our Lord, Jesus Christ. When summoning his disciples. Always made me wonder what he expected 'em to use for bait."

I scrawled: "Nothing else?"

He lifted the opposite shoulder. "Sure, now. I suppose you could take an unkind view of the term . . . attach it to some fellows you might meet up with over on the corner of Bourbon and Canal. Or along Rampart. Gamblers, ne'er-do-wells. Pickpockets, Irish robbers. Fancy-man coloreds. Fishing for folks' money, if not for their souls." He twisted up his mouth and tried the words again. "Fishers of men . . ."

As my host mused on the phrase, his servant, Constantine, captured my eye. Turning a corner with a plate of buns, he heard his master speak the words in question.

For an instant, the servant buckled. He nearly dropped his tray, although he recovered.

He saw that I saw him.

Mr. Champlain clapped his hands as the aroma of warm dough and cinnamon overwhelmed us. I knew I could not chew and the scent tormented me.

The other servant, Horatio, brought in more coffee. I could not drink it. That, too, was a sorrow.

"Better paint him up again, Constantine," my host told the servant. "Paint him back up while he's still awake. I'm afraid the good major's falling under the spell of that care-charmer sleep, the son of sable night . . ."

The servant went to fetch the pot of ointment and I scrawled out my last query: "What does the word 'pirates' mean to you? Anything in relation to Miss Peabody?"

That, too, baffled Mr. Champlain. "Well . . . I've heard some of your Yankee businessmen called that. And worse. General Butler's brother, for instance. The 'colonel.' I've even heard it applied to certain merchants on the other side of Canal Street . . ."

The servant returned with the pot and swab. Our host told him, "Once you've got him all painted up again, Constantine, you let him take the rest of it along. Wrap it up for him to carry."

The negro bent over me again. I opened my jaw as wide as the damage allowed.

After fussing for a moment, the servant stood up straight and said, "'Scuse, Marse Papa."

"What's the matter now?"

"I can't rightly see in this here light no more. Can you moves him yonder for me, over to the lamp, suh?"

The master of the household looked at me. "Major Jones? Would you kindly pass on over to that big lamp? So Constantine doesn't accidentally stick that swab someplace it shouldn't go?"

I trailed the ancient servant across the room. He stopped where a painted lamp perched on a table. Behind me, Mr. Champlain and Mr. Barnaby bantered about the quality of kitchen staffs.

Seating myself on a chair whose pride was past, I opened my mouth and allowed the servant to perform his ministrations. He cooed and tutted, as if treating a child, giggling now and then as darkies do.

Twas only at the very end, and only for a moment, that he dropped his smile and let his face grow somber. Affecting to apply a final coating, he brought his cheek close to mine. His breath chronicled old age, bad gums and coffee.

"Them fishers of men be everywhere," he whispered. "You gets home, you looks inside this here crock, marse."

$\mathcal{I}$ DID NOT LOOK inside the pot when I reached my hotel room. Not at first. Another matter distracted me.

The girl was gone. And the room was crimson with blood.

Now, when you are wearied by pain and wanting sleep, and when within a pair of days you have tumbled from a roof, been buried alive, bathed with snakes, suffered a queer paralysis, faced a slaughtering dentist, then met up with a fellow skinned alive, your enthusiasm wanes.

I could not summon the vigor to respond as boldly as I might have done. Blood seemed as common as water in New Orleans.

If the splashes of gore were insufficient to rouse me to a passion, I should have been shocked by the howl Mr. Barnaby raised. Twas a cry of misery so rich it would have moved the prophets and made poor Job feel lucky in his sorrows. Never had I heard such a wail from a white man, unless it come from that ruffian preacher whose son was killed in our fuss in Mississippi.

The hopelessness in Mr. Barnaby's bellowing should have pierced my soul. But it did not. As sad as it is for a Christian man to say, blood has been too common in my life. And I was wearied to the point of cruelty. He only made me impatient and disdainful. Here was Mr. Barnaby, a man who had dueled and killed, who had shot men in my presence the spring before, crying like a child and helping no one.

I found it preposterous that he should come to feel so for the lass in a spate of hours. Men and women do not love at a glance, but only want the shiny thing they see. Love untried by time is merely appetite. Had poor Juliet lived, she likely would have found herself abandoned as soon as fickle Romeo glimpsed Joan. The reckoning comes as the calendar's pages fall. We dally in the next one's arms, insisting that the stars look down in envy, and make our honor cheap as poor Marc Antony's.

I am no skeptic when it comes to love, but fear the strayness of infatuation.

Mr. Barnaby bayed like a hound, rushing from wall to wall. As if the girl were but hiding. He thumped the panels, again and again, in search of secret passages, and called her name as if they had been wed. I could not stop him from turning over the mattress.

Only blood.

Had we been out of doors, I would have drawn my Colt and fired it heavenward to shock the fellow back into his senses. But such things are not done in fine hotels.

"Mr. Barnaby!" I barked in my old sergeant's voice, still having a bit of a tussle with my jaw. "Stop this! Stop it now!"

He paused and looked toward me in astonishment. As if my presence had been plain forgotten.

"She's gone," he said, as if I had not noticed.

"Go you down and fetch us Captain Bolt. If you can find him."

He gazed at me. You would have thought him uncertain of my identity. I was about to repeat my command, when the poor fellow spoke again.

"I 'as to find 'er, Major Jones."

"Mr. Barnaby . . . get you down and summon Captain Bolt." When he did not respond, my temper blackened. "Do it *now,* man!"

"I 'as to find 'er, I does. I know she's alive, sir. Why take away a body what's already dead? She must be alive. Alive and wanting 'elp . . ."

"*Find Bolt.* Bring him here. Wake him up. Kick him, if you have to. Do whatever you must. But tell him I said he must come up at once." I squared my shoulders so he would not mistake me. "If you wish my help in the matter of your Master Francis, you will do as I say and remember yourself as a man."

That sobered him a bit, though not completely. Slowly, he began to stir to duty. "I 'as to find the lass," he insisted, pleadingly. "Before she's dead and done with." But his posture straightened as he touched the door.

His cries had drawn a crowd into the hallway. There were civilian officials with neckcloths undone, shirtless officers with their braces down, and one young woman painted bright as a mail coach. She giggled at Mr. Barnaby and myself.

I pushed my companion off on his way and told them, "Just go on with you now. Go along. There is nothing here that is your business. Go along."

I shut the door and sat me in a chair not badly bloodied, trying to make sense of the muddle of gore. And something struck me that I should have noticed the moment we entered. Blood there was, indeed, but no sign of a mortal struggle. Not a lamp was overturned, and the pitcher, basin and night pot rested unbroken. Nor did the pattern of bloodstains tell of a fight. The blood was spilled too evenly, as if to paint a slaughter where there was none. Twas probably not the missy's blood at all, but gore drawn from a dog or a sheep. Or a goat.

A kidnap there might well have been. But the butchery was staged.

The knowledge should have driven me to action. But I was so worn down that all things blurred. Ideas I had clutched an hour before, convinced I had made progress in my task, fled me as I tried to recollect them. I was not certain of a single fact, and the lass grew as unreal as a ruptured dream. I rested my cane between my legs and let myself slump down.

I should have been outraged and bent on justice. I should have burned with pity for the girl.

Instead, I fell asleep, still in my cape.

CAPTAIN BOLT SHOOK me awake with irritating violence. I rushed up from my slumber, calling for my old regiment to rally. Often, when I am startled out of my sleep, I imagine myself in India again. Sometimes, when I am glum, I fear I long for it.

"Hoo-ee, look out!" the captain cried as he swerved to avoid my blows. I think I took him for a murdering Pushtoon, although there was no ghost of a resemblance.

I mastered myself in a moment or two, but was in such a grump that I did not apologize. I even growled a bit.

"God Amighty!" Bolt called out, "I was only trying to wake you up, Major! You were snoring like a drunk Irishman and a sick mule sewed together . . ." He glared in Mr. Barnaby's direction. "This friend of yours says there's been another murder."

When we are hard asleep and too soon awakened, the world seems lurid with a nightmare truth. Our spirits fail. That is why our enemies strike before dawn. But discipline will tell, see. If my temper was poor, I restrained it and only said, "Look around you, man. The blood would seem to tell a tale, I think."

I did not explain that I thought the matter false, that the gore was not even the girl's, in my opinion. I wished to see what the fellow would say for himself. I should have offered comfort to Mr. Barnaby, there is true. But I was in a crank. And newly wary. I did not want Bolt blabbering in the streets. If we were meant to think Magdalena dead, no doubt the ruse had a purpose. The captain would be no help in finding it out.

I had another usage for him, though.

Bolt glanced about himself. As if noticing the great, darkening splashes for the first time. There was blood on the planks and panels, blood on the bedding and furniture.

"Who's dead this time?" he asked. His interest was not impressive.

"The maiden!" Mr. Barnaby interjected, fighting a sob. "The fair maiden."

Mystified, the captain looked at me. "He don't mean that high-yella gal? Does he? That scrawny thing you were snuggling yesterday morning?"

"Likely her," I said, too worn to be irate at his suspicions.

"If that don't beat all," Bolt said. "I swear to God." He was not quick of wit, to say the least.

My temper come up again, though. Not at the limitations of his character, but at his neglect of elementary duties. Aggravated by my rebellious jaw, my lecture was not gentle.

"Listen you," I said, "and listen well. It is tired I am of the doings in this hotel, which you and your soldiers have been set to guard. I am tired to a vomiting, Captain Bolt. If your masters have set you to watch me like a dog, you could at least observe my door often enough to keep stray murderers out. Look you, boy. Here is what you will do, and do not argue. Do not say a word until I finish. Or we can visit General Banks in the morning. To ask if you might not be rewarded with a posting to the front, where officers do not lounge about hotels, dreaming of fine dinners. Heed what I say, or I will see you become a soldier proper."

Grunting for emphasis, I reared up like the sergeant I once was. "The moment it is light enough to wake the residents, you and your men will search this cursed hotel from top to bottom. Do not pull faces at me, boy. Even if you find nothing—which is likely—it will tell these criminals their free run is past. You also will send a fellow to the paymaster to tell him I will come to inspect his accounts. Tell him to expect me in the afternoon. And warn him that I know the look of ledgers. If *he* objects, then he and I will visit General Banks. And you will go in your person to the provost marshal. To demand, in my name, any information he possesses about an organization called the 'Fishers of Men.' And he is not to put me off with Bible stories. He is to speak of men in their living flesh."

I stabbed the air with my finger, which is unmannerly. "Lastly, you will come down the stairs with me now, while I take another room. Where a fellow can sleep for a brace of hours without the creaking of secret doors or social calls by all the city's assassins. And you will post a guard upon my room, with orders that no one, living or dead, may disturb me until I am ready to be disturbed. And that will not be until the hour of noon."

Wheeling about, I faced poor Mr. Barnaby. I fear my temper was flowing in full flood. But who among us is perfect?

"And *you,* sir. You may sleep wherever you wish, then make inquiries anywhere you want. Ask about the lass, if you will. Living or dead or translated into gossamer. But you will also ask about these 'Fishers of Men,' and no nonsense. If you argue back to me and weep about a girl you have only laid eyes on, or waste another moment on penny romances, by God, sir, I will let your Master Francis rot in a Union prison a year beyond the end of this blasted war. Have I made myself understood?"

I looked from one man to the other, in a mood to devour raw flesh. Although I do not mean that literally, of course.

"Do you under*stand* me, gentlemen? Do you two understand what I have said?"

I did harbor some fear that they might *not* have understood me, given the impairment to my speech. But both men nodded, Mr. Barnaby pale as fresh milk and Captain Bolt as nervous as those brothers must have been when Joseph let them know the game was up.

"Good," I said. I took up my cane, then stomped out the door, marched along the hallway and paraded down the stairs. Followed by my well-chastised companions.

The clerk behind the desk was the same fellow I had upbraided the night before for lassitude. He did not like my looks when he saw me coming.

If nothing else, the fellow had sound instincts regarding authority and seemed to have learned that I must be appeased. I got my new room and half a hundred assurances that it contained no contraptions for shameful doings. I also got my guard from Captain Bolt.

Mr. Barnaby shambled off like a wounded pachyderm. He was glum as Mr. Carlyle pondering the deeds of Robespierre.

Now, you will judge me a hard man—and I have already admitted to my temper—but I saw full well that Mr. Barnaby by himself could enter doors where I would not be welcome. His fellows would speak more openly when not compelled to make a show for me. I wished to give him time alone which he would not take unless it were forced upon him. He was a lonely man and worried, too. Such fellows cling, Lord bless them. But I needed him to sink back into his city for a time.

It is like this, see: A stranger in New Orleans is an audience, for whom the city's natives play their roles. The place is a great theater, and every child and grampus is an actor. There are real theaters, and music halls, as well, giving plays and shows despite the times. But the performances of the foremost rank occur in the streets and parlors. And, perhaps, elsewhere. I leave it to you to imagine the intimate scenery.

As a member long admitted to their company, Mr. Barnaby could step backstage. Where I am told all theaters are sordid.

I watched the fellow's haunches recede through the doors that led to the terrace. The night gulped him down and I felt the stirrings of pity. After all, I am a lucky man, well married and well loved. But times there were when I believed that loneliness, not greed, was the root of all evil. Perhaps he was taken with the girl not because of a fullness he saw in her, but because of the hollowness echoing in himself. It is a hard enough life when we are loved. To walk the world alone is a terrible thing.

Well, we would find his missy, if she lived. In good time.

As I trudged up the staircase beside the guard who would post outside my door, the clerk come running after, calling my name.

Holding out a packet of letters, he told me, "Sorry, Major. I just plain forgot. Ship put in from Baltimore. Carrying the mails. Brought you these. Navy feller sent a letter, too."

Such lads expect a "tip" for merely doing their work, but the clerk got none from me. Such generosities only breed corruption.

Yet, I was pleased and there is no denying it. At the thought of news from home, the stench of bloody murder faded wonderfully. Exhausted though I was, I could hardly restrain myself from hunting through the letters there on the landing. But an officer must be dignified in front of the other ranks. I marched myself to my old room and gathered up my belongings in good order.

Annoyed I was at finding blood on my traveling bag, which had been a Christmas gift from my Mary Myfanwy.

It is a horrid thing to admit, but the stains upon the leather moved me more than the lot of the servant girl. I would excuse myself by pleading weariness and the heartless temper that overtakes us all, but the truth is that a tired man reveals himself. I am a sorry sinner, there is true.

I let the soldier bear my bag, while I carried a uniform. It had been returned, nicely cleaned, by the merchants who had dressed me head to toe. Concealed in the wardrobe, it had not suffered attack.

Halfway down the hall, that lass with the painted cheeks slipped by with a wink.

In my new room, which was haunted by cigars, I tumbled everything over a chair, bid the guard goodnight, and locked the door. Throwing off my cape and wrestling my new boots free of my ankles, I meant to have a hasty wash, if water there was in the pitcher, then to scour my letters and pay my debt of prayers.

I made the mistake of lying back on the mattress in my clothing. Intending only to gather my strength, I plunged into sleep before I could read one word. Nor did I thank the Lord for all my blessings.

My punishment was a dream of my wife and son. So real they were that it tore my heart in two.

TWAS DAY WHEN I awoke, with the city rumbling and squawking beyond the window-glass. I reached out for my darling, who had been so vivid while my eyes were closed, but found only an emptiness fouled by cigars.

The ache had come to visit my jaw again.

I spent a moment on personal matters, then pushed the pot under the bed. Water there was in the pitcher, so I scrubbed my hands and splashed myself to life. Quick as a miner under the eye of his pit boss, I bent to dig out the crock the servant had given me. My only purpose was relief from pain. I had forgotten the hint to look inside.

There was a message in the jar, scrawled on a slip of paper:

QUENE MANWELER NO EVTHIN

I took it to mean that some personage called "Queen Manweler," whoever such might be, knew everything that Papa Champlain had not been obliged to tell me. Perhaps the words were only darky nonsense, yet I regretted my hounding of Mr. Barnaby. If a "Queen Manweler" lived in the city, the fellow seemed likely to know of her. But I would not see him until the afternoon. Punished I was for being so heartless and hard.

Well, the intelligence had waited out the night. It could wait some hours longer. I dipped a finger into the pot and come up with a dab of green paste.

My wound was not complacent when I touched it.

After a shock that called tears to my eyes, I gently rubbed the concoction over my stitches. Then I coated the meat around the damage.

With my finger still roaming in my mouth, I recalled the stack of letters. I had been so worn down and weary that true events had blended into dreams, the letters consigned to a nether-world.

The missives lay beneath my cape, a happy dozen and more. Flipping from one to the next with the haste of a child, I saw that fully seven were from my darling, with one from dear Mrs. Schutzengel, a pair from our Pottsville lawyers, another from Matt Cawber, who had become a partner in our coal business, and, not least in value, two letters from my friend, Dr. Mick Tyrone. He was serving General Sherman, north of Vicksburg. With the Rebels stubborn between us, his letters had needed to travel a great, long way.

A note from a Navy captain intruded into the welcome stack. I laid it aside, unread. Once informed that I answered to Mr. Lincoln, the Navy men missed no chance to curry favor. I had been asked aboard many a ship for dinner, but my duty, as well as my interests, lay ashore. I had no time for fripperies and flatterers.

Now, a single letter from loved ones is a soldier's pride and joy, but to receive such abundance all at once promised me an interlude of happiness amid the horrors of Babylon. Nor could the timing have been more opportune. I had resolved the night before to cordon off the morning for rumination. Too much had happened too swiftly and I know myself well enough to understand that, while I may be deep of mind, I am not quick of grasp. I needed time to ponder, to let the facts arrange themselves—as facts will do when they are left to themselves. I also intended to give myself the pleasantest breakfast my wounded mouth would bear, then to engage my Bible for my soul's sake. My duty to our Union could wait for the afternoon. Every man has a higher duty still.

Oh, I love a letter when the news blows fair.

There is the queerness of it: I knew in my heart that the news would not be bad, at least not of my Mary, John or Fanny. There is still much that Mick Tyrone and his science cannot explain to us.

Oh, I was rich that morning! Joy gripped me before I cut a single envelope. Murder was naught, sin vanquished. All my thoughts were of hearth and home, of those I loved beyond reckoning. I yearned to read every letter at once, to devour all they contained.

Still, a fellow must not be weak or unmanly. My Mary says that a gentleman is someone who will not do in private what he would not do before the public's eye, although such a rule seems hard.

Leaving my Colt in my bag for the term of my breakfast, I allowed myself to choose three letters to take along to table, all from my wife. Then I warned myself that Southron indolence might well mean I would have to wait for my victuals. I took up the other letters from home, as well. Just at the door, I turned again and added the missives from Mick Tyrone and Matt Cawber. But I am not completely without restraint. I let the letters from the lawyers and the naval fellow wait.

The guard without my door had changed, but the new fellow looked alert, if a bit unkempt. He greeted me with a countryman's nod, which hardly suited military courtesy.

I said nothing. I wanted only my coffee and all the news from home.

To my dismay, I was far from the only officer in the dining room. They should have been at work, since it was Friday and after nine. But a dozen dawdled over their plates, like gentlemen at a club in Piccadilly.

I ordered coffee, soft eggs and bread with butter. It seemed a wise and careful choice that morning, although I found the smell of bacon tempting. A well-fried pig has a lovelier scent than all the perfumes of the Peshawar bazaar.

As soon as the waiter slouched away, I opened the first letter from my darling. The world faded away. The scald of coffee hot as guns in action drew little notice. The slop of eggs and moistened bread slipped down my gullet half-tasted. One after another, the letters carried me to a realm of goodness and affection, reminding me of all that makes this world worth enduring.

MY MARY MYFANWY, my darling, could pack more love in a letter than a corporal can stuff rations in his bedroll. The child was not yet arrived, of course, since the letters had spent long weeks coming by ship. But my Mary is not the sort to take to a day bed while awaiting her confinement. She wrote that she still spent some hours in her shop each day. Of course, that concerned me. Even if robust in constitution, a woman approaching her lying in must have some care in her doings. But my Mary has a head for business that rivals many a man's and, though I sought to persuade her to give up dressmaking after our fortunes turned for the better, she had grown a taste for being a proprietress.

Young John was ever larking about, and delighted in the snow. He sometimes asked where I had gone, which moved me. Little enough sense he had of me, his father gone off to war. Whenever I returned home, the lad spent the first few days in outright fear, though I am gentle. He was healthy and ever so clever, Mary wrote. Concerns that had been raised to me by Mr. Evan Evans on his deathbed found no credence in our young son's person.

Fanny was much praised by my wife, which was a pleasant change. My darling had not taken to her at first. An orphan she was, as I myself had been. As lovely as an angel dressed for Sunday, she hardly seemed of this hard world to me. Her voice might have humbled the cherubim and seraphim, for she made a hymn sound gentle as a love song, without suggesting any lack of faith.

Fair she was, our Fanny, with her auburn hair a tumult. Swift to obey, she was also quick to learn. Privilege had not been her domain and the poor thing lived in fear of being cast out, no matter how often I told her that was nonsense. She worked in the kitchen and washed our clothes in the tub in the backyard, applied herself to her letters to make up for years of neglect, looked after John when Mary was out and studied the art of the seamstress in my darling's shop. All vigor and glow our Fanny was. The life in her was pretty as May and heady as September.

But I must not be partial.

Other doings there were in plenty, with Mr. Gowen and his ilk still switching between offers to buy out the colliery holdings left us by Mr. Evans and clumsy threats of what might happen should we not agree to sell. Cowed they were now by Matthew Cawber's backing of our company, for he was the terror of all Philadelphia.

Matt's letter to me was confident. He wrote the lines himself, as the grammar and spelling attested. There was no word of Dolly Walker, whose partnership with us was best kept silent. Instead, he spoke of the boundless fortunes we were set to make, during the war and after, from the black gold of the anthracite fields.

I will admit that I do not object to owning earthly riches. I know the Bible warns us of wealth's perils, but might it not be a sign of heavenly favor?

Reading the letters from my wife a second time, I paused over the interest Mahantango Street society took in us. There had been plentiful invitations at Christmas, before I embarked upon my latest journey. Now Mary had been invited to join a number of clubs and circles. She was asked to tea by ladies for whom her shop provided dresses. I know that such behavior is hypocrisy, that only our wealth improved us in their eyes. But then I think of England and Wales, where not even money gives a man a chance. Oh, grab his funds the high and mighty will, selling off ruined estates at monstrous prices. They will let him make a fool of himself by aping a country gentleman and sponsoring undistinguished hunts for a bankrupt viscount's convenience. But he will never be master of the hounds, nor will he be fully master of himself. If he sits at a baronet's table, it will be on account of the nobleman's debts or a favor badly wanted, and his dinner companions will be the dreariest squires, not a London set. He may, if he is fortunate, be permitted to marry off his loveliest daughter to a penniless, titled fop in broken health.

No, I will take America and hypocrisy, if it means my wife can sit at the finest tables. We have our snobs, but they do not have titles. And loathe to admit it though they may be, even their money comes from sweat and not a dead king's favor. It is the fluid nature of our society that I like, as if it were a matter of hydraulics. A forceful man can rise and lift his loved ones. If Matt Cawber and I are not good enough for the highest families of Philadelphia society, our children will be. In Britain, the boy is doomed as his father's son.

Suffice it to say that all were well at home. Oh, how I longed to be there with my darling! My resolve to resign my commission, to turn my back on the war and death, redoubled. I had done my part for my new country. And any love I ever had for soldiering had perished during the Mutiny, in India. I was nearing life's meridian, like that Italian fellow lost in the forest, the one who was such a fibber. Twas time to devote my remaining years to my family and our business. To make a proper gentleman of myself, to read good books and take my darling out riding in our carriage.

I did not need more scars.

I needed to go home. As soon as I had done with Susan Peabody. I promised myself that even Mr. Lincoln would not win me over again. I would not ever purpose war, nor would I be its servant.

*   *   *

BUT WAR WOULD not release me quite so easily. My dear
friend, Mick Tyrone, was near despair.

He began well enough, describing his observations about
medical matters. The physiognomy of the brain had become
his consuming interest and his work as a wartime surgeon
allowed him to study the living organ revealed, to compare
the matter's conformity to the contours of the skull. His ex-
periments led him to question the laws of phrenology, which
I thought bold. Of course, much that Mick believed was hard
to credit. He speculated that bodily chemicals rule our deepest emotions—what you and I term our "souls," although
Mick has no patience with the word. And he did not think
our wills were all our own.

Twas when Mick got to the war itself that his temper
scorched the page. Even after General Grant was restored to
his command, the campaign lagged. Our troops advanced
into Mississippi, only to withdraw again. The desultory affairs that trailed our autumn successes brought us no closer
to victory. Vicksburg defied us proudly, interrupting strategy and commerce, with the results that Mick had witnessed
just after Christmas.

General Sherman had taken up positions north of the city,
where the Rebels had entrenched upon high bluffs. According to Mick, even a fool could have seen the formidable
cost in lives that must be spent, likely for naught, in any as-
sault upon the Confederate lines. But William Tecumseh
Sherman was a fellow not shy of a fight. I had quite liked
him, with his ginger hair and courage, as soon as I grew accustomed to his brusqueness. He was a lion on the field of
Shiloh. But a general must not let his energies flank his
judgement.

Leaving Mick aghast, Sherman ordered his men against

the heights, hurling them forward over bad ground and expecting them to scale the bluffs in the face of Rebel volleys.

Our troops did not fare well.

Mick, who had to clean up after the butchery, was unforgiving. He cursed Sherman. Then he cursed General Grant for not keeping closer watch on his subordinate. Instead of bringing Vicksburg under siege, our soldiers had retired toward Memphis. Leaving a number of dead sufficient to raise the enemy's spirits.

Had I been upon the field that day, I might have seen possibilities Mick's eyes could not detect. He is not a soldier, after all. But as I read his lines I felt my heart sink. Along with my regard for General Sherman. The day would come when I would think well of Sherman again, when his fierce determination brought us victory. But on that morning in the St. Charles Hotel, I found myself so troubled that I had to fold away my letters and turn to the newspapers strewn about the room. Unlike a letter from a friend, a newspaper account need not alarm us. Journalism is like a minstrel show, with every feature exaggerated and morality relaxed for entertainment.

The newspaper of the day only worsened my humor. Hardly had I opened the pages of *The Daily Picayune* when I met an advertisement posted by Dr. Fielding, who had done his best to devastate my jaw. Thereafter, the contents worsened. The Rebel commerce raider, the *Alabama,* which I had failed to prevent from leaving the yards, had been active off Cuba. She had taken a number of Union ships as prizes and had sunk our gunboat, the *Hatteras.* Whenever I read of the triumphs of Captain Semmes, I blamed myself for failing to do my duty.

I scanned on past advertisements for a show at the opera house, which promised English, French and German airs, along with a comedy by Kotzebue and two vaudevilles. I took a bit of solace in discovering that the French consul had been dismissed by his own minister for "complicity with the Rebels." The fellow must have been caught at something awful for the French to be embarrassed by his activities. I read that General Halleck had reversed an order of General Grant's expelling the Israelites from his department. And our ironclad, the *Monitor,* had foundered in a storm.

Twas not a happy time for Mr. Lincoln.

The Daily Picayune played up to both sides. While the columns described the Rebels as "our" troops, the scribblers did not gloat over Union losses and sought to please our occupation authorities. Whichever side won, the newspaper meant to be on it.

I read that incendiaries had been active, which I feared referred to my fuss of two days past. The port was busy as the world cried out for cotton. Ever more ships crowded into the wharves or waited along the levees. An Irishwoman had been arrested for drunkenness by the provost marshal's men and patriotic citizens had staged a meeting in support of our Union.

There was not a word written about the murders of the past few days, nor was there a hint of negroes going missing.

A queer place New Orleans was. Everyone had his secret reasons for doing what seemed unreasonable.

The last of the coffee was cold in my cup. I rose up with a sigh. My splendid mood had been picked apart and I slogged back to my room.

The guard was no longer in front of my door, which did not help my temper.

He reappeared before I could enter my room, hurrying down the hallway and banging a lonesome chair with the butt of his musket. He knew he had been caught out.

Without waiting to close the distance between us, he cried, "I'm sorry, Major! I know I shouldn'ta gone off, I know it. But if I hadn'ta gone, I woulda blown a hole right through my trousers."

"Well, do not leave your post again, man. Unless you call for relief."

"My whole insides was calling for relief, Major. I couldn't wait a minute, or I woulda. I was loaded with double canister and lit."

I did not require further details and went into my room.

Something was wrong. I sensed it, as an old soldier will do. There was no evident disruption, no sign of violence done. But certain I was that my traveling bag had been shifted, that the order of things was changed.

I dug into my baggage. Furiously.

My Colt was there. I saw no sign of tampering.

My letters of credit and authority to draw funds had not been stolen. Indeed, it seemed to me that my visitor had not found the item he sought. Whatever it might have been.

I should have sat me down and taken stock. Then I might have realized what had been taken. I should have possessed the presence of mind to count back through the letters I had left in the room. I might have seen that the note from the Navy captain had gone missing.

A pounding on the door robbed my attention.

It was Captain Bolt

My demeanor was not welcoming.

"For God's sake, man! I told you I was not to be disturbed. Until noon, at the earliest. Is the English language foreign to you?"

He shrugged, more baffled than concerned. "I didn't think you meant *me*."

I was about to lay into him like a cat-o'-nine-tails about the guard's dereliction, when he announced, "I can't say what it's about, exactly, but it sounds like more'n one thing.

Can't say what, though. General Banks wants to see you down at the Customs House."

"In good time, man. I have to—"

"I think the general means right now, Major. Judging by what he said. By the one thing he said, I mean. Although it sure sounded like there was more, I swear to God."

I tell you, I was fuming. I had believed that the general and I had reached an understanding.

"And what, pray tell, was this 'one thing' he said, Captain Bolt?"

"Well, it was about that paymaster you were going on about. Seems he turned up dead this morning. Over in Jackson Square. With greenback dollars stuffed down his throat 'til he couldn't breathe no more."

twelve

DAMN IT, JONES," GENERAL Banks welcomed me, "you're a menace to human life." Standing in a lozenge of light fallen from a window, he locked his arms across his chest, flaring the skirts of his coat. The epaulettes on his shoulders arched like caterpillars "It's bad enough when you leave a trail of dead niggers behind you, but when you start killing my officers, that's enough. That's the end of it. No matter what that letter from Lincoln says."

He burst into the artless motion of anger, fumbling with a box on his desk until he had retrieved a black cigar. Biting off its end, he spit the tip toward a cuspidor, missed, stabbed the roll of weeds into his mouth, plumbed his pockets in vain for a lucifer match, then hurled the cigar into a melee of documents.

"You've single-handedly driven this city to the brink of insurrection," he continued. Thumping down his fist, he made the steel pens jingle on his desk. A pitcher of water threatened an inundation. "Do you understand what it means when a Union officer *in* uniform is found dead in the most notoriously Confederate square in this damned disloyal pile of Rebel bricks? Right in front of the Catholic cathedral? With Federal currency stuffed down his throat? And all those Frenched-up bastards snickering away behind their perfumed whiskers?"

Unsettled by my presence, General Banks looked elsewhere as he spoke. "Colonel Feiger deserved better than that. A dog deserves better than that. They killed a decent man, insulted his uniform, and threw our national currency back in our faces. It's sedition, and it's murder." He returned his reluctant, disdainful eyes to me. "And I want to know what you had to do with it."

Now, I am one who respects rank and good order. I am the least rebellious man I know. But I do not like to be accused of murder, or the least complicity therein. And my jaw was still sufficiently pained to push me to temper's edge.

"Look you, General Banks. I did not even know your paymaster's name, not until you spoke it. I wished to speak to the fellow, there is true. And I made it known to your watchdog, Captain Bolt." I tapped my cane on the floor, demanding attention. "Perhaps you should ask young Bolt if he has been bragging? To killers who let an ass bray all he wants? The lad is a fool, and clear that is to anyone."

"The little you know," Banks snorted.

I took a breath so deep it was almost a growl. "As for my Christian self, General Banks, I cannot see much order in your city when a man to whom I wished to speak is slain as soon as I whisper my inclination." Shaking my head with Methodist solemnity, I declared, "Something is rotten, sir, and closer it is to us than the state of Denmark."

The general folded his arms again, smirking. "Jones, you don't know your backside from a wagon wheel. And you don't know me. I'm not going to let you twist this all up the way your Washington friends do. We're talking about a murdered Union officer. Of field rank." He gave the air a slap. "What gives you the right to annoy my pay department, anyway? What the hell and damnation would my paymaster have to do with this dead do-gooder of yours? What on earth could you have wanted from poor Feiger?"

"Someone in your pay office may have been tied to the murder of Susan Peabody." I considered things for a moment. "That same person may bear the responsibility for the death of your Colonel Feiger. If the colonel himself bore no blame."

"Don't talk in riddles."

"Well, riddles there are in plenty, General Banks. But I am not speaking in them. The fact is only this, see. Not long before her death, Miss Peabody received a sum from her father. Or perhaps from her own funds back in New York. I cannot say. But it is enough that the money arrived in this city. Because the New Orleans banks are in disarray, she entrusted the sum to your paymaster. Or, perhaps, to one of his subordinates. For safekeeping."

"You're blaming that woman's murder on one of my officers?"

"Perhaps other murders, as well. I cannot say that, either. Nothing is proven, not yet. I give you that. And I note that the person involved, officer or not, first acted while General Butler was in command. You yourself bear no responsibility for this business of the money. Or for the girl's death."

That calmed the fellow slightly, though not much.

"And where exactly did you come by all your intelligence? From that pot-bellied bummer who's been hanging on to you like a leech? A man with known Confederate sympathies?"

"If you speak of Mr. Barnaby, I do not believe him to hold Confederate sympathies. I should think the contrary true. Although he does have friends who are with the Rebels." I looked at the general. "As do many of our leading officers, if I do not mistake me."

"Then where *did* you get your information, damn it? This tall tale about money deposited with the paymaster. Which would contravene War Department regulations."

"I believe that General Butler's administration was less strict than your own about regulations. Any irregularities would have occurred before you took command."

"You don't have to repeat yourself. I understand what you're telling me. But I won't blame Ben Butler for every pile of slops in the streets. I still want to know where you got your information."

"Perhaps you might ask Bolt?"

He grimaced. "Captain Bolt doesn't have the least idea. Or I'd know it. And you know that I would." Bending toward me slightly, he said, "I should lock you up and see how long it takes for your cronies in Washington to realize you're absent from duty."

"Locking me up will not stop the killings."

"Who told you that the paymaster took the girl's money for safekeeping?"

"It does not signify. The person from whom I heard the report may be dead."

"That's convenient."

"Not for her, I do not think."

"You had it from a woman?" he said dismissively.

"I do not see that it matters. Especially if she was important enough to be murdered. Or kidnapped. Under Captain Bolt's nose."

"Forget Bolt."

"Well, whether or not the captain is forgotten, I should like to know what happened to the money."

"How much was it?"

"That I cannot say."

He picked up the cigar he had thrown down and lit it,

making faces and smacking his lips as he puffed the weeds to life. "There's a lot you 'cannot say.' Isn't there, Jones? You don't really know much at all."

"I know more than I knew yesterday."

"Presumably, the sum of money was a large one?"

"Enough to charter a ship, or ships, to carry freed slaves to Africa."

He laughed, but the sound was dry. "Oh, yes. The Peabody girl's fantasy."

"She subscribed to the effort. It was the scheme of a colored fellow. Who was murdered last evening."

"The one skinned alive?"

"For dreaming of taking his people to their homeland. *Or* because there was a great sum involved."

"All these murders . . . may just come down to money? Is that what you're saying now?"

"Much comes down to money, General Banks. Especially in a commercial city bankrupted by war. But no matter how much money Susan Peabody imported from New York, it would not have been enough to satisfy every party who learned of it. And greed is greed. Those who knew of the money are killing each other. So that the funds need not be shared among them. That is at least part of the wicked story."

He gazed at me through a pall of tobacco. "So the last one on his feet . . . would be the man behind all of your murders."

"It is too soon to say. So many parties are engaged in the affair and have taken so many risks that I cannot judge whether Miss Peabody's money is the cause or merely one factor of several." I transferred more of my weight to my cane, as if it might help me think. "To kill so blithely . . ."

His lips expelled a muzzle-load of smoke. ". . . in a bankrupt city . . ."

"There is another side to things that gnaws me," I resumed. "Logical enough it would be to look at the matter simply, to say that, because Miss Peabody deposited the money with the paymaster, he had her murdered in order to rob her funds. But that would be a foolish approach, and the colonel in charge of the pay chest is rarely a fool. Even the greedy are wary of the gallows. The guilty would have to summon another reason for Susan Peabody's murder. To divert us. To mask the simple greed."

"Maybe he was just stupid? Whoever killed her?"

I waved the thought away. "Unless we are speaking of Captain Bolt, I would leave stupidity out of the matter. No, the question must be asked as to how many people knew of the money, if money was the cause of Miss Peabody's murder. I know of at least four parties who had such knowledge. Two are dead. Another is either dead herself, or wickedly harmed and missing."

"And the fourth?"

"An old widow. With whom I mean to have another visit."

The remark refreshed his skepticism. "You're suggesting that an old woman killed everybody?"

"She may prove a victim herself, and not a criminal. That we shall see. But this much I will tell you. Black men and white men, Union men and Southrons, males and females, and every mongrel mix this city has to offer, Christian and otherwise, have their fingers in this affair. And I am not too proud a man to admit that I remain baffled." I looked at the spittoon next to his desk. Neither the general nor his guests had taken careful aim. "Even Miss Peabody is something of a riddle."

"Well, solve it and go back to Washington. I've got a campaign to fight up-river, trouble in the bayous, and a truculent city on my hands. And now a dead paymaster."

"Here is the matter of it," I went on, thinking aloud. "A

charitable plan was formed to send negroes back to Africa. But several of those involved in the scheme were killed. There was a sum of money in question, although that might only mislead our thinking. Negroes began to disappear from the streets, as if their freedom ships were sailing constantly. But everyone with a skin darker than yours or mine goes about in fear of being kidnapped. Or worse. And no one hints about a voyage to Africa any longer. Instead, there is talk of voodoo and '*zombis*' and such. Of pirates. And all I can draw from anyone is a muttered 'Fishers of Men.'"

Banks shrugged. "Frankly, I'm not concerned about scared darkies. If they're scared enough, they might stay out of trouble."

"Or will they create trouble? To fight against the object of their fears?"

"We can take care of any negroes who get themselves into an uproar. And the truth is, Jones, that I don't care a damn about the Peabody girl. Never did. There's a war on. I just want to know who murdered Colonel Feiger. And why." He folded his arms yet again, tucking his shrunken cigar behind an elbow. "Based upon your conspicuous successes so far, I'm not sure you're the man to find that out."

"I need to review the ledgers in the paymaster's office."

He smirked again. "If half of what you suspect is true, you wouldn't find the girl's money on the books. Couldn't be mixed in with Federal funds, anyway."

"But whoever accepted the money from Miss Peabody must have made a show of entering the funds into one record or another. To content her. Even if that record has been destroyed, my appearance will trouble the thoughts of the guilty person. And then we will see what happens."

A look of discomfort spread from the general's face to his

bearing entire. I knew what he was going to say before he parted his lips.

I spoke first. "If your colonel bore any guilt, then we will uncover it. And if he was an innocent victim, we will learn that, too, and protect his reputation."

His eyes searched the ceiling. "Oh, go down and look at the ledgers. Look all you want. Go ahead. Make a pantomime of doing something, even if you're not accomplishing one damned thing. Peek in every slops bucket in New Orleans, for all I care. Just get on with your damned investigation and finish it. So this city and I can see the last of you." He shifted his posture. He might have been holding a musket with bayonet fixed. "And don't blame Bolt for your own mistakes. I've got to have somebody keeping an eye on you. Since you don't seem to feel any obligation to keep the general commanding informed." He crossed his arms again. "Besides, you should be damned glad he dragged you out of that tomb the other night. Sounds to me like you're in the captain's debt."

"And if I am grateful, the lad is still a fool. And an annoyance."

"Tell that to his father, when you go back North. Old man Bolt controls more than his fair share of land, money and votes out West. And, from what I hear, half the shipping up-river of St. Louis. I'm just trying to keep the boy half-employed while he's playing soldier. And don't make that self-righteous face at me. It's your friends in Washington who gave young Bolt his commission, then made damned certain he isn't sent anywhere near the fighting. I have less control over him than I do over you. I'm just trying to get a little work out of him."

The general stubbed out his cigar and bellowed, "Crandall? Crandall, get in here. Bring the orders and those damned shoulder-boards."

"Then we are finished, General Banks?"

"I wish to Hell we were."

An adjutant tumbled into the room, bearing folded papers and a pair of lieutenant-colonel's epaulettes.

"I've received an order. From Stanton," the general said, with no pretence at satisfaction. "To promote you without delay. Your commission's signed by Lincoln himself, 'Lieutenant-colonel' Jones." His mouth writhed as if he had tasted something foul. "I'd call that fairly special treatment. For a volunteer officer who doesn't hold a command. Seems to me that you and Captain Bolt have a great deal in common." His distaste yielded to necessity. "Read the orders, Crandall. We'll get this over with."

"No," I said.

The two men looked at me.

"No," I repeated. "I do not accept the promotion. I do not want it."

"You—"

"I will not accept it, see. I will not be promoted."

I understood, of course. This was John Nicolay's doing. And Mr. Lincoln's canniness at work. It was an attempt to flatter me. To bribe me, to say things plainly. So that I would discard my intention to resign my commission and leave the Union Army.

"You don't want a promotion?" Banks asked, incredulously. "I would have thought that a man like you—"

"You would have thought incorrectly, General Banks. It is my intention to resign the commission I already hold, as soon as this Peabody matter is resolved. I intend to return to my family and my business. And I will not be lured into changing my mind."

A different sort of smile crept over his face. Twas small and hard. "Had enough of war, have you?" His voice was ice, but his eyes were colder still. He thrust a fresh cigar between his lips.

I understood what the fellow meant. He did not know my history, that I had seen more of war than a man should witness. He simply thought me a coward who, even kept at a distance from the battlefield, could not bear the danger, or even the inconvenience, of wearing a uniform. He thought me the same as countless others who had failed our country as the war dragged on.

There are times when attempts at explanation only worsen an honest man's predicament.

"Yes," I said, "I have had enough of war."

I WENT DOWN to the pay office, only to find it locked. I did not make a fuss, for an odd dismay had come over me. I decided the ledgers could wait a bit. Perhaps, I told myself, it might be better if I gave the guilty time to sweat. But the truth is that I turned away from the paymaster's door out of lassitude.

Sloth is unlike me. Nor does it become a Christian. Yet, I did not make a single inquiry in the neighboring offices, where clerks and captains crowded as thick as maggots on Navy beef. I tapped my way out of the Customs House and into the lively streets and brightened air.

A fine day had come at last, to speak of the weather. Warm enough it was to forgo an overgarment. Twas prancing April at the birth of February, with the sky blue and cloudless beyond the rigging of the vessels crowding the wharves. The city's pulse had quickened at the sun's debut. But there was ice in my blood.

If I failed to force open the paymaster's office, I should at least have returned to my hotel, to wait for Mr. Barnaby. I had much to ask of the fellow, not least about that message in the medicine pot.

Instead, I turned into the "Quarter," past merchants vending the bottled sins of France, by stationers and milliners, and along the walks where colored bootblacks sang. Even the beggars smiled with sunlit hopes. I wished to *think,* to "walk a turn or two," as Mr. Shakespeare put it. To see if I might find my vigor renewed by the freshening air. To bring some order to my teeming mind.

I would not be an honest man if I claimed no regrets at turning down that promotion. Although the Bible warns us of pride, over and over again, and cautions us that earthly station is naught in the eyes of Heaven, every man likes to see himself raised up. Nor do we shun the admiration of wives and the awe of children, or the gentle qualms of friends at our changed condition. Twas a wonderful thing to rise as high as I already had done, from a John Company private to an American major. Yet, I would have liked that lieutenant-colonelcy.

Still, I was proud of my firmness. I had resolved to have none of it, to take me home, once and for all, and leave soldiering behind. When the general insinuated that I was a slacker, I barely restrained an impulse to tear off my coat, to shed my unmentionables and let him view the scars upon my person. But I would *not* be confounded into changing my mind like a girl of seventeen.

I would go home.

I hated the morass of death and sin into which my peculiar service had introduced me. At least upon the battlefield, your enemy is clear, as is your purpose. But my duties to our Union had drawn me into circumstances that showed men at their worst. I think I feared infection, as a healthy man dreads entering a plague ward. Or, perhaps, as a man whose own health is doubtful fears the sick.

It also annoyed me that I had stolen the morning. It betrayed a certain deficiency of character. Selfishly, I had given my first attentions to letters from home, not to my Bible reading. Of late, I had been tussling with the First Epistle of Paul the Apostle to Timothy. Two bits stuck in my mind, from Chapter I. Paul, who was stern, was writing of matters of faith, but I could not help but apply his words to my own lot.

"Neither give heed to fables and endless genealogies," Paul tells us. Which made me ask myself if I had not been entranced by all the "fables" told in New Orleans. Paul bids us to have faith and avoid such complications and distractions. He tells us to go forward and not meander. Yet, every hour led down a doubtful path.

Still more immediate to my task was the charge that "we know that the law *is* good, if a man use it lawfully . . . the law is not made for a righteous man, but for the lawless and disobedient, for the ungodly and for sinners . . . for manslayers, for whoremongers . . . for menstealers . . ."

The Apostle meant God's law. I understand that. But might his words not apply as well to the laws laid down by men?

The bit that troubled me, of course, was "if a man use it lawfully." How shall we wield the law so that it serves the cause of justice and not power? Does all the justice upon this earth lie solely in the law? I saw how easily I might slip, because of a foul mood or a misunderstanding, and turn justice on its head. Or simply fail to see that which paraded before mine eyes, to see instead what I expected to see or desired to behold, instead of the meaner truth.

When does the pursuit of justice decline to selfishness, causing more harm than it mends? There's the rub, as that fellow says in the play. The evil must be apprehended and punished. But how do we select their pursuers with wisdom?

Was I fit?

When I thought of the many who had died in the course of my inquiries—not only in New Orleans, but elsewhere and often—I wondered if I had not done more harm than good. I had obeyed the letter of the law. Scrupulously. The cloak of the law had been my constant vanity. But had I violated the law's spirit? How many of my doings might be ascribed to pride, rather than to an honest sense of duty? Did I care more for approbation than justice?

In the end, of course, we only have our faith. Although it is not listed among the mortal sins, I wonder if discouragement were not left out through accident or haste.

I would not bow in the matter of promotion. But I would do my duty as assigned. This last time.

I wished myself back home in our dear Pottsville.

My wanderings about those streets were not entirely aimless. I tried to find the shop of Mr. Beyle, the old Frenchman who had told me his "fable" and trusted me with the sword cane. I worried that he might ask a thing in return that I could not honorably deliver. It seemed too queer by half that such a fellow would trust a stranger without asking a security. I feared he might seek my help in avoiding customs duties, or even in passing contraband through the lines.

I told myself I should return the cane, although I knew I would not.

My argument with myself come up to nothing. I could not find the alley that led to his shop. Now, I have found my way with skill in the Pushtoon hills, in secretive Lahore and deep in coal mines. Twas irksome to be stymied by a Frenchman.

I took me past the St. Louis Hotel, where French holds sway and no one liked my aspect, then rambled from the Mint back to the opera house. I marched from the old market, with its smells of decayed wares and weary fish, past the gloomy Roman church and all the way to Rampart

Street, which appeared still more unwholesome. Along my way, I recognized Mr. Champlain's house. Viewed by daylight, it wanted painting badly.

I went up one street and down another, with perfect method and discipline. But I could not discover that bent-over Frenchman's shop. Twas as if I had only dreamed of that room at the back, of the old fellow's treasures and stories of wild intrigues.

Giving up, I traipsed back to Canal Street. When I reached that broad expanse, I felt I had re-entered my own country. The shabbiness and languor of the Quarter gave way to well-kept shops. All the famous commercial names the world has come to know crowded together: Hyde & Goodrich, Mallard's, Levois's, Clark's and Laroussini's. Of course, men of high business did their trade on Tchoupitoulas, on the American side, but Canal Street was the artery in which the old blood mingled with the new, where civilizations tipped their hats to each other. I cannot say why, but the bustle lifted my spirits.

I arrived back at the St. Charles Hotel to find Mr. Barnaby shackled.

thirteen

"CAUGHT HIM TRYING TO break into your room," Captain Bolt announced to me and to every other person in the lobby. "Bold as brass. Trying to jiggle the lock. But we were watching, yes, sir. Just like you said." His eyes roamed the grand geography of Mr. Barnaby's person. "Now we know who's been sneaking around here killing folks."

Bolt wore the expression of a dog who has done his trick. Half-witted he was, and that is putting it kindly. I recalled the general's mention of a powerful, wealthy father, doubtless one of our self-made men of the West. What a sorrow it must have been for such a man to produce so feeble a son. Twas a caution to us all, a tale of generations risen and fallen. It made me think of my son John, about whom I worried helplessly. I prayed my boy would be stalwart, healthy and Christian.

"Take those irons off him," I said. I did not say it gently, but spoke in heat. Captain Bolt's nonsense had drawn a score of spectators in uniform—men who should have been laboring at their posts, instead of loafing about in a hotel. Each had his own opinion, but the pack of them quieted when they heard my tone. "Do it now!"

"But . . . this man's a . . . a *crim*inal! We caught him in the act."

I looked at Mr. Barnaby, whose face was wild and tear-stained.

"I only thought you was taking your rest," he told me, "and didn't want to be troubled. But I 'ad to trouble you, begging your pardon, sir. Things is topsy-turvy and worse, but the lass is still alive."

As he muttered that last phrase, his eyes ripened with another harvest of tears.

"I told you to take those blasted irons off him," I said to Bolt, employing language stronger than is my habit.

The captain nodded at one of his soldiers, a fellow I had not marked before. The lad produced a collection of keys that might have been the pride of the Tower of London.

"She's alive, I does believe it," Mr. Barnaby continued. "I'm certain and sure of it."

The soldier fussed about with the chains and manacles. I had never seen a convict so encumbered, not even in India.

"In good time, Mr. Barnaby, in good time. As for you, Captain Bolt, I countermand my order regarding my room. You and your men will keep your distance from it. In fact, you will not enter this hotel. Nor will you spy on me from the outside of it."

"But General Banks—"

"Raise the matter with the general yourself. Or with your father, boy. It does not signify. But you will not annoy me any longer." I might have added, "you bloody fool," but for the presence of those of subordinate rank.

"That man's a criminal," Bolt said, weakly but obstinately.

"So are we all sinners in the eyes of the Lord. Now get you gone, Captain Bolt. And take great pains that I do not find you near me."

Muttering as an officer should not do, he took himself off.

Leaving Mr. Barnaby unembarrassed by irons, his soldiers dragged along behind the captain, jostling and unruly.

A fool placed in authority is a hazard to us all. Yet, men whose rank exceeds their powers of judgement are as common as mules in a stable.

I led Mr. Barnaby upstairs to my room, which I found in good order. But our purposes were contrary. He wished to babble, while I hoped to calm him. I needed to ask his advice about the message in the medicine jar, about "Queen Manweler" and her purported knowledge. But the good man was excited to incoherence.

"She's alive, I swears it." That was the most intelligible of his remarks. "She's alive and waiting for us to find 'er."

"Sit down, Mr. Barnaby. Sit yourself down and calm yourself. *Please* sit down."

The afternoon was ill favored. The poor fellow obeyed me all too anxiously and plumped down upon the nearest chair, which was too delicately framed for his physique.

Looking up from the floor amid the splinters, he appeared as shocked as a preacher in a music hall.

"That 'asn't 'appened in years," he said, without attempting to rise.

I extended my hand to help the fellow up. Whether it was the shock of finding himself seated on the floor, or the subsequent contact of my flesh with his own, he seemed much sobered. Still, I thought it best to talk him round by changing the subject to something much removed. Indeed, I had been preparing my speech for some time.

I steered him to the bed, which seemed more likely to bear his manly frame, and settled myself upon a chair by the window.

"Mr. Barnaby," I began, hoping to distract him from his alarms, "there is a matter which I have longed to discuss with you. I fear I was unjust when we spoke in the spring. I condemned the reading of novels and was uncharitable. Even, I fear, contemptuous." I cleared my throat and disciplined my posture. "Since that time I have found reason to amend my prejudices. In fact, I have come to view the novel as a beneficial instrument, whose purposes may be salutary, if not misused. I speak, of course, of authors of firm morality. I wish to apologize to you, see. Indeed, I wish to recommend that you expand your reading. Instead of reading about Mr. Pickwick over and over as you have done, I believe you should read a more recent work by Mr. Dickens, *Great Expectations*. I think you would find it sound."

"Oh, I couldn't do that, begging your pardon. I really couldn't, sir."

"I know you are very fond of Mr. Pickwick. But there is a host of instructive characters, all waiting to introduce themselves. Really, Mr. Barnaby . . . Pip . . . Mr. Gargery— who is the very model of a Christian—the spurned old woman, the vain beauty . . . and Magwitch, who is wonderfully reformed . . ."

Mr. Barnaby shook his head, slowly but with decision. "I couldn't do it, sir. Really, I couldn't. It's all too awful and 'orrible. I couldn't bear to undertake the experience of more suffering. And people always suffers in a novel, sir, if it's worth the ink and paper." He battled the damp rebellion in his eyes. "I've even 'ad to give up reading about Mr. Pickwick, I 'as. I couldn't bear it no more, knowing as 'ow all 'is 'appiness is bound to be torn from 'is bosom. Not all Sam Weller's wits can't save the poor man, sir. 'E goes to 'is sufferings over and over again. Without end, sir, without end! As if that Charlie Dickens 'as trapped 'im up forever in the pages, so 'e can't never escape. It ain't Christian, if a fellow such as me dare point it out. It ain't near honest to pin a fellow down on the page so's 'e can't get up again, to make 'is sufferings eternal, so to speak, without no 'ope of recovery by and by. Even the voodoo lot ain't cruel as that. At least not most-wise." His features begged for a kinder world. "A writer fellow must be 'orrible wicked, sir, to go killing folks with ink and making everyone suffer for 'is pleasure. And for profit, sir! The scribblers takes money to make the innocent suffer in their books. It just ain't right to do a thing like that."

"Then read the Holy Bible," I advised him. Startled I was by the reversal of our positions. I could not think of anything else to say.

"I've tried that, I 'as. Reading the Gospels and what-not. But it's even worse than taking up a novel. What they done to poor Jesus, after 'e tried so 'ard to be nice to all of 'em. 'E wouldn't 'urt a fly, and look what they does to 'Im." His eyes gazed through the window as he recalled his collisions with the word of the Lord. "And as for that Old Testament, the parts what ain't Bedlam mad are mean enough to keep a fellow from ever trusting 'is neighbor, what with all those wicked kings and smitings and general misbehaviors. And it do take a terrible long time only to tell us we ought to behave ourselves better." He shook his head in the deep sorrow of memory. "Poor Jesus ends up even worse than Pickwick."

"The Gospels," I attempted to explain, "bear tidings of God's sacrifice for Mankind."

Mr. Barnaby returned his eyes and sagging cheeks to me. "But I doesn't *want* 'Im to sacrifice 'Is son, sir. It ain't 'alf right, that. When the poor lad ain't done nothing the least bit wrong. It's a punishment 'e didn't deserve. And I suspects 'e didn't ask for it, neither. No, sir. It's too much like this war of ours, started by the fathers in their pride and fought out with the blood of the lads they sired. There's been too much of that sort of thing, if you asks Barnaby B. Barnaby. I'd like the Gospels better, I would, if Jesus ended up old and plump and 'appy."

IT GREW EVIDENT that, for the present, Mr. Barnaby was no more susceptible to the beauties of our faith than Jimmy Molloy or even Mick Tyrone. Queer it is that so many of the fellows of whom I am fond will not be led to salvation. I hope in time to help them see the light.

Meanwhile, Mr. Barnaby had calmed sufficiently for me to risk a query or two. I would have liked to begin by asking about the message in the pot, but knew enough of men to see that first he would need to free himself of any news he had about the girl.

"What's this about the lass, then?" I asked. "Alive, is it?"

"I can't say exactly what's wherefore, sir. And I can't say precisely what 'appened. But I know she's alive, as sure as my father's own name was Barnaby Barnaby."

"But what evidence have you?"

He leaned toward me, making the mattress lament. "It was whispered to me, it was. Whispered in a crowd. I was making my enquiries among the lads I knows in the *Faubourg* Marigny—about your Fishers of Men, sir—when a negro comes up behind where I can't see 'im and whispers in my ear, 'She's alive, and she ain't been spoiled.' But when I turned myself about to confront 'im, sir, all I saw was the back of 'is wooly 'ead."

Considering the fellow's distraught condition, I asked, "Are you certain, then, that all was not imagined? Look you. Many's the wish so strong it plays with our senses."

He shook his head. "On my honor, as a gentleman's gent and one-time 'aberdasher. If I'm speaking of phantoms, may I never 'ave me appetite back again, sir. May I never see bread nor buttermilk."

"All right, man. If such words were, indeed, spoken, then why? Why should anyone tell you such a thing? If not to deceive us?"

He rolled his shoulders, which were considerably narrower than his hips. "What's the sense in anything anymore, sir? The whole world's at sixes and sevens."

"But someone may be trying to mislead you. To divert my attention."

"But she's alive, sir! That ought to count for something."

"Perhaps it is only a lie," I cautioned, although I believed myself that the poor lass lived, that the blood splashed about my room was a false concoction. I did not want to raise his hopes too high. "Why should we credit a whisper from a stranger?"

"Why doubt it, sir? Why doubt it? Ain't you forever preaching we must 'ave faith? It seems to me, it do, that the odds is even as to whether the fellow meant to do us ill or meant 'er good."

"Even so . . . what would you have me do?"

At that, he slumped profoundly. "I was 'oping you'd 'ave an idea yourself, sir. For I'm all out. The pockets of my brain are empty, and them what was willing to talk to me was them what had nothing to say. I ain't come forward an inch with your Fishers of Men, sir. Scared up and down the street, folks are. I never seen the negroes in such fear."

"Mr. Barnaby . . . if you please . . . we must set this matter of the girl aside. Do not be alarmed. I mean only for a time. There is another business to attend to." I walked over to the medicine pot, took out the message and handed it to my comrade. As for the jar itself, I kept it in hand as I sat back down, for my mouth wanted painting again, with the hurt resurgent.

"Can you understand the meaning of the scribble?" I

asked, fingering up a generous dollop of salve. "Who is Queen Manweler, can you tell me?"

"Oh, that's more odds than evens," he said vaguely, studying the paper with a confounded look. Next, he examined me anew, as I rubbed my finger over the meat in my mouth. I was not certain what to make of his countenance.

His features shifted unexpectedly, like mercury at play. Twas clear he was thinking hard before returning to speech, but that may be a virtue as well as a vice. It was the complexity of his expressions, their contradiction from one moment to the next, that concerned me. Mr. Barnaby's face had ever been a thing of India rubber, able to convey character or foolery. Now it told me less of him than at any time I recalled from our term of acquaintance. Instead of revealing the man himself, his face reflected the world beyond the window, all the secrets and loyalties of his city.

At last, he spoke. "White men doesn't know a thing about 'er. Not even 'er name, which"—he dropped his voice to a hush—"is Queen Manuela. Lord bless us." He crossed himself instantly, in the fashion of Rome, then scrutinized me with redoubled concern. "And you shouldn't speak 'er name out so plain, sir, begging your pardon. You ain't to know that such a body exists."

"But *you* know! And you are as white as I am myself, man. It does not follow that she is so great a secret."

He turned his head from side to side. Torpidly, as if degraded by opium. "You 'as to understand . . . that some things is always tucked away by the negroes, sir. And among them what's lumped in with 'em. It's 'ow they survives, 'ow they lives and gets on. There's doings what's only for show, and things what ain't. With the voodoo now . . . there's part of it what's only meant to draw in money from foolish folk, black or white. Most of the shows are no more than street-corner prancing moved out to the bayous. The truth is, begging your pardon, sir, that the voodoo priestesses, the most of 'em, is just as greedy as your Christian parson, expecting to be paid for praising one god or another and for squeezing you into their prayers. Most of 'em just knows a pair of mumbles, if that. They deals in poisons and potions made up of roots, in charms and such like. It ain't really supernatural at all."

He pause and eyed me as closely as a tailor judging not only a man's size, but the quality of fabric that must be offered. "But then there's them what believes, sir. What *really* believes. As sure as the Oxford Martyrs. They goes about it more quiet like, that sort, and they doesn't ever let a white man see."

"Then how do *you* know all this? Good Lord, I might as well be back in India."

"All's one, sir, all's one. My little Marie, now . . . you might say she was something of a chameleon, Major Jones. Whoever looked at 'er saw what color they expected to see. You, begging your pardon, would've judged 'er as white as Queen Victoria."

"You imply that your—"

"I never asked, sir. Never a single time. When a fellow's in love, 'e only makes a fool of 'imself and wounds them what 'e adores by asking questions. 'Let the past be,' that's my motto. My grandfather what served with Pakenham passed down that advice. And my father took it to 'eart and left it to me." He looked at me imploringly. "I know you doesn't approve of things slipping out of their regular traces, sir. But 'appiness is a rare thing in this world. I've never thought there was any sense in questioning it too close when it come knocking. I didn't care what my Marie was in 'er blood or in 'er background. It was enough and more that she made me 'appy."

"But your children . . ."

"Oh, they was lovely, sir! Lovely as Devon in May. I mourns 'em daily."

"Your wife . . . knew of these unholy rituals? Of this Queen Manuela?"

Mr. Barnaby looked about the room, as if there might be devils in the woodwork. "Don't say 'er name, I begs you, sir. It ain't to be said out loud. Nor even thought too plainly by the likes of us." He watched my lips as if they might transgress again. "But my Marie, sir . . . Marie was a proper Christian. She spent more time on her knees in St. Louis's than a maid spends polishing silver. It's only that she didn't see the point of betting all on a single number, sir. She always figured the odds, did my Marie. She wore 'er cross about 'er neck, but made time for Yermanja. Just in case us Christians 'ad it wrong. She didn't stint on praying to one or the other, Major Jones, but made plenty of time for both, and none's the worse for it."

There was no use in arguing theology with the man. Such lessons could come later. At present, I needed information. May the Lord understand and forgive me.

"And who is Yermanja? Another African snake god?"

"Oh, no, sir! Nothing of the like! African, I supposes, since it was only slaves and free negroes what took 'er up. Yermanja's sort of like the Virgin Mary, sir. She's the powerful goddess of the seas, begging your pardon, and she don't mind strolling ashore, when she takes an interest. She's for the sorts what takes up Candomblé. My Marie, now . . . she wasn't interested in casting spells on rivals and such business. She only prayed for 'appiness. And for me, sir. To keep me round and jolly."

His expression, then his head, then his shoulders sank. "Terrible it was. Too terrible for words, sir. When the Yellow

Jack took 'er and the little ones, neither Yermanja nor Jesus Christ was any 'elp at all. I suppose as Marie and the little 'uns wasn't important enough to be saved, sir. But they meant all the world to me." A tear blurred his eyes, but he met my gaze straight on. "I doesn't care what a man or a woman believes, sir, only whether their 'earts is good or bad."

"Do I understand you to mean that this Queen—this voodoo priestess of whom we have been speaking—worships a sea goddess?"

"That's what they says, sir. That's what they tells me. And not only 'er, but other spirits besides. But you'd 'ave to ask another to learn more, sir, for there's a limit to what I knows and we've already passed it by. But the lady whose name we ain't to speak . . . she's said to be a force for good, and strict in 'er observances. Not like Marie Laveau or that Marie Venin, the one what tried to poison you. They're more concerned with gold than with goodness of any sort. I won't say they 'ave no real powers, but what powers they 'ave come from the gullible themselves, that's what Barnaby B. Barnaby believes. From fear, sir. And from their knowledge of plants and such, and all the secrets they gather in from their followers. They're only frightful 'cause we makes 'em so. But . . . the lady of which we ain't to speak the name, sir . . . she's said to be so mighty that the other *voudouiennes* steers clear of 'er and won't say 'er name in a whisper."

"Do you believe she might 'know everything' about the murder of Susan Peabody? Or the other killings?"

"I can't say that, sir. Not one way or the other. For I doesn't know, to be honest."

"Where might I find Queen—I mean, this woman?"

"I couldn't say that neither, sir. Nor whether she's like to speak to you at all."

I looked at him more closely. A tone had crept into his voice that carried less forthrightness than I liked.

"There must be some way . . . some manner in which I might contact her?" Then I added, a bit cruelly, "Just as you hope that I will find a way to free young Raines."

Mr. Barnaby thought on that. And I let him think. For there are times when much is to be said for not saying much. Although it is a hard practice for a Welshman.

He pondered so long that the winter sunlight crept from one plank to another.

At last, he said, in a hushed voice, "Per'aps Madame La Blanch can 'elp us. Per'aps you might go visit 'er, sir."

"And who is Madame La Blanch?"

Mr. Barnaby chose his words with care. "She's a clairvoyant, sir. One of them sorts. What does up medicines, as well. We can call and see if she's in, for 'er rooms ain't far away. Just along Bienville, between Bourbon and Dauphine."

Now, I have little patience with clairvoyance, which I regard as no more than a parlor trick. I will admit to experiences of mine own which defy clear explanation, but on that count I agree with Mick Tyrone, who insists that the march of knowledge will soon conquer every aspect of our bewilderment. But New Orleans is hardly a place subject to science. The city celebrates each quirk and queerness, and you cannot move forward in the place if you demand to deal only with the rational inhabitants. They are a small minority, at best, like the Jains of India.

Anyway, I did not need Madame La Blanch to peer into my future, but only to help me locate Queen Manuela—who, for all her mystery, seemed a creature of flesh who lived among us.

"The address is in the Quarter, I believe?"

Mr. Barnaby nodded. "Everything what matters hides in the *Vieux Carré*."

MADAME LA BLANCH looked up from her soiled cards.

"Forgive my *deshabille*, Major Jones," she said. "I expected you this morning and had given you up en*tire*ly when you failed to appear with that promptitude for which you have become so famous among us. Indeed, sir, I had begun to fear the failing of my powers . . ."

"Afternoon, mum," I said, near choking on the scent that clouded the room. I might have been in the den of a Hindoo *fakir*. The untidiness made me careful of where I dropped my hat.

I was not much surprised at her knowledge of my identity. Anyone who poses as a clairvoyant must have abundant sources of information. Likely, some darky from Mr. Champlain's establishment had warned her that I might come searching for Queen Manuela.

"And Mr. Barnaby! Our Galahad!" She smiled gaily. "Or should I say, 'Our Gawain?' How *dread*fully long has it been, sir?"

"Pleasure to see you again, Madame La Blanch," my companion told her. "You ain't aged a day, I swears, and you looks as smacking 'andsome as you ever did."

The woman, got up in fraying frills, returned her attention to me. "Mr. B. is *ever* the gentleman. I always say that there is no man from here to Natchez knows how to honor a woman the way an English gentleman does! But really, Mr. B., I see right here in the seven of hearts that you have a most pressing errand! Don't you worry a bit, now. Your friend is in good hands."

Saying that, she took my right hand in hers so deftly that my cane clattered off the table's edge, coming to rest where the furniture met the wall. The woman drew me artfully into a seat cat-corner from hers.

"Lovely, lovely," Mr. Barnaby added as he took himself back through the door and into the street.

Now, "lovely" seemed to me an exaggeration. The woman before me did not look unmarred by the years, nor born to provide a special delight to the eyes. Yet, there was something about her that pleased, I grant her. You could not have told her age exactly, but the odder thing by half was that she made me recall what Mr. Barnaby had said of his own wife, that those admiring her saw what they themselves expected to see.

Like her age, her race was indeterminate.

I thought her likely a white woman, tawnied by some Spanish blood or simply French-complected. But I remained uncertain. She might have been one of those quadroons of whom so much is rumored, or even a proper negress painted pale by the quirk of an ancestor's affections. Her hair was black, but smooth in its plaits and cylinder curls, not made of negro felt. I thought her hair must be dyed to assert such an indigo, but could not judge with confidence. Her eyes were green, but edged with brown, and might have belonged to any race on earth.

Nor were her features written in clear ancestry. Rounded and turned up, her nose might have come of a negress dam, or from an Irish sire. Her forehead was nigh akin to Mr. Shakespeare's in that old plate a fellow sees, and such brows are not African, I do not think. Yet, her lips were full to an excess. They might have belonged to a princess of the Niger, or to a Welsh lass from the streets of Brecon. She looked pleasant, but not guileless.

Some peculiar force in her femininity did not allow me to draw my hand from her grasp.

"Madam La Blanch, I—"

She raised a finger to her lips, then laid a second hand upon my one, turning it over to expose my palm.

Tracing the highways and lanes of flesh with a fingernail, she smiled, parting rich lips. "You will live a long and happy life, although you will not realize how happy you have been until it is too late. You find discontents where others discover joy. You wish to have faith, but your faith is weaker than you pretend. What you call love of God is fear of the devil. And your devil wears human flesh. Like your own. You were born to doubt, which fits you to your work. But your heart is true and good, better than your temper. With the years, all these things will become easier for you, the fears will soften. You will learn joy, despite yourself. But you have no gift for stillness. Peace will elude you each time you think you have gained it. Few women love you, but those love without stinting. They would die for you. One has."

She looked at me. Smiling.

"She watches over you still," the woman continued.

I stood up. Abruptly. Tearing my hand free.

"This is nonsense," I said. A bit too loudly.

Her smile indulged me. "But of course it is! Mere webs of gossamer. You and I realize that, Major Jones. But I rely upon your honor as a gentleman not to give out my secret."

"I—"

"Sit down, sir. Please. You need not grant me your hand again. I fear I was forward. We're not so proper about such things as you Northern folk. Although we do love our social frills and fripperies. Our ceremonials, as they say. But you came to inquire about a certain person's whereabouts, not to indulge my silliness."

I sat down. Although my heartbeat had quickened to a throb and I wished to flee.

"What a strong man you are!" she said. "Every report I have had is true, sir! You must be an absolute pillar to your dear wife. And your son and daughter must positively *adore* you!" She read my face and asked, "But have I erred? You *do* have a little boy and an infant girl, do you not?"

The queer thing was that I could not say. My darling's letters, so long underway, had contained news of the past. I could not speak for the present.

These people learn infernal tricks, see. Like gypsies. Or gamblers who make their living from cards and dice. They know a hundred ways to read a man, to cheat him and beguile him.

"But I must re*strain* myself," the woman said. "I promised that we should play no more of my silly, little games. After all, Major Jones, you're a gentleman of importance, with pressing business. Not some poor little merchant's wife in search of titillation."

"I'm given to understand that you might help me contact Queen Manuela," I told her.

Her eyes scorched me. Fair flaming they were. But only for an instant.

"We do not speak that name," she said, quietly but sternly.

"But—"

"You must *not* speak that name."

She allowed our eyes to meet again. Or should I say that her eyes forced mine to show themselves? She had her proper tricks, did Madame La Blanch.

"I am only trying to help," I said. My tone was almost child-like. "The murders . . ."

"Are you brave enough?" she asked. Her voice had dropped in pitch, as if her new and unexpected gravity had weighed it down.

Twas not a ladylike question to put to a man.

"Brave enough for what, mum?"

"To help." There was no change in the light of the room, but her eyes gathered a shadow around themselves. All I could see were the burning spots in their centers. "To do what must be done. To fight the friend who is a foe and recognize the foe who is a friend. To face the coming fire."

That seemed a mumbo-jumbo. I told her, "It is my duty to do the things that need doing in these matters. As for bravery, mum, others must judge."

"Are you brave enough to meet *her*? At the time when she calls you, at the place to which she beckons?"

"If you mean Queen—"

She slapped her hand over my lips with so much force it stung me. And my jaw was none too happy to begin with. The lingering ache reminded me of the swelling of my face, the tightened skin, the discoloration that had greeted me in the mirror.

"Never speak that name again. It's very powerful. Too powerful for you. Even your best spirits could not protect you."

Of a sudden, my patience quit me. I am a Christian man and had already had too much to do with deviltry and shenanigans. New Orleans was a city of the damned. Or at least of those who did not dread damnation.

"You will excuse me, mum," I told her. "Excuse the interruption. I have been mistaken in calling."

I rose, took up my cane and put on my hat. But as I laid my hand on the doorknob, the woman said, "You'll let Magdalena die? You care nothing about the Fishers of Men? Or who killed your Miss Peabody? You're as false as the other men who wear blue uniforms?"

"I COULD PLACE you under arrest," I warned her. And I gave that action more than a passing thought.

Although I am a man of no great intelligence, I am not a fool on the order of Captain Bolt. I had seen with the suddenness of a shot how this woman had come to know so much about me. Doubtless, she had gained access to my letters before they reached my own hands. Those pages contained more than enough detail for her to spin a web of secret knowledge. I intended to give that hotel clerk a talking to.

"If you don't tell me what you know," I continued, "I can put you under lock and key. Until you think better of your behavior, mum."

The woman looked at me with the confidence of a saint on the Day of Judgement.

"Sit down, Major Jones. Please. Sit for a moment and calm yourself. I only wish to help you. Pray understand that. *She* possesses the answers, not me. Madame La Blanch only has the question she reads in your heart. If *she* won't speak to you . . . if *she* decides not to trust you . . . there's nothing I can do. Even if you send me off to some frightful Northern prison. Which I cannot believe that you, as a gentleman, would even consider."

She smiled, an aging flirt, and gave me time to weigh my course of action. For the first time, I looked around me properly. As if she had suddenly granted me permission to inspect her narrow parlor and its contents.

Now, I am a good observer, as a rule. Yet, until that moment, I could only have made my report of the woman's person and her words, adding that she owned a deck of cards and worked in squalor.

What I saw around me was laughable. Shelves rose half the distance to the ceiling, crowded with unmatched bottles, their contents protected by ancient corks or bits of rag in their necks. Gewgaws of the sort a butcher's wife buys on holiday crowded against reptiles ill preserved, withered and shrunken. A bust of Napoleon with the nose broken off was hung with cheap glass beads and trinket necklaces. The walls were covered with pictures torn from illustrated weeklies, Niagara Falls, table rappers, a fellow I believe was Garibaldi, and scenes of exotic climes. A hand-colored portrait of Jesus Christ hung beside a lurid sketch of some jungle god. The latter's frame was draped with wilting flowers. Words had been lettered on the wall, in black paint and in green, their meanings as inscrutable as the spelling was irregular. Hostile to fresh air and light, the whole place wanted sweeping out and scrubbing.

When my eyes returned to the mistress of the clutter, I found her smile unchanged.

"Mr. Barnaby will be waiting for you outside," she told me. "Please do send him in to me. As you leave. Unless, sir, you have decided to arrest me. In which case, his call would be superfluous."

"I am not going to arrest you."

She stood up. As a gentleman, I was forced to mirror her action.

"Then send in Mr. Barnaby. I will give him instructions. On matters that would be meaningless to you."

Her smile declined, then disappeared entirely.

fourteen

"THIS IS UNSPEAKABLE!" I told Mr. Barnaby.

He looked nonplussed as he sat on my dismayed bed. The fellow was trying to assist me, passing on his instructions from Madame La Blanch. But the proposition rankled. All the more since I knew I must accept it.

But I had my pride and did not mean to give in easily.

After leaving Mr. Barnaby to the clairvoyant's tutelage, I had wasted the rest of the afternoon with fruitless travels across the city and back again. That peeved me, too. I had returned to the pay office, hoping to find at least one dutiful clerk. The door remained locked. Next, I attempted to call upon Mrs. Aubrey, with whose assertions I had grown dissatisfied. A maid claimed that her lady was not at home. I could not intrude to challenge the poor girl's claim, since Mrs. Aubrey lived on a proper street and was respectable. Mr. Champlain was still abed, for he never rose until evening. Thus I could not profit from any knowledge he might have owned of Queen Manuela.

By the time I returned to the St. Charles Hotel, I had got myself into a state. Only to find Mr. Barnaby waiting, with a harried look on his face. He knew I would not like what he had to say.

"If that woman wishes to be helpful, she should deuced

well tell me what she knows and be done with it," I said after
hearing him out.

"She can't tell you anything, Madame La Blanch can't.
Not just like that. Not 'ow you means it, sir."

"Can't? Or won't?"

"All's one, sir, all's one." The poor fellow looked as forlorn as a child apt to be denied his dearest wish. "It ain't that
she don't *want* to 'elp you, it ain't that. All's to the contrary,
Major Jones. She does and she do! She wants to 'elp, and
she's trying." He rolled his stomach forward in great
earnestness. "It's a terrible privilege what's offered you.
Stunned me daft to 'ear it from 'er lips. The colored folk
what knows anything won't trust nobody. Not until 'e's been
given a proper look-over. And the person whose name we
ain't to speak not only knows more than all of 'em com-
bined, she ain't one to reveal 'erself to a white man." Sur-
veying the ways of the world, he shook his jowls. "It's a
proper shock 'ow she'd even consider putting you to the test,
sir. Whatever she 'as to say must be important. As important
as the news the Iron Duke scribbled from Waterloo."

"Then let her come forth and say what she has to say." I
cleared my throat, as if that might clear my thoughts. Which
were, I admit, disordered. "Mr. Barnaby . . . we live in the
nineteenth century, in modern times. Look you. All this
spooking nonsense will not do. Let the woman speak, if
speak she will. I'm weeping sick of all this city's nonsense."
I shook my head. "I am a man of open mind, ever ready to
weigh the views of another. I do not think any person could
dispute that. But I have no time for negro games and blasphemy. Listen I will, but I will not be led."

"It ain't that simple, sir, although I doesn't know 'ow to
make you see it. They're all afraid, every one of them, in ways
I never seen 'em. Something's 'appened what won't be told

straight out, not even by the boldest nor the worst. And there's more to it than the *Zombi* and such like." He looked down past his high-set girth to a spot where the Brussels carpet met the planking. "The truth is that they ain't sure they can trust you. For reasons Madame La Blanch won't even say. They 'as to be double sure of you, or they'll just stay pat and mum."

"Well," I said sourly, "she must not be terribly skilled as a clairvoyant. If she cannot even see into my intentions."

I had near bankrupted his hopes, for I can be stern to a fault. But Mr. Barnaby was determined to persuade me. "I can't say what she sees and what she don't, sir. But stone the crows, 'er offer is unusual. It's a right and proper honor, what with you a white man and not even pleasant." He sighed like a young swain watching his sweetheart flee. "You 'as to undergo it, sir. You 'as to give it a go. It might be our last chance, what won't come after."

He meant, not least, that it might be the final hope for Magdalena.

Well, selfishness shapes every human action. Unless we are in the company of saints, which did not seem to apply to New Orleans.

I scoured my throat again. My jaw was much improved, but still unkind. "How on *earth* is this . . . this pagan ceremony . . . supposed to prove a pack of darkies can trust me? It's preposterous! I am a proper Christian and—"

"They knows that, sir. And they doesn't mind it a bit. But they 'as to ask their own spirits if you're square."

"And if their 'spirits' tell them I am not 'square?' "

He buried his chin in generous layers of neck. "We wouldn't want to think like that, sir." His eyes popped up to meet mine own, though his hands continued to worry in his lap. "If all you've told to me is true, respecting your official purposes, sir, their spirits shouldn't tell 'em anything contrary. The spirits plays little pranks, they does, but they seldom tells a lie."

"Mr. Barnaby, I have been straightforward as to my purposes. As straight as Pall Mall. To suggest otherwise would—"

"I weren't suggesting nothing of the kind!" he said hastily. "Nothing of the kind, sir, nothing of the kind!"

"Then could you not assure them that I may be trusted?"

His eyes sank down again and his hands resettled on the thrust of his waistcoat. "It ain't the way things works, begging your pardon. The truth of it is that I don't quite understand it all myself, but they 'as acquired a dreadful fear of blue coats. They doesn't trust a single Union soldier."

"That's absolute folly!" I snapped. "We have come to free these people from the yoke of slavery. At not a little cost, I might add." I rearranged my bothered leg, a remembrance of Bull Run. "They should be trusting of our every word. And thanking us on bended knee each morning."

I fear my tone grew imperious. It is a queer thing, see, the way we are made. I possessed a measure of power over poor Mr. Barnaby and abused my position with relish, although I liked the fellow. I shudder to think how men would behave without the fear of God.

He made a face that did not wish to argue, but could not quite agree. "There's good folks and bad most everywhere, I believes, sir. And begging your pardon, I ain't convinced that every man what wears a Union coat is a heaven-sent angel."

"Why should I trust *them*? With all their voodoo foolishness and blasphemies? After one of their number tried to poison me? After those mongrel pirates or whoever they were hauled me up in a net, then buried me in a crypt? After they've skinned one of their fellows alive and threatened me with the same? Now they want me to go and join their rituals?"

"Oh, you ain't expected to join in, sir! They knows you're a Christian man. I warned 'em you ain't well-disposed towards the beliefs of others. Not even Catholics, I told 'em. They know your mind's locked up like Mohammed's daughters. But it ain't your mind what worries 'em. They wants to look in your 'eart. That's all. If you doesn't do anything foolish, but listens to what I tells you, you'll be fine, sir. For they takes their worshipping serious, as serious as you does yourself, begging your pardon. You can even take your revolver along. And your sword-cane. Although I can't say they'd be much 'elp, once you riled 'em."

I had run out of words that were worth the saying. I knew I had no choice but to acquiesce. But how it galled me!

My proper place was at home with my family in Pottsville. Not in this tawdry competitor to Sodom.

Mr. Barnaby leaned toward me with enthusiasm reborn. Likely, he sensed my wavering and called up his last reserves, as a general will upon the field of battle.

He pressed me as mightily as he pressed the mattress on which he sat. "Madame La Blanch ain't on the other side, sir. That's certain. As certain as mice in the bake-shop! And I don't believe that the person whose name we ain't to say out loud is on the other side, either. I swears it on my honor, sir. And . . . and on the mortal life of Lieutenant Raines . . ."

I grunted and folded my arms across my chest.

"I wish I knew who *is* on the other side," I said.

Before we left, I put on my clean uniform. It seemed to give me strength, like a suit of armor.

TWAS A DAY of one annoyance after another. Although Captain Bolt made himself scarce, and good riddance, the desk clerk took it upon himself to pester me as Mr. Barnaby and I tried to set off. The fellow come running after me, waving a dispatch. I hoped it might be a missive from home, celebrating the birth of a child and my darling's continued health, but saw in an instant that it was but another communication from that naval officer. I suspected some foolish point of protocol had been neglected, or that my favor was wanted after my return to Washington. An issue of promotion, perhaps, or the gain of a better ship. All braids and blather navies are. I had no time to waste.

"Hold it until my return," I told the clerk, without bothering to break the letter's seal. "I will see to it later, thank you."

"But the feller 'ut brought it said give it to you quick."

"Don't you understand the Queen's English?"

Mr. Barnaby and I went about finding a cab willing to brave back roads and miles in the darkness. None of the Frenchies would take us up and not a few seemed alarmed at our destination. Finally an Irishman agreed to transport us. Although I thought the fee he demanded was thievery. Nor were his manners especially accommodating.

"Ye can take yer arse along on your own two hoofs," he said in response to my protest, "if ye have to be so buggering miserly ye can't pay a man fair wages."

Mr. Barnaby played the peacemaker. And soon we were on our way.

We briefly stopped at an oyster bar before we left the city. Mr. Barnaby fetched stuffed buns for himself and a cup of glue for me.

"Gumbo," he said, as our vehicle rocked into motion again. "I thought as you might be able to suck on the broth and the other bits, sir. A man needs fortification, when 'e's going to stay awake until the morning."

Had I not grown desperate . . . had I not been worn to a nub and cranky with the bother to my jaw . . . I do not think I would have agreed to any of it. I had seen enough of deviltry in India, with bloody idols and men who were bloodier still. I am a great believer in the daylight.

I trusted Mr. Barnaby, but carried my loaded Colt and the Frenchman's cane. And a traveler's New Testament, shut in the pocket closest to my heart.

WE DROVE NIGH on two hours. Thrice we had to stop for pickets and outposts, manned by glum privates and sergeants as suspicious as a grocer asked for credit by a tinker. My papers passed us on our way each time. We traveled a lane of good quality for the first miles below the city. Mr. Barnaby called it the "Gentilly Road." But soon enough we turned into a byway, the ruggedness of which delayed our progress. Then we pursued a trail that was twice the worse.

Accustomed as we are to modern times, to gas lamps and the brightness of civilization, our spirits are ill prepared for the primitive dark. Despite my years of soldiering in India, whose darkness is of all too many kinds, I felt a bit unnerved by the inky air and the thickness of the foliage, which seemed avid to reclaim the earth from men. The cab's lamps sputtered on the verge of suffocation, as if the night were a smothering cloak pressed round us. The driver had to slow the horses, first to a walk, then a laze. The beasts, too fond of the city, shied and complained.

With a curse as harsh as the Dublin streets, the cab man dismounted, unhooked a lantern, and led his team forward on foot.

Winter though it was, the place was a jungle. Moss hung in mammoth shrouds and ragged tangles. Beyond the creak of the wagon's springs and axles, living creatures protested our intrusion. The black air smelled of rot.

The only habitation stood abandoned, gripped by vines. Although it pressed against the side of the trail, I might have failed to note the sagging wall but for the lamp's reflection on broken glass. Unless they are given fastidious care, properties mould swiftly in such climes, yet I could not suppress a sense that the dwelling had stood there longer than history allowed.

Birds called. Their cries were short and sharp, devoid of sweetness.

At last, the cab man halted his rig and poked his face in through the door.

"That's it, that's as far as we're going. At least, it's as far as you're going with Flinty O'Dair. For the ground's no more than a filthy mire, and treacherous as a promise from the Castle. If I can turn me wagon about, I'll be the luckiest man this side of Limerick. So get out with ye and I'll have me money, thanks, and wish ye good evening and go."

"Nothing of the sort, nothing of the sort!" Mr. Barnaby told him. "You'll wait right here, then. You'll wait right here. Or you shall not see a farthing! You'll wait right here until I return to go with you!"

I looked at my companion in the lamplight. "He can wait for me, as well," I said, not a little miffed.

"Oh, no!" Mr. Barnaby told me. "You'll be 'ere 'til dawn, Major Jones. And they wouldn't let me stay with you, I'm not to see what you're about to witness."

"Cajun colleens!" the driver cried. "So that's what the runty one's after! No bleeding wonder the bugger has to drive a good ten mile to find them what will have him, with the manners upon him and that low, Welsh look."

Outspokenness is a great fault in a cab man.

To my consternation, Mr. Barnaby did not contradict the driver's mistaken notion, but borrowed a lamp and tugged me along the track.

"Careful," he warned. "Just follow close after, sir. For not all the creatures is respectful of the season and they doesn't always keep to themselves like they ought."

Now, I have passed hard years in India's deserts and in the mountains of the Afghanee. I have made my peace with those cruel landscapes, I know their whys and wherefores. But I do not like the texture of a jungle, if the hinterlands of New Orleans may be called such. You cannot see what hunts you and the noises will mask an assassin at your back. You smell the world richly, but all scents displease. You feel as alone as a child locked in a cellar.

The moss brushed my face like the fingertips of spirits. Bravery is so fragile it is laughable.

After perhaps the quarter of an hour, I spotted a light ahead of us. Then one light became two.

"'Ere we is," Mr. Barnaby said. "Go gentle now, sir. And mind each thing you does."

After a few more stumbles amid thickets and briars, the path opened into a clearing lit by two torches fixed to trees. Veils of moss scorned the flames.

As my eyes learned the change of light, I saw that the plot was vacant but for five great piles of wood arranged as the points of a star. In the center of the clearing, where the grass had been worn away, a design had been laid out upon the earth. Intricate and faintly shining it was. An altar stood in the trickster shadows beyond, crude and bearing utensils whose like I could not determine.

"Be respectful now," Mr. Barnaby whispered. "For they're watching us, I doesn't 'ave no doubt. The guardians will 'ave their eyes upon us."

He led me toward the design marked on the earth, then halted so abruptly we collided. Soft he was, and fragrant with exertion.

"Begging your pardon," he whispered, as quiet as a little

girl abed, "but if you 'as to perform your natural functions, sir, best to do it now. Step back along the trail, and none's the wiser. For you won't 'ave another chance 'til morning, or close to it."

I was dismayed. I did not like the circumstances into which I had let myself be cajoled. With one nasty revelation chasing after another. I began to wonder whether he expected me to be cooped, or tied, or shackled. There was a limit past which I would not submit.

I did as he suggested, stepping back along the trail and out of their ritual ground. I did not take the lantern, but left it in Mr. Barnaby's hand. For although I have been a soldier, with all the raw experience that implies, in general I remain a friend to modesty.

As I paused at my baseness, limbs shifted in the shrubs.

Still, no one appeared to greet us. Emptied for the ordeal ahead, I followed Mr. Barnaby to the spot where their devilish pattern glittered.

It was a circle of about five feet from its empty center to its outer rim. Made of broken oyster shells it was, speckled here and there with colored glass. It put me in mind of the symbols Hindoo holy men draw in the sand, their markings so ancient that the *fakirs* themselves do not know their origin. Or even their proper meaning.

"Step in there, Major Jones," Mr. Barnaby instructed. "Right to the middle, where they 'as left you a proper space. No, *no!* Don't step across the lines like that, sir, that won't do at all. Slip in right 'ere, where the spirits 'as left you an opening, like."

"Mr. Barnaby . . ."

"Please, sir. This ain't no time for arguing. It's too late now. Just do as I says, I begs you. Or they might not look with favor on either one of us."

I did not restrain the impulse to feel the outline of my Colt beneath my cape. Tracing its solid outline with my hand, I stepped into the circle.

"Now *stay* there, sir," my companion told me, his tone half a plea, half an order. "And don't say a word to whoever comes out of the bushes to close up the circle. Don't say a word to nobody, no matter what you sees. Just stay mum. Pray, if you likes. But don't make a fuss of it, neither. Stand up as long as you can. But whatever happens, whatever you sees, don't lay so much as a fingernail outside the circle. Don't even touch the shells, if you can 'elp it."

I had to wonder, as you yourself would have done, how on earth I had allowed myself to enter into so unsound a situation.

"Please, sir," Mr. Barnaby said again. "Whatever you do, and whatever you does . . . whatever you sees or you don't . . . don't even hint that you're like to break the circle. It's for your own good, sir. Bless me and you both, it's for your own good. Even if they seems to be speaking to you directly, don't answer. For it ain't them speaking at all, and it ain't your mouth that the spirits expects to reply. Don't make a move you doesn't 'ave to, and don't say a word, I begs you."

I began to ask a question, but found my mouth peculiarly dry. "You really intend to go? You won't be watching?"

He shook his head decisively. "They'd kill me dead if I so much as tried, sir. For though they doesn't dislike me the way they generally does a white man, my credit ain't good out 'ere and they'd treat me unpleasant. Before they got around to killing me proper."

"And . . . and how will I know . . . that is, when will I be able to leave this ridiculous circle?"

"When it's all over, sir, when it's all over. One of 'em will come back and open the path again. But don't speak to 'im, neither. And step careful, sir, step careful even then."

"But . . . if I am not to speak . . . how will I ask questions . . . or come by answers?"

"*She*'ll take care of that, sir. In 'er good time. We can't be too demanding, under the circumstances."

"But will this . . . this woman actually—"

"I 'as to leave you now, sir. I can sense 'em and they're growing most impatient. They wants to start their business, sir, and it won't do to delay 'em."

With that, he turned abruptly and strode off, lantern bobbing. He did pause for one last moment, turning just enough of his formidable person to whisper, "For God's sake, Major Jones, stay in the circle!"

His bulk obscured the lantern and, for a little time, his silhouette glowed orange. Then he reached a bend in the trail and disappeared entirely.

The night did not feel welcoming. Under the draping moss, the torches crackled, their noise akin to mockery. Again, I laid my hand upon my Colt, clutching my sword-cane tightly with the other. Queer it was. My left hand had taken a wound from a blade the past autumn. Although it had healed nicely, I had not yet been able to make a solid fist. That night, my paw relented, gripping my cane so tightly that you might have mistaken my fist for an old Seekh cannonball. Yet the wound itself, which I had received from a madwoman, ached peculiarly, with a cold, sharp pain that seemed a thing alive.

I considered abandoning all the nonsense before me and taking myself along behind Mr. Barnaby. As quickly as I might go.

A form materialized at the edge of my vision. It was not Mr. Barnaby returned.

A black fellow, big and fierce as a heathen idol, come strolling straight toward me. He did not look affable. Despite the chill of the winter night, his attire consisted of only a colored handkerchief draped to conceal his embarrassment. For a worrisome instant, I thought it might be that great colored fellow with the scars upon his face, the one who had chased me from the rooftop down through the fancy house. But the approaching negro soon looked a less kindly sort.

He engaged my eyes for an instant's disapproval, then dropped to his knees at the outer edge of the circle. Deft as a veteran seamstress at her stitching, he rearranged shells and sparkles of glass to complete the inward pattern of the design. Then he closed the circle and pushed back to his feet with an angry grunt.

Towering above me, his person was of such developed musculature that you might have judged him impervious to bullets.

Then I heard them. The way you hear Afghanees creeping toward your camp in the heathen dark.

The drumming commenced, meant to entice, not terrify. Instead of booming through the night, it slapped and tapped and teased in rhythms that had no civilized origin. From out of the maze of crippled trees, the musicians themselves appeared, to the number of three, approaching the flank of the altar. One of the drummers affected the same state of undress as the negro who closed the circle, but the others wore long white shirts over bare, black legs.

None was shod.

Twas not a setting for the weak of heart. In ones and twos, then in silent packs, the celebrants entered the clearing, phantoms out of the wintering swamps, their eyes thirsting for the torchlight. You might have thought them risen from their graves on the Day of Judgement.

Motley and immodest, the women appeared as shameless as the men. Some wore loose frocks of white or butter-muslin, while others wore only skirts and, forgive me, nothing above but blue cords round their waists. A minority of the negresses had chosen raiment identical to that of the nearly naked men.

Twas winter, mind.

First one man, then a second, seized the torches from their sconces on the tree trunks and began to prance about, playfully thrusting the flames toward their companions, who made a game of leaping from their paths. As they jollied about the clearing, the torchbearers lit the bonfires, which must have been prepared with pitch or the like. The pyres blazed so readily that waves of unleashed warmth swept over the clearing.

The lot of them began to chant to the tapping of their drums. It was no outcry, but a mighty whisper, all the more unnerving for its restraint.

Gourds passed from mouth to mouth. Some drank from bottles.

They began to form themselves into unkempt patterns, dancing in and out of the star of bonfires, flexing their limbs and paying each other not the least untoward attention. Despite the alarming nakedness of full-grown women and girls coming into their figures, the men pressed no indignities upon them. In return, the females ignored the males, but brought increasing vigor to the dance.

Even as the fires blazed, turning brown flesh bronze and scorching the air, the volume of the drumming remained subdued. The fire-glow must have been visible from afar, above the wild trees of bayou and swamp, but the worshippers did not wish to be heard.

At least not yet.

I believe they were in number almost a hundred, perhaps more, with the females in the advantage by two to one.

I remembered, of course, that I had been singled out to become a "goat without horns" by some of their fellow pagans. But for the moment I might have been invisible for all the interest the celebrants took in me.

They chanted and danced, and drank without breaking stride.

As the fires blazed, I got a better look at the altar's clutter. A great wooden bowl took pride of place in the center. To the right stood a Catholic statue. I believe it represented the Mother of Christ. Beads and baubles adorned it and I thought it seemed familiar. On the other side of the bowl, a creature carved of wood depicted Nightmare.

The pattern of the drumming changed, taking speed as the cavalry shifts from a trot into a canter. The dancers compacted themselves into the yard between the bonfires. I noted that not one approached the altar.

I felt a nasty chill, almost a panic, but fought it down by reciting my favorite Psalms under my breath.

The congregants took as much care to avoid my circle as they did to shy from the altar.

To my relief, there were no white women present. Of that, I can assure you. Rumors of such racial mixing had troubled me, as they would any Christian man.

Yet, not all those assembled were the cinder-black of Africans in picture-books. Some of the women, especially, were light as caramel or even as pale as milk coffee. The men tended to a darker hue, but not a few of them might have passed for Rajputs, had their features been less broad and their manners more decorous. I wondered what pursuits they followed by day.

One of the men erupted in a fit, demanding the attention of all present. He was a queer fellow, muscled like a half-starved stevedore, ropey, strong and hungry-looking as Cassius. At first, I thought him a victim of Caesar's affliction. He stomped madly, arching his back until it must break, then flopping forward to curl over his belly. Next, he flung wide his arms, eyes rolling madly, then closed himself into a fist.

Sleek as a dolphin spotted off the Cape, he leapt high in the air, twisting about between myself and the altar. He dropped from his heaven-ward flight straight to his knees, striking the earth so heavily the pain echoed in my limbs.

He did not rise, but dropped his forehead to the earth like a Musselman.

All of the others followed his example. Hastily. Groveling on the soil. With no regard for white skirts or snowy blouses.

They barely paused to plug up their gourds or stuff corks into bottles. As they bent and writhed about, a fellow saw much that was not meant to be seen.

Even the drummers fell to their knees, although they did not press their faces in the dirt. They bowed to the altar in rhythmic waves, slapping away at their instruments all the while.

Twas then I saw her. Emerging from some morbid bower or grotto. I felt the sort of surprise that transfixes a man, that makes no rational sense. Twas a shock far greater than it should have been, of the sort that none of our doctors can explain.

Madame La Blanch it was who appeared from the shadows. She no longer wore her dress of tattered frills. Instead she wore a gown of purple satin that made her face look regal, hard and deathly. The palest of them all she was, but revealed now unmistakably as a negress. Perhaps it was the turban she wore, tied up like the rags of a Peshawar mullah who has done his Haj and wears his badge of honor. The cloth of her headdress was parti-colored, so rich and tumultuous in pattern that I only saw the snake when it thrust its snout some inches beyond the fabric.

She carried a snake in her turban, and not a small one. Curled about her head like a fancy bonnet, making of the woman a willing Medusa. I had never seen the like even in India.

But that was not the queerest of the business. She led a fellow on a golden chain, a towering negro whose skin gleamed as maroon as Spanish leather.

He looked like a walking corpse, dead to the world but still maintained in motion.

Twas not that his physique was foul or withered. His flesh looked plump and strong. But there was nothing in his eyes, no spark, no soul. His movements were stiff, as if he were a machine in need of oiling.

Except for the chain about his waist, by which he was led as a prisoner, the fellow wore the innocence of Adam.

As Madame La Blanch approached, her congregation began to moan and plead. I could not understand a word they uttered. Their language was as foreign as the shores of Death. Perhaps it was a ruined child of French.

Madame La Blanch was the first of the lot to look me over properly. Vivid with firelight, her eyes burned the air between us.

Hereafter, I shall call her Queen Manuela.

Behind the empty-faced fellow she led along, a single fully-dressed male appeared, got up like a king in an amateur theatrical. He carried a drowsing lamb in his arms and rocked his head from side to side as if to a strain of music none other could hear. The "king" wore a goat's beard on his chin, but no moustache or whiskers. His eyes would have frightened a cobra.

Of a sudden, Queen Manuela cried out. The sound reminded me of the calls of tribal women perched above the Khyber. At once, her followers hushed and cowered as if they wished to hide themselves in the earth.

She did not secure the leash by which she led her naked slave, but merely left him standing by the altar, dead-eyed and grim. Plunging into the midst of her flock with exaggerated strides, she took no care of where she placed her feet, but let the worshippers squirm out of her way. Producing a pouch from the folds of her gown, she tossed a handful of dust in the nearest bonfire.

Her offering flared green, sparking and sizzling. I caught a scent that might have put me in mind of India's incense, had it not conjured up a matching odor of death.

With the mass of worshippers teeming against one another, careless of indecency, Queen Manuela proceeded from blaze to blaze, offering a tribute of dust at each. I saw bright clouds of purple, rose and blue, then green again.

The aromas grew confusing and complex. First, they bid you breathe deeply and take your pleasure. Then they gagged you like a pit of corpses.

Queen Manuela paid me no further attention, but paced thrice round her star of roaring fires. With the snake rising up from her turban, as if on watch for dangers to her rear.

Returning to the altar, she began to chant in a voice as strong as a man's, leading her flock through a queer, corrupted liturgy. Spreading her arms in mockery of a priest, she let her purple vestments trail like wings. Eyes closed, she raised her face to greet the darkness. The way an honest Christian greets the light.

Beside her, the tethered negro stood inhumanly still, while the tatterdemalion king stroked his lamb and smiled.

The queen raised the empty bowl to the sky and shrieked.

Her adherents roared out a sudden response so mighty it made me recoil. I had to remind myself of Mr. Barnaby's warnings to keep myself upright and within the circle.

The incense changed aromas as it burned, beginning to smell of nameless fruits gone off. The fragrance hinted of lures, of intoxication.

A prayer broke on my lips. I retreated to the greater strength of the Gospels.

Back and forth they went, the queen and her congregants, in call and response that might have suited the noisier sort of Baptists. The sound was disconcerting. It carried a sort of undertow, like the tides of the Bristol Channel. I laid my hand over my breast pocket. Where my Testament resided. As if I feared to end a drowning man.

She must have called to the mock-king with the lamb. He bowed his head and, bending low, meekly approached the altar.

I expected a blood sacrifice, for that is the general practice of primitives everywhere. But the meanness of their actions soon astonished me.

Queen Manuela stepped toward the king, who seemed to shrink and cower. Slipping to his knees, he offered the lamb. Standing before the trembling fellow, the voodoo priestess raised the skirts of her gown, allowing him to slip the animal underneath the folds.

Queen Manuela screamed, as if in agony. Gingerly, the king withdrew the lamb.

Twas a pantomime of birth.

Then he placed the beast upon the altar.

Animals have more sense of things than we credit. The little creature trembled so hard that I could see it quivering from my circle. All beings want to live.

I thought that one of them would cut its throat. Instead, the priestess took the great, insensate fellow by the leash and drew him behind the altar, until his massive torso framed the lamb.

The queen had lowered her voice, whispering secrets to her soulless slave. I never saw him blink. Stiffly, like a great mechanical doll, he extended his arms and took up the lamb, lifting it to his mouth.

I will spare you excessive description. Suffice to say he skinned the beast alive. With his teeth. Over the altar bowl.

The poor thing bleated longer than I thought possible.

The snake in Queen Manuela's turban rose to watch the world beyond the sacrifice, as if it were a sentinel in a tower.

The meat and bones and pelt of the lamb were discarded. Twas only the blood that mattered. The priestess thrust her slave back into the shadows, rudely and confidently. Gore trailed down his jaw and over his chest.

The king turned from the altar, scurrying off like a child who fears a beating. The worshippers had grown ever more restive, some of them trembling like the lamb, others writhing in torment and demanding some vague blessing of the darkness. Choosing the most demented among them, the king tapped one head then another.

The fortunate crabbed their way toward the altar.

Queen Manuela lifted the bowl of blood and filled her mouth, then set the vessel down reverently. Lunging forward, she spit quick streams of blood onto her disciples, staining their faces and frocks, their heady nakedness. Each took the unholy baptism as license to a frenzy.

The maddest rose and danced. Others chanted, raggedly but fiercely. The drums surged. There was no fear of intruders now. Their spirits had come among them.

The priestess drank again. And then again. Treading among bodies as tormented and bloodied as soldiers in a field hospital. Yet, for all the intoxication, I noted that a few of the men remembered to add more wood to the bonfires.

The gourds and bottles of liquor reappeared. Splashed from mouth to mouth, their contents glazed over chins and down dark necks.

By the time she had drained the last blood from the bowl, Queen Manuela's features were slimed crimson. As she moved about the crowds, men and women alike caressed her legs below the knee, moaning and begging.

Her eyes were not of this earth.

Now, I have stood punitive hours on parade. I know that a fellow must bend his knees to avoid toppling in a faint. I drew on my soldier's tricks to remain erect. But queer it was. I had to fight back wave after wave of dizziness, as if I had been plied with their savage liquors.

I did not want to lose my footing or, still worse, my consciousness. I was not certain I would be allowed to rise again.

The world lost its clear edges. They danced and drank, calling to the darkness and each other. The fellow got up as a motley king had fulfilled his liturgical function. He stripped himself down to obscene, excited nudity, then plunged into the round.

Time lost all its dignity and order. It answered to the drums, not the other way round. Some among the dancers reminded me of a corporal who had been gnawed by a rabid dog near the Lahore cantonment. The regimental surgeon ordered the poor fellow bound up, he had no choice. The corporal took a long time to die, reduced to a raging animal, shrieking in pain and anxious to fix his teeth into the flesh of his fellow man. Even the bravest men watched from a distance.

Twas odd. Our regulations would not let us put him out of his misery. There was no provision for such a case, although the lads agreed he should be shot. In the end, some Mussel-man fellow cut the corporal's throat in the night. Perhaps it was only to put an end to the screams, which could be heard far away, among the natives. But I like to think it was done from human kindness.

Let that bide. The demonic possession of my fellow crea-tures was unlike anything I had ever seen before. Even the vigor and savagery of battle has purpose and some wild order. But the dancing, if so I may call it, grew crazed and lurid.

The men and women became less careful of the distance between them. Clothing fell away, what little there was of it. Pairs declined to the earth. Some staggered to the far side of the bonfires, still possessed of a vestigial modesty. The brutes among the crowd dropped where they pleased.

No Christian man should witness such events. Nor did I wish to watch, nor did I gloat. I turned my eyes away from the vilest acts. But I feared to shut them. I feared it as I rarely have feared anything.

And strange it was. I could not dismiss the foulness be-fore me by telling myself that, after all, they were negroes. I had a hateful sense that what I saw lurked below the accident of skin. Lads in my own regiment in India did things to na-tive women that no man among us ever will write down. And they were boys from Chepstow or from Chester. I did not wish to remember those things, but I did. How bright-faced boys tormented brown-skinned lasses during the Mutiny, killing them after their pleasure was all spent.

For all the devilish doings that night, the only creature killed was that poor lamb. At least thus far.

They rushed at me without warning, spurred by some

command I did not hear. I had no time to draw my Colt and barely raised my cane.

My pale attempt at defending myself was useless. Crazed and crowding, male and female, spattered with blood and reeking of fleshy sins, they raged about me, dancing and shrieking, shaking tawny fists.

I could no more have stopped them than I could have stood against a locomotive. The truth is I was helpless as a babe.

Yet, not a one put a toe inside the circle.

They howled and screamed, ogling me as if that lamb had merely served as practice. Plunging about and snarling, the mass of them might have torn me limb from limb. They seemed to long to do it.

But not one finger violated the circle. For all their wildness and savagery, they had a certain grace, that I will give them. They danced to the edge of insanity, pressing themselves within a fraction of an inch of that outer ring of shells, artful in their abilities to come ever so close, yet still avoid desecration. Male and female alike, a number revealed their body's parts to me, mocking, teasing and threatening. Some laughed, while others raged.

I lowered my cane. Useless it would have been to attempt to wield it. There was no sense in provoking them even further. There are times when a fellow simply has to stand erect with whatever aplomb he can muster. It is one of the few things Englishmen are good for, and although I am a Welshman born and bred, I never was too proud to take a lesson.

The negroes smelled of life, proud and unembarrassed.

I cannot say how long the trial endured, but it ended with a sort of ragged swiftness, as one then another retreated from the ring.

Twas then I saw her again. Standing in her purple robe,

staring at me directly. As if nothing else in the world could draw her interest.

Her congregation grew sober with a suddenness more unnerving than their exuberance had been. They formed themselves in a great, uneven circle, with me at its center.

The drums relaxed, but did not quit. The rhythm slowed to the pace of a human heartbeat.

With dried gore crusted on her cheeks and her purple robe disheveled, Queen Manuela approached me. I do not know that I have ever suffered such a gaze. I have killed men, face to face, whose eyes had less intensity as we struggled. The dizziness welled up again, until I thought it would topple me from my feet. I leaned upon my cane, but felt as if unseen ropes and cords wished to pull me one way or the other. To tug me down and drag me from the circle.

Her stately progress aroused a greater fear in me than all the shouting and raging of the pack of them. The hands below her sleeves were a raptor's claws.

But she, too, paused when she reached the edge of the circle. Still, she looked about to devour me whole.

The serpent in her turban rose. Looking toward the fires, not at me.

The priestess began to moan. Until the moan became an incantation. To my relief, she closed her eyes and looked about to swoon. As if a greater power had descended and put her in her lesser, mortal place. I cannot say why, but I felt the way a fellow feels as he bursts to the water's surface and breathes again. Gasping I was, although I hardly sensed it.

Deliberately, she pulled apart the bodice of her gown, displaying her dugs and muttering at the sky. She rubbed first one, then the other, of her breasts, but their age of excitement was past and soon she covered herself.

She shrieked at me then. I almost tumbled backward. Again and again, she shouted in some foreign, satanic tongue. They were questions, judging by the tone, and I felt compelled to make some attempt to answer. But I recalled, in time, Mr. Barnaby's warnings.

I only wanted to see some hint of the blessing of God's daylight.

I could not say how many hours had passed, for time had lost the constancy of angels. We say time speeds or slows, depending on our terrors and excitements, on loneliness and absence from our loved ones. But that, I think, is only an illusion.

That night was different. Time cast aside its laws.

She turned from me and called into the murk beyond the fires. Bidding her slave approach her. He responded slowly, with the stiffness of the ancients. But come he did.

As he neared, he looked to me a giant.

She led him around my circle, anti-clockwise, seven times. Then she spoke to the darkness above the trees.

Her worshippers edged rearward. As if they had been warned of poisonous serpents.

Queen Manuela stepped back herself, but did not break the stare she fixed upon me. She eased toward the altar, but stopped before breaching the circle of her followers. At last, she unwrapped the snake from the folds of her turban.

Holding the creature above her head, then clutching it to her bosom, she finished by displaying it to her left side and her right. She did not replace it in her turban, but released it onto her shoulder. The creature docilely made its own way back atop her head, as calmly as a cat returns to its favored spot by the hearth.

They all chanted together then, the priestess and her flock. They did not dance, but trembled where they stood.

With neither warning nor provocation, the great, stiff fellow broke into a struggle against an invisible opponent. Twas as odd a thing as any I ever saw. The massive negro recoiled as if taking mighty blows from an airy nemesis, then pounded back at his ghostly, unseen enemy. The worshippers watched as raptly as privates at a boxing match upon which they have staked all their back pay. Their eyes were huge and grew wider still as the big fellow tumbled to earth in a death-grip with the transparent wraith he was wrestling.

You will not credit this, although I tell it you. And I will admit that I may have been deceived myself by the madness of the night. But the mighty negro was bleeding from nose and mouth, with claw marks elsewhere, as if he had been pummeled by a creature half-man, half-beast. He did not injure himself, I tell you, but recoiled from magical blows until he oozed gore.

By the time he had lost his fight with the spirit, one of his eyes was swollen shut and even one ear was bleeding.

The congregation moaned in desolation. At Queen Manuela's command, a flock of women lugged the poor fellow off.

She approached me again, once her slave was gone. Her face was terrible. I cannot say if her features reflected awe or grief or ecstasy. Her soul was gone beyond our common emotions. Her eyes retained no symptom of humanity.

Reaching into the deepest folds of her garment, she drew out a pouch the color of negro skin. In a movement so quick that my eyes could not follow, she scooped out a handful of powder and dusted it over me.

That is the last I remember of the ceremony.

I WOKE WHEN a child tried to pick my pocket. I gave a great jump, as if to avoid the thrust of an enemy bayonet, swinging my arms about.

The lad who had annoyed me leapt away, eluding my blows. Lean and brown and ragged, he had a mischief-maker's smile in his small, round head. A meager lass stood behind him, prodding the earth with my sword-cane.

Twas morning.

I bellowed to fright a pack of Irish privates. The boy danced off, pausing briefly by his unmistakable sister. Then they fled. Laughing. The lass let go my sword-cane and it fell to earth. Twas only a game, I think, not proper robbery.

They ran grandly, crying out with glee and pretended terror, until the swamp concealed them.

I looked about. My head was thumping like those blasted drums.

And I remembered.

In that unreasoned panic which afflicts a man surprised between sleep and waking, I nearly buckled. Staring about in distress. Looking to see if I had broken the circle.

But the circle was gone. There were only a few truant bits of shell and the freckled earth where the runes had been swept away.

I had a sickly feeling, with a clamoring in my head that recalled my Indian days, before I turned to Our Savior. Back when I was a heedless lad who did not always resist the lures of liquor.

Cold it was, with that morning chill soldiers know. The sky was pearl and mist roamed from the swamps, which stank. Five blackened patches upon the earth were the only relics of the past night's revelry.

I felt beneath my greatcoat. And found my Colt in place, as well as my purse and my Testament. My fickle watch still swelled my waistcoat pocket. Nor was there any suggestion that the congregants had interfered with my person.

After shaking myself as a hound might have done, I

rubbed my eyes and went to retrieve my cane. Stiffness infected my thirty-four-year-old bones, worsening my limp. The earth is an unkind bed for a middle-aged man.

I stooped to pick up my cane. As I rose, I saw her.

You would have thought her out for a morning stroll. Her purple robe was gone, along with her turban. And the serpent. Her face was clean and still above her cape. With her out-of-season parasol, she looked a lady come down in life, not a pagan priestess.

Still, my flesh defied my will and shuddered.

She kept a distance between us, as if we must speak from the opposite banks of a stream. Perhaps that was the case in a deeper sense. For our two shores of faith would never reconcile.

I was unsure, almost unsteady. I wanted coffee and time to arrange my mood, which was snappish. The whole affair seemed shabby and cheap in the daylight. I wondered if I had been played for a fool.

"You," she said, in a voice not free of weariness, "have a great protector. Papa La Bas, he can't touch you. You're a lucky man."

I am a Christian man. That is my protection.

"She's very strong, stronger than me," Queen Manuela continued. Or perhaps I should call her Madame La Blanch again. "She must have died young, your haunt-girl. To be so strong."

Such nonsense riles me.

"I have questions," I told her. My voice meant to be stern, but had a wheeze. It had not yet been tested by the day. "I did as I was asked, mum. Now it is my turn to—"

"Five askings," she interrupted. "You get five askings. Then no more."

"Who are the 'fishers of men'?"

"Union soldiers. Pirates. Negroes who hate their own skin. Marie Venin." She followed the name with a clot of spit. "A white devil-woman."

"What do they do? Why do the negroes fear them?"

"They steal black folk. Take them away. On ships."

That baffled me. "But where? To Africa? Why on earth would they—"

She shook her head, as solemnly as if standing over a grave. "Not Africa. Somewheres. The spirits don't say. They know, but they won't say. No one ever comes back, that's all we know."

She chose her words with the care of a soldier on court-martial.

"But why? To what end?" I demanded. "What would be the sense of kidnapping negroes, for the love of God? They're worthless now. They're free." My head still throbbed. I could not think as crisply as I wished.

"I can't tell you that. Maybe you already know. The spirits say you know plenty of things. But you fight against knowing them."

For a moment, I thought she might step closer, to impart an intimacy. She seemed to waver. But she held her ground.

"Palms been crossed with gold, not only silver," she told me. "Listen now. You only got one asking left. Just one now. I'm not allowed to give you no more than that. Think hard, white man."

Twas all a hocus-pocus, of course. A way to feed me little bits and pieces. Perhaps, I suspected, to lead me astray again. Likely the pagan revels had been no more than a ruse to steal my time. While wickedness proceeded back in the city.

Skeptical I was, and sore of body. Far from the world of airy spooks, my bowels began to protest my neglect, for they are as reliable as the company bugler.

Yet, I thought me hard before I asked that final question. Only to surprise myself and put a trivial query. Surrendering to morbid curiosity, perhaps to a sort of vanity.

"Was Susan Peabody . . . a virtuous woman? Was she—"

"She was a woman. Like any other."

Madame La Blanch shook her head again, as if she pitied me deeply. As if I were a small and foolish man, after all. She made no further mention of great spirits.

"Man who won't see might as well be blind," she said brusquely. "Can't lead a mule who won't go. Play a fool to make a fool, then see who the fool is."

Finished with her epigrams—as trite as a fortune-teller's at the fair—Madame La Blanch strode off. I was dissatisfied and moved to follow her. But she sensed what I intended and turned about.

"You stay put," she snapped, eyes blazing again for that instant. "You stay right there 'til I'm gone. Then you skedaddle. There's things in this life you don't want to know."

fifteen

$\mathcal{J}$ WILL ADMIT THAT I was in a dudgeon. I had submitted myself to pagan follies, only to be mocked by a blaspheming negress. Nor was I content with the clumsiness of my questions.

Madame La Blanch had indicted almost everyone in the city, our Union soldiers and pirate gangs, a voodoo rival and even fellow darkies. Along with a "white devil-woman." It struck me as a crude attempt to employ me in a reckoning with her enemies. All the world could not be in conspiracies.

I marched me back along the trail by which I had arrived the night before. Stabbing the earth with my cane like a sulking child, I grumbled but did not dawdle. For I had an urgent purpose. One that had nothing to do with the fate of Miss Peabody and everything to do with mine own comfort.

I scooted on my way and did not look back.

Why on earth would anyone steal negroes? Slavery was finished and their value had expired. They could be hired in dozens for a dollar. And that might not be a dollar wisely spent.

Nor were we drafting Africans into our army. On the contrary, General Butler, of whom much ill may elsewise be said, had led our efforts to recruit them honestly, meeting with great success before his removal. We had more colored volunteers who wished to wear a blue coat than Washington could regulate or arm. Indeed, many a high, distinguished voice remained reluctant to back negro recruitment, viewing the black man as worthless in a fight or worrying that we would antagonize Mr. Davis.

Meanwhile, runaway "contrabands" crowded our camps and slept in the city streets, hazarding the general health and, certainly, themselves. Freedom had levied a tax in human misery.

Yet, I would be just: Who among us would not prefer to live in confounding freedom over the certainties of the slave? The worst among us then were men of privilege, who, having kept the African chained and ignorant, complained that he was ill prepared for freedom. I would not raise the black man upon a pedestal, nor do I quite propose him as our equal, but every man deserves an honest chance.

Freedom may not guarantee our nourishment, but I never met a man whom it had poisoned.

I pitied the negroes, but knew not what to do with them. Such matters were better left to wiser men.

Twas all a blather and a bother, anyway. After I had gone a hundred paces, the only thing that mattered was my bowels.

I beg your pardon for my frankness, but history must be recorded truly. I paused on the wretched trail and looked about me. Lazy vapors eased between great trees, caressing the moss. Black water steamed in the cold, its surface as unmoving as the earth. The swamp smelled of an undrained family bath and wet-rag air annoyed my exposed skin. Odd birds called, but hid. I saw no trace of other human beings, but had no confidence that I saw all. I do not like to think my modesty compromised.

An earnest survey found no trace of alligators, which I am told are prevalent in New Orleans.

I found a not unwelcoming spot a few steps from the trail and peeled off my greatcoat. Further actions do not require description. Although I will admit to scanning the foliage for reptilian intruders and such like.

At the very moment of my satisfaction, I felt that I had been bitten hard, indeed. Not by a creature of our American Nile, but by the realization of my stupidity.

I saw it *all*. The sense of things, I mean. I nearly leapt directly to my feet. Which would have been ill judged.

I fear that I used language to abuse myself that never can appear upon the page. My comments upon my unbelievable blindness were so strong that I shall have to answer for them on that day when the sternest questions are posed.

The kindest word I spent on myself was "idiot."

I tidied myself as swiftly as I could, grateful for the broad and bountiful leaves the Lord provided even in mid-winter. And then I set off at a run, like a hobbled horse at the races, too impatient even to don my greatcoat, fair hurdling with the help of my cane and begging every power in Heaven to let Mr. Barnaby be there waiting, with a vehicle ready.

And waiting he was, the good fellow. With that sour Irish cab man still in thrall.

Mr. Barnaby waved and stepped toward me the instant he marked my approach. Even at a distance, I could read the bright relief upon his face. He cried out, "Tally-ho!" and danced a jig.

As I come up to him, he added, "Bless me, Major Jones, you're still alive!"

Tears welled in his eyes, though he was jolly.

"I brought you a nice, soft bun," he declared, "in the 'opes that you could chew it. You must be—"

"No time!" I snapped. "Get in the cab. *You*," I called to the cab man, "fifty Union dollars if you drive the horses like they're running at Epsom! Take us to the Customs House, to Union headquarters!"

I stormed the interior of the cab like a rush of fusiliers taking a redoubt. Mr. Barnaby followed me with all the alacrity his doughty girth allowed.

Despite my cajoling and the cab man's greed, we could not go too swiftly on the trail. I leaned forward on the bench, as if my weight might lend us more momentum.

"What's 'appened, sir, what's 'appened?" Mr. Barnaby begged of me. "Did the one we ain't to name tell you 'er secrets?"

I swung a dismissive paw at the great, wide world. "Later, later. Did you, or did you not, say that slavery is still in practice on the Spanish islands?"

"That it is, sir, that it is! As legal as ever it was hereabouts, and twice as mean or worse, the way they treats 'em. The high-seas trade ain't legal, God bless the Royal Navy, but what slaves they 'as already got is bound to be slaves forever. Even in Brazil, among the Portugee, it ain't been abolished, though we pretends to live in civilized times. Why, in Cuba they—"

"The *bas*tards!" I shouted, including myself in the curse. Oh, Madame La Blanch had been right, indeed, that a man who embraced his blindness would never see. And right she was that I possessed the knowledge I needed, but had been too proud and cock-sure to make sense of it. "The low, wicked *bas*tards!"

It took me another moment to force the rueful conclusion from my lips. Mr. Barnaby's face absorbed the fervor of my tone and shifted from concern to expectation. He knew I was not given to strong language and my outburst promised a revelation to come.

"The bastards are selling negroes back into slavery," I explained.

*   *   *

THE REGIMENT OF clues paraded past, laughing at me from their perfect ranks. I smashed down my fist on the battered seat. Hammering the bench I was, and groaning like a mad, tormented animal.

My pride, my pride! Vanity had closed my eyes more tightly than a blindfold. Now they were opened, to my terrible shame. The matter had become a magic puzzle, putting itself together on its own. One connection led to another, until it all seemed so obvious than even a fool should have seen the lie of the land.

What had Madame La Blanch said to me? As her parting admonition? "Play a fool to make a fool, then see who the fool is." Well, there was no question as to the identity of the greatest fool in the matter. Twas me. Not least because I had let a dissembler play the fool with me.

Captain Bolt was no more a simpleton than Mr. Aristotle. He must have been the cleverest of men to play the ass so aptly, to pander to my pride and superiority.

All of it had been laid out before me, plain as a Methodist chapel. I should have got it the instant Madame La Blanch mentioned negroes carried off on ships.

No. That is too generous. I should have seen it days before, without the need of instruction from a heathen.

Consider what I had learned, only to ignore. Negroes disappeared without sensible cause. A white girl, then a colored man, both of whom championed negroes, were foully murdered. To terrorize any who might interfere. And if the negro had no value in our United States, where did he still hold monetary worth? How could he be gotten there? Who owned ships and suffered no embargo? Mrs. Aubrey, of course, who was so anxious to slander Susan Peabody. But who might connect her to the power of our Union authorities? If not the son of the man who controlled the riverboat shipping on the upper Mississippi, as General Banks himself had informed me? A young man who likely would have been known to the woman who owned the finest hulls on the river's Southern reach?

Who had been given a generous writ to spy on me, to hound me? I did not suspect General Banks of any complicity, but sensed that he, too, had been fooled into giving Bolt license.

Of course, Bolt had known which tomb to seek me in. His co-conspirators had put me there. Oh, I remembered all too well how "clumsily" Bolt had behaved after freeing me. Firing from behind to pin me down to give the mock assassin time to escape. I had frustrated him that evening, but he had more than gotten his own back. He had known the numbers of my rooms, the hours of my baths, the purpose of my journeys, the subjects of my visits.

And he had known that I meant to question the paymaster. Whose murder passed with shameless speed thereafter. While I, the "great investigator," had no least suspicion of the culprit.

I wondered if Bolt had done that deed himself. *He* could have lured the poor officer out in the small hours on any number of pretexts. Or Bolt might have ordered him to present himself, holding over him the power of his plunge into corruption.

Mr. Champlain had been right about the enduring power of money. But . . . why had he helped me, to the degree that he had, and what, if any, role did he himself play in these affairs?

There were so many dead, from a bath attendant to an educated negro, from the enigmatic Miss Peabody to a dirty-fingered colonel.

God knew how many others.

Supposed by my superiors to be a man well skilled in investigations, I had become the puppet of a scoundrel. Of a pack of scoundrels.

Were I a fellow from any one of Mr. Shakespeare's plays, it would be Bottom, who was turned into a jackass. In that play with the fairies and disobedient girls.

Magic? Voodoo? Spirits? Not a bit of it. Marie Venin had been hired on by the conspirators to terrorize the simple, country negroes flocking to town. And many among the longtime residents, too. But it wasn't the "Grand Zombi" who walked the streets to steal their souls. Twas a press-gang sanctioned by our own authorities that swept their bodies into outbound ships.

I did not remark on the matter to Mr. Barnaby, but it seemed to me a miracle that Magdalena had not been murdered long before she reached us. Marie Venin had not come to the convent only to lure me out. I was a minor prize compared to Miss Peabody's servant, who knew more than the conspirators could risk.

The lass almost spoiled everything for Bolt and his "Fishers of Men." If nothing else, she knew enough to cast doubt on the stories blackening Miss Peabody. She did not know the sin, but knew the sinners.

Poor Mr. Barnaby, to whom I had been so ungenerous, sat in ponderous woe on the opposite bench. He did not attempt to banter or to satisfy his desperate curiosity, although he must have been yearning to ask if I had learned anything of the lass. He was a man whom life had taught to wait on the whims of others. He simply sat and watched me grimace and growl as I scorned myself like Lear upon the heath.

Not that I would compare myself to a king.

"It's Bolt," I said at last. "Captain Bolt. He's in it up to his whiskers, the bleeding rotter. Bolt and that damnable Aubrey woman, the two of them."

"Can't say as I fancied either one," Mr. Barnaby allowed.

I ground my teeth, reminding myself in an instant that my jaw remained convalescent.

"I can't believe . . ." I said, ". . . I cannot *believe* the wickedness of it."

That observation did not impress my companion.

"I finds," he said, "it don't pay to put too much faith in others, begging your pardon. If you doesn't expect too much, you'll 'ave yourself a pleasant surprise now and then. But if you goes about expecting goodness, you'll end your days a disappointed man."

"But . . . but you have put faith in me, Mr. Barnaby. You trust me to keep my word about Lieutenant Raines."

"Oh, you doesn't count among the common sort," he told me. "You're too afraid of yourself to misbehave."

I let the observation pass. Another sickening revelation had rippled through my belly, mind and soul.

"Dear God," I said, dropping my face into my hands. My sword-cane clattered to the floor of the cab. I clenched my eyes shut in shame, hiding them with my palms.

"I didn't mean it insulting, like," Mr. Barnaby assured me. "What I said about—"

"The *letter*. The blasted letter. The *letters*. Two of them. I ignored them both." I dropped my hands away from my eyes and looked at him across a slough of shame. "I've been . . . Good Lord . . . such a fool . . . a perfect ass . . ."

I might have found it friendly, had Mr. Barnaby seen fit to contest the latter description of myself. But he did not.

Doubtless chock with questions of his own, he sat before me full of concern but determined to be amiable.

"I had letters, see," I explained. "From a Navy fellow. The first come the night I was rude to you. When I sent you off and told you not to trouble me until the next afternoon. I had a dozen letters, that is the thing of it. Most had arrived from the North, from home. But there was one from a naval officer." The pain of the remembrance was almost physical. "I laid it aside. To read my personal mail over my breakfast."

The carriage turned from the trail onto a back road. We gained a measure of speed.

"I'm afraid I doesn't follow you, Major Jones."

I wiped imagined sweat off of my forehead. "While I was dallying over my coffee, the letter disappeared from my room. Oh, *damn* my stupidity, man. I missed the theft entirely, although it should have been the first thing I noticed. It was gone, and I failed to even think of it. A message from the Navy did not fit with my opinions, see. I could not squeeze it into the scheme of things, a scheme I had already accepted. Then, last evening, the hotel clerk brought me a second letter. From the same Navy fellow. And I dismissed it out of hand. As I had the first. You were there. You heard me."

The poor fellow must have had only a bit more sleep than me, but now he saw it. I watched the grace of knowledge cross his brow.

"If ships is sailing off loaded with negroes," he proposed, "per'aps the Navy lads seen something queer?"

"Exactly! It might have been almost anything. A bill of lading that made no sense. Some subterfuge, suspicious behavior. Whatever it was, they connected it to me. The Lord only knows why. They tried to alert me. But I paid them no attention. None at all . . ."

Mr. Barnaby chewed upon the notion, then produced the promised bun from his pocket at last. "You must be deadly 'ungry," he said in a kindly tone. "You 'as to eat for your strength, sir. And your swelling's gone down most admirable. Do 'ave a try."

I accepted the bun, for I was properly famished. I gnawed it, almost reveling in the jolts of pain that still surprised my jaw.

The truth is that I saw more clearly than Mr. Lincoln, who placed more faith in me than I deserved. I was not meant for grand investigations. Nor was I suited to remain a soldier. Time it was for me to return to my family and our new-found business concerns. I told myself, for the hundreth time, that I had done my bit for my new country. As soon as I could sort things out, I would resign and go back to my wife. To be a proper father to my son and to my ward. And, perhaps, to another son or daughter by now.

I wondered if the babe already lay in my darling's arms.

The truth is that I wished to hide away. To bury myself in my family and honest work, hidden from every misery beyond the common sorrows of those I loved.

I know that a good man will not shirk his duty. But there must come a point when his duty is done. Nor was I entirely sure I was a good man.

"My grandfather, Lord bless 'im," Mr. Barnaby said, "what fought under Pakenham and thought 'im a dreadful fool and daft besides, always told me to 'ave respect for sailors and to listen to 'em until they got round to the truth, which they would in time. Although 'e warned me to step clear of Portsmouth." He canted his head, musing over his memories and my recent revelations. "I only 'ope that second letter's still waiting at the 'otel."

I LEANED OUT of the window and shouted to the cab man to take us first to the door of the St. Charles Hotel. He grumbled and whipped his horses, sorry that he had ever seen my face.

I fear I had allowed my hopes for the contents of the letter to exceed the bounds of reason. I longed for it to offer a clean solution to the filthy problem that still lay before me. I wanted the letter to do the last work for me, see, since fresh doubts had come to plague me as as we drove.

First, what proof did I have of anything at all? Everything made sense as I had finally pieced it together. But sense is not evidence. How could I march up to General Banks and tell him to arrest the richest widow in New Orleans, a well-respected matron who might call on those more powerful than either of us? What could I even prove against Captain Bolt?

Mr. Aristotle favors logic. But logic never rules in human affairs.

The evidence convinced *me*. But I was man enough to see that, after my string of follies, I longed to be convinced. Was I to hurl some dozens into prison because a voodoo priestess communed with her spirits on my behalf? Even Mr. Lincoln's sense of humor would not extend to a toleration of that.

After the recent fuss about freeing the negroes, Mr. Lincoln would not wish himself more trouble. He was a man who never could please all. Whatever he did, some high and mighty faction damned him as a simpleton or worse. They said he squandered lives and wrecked our laws.

I wonder if he ever felt as I did, wishing he could go home and be shut of his cares. What had his service brought him beyond sorrow and the mockery of those with ink for blood?

After reaching the main road, we gained a proper speed. But my worries increased as the miles fell behind. Certain I was that I was right, but I had no means to prove it.

For all the false moves I had made, mine enemies had made none. I knew who stood behind Susan Peabody's murder and the subsequent deaths. But nothing could be proved in a court of law. Or even to a military tribunal. The thought of my ineptitude was not conducive to an even temper.

Although I had reason to be grateful to Mr. Barnaby, on many counts, he was the only person present against whom I could aim my loaded mood. Of course, I told myself at the time that my admonition would be for his own good.

"Mr. Barnaby," I began, in a tone that should have warned him from the outset, "despite my respect for your good heart and your intentions, I cannot overlook your toleration of abhorrent practices. The orgy I witnessed last night would have shamed the Romans and—"

He moved to cup a hand over my mouth, as we do to children when their speech errs gravely. He just refrained from touching me, but whispered above the clatter of the wheels, "I shouldn't say a word, sir, not about such matters. Nor mention names nor places, nor any least details of the goings-on."

"Mr. Barnaby . . . I find all this secrecy preposterous. Suffice it to say that, speaking as a Christian, I cannot understand how you, who were raised, however irregularly, in the Christian religion, could approve of pagan rites and devil-worship."

"Oh, I doesn't approve and never did," he told me with aplomb. "Church of England, I was raised, and if that ain't Christian, it's the next-best thing."

"But your own dear wife—"

"She was a Christian, too, sir. As I been telling you. Regular to mass as a thirsty priest." He looked at me almost pityingly, as if I were the one whose soul was endangered. "But my Marie always put it like this, sir: She said that every bed needs its own blanket. And on the coldest nights, it might need two."

"We must have unswerving faith in a single God."

"But, Major Jones, the priests and parsons also wants us to believe in Jesus Christ and the 'Oly Ghost, as well as the Lord 'Imself. Don't that make three? And the Catholics 'as more saints than the 'eathen 'Indoos. All's one, sir, all's one! The *voudou* folk don't no more agree with one another than Lutherans and Baptists. Some believes they're worshipping the 'Oly Ghost, that 'E come out of the African bush, where 'E 'ad another name. Others 'as a fondness for Mother Mary, who wears more names than a red-headed riverboat gambler. And even if they worships an African god, who's to say 'e's not the old fellow we're fond of? 'Ow can we know they ain't all the same, only speaking different languages, just like men do?"

"The rites I saw last night were . . . there was nothing Christian about them, I assure you."

"I didn't say there was, sir, begging your pardon. Nor that there wasn't. It's only that I doesn't feel fit to judge. I mean the negroes, sir. Many's the colored Christian, sir, who's as devout as any of your Methodists. They goes about things regular, except sometimes they sings a little louder. But I 'ave to ask myself 'ow I would look at things, if I was in their shoes, sir. Speaking of the ones that 'as shoes of their own. They was raised up on plantations or in city houses where the master and the mistress told 'em about Jesus and the raising up of the meek, then beat 'em when they dropped a stitch or sold 'usband from wife to pay off a gentleman's note." He shook his doubting head. "It's a wonder that a one of 'em believes in the 'Oly Gospels, sir. After 'ow they been treated by proper Christians. Turned away from churches, whipped and scourged." He looked at me with formidable earnestness. "Who among us 'as suffered like Jesus Christ, sir, if not the African?" He glanced out at the raw, ungiving landscape and spoke his last words as if to himself. "Sometimes I thinks that we're 'is cross to bear."

"Suffering is our lot upon this earth. For every man. To prepare us for the joys of eternal salvation."

"True enough, sir, true enough! And suffering's one thing what ain't in short supply! But there's suffering, and there's suffering. It always seems to Barnaby B. Barnaby that it's easy enough for a fellow like you or me, all fancy free, to talk about our sufferings over a toddy. But I wonder 'ow we'd feel if we was negroes."

"But you have suffered a great deal yourself. You lost your wife and children. Your business. And now you worry about Lieutenant Raines . . ."

"Begging your pardon, sir, but I sees it different. Marie and the children was taken away by the Yellow Jack. The 'And of God, you might say. But the negro suffers at the 'and of man. At Christian 'ands." He leaned toward me, which always involved some effort on his part. "Major Jones, I ain't as learned and clever as many another, but it seems to me that folks needs to believe. In one god or another. Otherwise, the bad times would be unbearable. We needs to believe that there's some great sense to the mess of things. Assuming that the Good Lord made us that way, maybe it don't matter exactly 'ow we believe in 'Im, or what we calls 'Im. As long as we believes with all our 'earts. And behaves ourselves tidy."

"I witnessed copulation. And animal sacrifice."

"Well, I ain't excusing any such goings-on as that, not entirely, and I doesn't mean to imply it, sir. But if a body 'asn't got the two bits or ten dollars for a visit to any of a 'undred fine establishments in the Quarter, and if that body lacks a roof over is 'ead, I suppose the body'll do what we all do someplace where it 'appens to be convenient. We're all the same in that way, if no other. If you're asking Barnaby B. Barnaby. And as for animal sacrifice, ain't there a terrible lot of it in the Bible? And wasn't Abraham 'imself tempted to cut the life out of 'is poor son?"

"The Lord was testing Abraham."

"And a nasty test it was. God ought to be ashamed of 'Im-self for that one. And if it's brutality you wants, you doesn't 'ave to go far. Could anything be crueler than this war, sir? Or any war?" He reclined again, and sighed. "Oh, Major Jones," he told me, unrepentant, "if only folks doesn't do one another a damage, I'm inclined to let them go any way they wants."

"Our only hope of salvation lies in Christ."

He nodded. "Don't that seem a bit selfish and vain on 'Is part?"

He was hopeless. I only know that, without my faith, I could not endure another God-given day.

But let that bide.

Now you will say: "Abel Jones, you are too lax and tolerant." But I will tell you: I believe in spreading the blessed message of Jesus Christ, but I do not think conversions come through nagging. And, truth be told, when I was young and green, there was a dear person in India, a Musselman, whom I never tried to convert. Of course, those were the days when I had strayed. I was little better than a heathen myself. But her heart was good, far better than mine own. Her tawny skin could not conceal her virtues. I cannot bear to think the sad lass damned.

I let the air between us rest a few minutes. Raw and squalid, ever more signs of settlement broke the countryside. Even the finer houses looked neglected. Perhaps it was only the effects of war and winter, but I did not find their Southron world appealing.

My papers passed us through a Union guardpost. The smell of cooking coffee made me want.

"Speaking of negroes," I began anew, "I noted a curious thing about Madame La Blanch."

"Oh, I'm glad to 'ear you call 'er that, for any other names should be forgotten."

"You *knew*! You knew her identity all along!"

He squirmed a bit. "Oh, I wouldn't say that, sir, I wouldn't say so much as that. I had my suspicions, I did. That I admits. But suspicions and no more. For it doesn't pay to know what we're not to know. Not even if we knows it."

"Be that as it may, perhaps you can explain a curiosity."

He looked at me warily.

"Yesterday, at her *'atelier,'* as I believe you called it, Madame La Blanch seemed to give herself out as a white woman. Not that she made any specific claim, that I will grant you. But her speech during our interview was that of a Southron gentlewoman. If not one of the finer sort." I re-arranged my person on the cab bench. A certain attribute of my anatomy is not well padded and I had grown sore as the vehicle jounced along. "Yet, last night she seemed unmistakably a negress. Indeed, she gloried in the role. And her speech, when it was not indecipherable, had an accent not of this world. Or, perhaps, of old Africa. Then this morning . . . this morning, when she appeared in civilized dress again, her accent resembled that of a colored maid." I tapped him on the platter of his knee, asking his thorough attention. Clear it was that the subject made him uneasy. "What am I to make of that? One thinks the woman unlikely to be honest. Who is she, really?"

I believe the pity that filled his eyes was for Madame La Blanch, not me.

"I ain't sure as she knows the answer 'erself anymore," he told me. "Not that I knows 'er all that terrible well, sir. But she always seemed unsure of where she fit." He smiled sadly. "Like every other negro in America."

AS WE RATTLED up to the St. Charles Hotel, with the tardy sun sweeping the streets, I ordered Mr. Barnaby to hold the cab man at bay while I fetched the letter. I was ashamed of my appearance, unshaven and stained by a night spent in the wild, but there are times when we must forego propriety.

I rushed up the stairs and into the lobby, aiming for the hotel desk as directly as a rifle ball. I meant, of course, to demand that the clerk on duty produce my letter.

I was forestalled.

A Navy captain, in full, braided regalia, appeared from behind a column and grabbed my sleeve. Discourteously. Gray-haired before his time he was, and handsome in a ruddy way. You would have thought him suitable for display at a royal court. But he did not look pleased.

"You Jones?" he barked, keeping a firm grip upon my arm.

"I am Major Abel Jones, United States Volun—"

"Then *you're* the high-hat sonofabitch who's been authorizing ships to sail without proper inspections." Had he not been a gentleman, I think he would have spit upon the parquet. "Just like the goddamned Army. Isn't it just? You a Butler man? Is that what I'm up against? The clerk said you wouldn't even open my damned letters."

There are times in life when apologies do not suffice.

sixteen

"CAN WE CATCH THEM?" I asked the captain. His name was Senkrecht and he was a Farragut man, the sort who wishes the enemy had a proper fleet so he could steam out to fight it. "Can they be overtaken?"

Perhaps my avidity convinced him that I was telling the truth, that I had issued no letters authorizing ships to sail without review of their cargoes. That any papers bearing my name had been forgeries.

He muted his anger to the common gruffness sailors affect. "You won't catch the *Barbara Villiers*. She's as sleek a hull as I've seen upon this river and fully seaworthy. She's two days gone and out on the open waters."

"But the second ship you spoke of, the *Anne Bullen*?"

"Well, if we weren't standing here with our hands down our trousers . . . she's fast by the looks of her, but not too fast for, say, the *Cormorant*. Not while she's still on the river. She only left harbor this morning. A side-wheel gunboat *might* catch her. And outmaneuver her. With a shallower draft in the channels, we could——"

If he had been rude to grasp me by the forearm, I was twice as discourteous to tap him with my cane. I was already moving and only wanted the fellow to hurry himself along.

I did not wish a lecture on naval affairs. I only wanted to know if we had a chance.

Look you. I was set to have a terrible load upon my conscience. If we could catch one of the slaver ships, it might be reduced by half.

But think on it. Because I had read my letters from home, instead of attending to duty, a ship full of kidnapped negroes had set off from the city's wharves under our noses. Because of my inattention, men and women—perhaps children, too—who should have enjoyed freedom would live the rest of their lives under the whip.

It made me little better than a slave-trader myself, may God forgive me.

I wished to catch that second ship, the *Anne Bullen,* almost as much as I have desired anything in my life.

I dragged Captain Senkrecht behind me by force of will.

"So, we *can* catch her, then?" I repeated, as if I distrusted the confidence of his answer.

"Good chance. Very good chance. She won't be running at maximum speed because she won't want to draw attention to herself. She's fast enough, but if we can get the *Cormorant* underway in, say, two hours, we'll have us a horse race. She's been patrolling the coast and has Marines aboard. I'll double the complement while her skipper's rounding up his strays and raising steam. In case your friends decide their contraband's worth a fight. Which would be a damned fool choice for a merchant hull."

That sounded wise. About the Marines, I mean. For well enough I knew my opponents were deadly.

I had first encountered American Marines the spring before, when I sailed to England on a mission that failed, leaving that pirate Semmes to prowl the seas. I do not think I ever saw a nastier lot. The Marines, that is. The barbarian guards hired on by the Roman emperors cannot have been more fearsome in their aspect. Indeed, with all respect to Mr. Gibbon, I suspect the barbarians were gentler. No sailor dreamed of mutiny with a squad of Marines aboard.

I am told they frightened the Barbary pirates.

Rushing back to the cab and Mr. Barnaby, who was trying his legs on the paving stones and, doubtless, indulging in thoughts of a proper breakfast, I waved my cane and called his name, as impatient to have a go at the world as was my naval companion.

I would have liked to explain what I was about, to let him know the import of those letters. But there was no time. I simply grabbed the fellow by the lapel of his well-worn coat.

"I must be off. And you must do as I say. Do all that you can to uncover any connection there is or ever was between Mr. Champlain and Mrs. Aubrey. Move heaven and earth. But find out."

"I thought—"

"*Find out.* Then meet me here." I looked to the captain. "How long shall we be out?"

"Depends on how long you stand there dawdling, Major. Two days. Three, if we get the slows or things turn unpleasant. If we can't overtake her before she leaves the river, we'd waste our time out on the open seas."

"And I want to know where I can find Marie Venin," I added to Mr. Barnaby. "To arrest her. She will never frighten another negro again."

"What will you—"

Already leaping toward the cab, despite my bothered leg, I told him, "Just do as I say, man! And pray for our success. If she's still alive, I'm going to bring that servant girl back with me."

"Magdalena?" he cried.

There was such hope in the poor man's voice and on his face that it would have broken the heart of Herod Antipas.

The Irish cab man was not pleased to find himself charged to embark on a further journey. But I believe that, had he not obeyed the captain's instructions to drive to the wharves, I would have knocked him off his seat and taken the reins myself. Which, given my dislike of the horse, was a mark of my resolve.

We clattered off at a speed that made a spectacle. The team must have been weary, but the whip kept them in play. All Poydras Street fled from our reckless path. We nearly slew a workman rolling a barrel.

"Have you pencil and paper?" I asked Captain Senkrecht, although I thought it unlikely.

"What do I look like?" he asked, glancing down at the splendor of his own uniform. "A damned clerk?"

I never quite fathom the disregard in which otherwise sensible men hold honest clerks. I have been a clerk myself and a good one. I never saw the shame in it.

I let the matter drop. The curious thing is that, once we had decided on a course of action, Captain Senkrecht asked no further questions. He did not ask about the cargo of the *Anne Bullen* or even about my greater purpose. He seemed to accept completely my explanation that my name had been forged on any documents that had been shown to him. Navy fellows are like that, see. Give them a chance at action and they will not waste their energies on thinking.

Regarding my instructions to Mr. Barnaby to peer into the relations of Mr. Champlain, twas not mere curiosity. Nor was it, to be honest, an inspiration. Bits and pieces of the puzzle continued to fall into place, in an order all their own, and I had seen yet another thing that should have been clear as day some time before. The note put in the medicine pot to steer me to Queen Manuela had been put there by Mr. Champlain, not one of his negroes. The servant had only played his role in a piece of homely theater.

No colored fellow would have dared to write Queen Manuela's name. I saw that now. They would not even speak it, let alone put it to paper. If they could write. But Mr. Champlain had suffered no such qualms. Or at least he had judged the risk worth the reward.

And that was queer. I did not think him likely to be involved in the slaving scheme, not in the least. In his sly and playful way, he had done much to help me uncover the plot. But that meant he already knew that the plot existed. And wanted it brought to an end for his own reasons.

Forgive me if I am uncharitable, but I did not believe he acted out of justice. That is not the pattern in New Orleans. All feuds are personal. Justice is a mask, sometimes convenient.

Given their social positions and Mr. Champlain's remarks, I thought the likeliest tie would be found between him and Mrs. Aubrey. Although I could not say what that tie might be.

I did not foresee the sorrow I would find.

But I must not go too swiftly.

The wharves were a great bustle, with deep keeled ships crowding in to load cotton for the hungry mills of Manchester and the looms of Massachusetts. You would have thought catastrophe inevitable, but the great hulls moved with the grace of a Hindoo dancing girl, their side wheels thrashing the water as they turned, assisted by small boats flirting with danger. The riverboats, in need of a scrub, were reduced to the lot of stepchildren, lined up along the levee farther on. The Rebels still had a choke-hold on the river to our north and the flat hulls dreamed idly of Memphis and St. Louis.

But the ocean-going ships were in their glory, their holds devouring cargoes for all the world. Hard it was to believe the city had been reduced to beggary, for the docks were paved with silver, if not gold.

Why traffic in slaves when wealth could be made from shipping wartime cotton? Was it simply that greed is mankind's bane?

The one time Jesus got into a fit was with those moneychangers in the Temple. Knowing what I know of men and looking back on the cruel end of Our Savior, I do suspect the Hebrews have been maligned. Were I the sort who wagers, I would bet it was those Jerusalem bankers, not the common people, who bided their time until they could take their revenge. For Christ's mistake of spoiling their accounts.

And do not say the moneychangers were Jews and there is an end to it. That makes too simple a tale. Christian bankers are no models of charity. I do not pretend to be a learned man, but I cannot believe that the simple folk of Jerusalem desired the death of Our Lord Jesus Christ, who did no harm and must have seemed a good fellow. That is not the way that these things go. No doubt those Temple bankers packed the assembly with troublemakers and staged a nasty scene to worry Pilate, who only wished to keep the peace and be done with it. Public officials, after all, value order above all other moralities.

And I served in Washington long enough to know how men of finance rule politicians.

If anyone grinned at the foot of the cross, it was those moneychangers getting their own back. I doubt that many bankers go to Heaven, whether they are Christians, Jews or Hindoos.

The captain had the cab pull up at the wharves reserved for our fighting ships. The yard stank of tar and burning hemp, of canvas set to dry and tamped-down boilers. Bluejackets swarmed about the dock, bossing negro stevedores and inspecting stores delivered by white chandlers. Some fussed with ropes or slathered hulls, while their idler comrades swaggered in wide-bottomed trousers.

At once, Captain Senkrecht was off and barking, leaving me to follow in good time. I noted how the sailors fled his path, how junior officers cracked their heels and saluted. I should explain that a naval captaincy is a higher rank than a captaincy in the Army. Do not look for the sense of it, but think of a seagoing captain as a colonel.

Those naval fellows always do things differently.

I wished to hasten after the captain, but first I had a matter to resolve, an issue of some delicacy. I had but little money upon my person. I needed to draw funds, but lacked the time.

Approaching the cab man and keeping an eye on his whip, I told him, "You shall have to wait for your pay until I return."

Now, when you anger an Irishman you are lucky if he does not resort to fisticuffs. Fortunately, the fellow was sober and weary.

Still, his language turned the sailors' heads.

"You shall have your pay and . . . and even something extra," I said to placate him.

Between his imaginative, even lyrical, obscenities, he managed to say, "Ye promised me fifty dollars, ye low, dirty taffy, ye skulking, low Welshman, ye bummer. Fifty dollars it was to be, and that atop me wages for last night, for taking ye out to yer filthy doings with those Cajun lasses in the swamps . . ."

His voice was raised to stir half of the city and my embarrassment was undeserved. Fumbling, which was unlike me, I drew out my pocket watch and offered it to him in pawn until my return.

He did not even deign to take it up. "'Tisn't worth five dollars, that piece o' tin. Ye dirty—"

Now, I am ever a just and temperate man, but I will admit that, in the past, I have not always thought generously of anyone who chose a life at sea. For I have always been a proper soldier, who kept his two feet nicely in the mud. But on that day my thoughts embraced amendment.

A lieutenant of Marines appeared at my elbow, along with two fellows in uniform who looked like white-skinned cannibals afflicted with indigestion and bad tempers.

"You," the lieutenant told the cab man. "Shut your mouth. And get out of here. Or I'll arrest you for interfering with military operations. After I shoot your horses."

His tone did not encourage indecision.

At once, the officer turned to me and snapped his hand to his cap in a perfect salute. "Lieutenant Gray, sir," he reported. "Captain Senkrecht invites you to come aboard."

That was the day I began to like Marines.

TWAS ALSO THE day my luck began to turn. If I may speak of luck and not God's mercy.

I was scribbling out a note to General Banks and trying to keep out of the way of the sailors, who had a great deal to do before we could sail. In truth, I understand no part of the bluejacket's life, but it seems an awfully complicated thing. There are ropes enough aboard a ship to hang a century's murderers, and not a few members of the crew on any deck look fearful of the noose. They scramble about as if pursued by Death, while their officers keep an eye on things and preen.

The ships with which we fought the war were queer things. I do not speak of the ironclads in the illustrated weeklies or of the turtle gunboats on the rivers, all of which were strange enough in their ways, but of the warships that patrolled our coasts and the oceans. They were, like all of us, caught between two ages, one of wood and wind, the other of metal and steam. The smokestack of the *Cormorant* rose straight between her masts, a confident brat between two hapless elders. The humps of her twin wheels gave the vessel a muscular look, as if her strength were clenched to spring on her prey. You could not doubt her. And yet, for all her polished brass and the shining bronze of her guns, the *Cormorant* lacked the grace of the older vessels creaking and sighing along the commercial wharves. The gunboat was a creature of our times, which value power and do not pause for beauty.

Of course, I stand for progress and only mean to offer you a picture. Nor could I much dislike those leviathan boilers, since many were powered by our Pottsville coal. But we were all in the middle then, caught in the very war that made us modern. None of us could see what was to come, but all sensed that the past could not return.

My note to General Banks was nearly finished, counseling him to apprehend Captain Bolt and confine him on the charges of murder, kidnapping and conspiracy against our government. I had all but signed my name when the bulk and churn of a vessel lifted my eyes. 'Twas just coming up on our stern, alive with uniformed men and flying our nation's flag, with a big Dahlgren gun on her deck. She seemed so near I feared we must collide.

Captain Senkrecht hailed the vessel through a speaking trumpet as bright as the helms of Mr. Homer's Greeks.

"Ahoy, *Hermes*!"

"Ahoy, *Cormorant*."

"Did you pass the *Anne Bullen*?"

"Aye. The *Anne Bullen*. Fifteen miles downriver."

I saw a look of surprise cross the captain's face. The *Hermes* plunged along, roiling the waters. Our own deck rose and fell as cold gulls swooped. After a lapse, the captain called out again.

"Was she under steam?"

"No steam up. Under sail."

Captain Senkrecht did not even bother to end with a salutation, but turned to me at once and said, "We've got her! The damn fools must be mad not to be under steam. They've barely got enough wind to let them steer." He smashed his fist into his palm and looked as pleased as Lord Nelson at the Nile.

But now that my intelligence had finally cast off its slumbers, another possibility occurred to me. I wondered if we were being given a chance. If some of the better, or braver, souls among the New Orleans negroes had interfered with the *Anne Bullen*'s machinery. To give their dusky brethren a last chance at freedom.

I did not voice my suspicions to the captain. All that could wait. I descended to the wharf to dispatch my message and nearly toppled into the river before I reached solid ground. A shudder had wracked the ship. But when I looked back, I could not complain of endangerment. For the tremor that had nearly spilled me over had come from the first great belch of the fired boiler.

A black cloud rose between the masts, as if the vessel itself had been angered and yearned to get into a fight.

It had taken but an hour and not two to trim the ship for the chase. Say what you like about Navy men and all their suspect habits, they rush to a scrap as other men rush to sweethearts.

I barely had time to impress my note on a guard, with the warning of frightful penalties if General Banks did not receive it as quickly as the poor fellow's legs could run.

*   *   *

THE DAY WOULD not decide to be fond or foul. Bright sun struck brown water, promising warmth. But each time I thought to remove my greatcoat, a contrary breeze swept up the river to stop me, shifting clouds whose shadows harbored winter. The air on the river was wet as a mine that has not been pumped out, even when the sunlight warmed my face. Twas a sickly climate.

Along the banks, beyond the useless forts and unkempt levees, the few plantation houses looked bereft. Some had burned, in all or part, casualties of war. Lean children failed to wave. Elsewhere shanties perched at the edge of swamps, as if their occupants meant to reverse the theories of Mr. Darwin. Unbothered by the modern life on the river, their freedom seemed the liberty of the poor, to breed, quarrel and fail. That is the queer thing, see. Setting aside the high and mighty landowners, I never understood what the Southrons were fighting for.

When I explained to Captain Senkrecht that the *Anne Bullen*'s cargo consisted of kidnapped negroes, he looked crestfallen. As if he would have thought it more in keeping with his station to apprehend an illicit load of cotton.

The Southrons fought to keep the negro enslaved. Reluctantly at first, we fought to free him. He began as a cause and became an inconvenience.

The captain convened a council of war in a cabin below the wheelhouse. Included were the commander of the *Cormorant*—a younger officer with a fine moustache—as well as a river pilot and Lieutenant Gray, who had charge of the detachment of Marines. Charts I could not read covered a table, overlaid with instruments fit for astrologers. The cabin smelled of tobacco, oil and paraffin.

Earlier, I had judged the captain falsely, thinking him a plunger and no strategist. But as he and his officers studied the

charts, he proved himself to be a lively thinker, weighing his
enemy's possible actions and plotting his course accordingly.
He would not have been liked in our regiments in India. Nor,
I fear, in our Army of the Potomac, where genius is employed
to explain failure, not prevent it.

Abruptly, Captain Senkrecht looked up from the talk of
depths and currents.

"If we have to choose, which is more important to you?
Capturing the crew or freeing the niggers?"

"The negroes," I said. Although the crew deserved hanging.

He made a sound deep in his throat, neither approving nor
disapproving. Turning back to his subordinates, and with especial attention to the pilot, he said, "If she still isn't under
steam, we can probably overtake her here." Placing a forefinger on a map of the river, he traced a course. "Or there, at
the latest."

The pilot nodded.

"I don't want to run past her," the captain continued, "in
case her crew decide they'd just as soon ram us. Given what
they're carrying, they might feel desperate enough. We'll
come alongside . . . say, here . . . and edge them toward that
bar." He looked at the pilot once more, who nodded and
sucked on an unlit cigarillo. "I believe they'll choose to run
her aground, gentlemen, as close to shore as possible. Once
they realize we're onto them, their prime concern will be to
escape the gallows. They'll want to get off that ship. So
we'll encourage them." He shifted his eyes to Lieutenant
Gray. "Place your best sharpshooters in the masts. Shoot the
crew in the water, if they won't surrender. They've forfeited
their right to be called human. Should any of them reach the
shore, shoot them before they can slip into the swamps."

"They won't much like it in there, anyhow," the pilot
interjected.

"I want two longboats ready to lower the instant we mark her turning for the bar. Swiftly, gentlemen, swiftly. Lieutenant Gray, you will divide the remainder of your men. Half will pursue the crew if they flee and gather up any wise enough to surrender. The other boat will ferry the boarding party. I don't expect much of a fight, but we'll give them one, if they want it."

He turned again to me. "Lieutenant Gray will be master of the *Anne Bullen* until her crew has been secured. Thereafter, Mr. Fox will take the vessel, but he and Lieutenant Gray will give you every assistance in freeing the contrabands. If her crew runs the *Anne Bullen* aground, we'll take the darkies off before we leave her." He took a manly breath and spoke to all of us. "It's all straightforward, gentlemen. But pay attention, in case our quarry indulges in any foolishness."

"Shall I run out the guns, sir?" the fellow in command of the *Cormorant* asked. "For effect?"

Captain Senkrecht shook his head. "They'll know we don't intend to sink her." He grimaced. "They probably wish we would. To get rid of their cargo. No, Mr. Brock, if they don't obey our order to lay by, the sharpshooters will scour her decks. Then we'll board her."

They all seemed to think it a fine plan. But I did have one question, of course.

"And if they are under steam?" I asked the captain. "And we do not overtake them as your plan supposes?"

In his element now, he was imperturbable. "Then we're in a race to the Gulf of Mexico," he said. "In a deep channel, we've got fourteen knots to their ten or eleven."

But we were not in a race to the open sea. I wish I could report a ripping chase, but we come upon our quarry precisely where Captain Senkrecht thought we should. There

was still no hint of smoke from her bowels as she floated
slowly downstream, lazy as Cleopatra's royal barge. The
wind had taken the side of the Union and justice, putting so
little swell in the slaver's sails that they looked like untucked
shirts.

The captain and I stood just outside the wheelhouse as we
closed on the *Anne Bullen*. He peered through a pair of those
newfangled spyglasses, moving his lips just slightly, as if
asking the air a question.

"She's busy amidships," he told me. "My guess is that
they've been having problems with the engine all along.
Only explanation for it. Contraband boat doesn't want to
draw attention by running all out, but she doesn't dawdle, either. And that canvas isn't doing them much good."

We were not yet in hailing range and the captain wished
to surprise them, so we made no more show than any Federal vessel to-and-froing on the Mississippi. But the sharpshooters were crouched in their buckets atop the masts,
while the Marines and sailors to man the boats sat quietly on
deck, concealed from the *Anne Bullen* by our gunwale.

Captain Senkrecht passed me the glasses. With the aid of
the lenses, I began to make out faces. The crew were as
mixed as the lot who had tried to capture me on that rooftop,
black and white and every shade in between. Busy they were,
indeed, although there seemed to be some fine confusion.

Then I saw him. The gargantuan colored fellow with the
scars cut into his cheeks. The one Mr. Barnaby referred to as
Petit Jean.

I do not know if he was a proper sailor, but he seemed to
be in charge of the doings on deck.

"We may be in for a bit of a fuss," I warned the captain.
Passing the glasses back to him, I added, "You'll see a tall,
brown fellow. He likes a scrap."

The captain raised the glasses again, although we were coming on at such speed that we could see much without them. The chaos on the *Anne Bullen* only increased.

"Good God!" the captain said. He was a steady fellow on the water, strict and stalwart, with a voice long practiced not to rise until necessary, in order to keep secrets from the crew. But his tone at that moment was such that it alarmed me.

I squinted to see what he might mean. I did not think the mere sight of Petit Jean could have much disturbed him.

"They're splashing pitch on the decks," he said in a sharpened voice. "Pitch and maybe oil. Can't tell."

I nearly grabbed the glasses from his hands. I understood, see.

"They know we're after them now," he said. "They're going to burn her."

He swept into action, ordering Lieutenant Gray's sharpshooters not to wait for his challenge, but to start shooting down the crew as soon as they could. Ordering the longboats into the water, he advised me to join the boarding party immediately.

Before I climbed down to the main deck, which was a minor trial with my leg, I saw the *Anne Bullen* shudder and halt a rifle shot ahead.

The captain had been right about that much. Her crew had run her aground. Not a hundred yards from shore.

But not a one of us had foreseen that the slavers might burn their human cargo alive.

Atop the masts, the sharpshooters opened fire.

I hastened to the boats, expecting to find the confusion that attends a plan rushed forward. But the Marines were crisp and the sailors were methodical.

"This one, sir," Lieutenant Gray called to me. "In this one, with me."

I passed my greatcoat to a sailor who would remain aboard. I meant to fight.

Now, I am a fellow who can prance about with bayonet or sword. Despite the bit of bother to my leg. But that is on dry land. Although the river was not so turbulent as the ocean seas, I was not at my best while clambering into the boat.

The Marines were of assistance, for which I was grateful, despite a shade of soldierly embarrassment.

Tugged along on a line at first, our longboat was a play-thing for the sidewheel. The mighty instrument churned and groaned, creating a choppy, artificial tide. I held to the side of the boat and took a splashing.

The crackle of shots from the sharpshooters come regular as drill. Our sailors sat erect, with oars raised high. When the sidewheel sent us a nasty wave, the Marines shielded their rifles, not themselves.

As the *Cormorant* maneuvered close, I saw the first men leap from the *Anne Bullen*. They struggled with the current and strove landward.

A cloud of smoke rose from her deck. It was not from her boiler. The pirates had fired their ship, as the captain feared.

Furious and sick inside, I was about to shout at Lieutenant Gray. But he forestalled me. Ordering the line cast off, he told the sailors to speed us to our goal.

A bluejacket who looked as though he had surived all the world's diseases called the rhythm as the sailors rowed. We rose and fell from atop a last wave fashioned by the side-wheel, which had already creaked to a halt.

I looked, again and again, to see if Petit Jean would jump from the ship. I could not spot him. Soon the *Anne Bullen*'s stern blocked my view of the landward side.

The sharpshooters kept up their fire from the *Cormorant*. Twas queer. A bucket bobbed by. Then another.

"Scum," Lieutenant Gray declared. "They've heaved their buckets overboard. So we can't fight the fire."

That fire was running high, if flaring unevenly.

Just before we closed with the hull, I heard the first cries of terror, then of agony. There were only scattered voices at first, like the opening shots of a skirmish. Then the ship before us shuddered again, this time with a roar of human fear.

The poor creatures in the hold knew the ship was burning.

The *Anne Bullen*'s gunwales did not ride high, for she was new and sleek, but the Marines still had to swing up hooks as we bobbed by the hull.

I smelled the fire and felt its warmth before I reached the deck. But more than anything else, I smelled the fear.

The wailing from the hold grew so loud that the Marines could hardly communicate one to another. I heard the unmistakable rattling of chains, a sound that seemed colossal.

Now, I am a strong enough fellow. In my salad days, I could climb a rope like a mischievous temple monkey. But that had been on land, before I was encumbered by a cane.

Fair raging at my awkwardness I was. I feared I would drop my stick into the river. And the Lord only knew what price that ancient Frenchman would demand once he learned I had lost it.

After watching me fumble and bumble, a red-haired Marine reached down and grasped my encumbrance. "Come on, sir," he called, "for she's burning like Betty's behind when the fleet comes in."

Relieved of my cane, I scaled the rope quite nicely.

The deck was a maze of fires through which a man roamed at his peril. One sail had caught, as well. Beneath our feet, the vessel shivered and shook with the cries of the negroes.

Stick in hand once more, I trailed the Marine. He plunged

into a vertical hatch, disappearing into shadows. I could not go as quickly as him, for the steps were steep and treacherous, but I did not waste a second more than I needed.

Below decks, I bumped into Lieutenant Gray, who was plunging back through the smoke. Even though the loss of light had addled my eyes, I could tell the lad was shaken by what he had seen.

"Axes," he shouted against the shrieks and the clang of chains. "Hammers."

That was all he said. He rushed past and climbed to the main deck, followed by another Marine, who was coughing from the smoke and cursing roundly.

The fellow with me hesitated, unsure whether he should follow the lieutenant.

"Come on," I ordered. I needed to judge the matter for myself. And I did not know the ways of the ship or just what might be waiting.

Sidling along a passageway, I smelled a stink that I knew all too well.

The roasting flesh of Man.

I should have drawn my Colt, but was too maddened. All my years of soldiering counted for little in the face of this.

Down another half-flight of steps, I found the stuff of nightmare.

Oh, light was not a problem any longer. I stared into an inferno in the middle of a long hold. The smoke swelled black, but could not hide the scene. Above the flames, an open hatch mocked the doomed with daylight.

The pirates had poured pitch or the like directly onto the negroes below the hatch. Then they burned them. Perhaps only twenty or thirty were splashed of the hundreds crushed together, but those human beings—we all must allow them that claim—had become animate torches, raging with pain and struggling wildly against the chains that held them in their places. Many were already dead of course, for the body does not like the shock of fire. But others still squirmed in burning rags, helpless even to rise up to their feet.

Their brothers looked on, howling, as they waited for the fire to spread.

I coughed. From the smoke. And the smell of burning man-meat.

At the sight of me, the nearest negroes erupted in lamentation, struggling to raise chained hands to strengthen their pleas. The altered tenor of wails spread like an infection. Until the entire hold became a begging, clanking maelstrom.

Rails had been fixed lengthwise in the hold and the prisoners had been chained to them, ankles and wrists together. Left to relieve their bodily needs in their places. Yet, such discomforts must have seemed a heaven compared to what they suffered now.

For a terrible moment, I knew not what to do.

The Marine at my side said, "Jesus."

Lieutenant Gray had been right, of course. We needed hammers and axes to do any good.

But I was on a still-unfinished quest. And all the negroes in that hold were males.

Beckoning the Marine to follow, I struggled through the ranks of desperate men, doing what I could to escape their grasps and their pleas that each might be first to be freed.

I believed that I had heard another sound. And I had a promise to keep.

To get round the burning men and corpses, we had to step among the rows of prisoners. I promise you I had no choice, but I beat men with my cane to keep them off me, while the Marine employed his rifle's butt and barrel end. I feared they would seize me in their thoughtless terror, the way one drowning man pulls down another.

Their faces. Dear God, I shall remember their eyes beyond the grave. Their terror would have suited the Day of Judgement.

Up on deck, beyond the hatch and the snapping of the flames, white voices railed in frustration.

Thrusting myself through a doorway at the end of the long hold, I felt a craven relief. I had been right, my hearing had not failed me. The other shrieks were clearer now, close by. The wails and cries of women.

My relief did not last.

He stood before me, revolver in one hand, a cutlass in the other. He was so tall he had to stoop in the passage.

He smiled at me before he pulled the trigger.

Even then, Petit Jean underestimated me. He shot my companion, judging him the more dangerous of us. Despite our rooftop battle and bordello duel.

The falling Marine called out for his beloved.

Before he could work the action on his pistol, I had my blade free of the cane and swept it down across Petit Jean's wrist. I struck with such ferocity the blow revealed white bone. The revolver clattered into the shadows and smoke.

The fellow roared.

What saved me? What made him an instant too slow? Fate twists and turns. I had been saved not only by Petit Jean's flawed judgement, but by the madame of that bawdy house. You will recall that she shot him through the arm when she interrupted us. It had not done me much good then, but now I was paid with interest.

With a growl, the giant lunged at me. He appeared so vast in the cramp of the hold it seemed he might simply engulf me if his blade failed to find my flesh. But sometimes the Lord favors men of lesser stature.

Bad leg or no, the advantage of size was mine now. I could squirm about, while Petit Jean banged into boards and beams. He used his arm and the cutlass as a scythe, but could not harvest me.

All the while, the screams only grew madder, the deep roar of the men to my rear and the high pleas of the women to the fore.

We dueled. Like two fellows in a tale of Mr. Scott's. He did not give me leisure to draw my Colt and I did not give him space to pick up his revolver.

Steel it was, to the end.

Twas no easy struggle, that I grant you. If I was not slashed, I was not unscathed. My bones took a nasty battering on the timbers as we clashed and feinted in the smoke.

Fire began to spurt from a side compartment, threatening worse.

I believe I would have won in the end. For I was an instructor of the bayonet in my regiment in India and am a doughty fellow in a fight. But I will never know.

A pistol roared at my ear. Petit Jean fell.

Lieutenant Gray put another ball into my enemy, who was twisting on the floor and clutching his guts. The second shot stilled him.

"Big bastard, that one," the lieutenant said.

I was already rushing past the corpse. Toward the women and their frantic cries.

The door behind which the women wailed was padlocked. I got out my Colt and tried to shoot it open, with no success. I was just about to turn back to the corpse of Petit

Jean, in the hope in a thousand that he might have the key, when Lieutenant Gray fired from another angle.

The lock sprang free.

The women were packed as densely as the men, though in a smaller hold. They were not chained. Perhaps they were kept so at the pleasure of the crew. Beyond that, I shall not speculate.

"Magdalena!" I shouted through the smoke and the squealing confusion.

I could not hear anything clearly, not after that pistol had gone off at my ear. Twas all a great roar that refused to break into parts.

"Magdalena!"

Foolish women hurled themselves at my person and the lieutenant, pleading for rescue. Their wiser sisters slipped by us to flee on their own.

I fear my roughness was ungentlemanly. I spoke strongly, admonishing them to get themselves along and save themselves. Lucky they were to bear no chains, unlike their tormented brothers.

Dizzy from the smoke and with my hearing spoiled, I felt pressed toward madness. Now, I was ever a cool one in a fight. But not that day. Every burning man was on my conscience. Yet, I had turned my back on them, as purposeful as a beast.

"Magdalena!" I cried again, pushing raving negresses out of my way. The stink come high. You smelled it through the acid of the smoke. For they had been granted no greater allowance of sanitation than the men.

I saw her at last, toward the back of the hold. Collapsed against a wall, given up by her sisters. Her face was swollen from beatings. And she alone had been chained.

She *must* have heard me call, despite the ruckus. But she

had not responded. Her eyes were shut, but she could not have slept through the tumult. Perhaps she had thought me yet another tormentor, come for a favor. Mayhaps her hopes were quit.

Her dress was ripped and ragged. All of her person was in disarray.

As I brushed aside the last confusion of lasses, she opened her eyes and saw me. God knows how I appeared amid the smoke.

But how she changed! Her tan face brightened as if she had gained a glimpse of the highest Heaven. Bruised and battered, she did not quite speak, though she tried to mouth a word.

I rushed to her and tore at the chains, which had been driven deep into a beam.

They would not give, of course. I roared in outrage, scorning all pain that might revenge my clumsiness. In a fury I was, made stupid. I did no good at all.

I tried to shoot the chains free of the wall. But that was hopeless. It only endangered the lass with ricochets.

So fast, it all happened so fast. I resolved that, if I could not free her, I would put a bullet through her forehead, rather than let the poor thing burn alive.

I did not think of the misery of hundreds. I forgot Lieutenant Gray. Who can tell the reasons of our hearts? My time might have been more wisely used to free others. But I had made a promise to Mr. Barnaby, a quick, unconsidered remark meant to lift his spirits. Now it was a crisis in my soul.

Perhaps it was my own knowledge of loss, my memories of India. The pain of the flesh is here and gone, the common coin of martyrs, but the miseries of the soul haunt the longest life.

God bless the United States Marines. The lieutenant had

gone back through the smoke and brought not only a sledge-hammer but a brawny Marine to wield it.

That hammer had been at work in the burning hold, saving the many. But the lieutenant had ordered it carried to my aid.

"Stand back," he told me. When I failed to respond, he shoved me out of the way.

Perhaps that Marine once broke rocks for a living. He had a way with a hammer. I thought him wild and feared he would finish the girl. But each blow fell precisely, splintering the timber where it had embraced the fixture of the chain.

The poor child closed her eyes the while and wept.

Bless him, he freed her in a pair of minutes. Which was fortunate for all, as the fire was spreading and wrapping us in smoke.

Giving up the hammer to his lieutenant, the stout Marine drew the lass over his shoulder.

Gray and I followed, stepping over the carcass of Petit Jean. I recovered the sheath of my sword-cane and gave the corpse a last glance. What a tortured soul must have been his, not only to sell his brethren back into slavery, but to burn them alive instead of letting them live. Did he hate them so? Or did he hate himself?

He was a minor player in the drama. But I think on him.

Back in the main hold, horror flourished. The negroes were chained to the long rails with individual shackles. The rails could not be broken out and the prisoners had to be freed one at a time. The Marines had only found a pair of hammers. The others had likely been cast overboard with the buckets. All with an aim of letting the prisoners burn.

As we struggled back through the mass of them, one poor sod dug his fingers into my trouser leg so fiercely he cut the fabric and broke open my skin, as I found later. His eyes were huge and he would not let me go.

I had to thrash him over the head with my cane.

He wanted to live, as all men do. But I moved on. The smoke was deadly where he sat. I needed air myself.

The clamor and din were patterned after Hell.

Lieutenant Gray was younger by a decade, but I had the better shoulders of the two of us. One Marine was swinging away to free as many negroes as he could. I tore the other hammer from the lieutenant's hands. Gasping, I told him to call for more tools from the *Cormorant*.

"I already did," he assured me.

"Then get you out of my way until they come. Here. Take my cane. And get yourself into the sunlight. Go away, man!"

You understand me. I could not stand by idly as they burned. I had to employ my own muscle, my own breath, to free as many poor souls as I could.

I began where I stood, to the joy of a poor, fat fellow who cried his gratitude unto the Lord.

Another negro, down the line, shouted that I should save him because he could read.

How do you choose? When you know that you cannot save them all, only a portion? How should we play God? Do we choose the comeliest? The strongest? The one who begs us nicely? The young? The old?

I refused to think. I surrendered sense to labor. I worked in order from the spot where I found myself, freeing one after another down the line. Ignoring cries, pleas, screams, jibes, curses, all the dissonance of human torment.

I tried not to look into a single face.

As a young lad, before I ran off and signed for John Company in Bristol, I had worked down in the pits for a pair of seasons. I know how to use a hammer, if not so perfectly as that bold Marine. Yet, I was in haste, half maddened and gagged with smoke. I smashed a poor fellow's hand, instead of his shackles. Even then, he did not complain but begged me to strike again.

Men burned. Or suffocated. The clangor of chains and the failing cries surmounted the worst miseries of India. Or even the lot of the lads who burned at Shiloh.

I near pitched over. All of a sudden. Bleary and dizzy. I could not get the air back into my lungs.

I swung again, determined to do good, and broke a poor devil's leg.

As I wobbled, dark hands grabbed for the hammer. Manacled, not one of them could have swung it. But each one hoped the tool might save his life.

I could hardly see any longer, barely grip.

A flurry of hands grasped me. Not by my legs, but higher. I tried to struggle, but could not.

Despite the thunder in my ears, I heard a white man's voice say, "Get him out of here."

They carried me off, and I did not protest.

Swooning, I heard the devil's orchestra playing. For that is Satan's tune, I do believe. The sound of human beings dying slowly, in great pain.

I am unaware of precisely how they got me back to the *Cormorant,* but when I awoke I had exceptional bruises.

I cannot say for certain. And am not confident that I wish to know. But I wonder if the fading of my consciousness down in that hold come honestly from drinking smoke and that infernal heat, or from the cowardice lingering in us all. Was it just exhaustion and no air? Or was I fleeing?

The *Cormorant*'s medical fellow brought me around with smelling salts, just as he would have awakened a dismayed dowager. I rose, stiff as a grampus and dizzy. I felt as though not a few of the hammer's blows had landed on me. My uniform reeked as sharply as the salts, smelling of ashes, sweat and the blood of strangers. But my cane stood waiting against a chair, preserved by the lieutenant. Twas good of him to save it. And kinder still to save me.

The dark was down, enlivened by the blaze consuming the *Anne Bullen*. We had only just begun to steam away. The wheels propelled us northward, back to New Orleans.

When I made my way out onto the deck, staggering like a drunkard, the river was livid with firelight in our wake. We had gained some distance, so I could not hear the concert of flames above our engine and paddlewheels, but I did hear muted sounds of shock and sorrow. Twas the rescued darkies, shivering in the cold upon our deck.

A lone voice rose and called upon the Lord to come unto the children of Israel and succor them. Fervent and rasping, he spoke as if expecting God to answer.

A sailor cursed and told him to be quiet.

I learned that we had saved thirty-nine women and fifty-five men before the smoke and flames drove our lads from the ship. Perhaps a hundred and fifty burned alive.

seventeen

$\mathcal{M}$R. BARNABY, GOD BLESS him, did not follow my instructions. Rather than waiting at my hotel, he stood, anxious and shivering, just beyond the sentries at the wharves. Impatient as a child he was, for he had a tale to tell.

I did not spot him from the boat, of course. I was bedazzled as our paddlewheels fought the muscular river. The city glowed ahead of us, as if it were Jerusalem, not Babylon. Gas-lit, lamp-lit, torch-lit and finished with candles, New Orleans looked a miracle at night, a muster of stars that had deserted Heaven. How could it be that such a thing of beauty could bear our shabby, vicious, human selves?

As I debarked, after some last formalities, I heard two sailors speak of bought affections. They both looked forward to some hours of liberty, though one complained of discomfort from past forays.

And yet, I would be just. My purposes led me among the worst of mankind, not among the simple folk who doubtless live as quietly in New Orleans as they do in Merthyr Tydfil or in Pottsville. The vicious steal our attention and make the entire world seem wracked with sin. The reverent and kind attract less notice.

I had a good deal to do and as many questions to ask as a Dublin judge. I did not expect to encounter Mr. Barnaby as

I wobbled along the wharf, refreshing my legs with the feel of solid ground.

I could not be a sailor for the life of me.

And there he was, unshaven still and bleary in the lamplight, a great, fat man whose strength was on the ebb. Ever dapper he tried to be, but now his features looked as frayed as his cuffs. The thing of it is, you see, that he was honest. Such men do not prosper during wartime.

"Major Jones!" the good man cried, "Captain Bolt 'as shot the moon and Marie Venin's as dead as Napoleon Bonaparte!"

Twas more than I could take in at once in my weary, unsettled condition. I nearly cast humanity aside and demanded every detail of his news. But proud I am to say that I remembered myself. He wanted news himself. Of Magdalena.

I do believe that duty must come first. Yet, there are times when mercy asks pride of place.

"It is good news, see. Your . . . your acquaintance . . . has been rescued. She is as safe as barley in the bin." At that the poor fellow's face grew brighter than all the lamps and torches on the waterfront. "She will be fit and fine, but wants a rest," I added.

He looked down at the mucky way and grew shy as a schoolboy. "I should like to see 'er, I should." Twas barely a whisper.

In that regard, I had to disappoint him.

"In good time, Mr. Barnaby, in good time. Miss Magdalena is sleeping, see. One of the boat's officers has given up his bed for the lass's comfort. She must sleep the night through, for her health's sake. She suffered some . . . indignities . . . and wants a proper rest to set her up."

He grew alarmed to a point inviting ridicule. "But

she's . . . she's all right? She isn't . . . she wasn't . . . she ain't . . . that is—"

The truth is that I was not entirely certain of her condition. The medical fellow on the gunboat had assured me her basic health was sound. But as for matters beyond that, as for the final toll of all she suffered, even she herself could not yet know. The devils that enter us like to hide for years.

"You shall ask her yourself. Tomorrow," I said briskly. "Now, you have had your news, and on to business. What was that you said of Captain Bolt?"

"'E's bolted, Captain Bolt 'as. Shot the moon, and no one knows where to find 'im. I knows it because they're 'unting 'im all over, rooting in cisterns and cellars and such until the entire city's topsy-turvy. They say your General Banks is mad as a wild pig what's been bothered at 'is dinner. 'E even sent the invalid soldiers to comb the streets and alleys. Though I shouldn't think they'll 'ave much luck at finding 'im."

"Why is that, then?"

"Well, sir, begging your pardon, New Orleans swallows bad men whole and doesn't spit 'em back out on command. It's a marvelous place to be a wicked fellow. A rogue delights 'em far more than a preacher, though they lets on it's the other way around. Why, even a bloke what's been 'orrible bad won't be given up at the first rap of the peeler. They likes things slow and savory down 'ere, sir. Even crime. But all's one, sir, all's one. I should think the captain's taken 'imself right off, quick as Paddy's pig. For 'e don't understand New Orleans no more than you do. 'E'll think it's safer to run, which ain't the case. Although it means your soldiers is wasting their time 'ere in the city."

"Where would he go, man?"

He scratched his forceful belly, then re-settled his hat on

his head, gestures that seemed to ease the process of thought. "Well, if 'e was a fool, 'e'd set off north and try to pass the lines into the Confederacy. Such of it as remains. But Bolt ain't a fool, not in that sense, so I suspects 'e's waiting out in the swamps for things to settle. Until 'e can find 'im a berth on a ship putting out for the Spanish isles. That, or 'e's already 'eaded west for Texas. Which might not be as friendly as 'e expects."

"*Find* him."

He looked nonplussed. "I . . . I would if I could, sir, begging your pardon, but—"

"I do not mean you personally. Employ the negroes. By whom you are befriended. Excite them, rouse them. Raise the negroes, since they seem to be better intelligencers than our agents. Remind them of what has been done to them by Captain Bolt and his colleagues. And tell them there is at least one Union officer they can trust in this rancid matter. Ask them to find Captain Bolt for us. Otherwise, he may not come to justice."

He let a sigh so great it might have bulged a clipper's sails. "I shall ask 'em, sir. Ask 'em I shall. But that's all I can do, for they're most particular. I doesn't say they won't do what you're asking. But I can't say as they will, not 'til I asks. For they've been bothered and bruised, sir. In ways white men can't imagine. They doesn't trust the same as you nor I, sir, and when they 'as the liberty to say no, sometimes they does. For every fellow likes to enjoy 'is choosing, even when it ain't to 'is own benefit."

That was too convoluted a doctrine for me.

"Do your best," I begged him. "Please. Persuade them. Tell them that we must bring Bolt to justice. For what he and his like have done to them. Convince them, Mr. Barnaby. And what is this about Marie Venin? Dead, is it?"

"Dead as Holofernes! Dead as poor, old Chatterton! Dead as General Johnston 'imself upon the field of Shiloh in 'is glory!"

He spoke with such glee you would have thought him a colored fellow himself, avenged at last on the woman who feigned secret powers to re-enslave her race.

"What happened? Are you certain?"

"I can't say as I've seen it with my own eyes, but the negroes are certain as greed on Tchoupitoulas. They say she was last seen alive at the crossroads out by the Metairie Cemetery, crawling about on 'er 'ands and knees, and foaming at the mouth. Snapping like a dog what's in its death throes. They all believes the devil come up to collect 'is bills with interest, but I suspects she was slipped a draught of poison. The way she almost done you in 'erself. They're wonderful poisoners, every one of the *voudouiennes*."

"What about the corpse, then? Is there any proof that she is dead?"

"They tell me she's still lying there, in the middle of the crossroads, for there ain't a colored person between here and Africa what's willing to touch 'er."

You see now how a criminal scheme comes undone. One day it appears unassailable, perfect in its arrangements and successful in its defiance of the law. And overnight their plan unravels, leaving them lying about their stage as if Mr. Shakespeare had written their final act.

For all his breathless talk, Mr. Barnaby had not alluded to the query with which I had left him.

"And did you learn anything at all of the relations between Mrs. Aubrey and Mr. Champlain?"

He took on a damped-down look and hardly met my eyes. Like a lad who has left his daily chores unfinished.

"I can't say as I've found out anything much, sir. Nor

nothing at all, to tell it to you honest. That is, I asked 'em, sir. Them what should know. And not just among the household Negroes. I even asked the *gens libre de couleur*. And no one could draw a single line between 'em, sir. Not a single connection. Excepting the normal doings of society. And even in society, they kept apart. Of course, given as *Père* Champlain don't leave 'is 'ouse and 'asn't done for years, that ain't surprising. Folks almost forget that 'e exists, they see 'im so little these days. Withdrawn 'e 'as, withdrawn. Although Mrs. Aubrey ain't half so retiring, for 'er part. She lends 'er name to charitable causes . . . although she don't give anything 'erself."

He paused, reviewing all the day's encounters. "The queer thing, sir, is that I think you're right. It's the old negroes what gives me cause to wonder, the ones what lived so long they know that most things are best forgot. Oh, the young folks would 'ave told me, if they knew. For the young do love to let us know 'ow wise and worldly they are. But nothing they 'ad to say was anything much. Speculation, sir, worthless speculation. But the old ones, now . . . they knows something, they do. Whatever the connection was between the Widow Aubrey and *Père* Champlain, it's buried in the past, sir, dead and buried."

If Mr. Barnaby was right that I did not know New Orleans, I had observed enough to grasp that nothing was ever quite buried in the place. Not even the dead, who rest above the ground. I knew no other place outside of India where the past was so determined to be present.

The truth is that Mr. Barnaby had done a yeoman's work during my absence. And however dubious his late wife's attributes may have been in certain respects, the ties she had allowed him to forge with the negroes of the city had aided me greatly. The world is not as simple as we wish it.

And clear it was that his wife had made him happy, while she lived. He mourned her still, as suited the best of Christians, and I did not think the appearance of the servant girl had changed his heart, except to give him hope. Loathe I am to say such a thing, for it insults true religion, but I wonder if virtue always must be perfect?

"All right," I said. "You have done well, Mr. Barnaby. And I am grateful, see. But I must ask you to forego your rest a while longer. Until you have set the negroes after Bolt. As best it can be done so late in the evening."

"Oh, the dark's the perfect time for communications, sir. With the colored folk, I means. Once the master's drunk 'is draught of Madeira and the lady of the 'ouse is dozing off to dream of all the *beaux* she declined and wishes she 'and't, that's when they 'as a bit of time for themselves, the serving classes. And then there's some what ain't in service at all. The sort what comes out at night, if you take my meaning."

"To it, then, Mr. Barnaby. And Godspeed. Call on me in the morning, at the hotel. I have a bit of business to do myself before I sleep."

"Off to call upon the Widow Aubrey, sir?"

His insight perplexed me. "How did you know that?"

"Oh, it's only 'ow you does things, Major Jones. You're like a terrier, begging your pardon, what won't let go even when you take a stick to it. And when the answers you want don't come to you, you go straight for 'em, whether they likes it or not. And Mrs. Aubrey still ain't answered up."

"Well, I will tell you what comes of my visit tomorrow."

I meant for him to take himself off. Midnight had caressed the dying day. But the good fellow hesitated, shifting about from foot to foot and not quite meeting my eyes. He even doffed his hat and stood before me truly hat in hand.

"Begging your pardon, sir." Even in the torchlight, he

looked flushed. "But if Magdalena needs a bit of nursing . . . or even if she don't, she'll still need a home. I mean, a safe place to recover and then get on, sir. For she's all but defenseless, she is. She doesn't even speak the local talk, sir, and couldn't 'ardly get 'erself a loaf without a gentleman's assistance. There's 'ardly anyone left 'ere who speaks Spanish, sir, and even fewer what speaks the Spanish creole thick as 'erself."

The fellow had briefly met my gaze, but looked away again. "I shouldn't want you to think of me as a sponger, sir. Or as any sort of bounder, not Barnaby B. Barnaby. It's only . . . it's only as I'm utterly out of funds, sir. I'm bust. I doesn't even possess a Confederate dollar. Not a nickel. That cab man put upon me this afternoon and swore you 'adn't paid 'im. And he swore more than just that, sir. I gave 'im the last coins from my pocket, not that it made 'im 'appy."

He summoned all his manly resolve and met me eye to eye. "It ain't for me, sir. Or I shouldn't never ask it. But . . . if you . . . Lordie, I'm so ashamed to even ask. 'Ow the mighty are fallen, as they say. But if you could see your way, per'aps . . . that is, despite you being a Welshman and all . . . if I could prevail upon you for a loan, sir, I'd—"

The truth is that I should not have let him speak as long as I did. The poor fellow was sick with humiliation, for he had a peculiar pride he never lost. I should have put a quicker end to his suffering. Twas only that I am awkward in such matters. But the Good Lord did provide an inspiration.

"Mr. Barnaby, you embarrass me."

"Oh, I didn't mean to do that, sir, I—"

"No, no. I did not mean your request, see. I spoke of my own negligence. I forgot to tell you, there is true. The moment you began to assist me, I put you down on my special agent's payroll. At . . . at ten dollars the day! Including Saturdays. And the Lord's day. Look you . . . with a fair advance on expenses . . . would a hundred dollars be of some assistance?"

Yes, I know. I told a lie. But that is on my conscience, not on yours. Nor did I intend to lay a charge to our government. I meant to pay the fellow from my own funds.

I will admit it pained me. But what is the purpose of wealth on this earth if not to help the deserving? What progress, if any, would I have made without his able assistance?

Still, I will admit to wondering whether I should have offered him fifty dollars and not an entire hundred. Generosity must not become indulgence.

"I . . . I didn't realize . . . didn't know . . . I mean, I wasn't 'elping you for wages, sir. It was all for Lieutenant Raines, for Master Francis. Although I shouldn't like to refuse what's proper."

"Well, right and proper it is, Mr. Barnaby. Right and proper. I shall draw funds in the morning and—"

"Begging your pardon, sir, begging your pardon. I doesn't mean to seem ungrateful and nasty . . . but if I could 'ave but two dollars tonight . . . you see, I've been turned out of the place I was boarding, sir. I never thought I'd live to fall so low . . ."

The fact is that my own pockets were empty, and had been for some time. Had I been better organized, I would have seen the need for funds in my purse.

Embarrassed I was for the fellow. Twas as I said before: The honest do not prosper during wartime.

"Wait here," I said. I saw one forlorn hope.

I took me back aboard the *Cormorant*. Captain Senkrecht was gone off, but I asked for the gunboat's commander. In his stateroom he was, which hardly deserved so eminent a name. He worked at a stack of papers by a lantern's light. After a battle of shot and shell, the long campaign of ink and paper begins.

He was a fair young man. Had he not been so intelligent, he might have been well-suited for the cavalry.

"Major Jones?" he said in some surprise. He had thought himself rid of me. His face bore the look of a man wrenched from deep thought, the confusion of leaving one world for another.

I produced the letter prepared by Mr. Nicolay and signed by Mr. Lincoln. Granting me authorities that even I found excessive.

"I am in need of funds. Urgent need. Have you a hundred dollars on board? No, a hundred and fifty?" I decided that I might have needs myself before I had time to call at the pay-master's office. Where corruption had reigned of late.

"Of course, this is irregular . . ."

"I shall pay the money back in a day. Or in two days at most."

He finished scanning my letter, then said, "Yes. Of course. I didn't realize . . ."

I find I lack the rigor of my youth. And, perhaps, the strictness befitting a Methodist. I am uncertain, even now, that it was proper of me to draw funds from the *Cormorant* for purposes that were but half official. But no ill come of it. And lest you wonder, I paid the fellow back.

I returned to the wharf well satisfied that I had done a good deed, if by flawed means.

Mr. Barnaby, despite his bulk, looked haggard and hard used.

"Did you see 'er?" he asked eagerly. "Did you see 'er, is she all right?"

I wanted a moment to understand his meaning.

"No, Mr. Barnaby, I did not see the lass. She is sleeping, see. And that was not my business." I drew him away from the brightness of lamp and torch to a spot where I might pass him his funds discreetly.

Now, Mr. Barnaby had always maintained a demeanor of handsome dignity. But that night I feared the fellow would kiss my hand.

This life of ours is not a fair one. Our Savior Jesus Christ accepted that and specified that our reward is to come. Yet, it troubles me at times that, even in America—which is the best of countries on this earth—the contents of our pockets shape our fates. I wish that goodness counted slightly more.

Twas then I got my comeuppance, well and true. No sooner had Mr. Barnaby set off, than a flood of shame swept over me. In the emptiness he left behind, I saw a thing I should have seen long before I let the poor fellow embarrass himself by admitting his funds were exhausted.

I recalled the first evening of our reaquaintance. When he spirited me off to that voodoo hag who got the poison out of me. He had laid seven coins upon the floor. Gold coins. From his own purse. As the price of my restoration.

In the press of events, my debt had escaped me entirely. Those coins must have been his last wealth on this earth. Yet, even in his present destitution, reduced to begging a loan, he had been too much the gentleman to remind me of my financial obligation.

He was a splendid fellow, Mr. Barnaby was. And here is the nut of it: He hardly took an interest in religion. At least not in a proper Christian way. And yet I think Our Savior must have been fond of him. If there were no hymns upon his lips, Mr. Barnaby had a Christian heart. And a better one than many a man who praised the Lord and pocketed his rents.

*   *   *

I COULD NOT pause for revery and regret. I had a task before me, and a grim one. But as I set off to locate a conveyance, a fellow come trotting along the wharves, shouting, "Major Jones! Major Abel Jones!"

I turned to respond and waved from an eddy of lamplight. I did not call out, since the smoke in the slaver's hold had scorched my throat. And I would have more need of my voice before dawn.

At least my jaw had improved, though it still gave me needles.

My summoner was a major like myself. I must say he looked untucked, as if he had risen in haste from his couch, if not from a site more intimate.

"Major Jones?"

"I am Major Abel Jones."

"Thank the devil . . . we just now heard the *Cormorant* put in . . . didn't expect you back as soon as that . . ."

"Well, I am here. What is it?"

"General Banks. The general wants to see you. He said it didn't matter, day or night, he wants to see you. He's been roaring like a bear with his hind leg broke."

"Well, then we will go to the general." I began to step out toward the Customs House, which was but a stroll away.

"No . . . he's at his quarters." The untidy major seemed at sixes and sevens. Indeed, his shirt was incompletely stowed and his waistcoat was ill buttoned. He had come out without his greatcoat. Thankfully, the nights had warmed a bit.

We waylaid a sergeant and private driving a buckboard. They were not pleased that we interrupted their business, but, then, I was not certain their purposes on the wharves in the depths of the night were fully legitimate. The sergeant complained, but complied.

And we were off, jouncing away from the Frenchy part of town. Headed for the pleasant reaches of the American side, where the houses of the gentlefolk stood primly apart from each other, shunning the intimacies of the *Vieux Carré,* where even the dwellings embraced each other wantonly.

"I need your help," I said abruptly. The very lack of comfort in the back of the little wagon seemed conducive to thought. "I believe the general will support my request."

"General Banks says you're to have anything you want."

That was a pleasant change.

"While I attend the general, go back and find me ten or a dozen soldiers. Select the most unpleasant ones you can find. Brutes, the sort you would not trust behind you. For that matter, just choose Irishmen. And place them under a vicious sergeant, the type who makes himself hated by all he rules."

I had forged a plan, see. To improve my chances of a successful visit with Mrs. Aubrey.

The major thought the request less peculiar than I expected. Perhaps he had been a long time in New Orleans.

The general received me in his nightshirt and cap, made decent by a handsome velvet robe. He still looked rather a dashing fellow, although not quite a general in his sleeping duds. But that is the usual way of things. When you strip off an officer's uniform, you always find him smaller than he seemed. Generals are especially diminished.

He had taken himself a lovely house, the parlor of which would have delighted my darling. An aide and an orderly fussed about, searching for papers and promising to cook coffee.

The general told them both to get out. And they did.

We sat in that commandeered parlor, rivals in weariness. When the sliding doors clapped shut, with a worrisome quiver of glass, he leaned toward me and ran a hand over his nightcap.

"You were right," General Banks said. He sounded as if he were tearing out his own liver as he spoke, for such admissions are painful to a general. "The paymaster was in it with Bolt, the two of them thick as thieves." He rubbed an eye and corrected himself. "Well, I guess they *were* thieves, for that matter. One of the clerks gushed it out the minute we pressed him. Just puked his guts out. Scared out of his wits he was going to be the next one to turn up dead in Jackson Square. And for all his troubles—keeping your Miss Peabody's money hidden away—the only thing that damned clerk's going to see is a prison."

"The money has been recovered, then?"

"No, damn it. Bolt has it. Made off with it first thing in the morning, bold as brass. That bastard. Look. I'm sorry. Believe me, I had no idea . . . all I was trying to do was to keep him out of trouble so his father wouldn't raise a stink with his friends in Washington. The bugger had me fooled from start to finish. I never dreamed—"

"No matter, sir. But Bolt has funds, does he?"

"A hundred and fifty thousand dollars. I damned well couldn't believe it. She was going to waste all that shipping niggers back to Africa. Hell, she could've just bought them a piece of Texas and marched them over." He snorted. "I guess that was a sum worth slitting throats over." He grunted. "And it's plenty to see Bolt down to Mexico. Where the French'll be happy to help him out, for a price."

He shaped his hands over the tops of his knees. "Apparently, he's got other money, too. From this slaving business. It seems to have been going on since last September." He pointed a finger at me. "But let me tell you this, Jones. If Bolt's anywhere in this city—or anywhere around it—we're going to find him. If I have to send out every last soldier between here and Baton Rouge, then hold up a lantern myself."

"Call them off," I told him. "Call your soldiers in."

"What?"

"Call them off, sir. They will not find him. They may do more harm than good."

"*You* know where he is?"

"No, sir. But if you give me a bit of rein, I will find him. If found he is like to be."

He thought on the proposition. "What makes you so cocksure of yourself?"

"I am not sure of myself, sir. I am only certain your soldiers will not find him. Perhaps Captain Bolt has already escaped. I cannot say. But I will do my best, then we will see."

He shrugged wearily, then shifted his person from one uncomfortable position to another that looked equally unpromising. The parlor chairs were cruel, but such is the fashion.

"What happened on the river today?" he asked as he straightened his robe.

I told him. Everything. At one point, the orderly rapped on the glass of the parlor doors, offering us coffee. Snarling, General Banks said none was wanted. Which was not completely true, for I would have valued a steaming cup myself. But generals assume that, if they do not want a thing, no one else wants it, either.

I do not wish to exaggerate, but as I told the general how the slaver burned, he paled and looked near a sickness. Offered my guess of how many cooked alive, his hands twitched in his lap.

"This . . . this can't become known," he said. "It's unthinkable."

He was a man like any other, fearful for his position. Still more than that, he saw the effect that such a tale would have upon our Union. The newspaper fellows are shameless in their pursuit of all things lurid. As if the facts were not harsh enough, they would have increased the victims a hundred-fold. To read a newspaper properly, a fellow needs sound mathematical skills. Especially the knack of long division.

Yet, I had some hope of keeping things quiet. The crew did not much care about the negroes and seemed to think the Marines had saved too many. And I had promised a special payment of prize money. While stressing that our purpose had been secret.

"Mr. Seward will not raise a fuss," I assured the general. "Nor will Mr. Lincoln. Not now. Not after I have explained matters." I set both hands atop the hilt of my cane. "I do not see any blame in this for you, sir. Nor do I expect discord from anyone else. Mr. Seward will speak to Miss Peabody's father, and he will settle things. The fellow loved his daughter, see. That is what sent me down here. But there are things no father wishes to know. Or wishes known." I monkeyed my shoulders up and down, refreshing my wakefulness. Stiff as old timber I was from the day's exertions, "But there is more to do here in New Orleans."

"For instance?"

"Mrs. Aubrey. The shipowner. She is in this deep. If not the originator of the entire scheme."

"Well, we'll arrest her. And see how she likes that."

I shook my head. "No, sir. That will not do. First, because we do not wish a public spectacle. Beyond those we have already endured. We do not want the South to win with barristers what they have not won in battle. Second, because we cannot prove a thing. And she knows it. She has been crafty, that one. We know her to be guilty, and she knows that we know it by now. But all she need do is to keep up her manners and go about her business. The witnesses are dead. There are no documents. At least, none we have discovered. Only Bolt could name her, and he's gone."

"You mean to let her go? Without a penalty?"

"No, sir. Not exactly. I hope to see justice done. I intend to visit Mrs. Aubrey tonight. In the company of soldiers. If we cannot break her story, we can at least break her furniture. I do not think she will put a claim for damages."

"That's hardly justice."

"I hope there will be more justice than that. But I must begin somewhere. I give you that I am being common and vengeful. In doing her material goods a damage. But there is a sense behind it, not mere nastiness."

"I don't care if you burn her house down, at this point. But the law has to count for something."

I shook my head again. "Burning there has been enough for one day. And for many days thereafter. I still believe the law may count for much. But I will go to her and have my say. Then we will see."

"And Bolt? You really think you can find him, Jones? That fat friend of yours involved? The Confederate?"

"He is no more a Confederate than I am, sir. But look you. New Orleans is a curious place. You cannot fight against it. For when you press in one spot, it only bulges outward in another. Our only hope is to let the city fix itself."

"That's a bit cryptic."

"Well," I said, quite cleverly, if I do say so myself, "it is a city of crypts. And, God willing, we will live to see this affair well buried."

He sighed, then yawned, then cursed. "Well, come to headquarters and see me in the morning. Tell me how Mrs. Aubrey liked your visit. Meanwhile, I intend to round up every last bastard who helped Bolt in any way, whatsoever."

"Do not arrest them, sir," I said. "There is a better way to punish the guilty."

He raised an eyebrow.

"Transfer them to fighting regiments. Take them from the comforts of the rear and send them into the lines. Let them do their part to save the Union."

He grumped a bit, but clever enough he was to see the sense of it. Making soldiers do their honest duty would do more good and make less noise than lining them up for courts-martial and having them talk.

"Well, then, if you will allow me, sir, I will go and call upon Mrs. Aubrey." I glanced out through the part in the velvet drapes. Into a darkness faintly tempered by streetlamps. "Let us call it a 'morning visit.' In keeping up our manners."

The general gave me a searching look, tired, exhausted and still far from content. "I swear to God, I don't know what to make of you, Jones. You do everything upside down and backwards. But here we are. And I'll say it again, damn it. You were right. And . . . I was wrong." He looked at me like the friendliest of enemies. "I don't suppose you've reconsidered that promotion?"

"It was not a proper promotion. It was a bribe."

"The devil you— just what the hell does that mean? Oh, forget it. I'm not going to argue with a man about what's good for him. I'm going back to sleep. If I can escape having nightmares about that slave-ship business."

He took himself off, trailing the belt of his robe and a whiff of pomade. The major had not yet returned to furnish me with the soldiers I had requested, so I wandered about the house in search of the orderly. I discovered him sound asleep by the stove in the kitchen. He did not like being disturbed, but I had no sympathy. His berth was not a hard one for a soldier.

I had him fuel the stove and heat that coffee.

eighteen

$\mathcal{G}$LASS SHATTERED AS THE soldiers broke open the door. I had not troubled Mrs. Aubrey with a tug on her bell or a rap, but ordered the sergeant to smash the lock and enter.

The soldiers, who looked a wonderfully nasty lot, rushed into the house with their lanterns and muskets, careless of any objects in their path. I had given them two instructions, and two only. First, they were to search the house for any suspicious items. I did not explain what "suspicious" might include, but simply observed that damage might not be avoidable, a suggestion they greeted warmly.

I wanted them destructive, on a rampage.

Second, I warned them sternly that they must do no harm to the servants or their possessions.

At first, the soldiers could not believe their good fortune. But their sergeant, still possessed of half his teeth, grinned and said, "Go to it, boyos. Damnation to the Rebels!"

I do not think I can describe the uproar. The crack of smashing china sang soprano, while the thump of furniture overturned sang bass. Between those two extremes of pitch, the alto and tenor of destruction followed the rhythm of boots on carpet and wood.

Do not think me converted unto barbarism. Harsh my actions were that night, but there was method in them. I wanted to penetrate Mrs. Aubrey's composure, which experience had shown to be nearly impregnable. The concert of breakage was all part of my plan.

I followed behind the leading soldiers, reminding them not to annoy the servants, a few of whom were already up and shrieking.

"Come on, lads," I bossed, speaking to the pair of privates whom I had selected for my special guard. I would not have trusted them with an orphan's stockings. "Hurry along with you, come along."

I do not believe that I have climbed a flight of stairs so swiftly since Bull Run. I vaulted over my cane, almost outracing the cast of the lantern carried by one of the soldiers.

I could not know which door led to Mrs. Aubrey's bedchamber. But she assisted me. Erect and stalwart, she stepped into the hall in her retiring costume, bearing a candle in a silver holder.

When she saw me, her glare rivaled Medusa's.

"How *dare* you?" she demanded.

"She one of the servants?" a private asked me. Twas clear he did not fancy her tone of voice.

I ignored the lad and spoke to Mrs. Aubrey.

"Stand aside, if you please, mum. We are looking into a crime."

At that, she smiled faintly, a cat recalling herself in front of a mouse.

"Would you invade a lady's intimate quarters?" she asked in a voice she had forced under control. "Even *you*, sir, should—"

"I am not certain you are much of a lady," I told her. "Step back from the door, or the soldiers will remove you."

Even as I spoke, I had a blessed flash of inspiration. I am not always utterly dull of wit.

She stood across the door-frame, defiant as Miss Fritchie of Frederick, Maryland. Although the latter served a better cause.

Mrs. Aubrey met my expectations.

"I shall *not* move," she said. "You must have the decency . . . the common decency to allow me time to dress."

I pretended to hesitate. The soldiers beside and behind me seethed at my lack of resolution. Although she did not sound much of a Southron, to them she was the sum of all New Orleans. Where they had suffered mockery enough. I think they would have beaten her to the floor, had I allowed it.

I am no skilled dissembler, but I made what show I could of weighing my course. At last, I answered. Struggling to look stern and show no smile.

"Well, then," I told her, "you shall have five minutes. But no more. Dress yourself, mum, get yourself up proper. For you and I have matters to discuss."

Oh, she thought she had me then, the witch. Begging your pardon.

Before she could shut herself back inside her bedchamber, a colored lass fought her way up the stairs and called, "Miz Aubrey, the Yankees is into the silver cab'nit and stuffin' spoons an' forks down their bee-hinds."

With a look of wondrous insolence, her mistress told her, "See that each one gets his thirty pieces."

Mrs. Aubrey slammed the door behind herself, leaving the servant girl to puzzle her meaning.

Wise enough the lass was to recognize an officer. She addressed her disquiet to me.

"All this 'mancipation don't do *me* no good. I gots to clean this up, what y'all be doing."

She trudged back down the stairs, shaking her head. The servant in every land is freedom's surveyor, taking its indisputable measurement.

The soldiers grumbled. One even asked, "You going to let that old crow just get all ignorant with us, Major? While we stand waiting on her like she's some damn queen?"

"Now, now, lads," I told them, restraining my impulse to smile. "I do not think you will be disappointed. Look you. I will stand the guard upon her door. Leave me the lantern. You may search the other bedrooms. But come when I call you."

They did not ask for further clarification, but took themselves into the neighboring rooms. You might have thought that loot would be their foremost goal, but the sounds that issued from the interiors told of pure destruction. The soldiers had enjoyed their fill of Southron haughtiness and meant to avenge each slight that had been paid them.

I never would have condoned such behavior, had I not hoped to unsettle Mrs. Aubrey. I trust you understand that. I am a friend to discipline, among soldiers and within families. Anyway, nothing that transpired that night was half so shameful as our doings in India.

Mrs. Aubrey did not consume her five allotted minutes, but emerged in hardly four, if my watch was honest. Glad I was that the cab man had not accepted it in pawn. Her haste only confirmed my inspiration.

Dressed she was, but not with her usual care. She had wiggled herself into a gown so thick and full it might have done for a ball.

"Now, sir," she said, as if she were a queen, indeed, speaking to a stinking, itching commoner, "you have the liberty of my bedroom. I trust your every interest will be satisfied."

"Thank you, mum. I'll have my look in a moment."

I called out to the lads. In my old sergeant's voice, not in the gentler tone befitting a major.

They come out into the hall with their pockets bulging. Two more come up the stairs when they heard me bark.

"Undress her," I told them.

Doubtless, they would have responded with more alacrity had she been young and fair. Or perhaps they possessed their own notions of propriety. None of them moved.

Mrs. Aubrey raised a hand to slap me.

The sergeant, who had come up to have a look-see, caught her wrist.

Mrs. Aubrey's burning eyes showed less love than a cobra's. She spit and said a thing so foul it shocked.

That was an error. Her language broke her spell over the soldiers. Two grabbed her arms and one gave her gown a rip.

They hesitated again.

"You don't . . . you mean *all* the way down, sir?" the sergeant asked.

"I will tell you when to stop."

Wise enough she was not to resist. She stood so stoutly you might have thought her one of the Oxford Martyrs.

Staring at me with a fury that would have killed and called the killing good, she did not say another word as the soldiers ripped away her velvet and lace.

As her skirts come off, a picture frame fell to the carpet. Glass tinkled and spread. Twas only a small frame, the sort we place on a table near our beds, but large enough it was to make her scream.

She found the strength to tear free of the soldiers. Shrieking, *"No!"* She hurled herself to the floor, protecting the image.

"Get her up," I said coldly.

She fought. Scratching and snapping at the lads with the teeth that still remained to her. It was no sensible strategy with ruffians. She only worsened their tempers.

How she screamed. *"No!"* Over and over again.

She bit a soldier and he slapped her face. Hard. Still she would not give the picture up.

"Stand away," I ordered. "Stand off her now. Let her go."

They were unhappy and relieved at once. As the lads took their hands away, Mrs. Aubrey cowered on her knees, weeping like a lass who has lost her sweetheart to the rival she hates most.

Against a lull in the tumult and breakage, I told her, "I know the portrait is of Mr. Champlain. Give it to me now. I will not keep it."

She wept as bitterly as Mary Magdalene upon the day they nailed Christ to the cross. Had I known any less of her cruelty, I would have pitied her much.

"Give me the portrait now," I repeated. "Or I will have the lads take it from you and your treasure may suffer a damage. Give it to me. You shall have it back before I leave."

She hesitated as if asked to give up the life of her first-born. Although that was not her relation to Mr. Champlain.

I did not say another word, but let her take her time. All but one of the soldiers soon lost interest. They took themselves off in search of more advantage.

The old woman's face—for she was reduced to nothing but an aged, broken creature—humbled itself inches from my boots. As if the weight of her tears pulled her brow to the carpet. Her hands were bleeding from the broken glass, yet she clutched the portrait as if it were alive. As if it were her only source of comfort.

"A man like you could never understand," she said.

I ALLOWED MRS. AUBREY to dress anew and recollect her composure. Meanwhile, I studied the little oil portrait of the youthful Mr. Champlain, picking away what bits of glass I could. A shame it was that the photographic image, that wonder of our age, had not been extant in the days of his youth. The painting showed a rather dashing fellow, robust and not yet corpulent.

The artist's brush must have been very fine. Despite the medium's crudity, you saw a lad intelligent and reckless, with a strong, determined forehead shadowing lips that would have suited a woman of temperament. His hair was long, in the style of my parents' day, a fashion lost but for illustrated books. It would not suit our close-hewn, modern age.

Now, you will think me addled by my newfound taste for novels, but as I studied the portrait I imagined that it captured a golden moment, a life's premature meridian, when the young man fixed in brushstrokes must have felt that all before him would be triumph. Although his sun was tipping into decline.

I do not wish to moon about the matter, but I felt that the portrait, for all the sitter's dash, foresaw some tragedy. As if the painter had realized more than young Champlain in his gilded hour of glory. Of course, artistic people, although generally unsuitable, seem to have a knack for that sort of thing.

What mattered was the question of identity, of course. For all the deformity of flesh that had accrued to Mr. Champlain over the years, you did not doubt that you saw the very same fellow.

Prince Hal had become Falstaff.

Mrs. Aubrey reemerged from her bedchamber attired in black and markedly subdued. Still, a docile viper remains a viper.

I offered her the portrait. She took it, calmly, in a hand wrapped in a handkerchief. A crust of blood formed at the edge of the cloth.

"Now we must have a talk," I told her, "the two of us."

She did not speak, but started down the stairs.

I had the sergeant gather the soldiers and drive them from the house. They clanked with booty, much enriched, though still greedy for more. They grumbled, but went out.

A private as Irish as hunger lugged a ham, into which he had already gnawed a cavity.

In the parlor, I set two chairs to rights, then placed a lantern on the floor between us. As Mrs. Aubrey took her place, the light from below gave her a devilish look. But her aspect no longer menaced. Instead, it seemed the stuff of clumsy comedy. She was a devil fit for Punch and Judy.

"You have no proof," she said cooly. "You can't prove anything. But you know that, of course. That's why you indulged in this . . . this performance."

"No, mum, there is true. I have no proof. At least none that will do for a court of law."

"Still, I underestimated you, Major Jones. The error disappoints me. It was as foolish as it was ungracious."

I glanced at the ruin around us. Convinced their luck could grow no worse, the soldiers had smashed a great mirror, as well as tearing paintings with their bayonets. The ships that had cruised her walls would sail no more. There were so many bits strewn on the floor it looked like the Apocalypse in Staffordshire.

"Well, we are quits," I lied. "Woman or no, I would hang you if the law allowed me to do it. But I have taught you a lesson, there is that much, and you will not engage in such trade again. We will be watching, mind." I gestured toward the wreckage. "And you will have this evening to remember me by."

"It must be a great annoyance," she said, become the cat to my mouse again. "That you can prove nothing."

"It will not annoy me long. I have done enough, see."

"How did you know? Did *he* tell you?"

"No, mum. He did not tell me. Although enough was said to help me onward."

She shook her head. Somberly. Unpainted, her cheeks looked hollowed by the tomb.

"I didn't know he hated me so much," she sighed. "Even now."

"Whatever did you do to him?" I asked carefully. "It is curious I am."

"I broke his heart," she said matter-of-factly. As if she spoke of spilling a cup of tea. She appeared to meet my eyes, but her thoughts had flown. "He was an absurdly romantic young man, you understand. Completely impractical." She smiled with half her mouth. "He wanted me to run away with him. To South America. He was going to join some revolution or other and carve us a kingdom from the Spanish empire. That was forty years ago. No. Longer."

She tilted her skull to the side. "Frankly, he was an ass. If an endearing one. Comical, really. He was a strong young man who imitated the weakness fashionable in Europe some years before. But his . . . energies . . . were very much of this earth." Her smile grew, though not nicely. "He affected to like the most execrable poetry. All fairies and airiness, love beyond the grave. I found it common of him."

Her voice warmed half a degree. "He had a blue coat and buff pantaloons made for himself, in imitation of some fool in a German novel. He was hardly *à la mode*. Such gestures belonged to a previous generation even then. But he was always in love with the past, you see. At least with the past as he imagined it. The trait is not unusual among the people of this city." Her rasp hinted a sigh. "He did cut rather a figure, I grant him that. The country girls were mad for him."

She looked away, into the relentless past. "But he was mad for me. That was his tragedy. If so elevated a word suits his situation. He loved *me*. But his family had fallen terribly low. I could not take his offer of marriage seriously, no matter how avidly—and repeatedly—he pressed it. I was a few years the elder and had some sense of the world. I wanted a future, Major Jones, not merely a past. You've seen his house? His 'mansion'? He hasn't made a repair in forty years. And his family did nothing for twenty years before that. It just rots away. Emblematic, I should say. He's turned himself into a creature of ridicule, a grotesque masquerading as a *Vieux Carré* eccentric."

The skirts of her dress shifted all of their own, as if an invisible weight had become insufferable. She rearranged them with a practiced hand. "But I didn't know he still hated me so deeply. I should have thought him given more to revery. With his bent for the romantic, for the maudlin."

"And so you married Captain Aubery?"

"*Admiral* Aubrey. But no. That was later, you see. When I had grown even more realistic. I first married Eugène Charboneaux, a promising man who had read sufficient law to understand its weaknesses. He might have done great things, Major Jones. Really, he was a perfectly suitable companion. Family, some wealth, charm . . . and good sense. He died of smallpox while in Cartagena, pursuing a claim. You see, Major Jones, in death and business we always have looked southward. Never to the north."

"And Admiral Aubrey?"

She waved her wounded hand. A loose end of handkerchief fluttered. "Great wealth and great age combine wonderfully in a man. His person wasn't intolerable."

Yes, wealth. "Why do it, then?" I asked her. "Why risk so much, when you already own such wealth? Why sell human beings back into slavery? God forgive you."

"I shall take my chances with God. Whom I have always suspected of inattention. As for your 'human beings' . . . really, Major Jones! If cant were a capital offense, you would hang long before I might. Can you truly believe that negroes are our equal? That they are fully developed in their faculties? In their intelligence? In their feelings?" She looked askance at the follies of the world. "Of course not. You don't believe it for an instant. You're merely conforming to a transitory fashion."

She rolled her eyes in a most unladylike manner. "As for their 'abilities' . . . they imitate us like monkeys, like clever apes. Pretending to feel affection. Or pain. Really, Major Jones, I've had dogs who felt more profoundly. Slavery is a blessing for them. It frees them of the need to fend for themselves. Which they could never do in a civilized country."

Raising an eyebrow as if raising a teacup, she continued, "As for your Miss Peabody's ludicrous notion—advanced to her by a nigger—of sending them back to Africa, why, they'd be eaten by their fellows in a fortnight. If any blame attaches to us, it's only that we've unfitted them for their native realm and spoiled them. Yet, they'll never be more than servants to our race. Of course, the servant's lot must be greatly preferred over the squalor of the jungle, the life among beasts." Her aged face judged mankind. "I think them quite fortunate, all in all."

She smiled. "As for any risk attached to my ventures . . . I haven't come off so badly. Do you think? I had already determined to replace my furnishings, from Paris, now that commerce between nations has been restored to us. You've simply quickened my resolve."

"You lost a ship. Today. The *Anne Bullen*. Burned on the river. You lost that much, at least. Even if the lives aboard meant nothing to you."

Her smile was as cruel as a three-sided bayonet. "No such vessel has ever been on my lists."

"But *why*? Why do it? When you're already so wealthy?"

"My dear Major Jones! A man accustomed to wealth himself would never ask such a question. Wealth is the only joy that never palls."

"Well," I said, in sourness only half-feigned, "you have your wealth, mum. But if you try such a business in the future, you may not fare so well. Our authorities will keep an eye on you, from now on. Your every venture will be scrutinzed. Twice over."

"I should be disappointed, were it otherwise."

I left her that way. Smug, and convinced that she had triumphed over me. That the only price she had to pay was a few broken chairs and torn draperies, some moments of shame and the loss of the household silver.

The proof, if any more were needed, that I was not fit for the work assigned me was that I understood what was to come. And I did nothing to stop it. She did not reckon how much her world had changed, that all her wealth could no longer protect her. The ranks of her world had broken, and all that remained was a series of rearguard actions against the future. I do not mean that the rich could no longer dominate, but that they had to do so by new rules. She did not see it. But I did.

Mrs. Aubrey thought only of the law, and not of justice. Like that first husband of whom she had spoken, who knew enough of the law to spy out its weaknesses. But there were parties in her city who would not rest until they had found justice. And war will cover much, as her own doings should have warned her.

Were I the man I long professed to be, I would have stopped it. I always thought that I cherished the law. And yet

I walked away, convinced that the law would be broken and that justice would take its course.

Now you will say: "Who are we to determine what is just?" I know the argument. I even believe it. And yet I walked away from Mrs. Aubrey's door that night, rejoining the merry soldiers in their wagon.

I had seen the ham, but had not spied the bottle.

They thought me a splendid fellow, for an officer. I did not reprimand them in the least, nor did I question the sacks they bore or the bulges in their pockets. That, too, was wrong of me. For an army is but a mob when it loses its discipline. I broke that rule, too, for that one night.

The news followed me back to Washington and beyond. Mrs. Aubrey was dead within two months. The negroes had been far too wise to kill her in her bed or in her own parlor. She was found with her throat slit wide and deep, in the ladies' retiring salon of one of the grandest houses in the city.

But I have more to tell you of New Orleans.

nineteen

THE EXTERIOR OF MR. CHAMPLAIN'S manse was illumined as if for a ball. The torches would have done equally well to fend off the miasma of a fever year. Queer it is how joy and grief ask similar tributes of us.

I told the cab man to wait. Thankfully, he was not Irish and truculent.

The servant named Horatio announced me and Constantine guided me in. Mr. Champlain sat on his throne as usual, in the center of the room, at the eye of his world. His flesh no longer spoke of lordly appetites, but of ruin. Youth, health, vigor, all had been vanquished. I had thought him a glutton, of course, and had been wrong. What he had done to his person down the decades must have taken a discipline no less than that of the anchorite in the desert, the saint gone awry.

He grinned, as he did always. "Major Jones! Been expecting you! Come right in, *cher*, come on in. Take a seat. My, my, that salve does work wonders! You look fit for a nibble, keep an old man company. Sit down, sit down!"

I sat.

"Simon-Peter?" he called to yet another liveried fellow. "Where are those *beignets*? Bring another cup for the major's coffee."

I almost told him that I wished no refreshment. But it would have been a lie. Besides, I had come to suspect that I placed too much importance on easy sacrifices, such as declining a mug of coffee, instead of facing weightier concerns. And rudeness is the least useful form of selfishness.

"Yes, Major Jones, I *have* been expecting you. Tonight, tommorow night . . . knew you'd stop by to pay your respects. And I am honored, *cher,* profoundly honored, that you feel at home enough to come on over all by yourself. Not that Mr. Barnaby isn't welcome, acourse—you're feeding him better, I hope?"

"You lied to me," I said.

He smiled indulgently. "Now, you're just heated up. You know that isn't true. I won't deny a certain amount of . . . of going at things roundabout. But a man takes the course he thinks best and—"

"Had you spoken to me forthrightly, many lives would have been saved."

Constantine, the servant who seemed the chief of the lot, never flinched. Of course, that is the servant's proper attitude. Mr. Champlain paid the fellow no regard, either. Nor did he allow the reappearance of Simon-Peter with a tray of food and drink to interdict the flow of our conversation.

"Well, now . . . I'd say you're assuming a great deal, sir, a great deal. I knew some things. Didn't know others. But I did have the sense to point you where you needed to go. I will accept that blame, *cher,* if blame has to fall upon my head. Don't be shy now, have a little feed. You won't get *beignets* like that the other side of Canal Street, let alone back up North. Men eat together, they can hold on to their civility that much easier. Simon-Peter, if that coffee's not warm enough for the major, you go on down and get us up another pot."

The servant poured, the coffee steamed. I drank.

"I was saying, Major Jones . . . you've been in this city long enough to know that nobody knows everything. Damnation, none of us even know half of what we think we do. Five men living along Villere going to give you six different answers, you ask them a simple question. Been living here all my life and I don't know the half."

"You used me."

He frumped his grandly padded chin and nodded. Flesh rippled downward. "Now, that's another thing entirely, *cher*. Acourse I used you. I won't deny it. And you used me. Didn't you? We enjoyed ourselves a transaction of mutual benefit. That's the thing you have to understand about us down here . . . we take it for granted that life is made up of using other people. Instead of being hypocrites about it, we put some manners on it. Try to do it gracefully, if not graciously. Folks down here have realistic expectations of their fellow man. Say nothing of their fellow woman." He grinned, with a dough-ball suspended before his mouth. "You got what you wanted. Now, didn't you?"

Yes, I had gotten what I wanted. But I had not wanted it to be gotten so.

He barely chewed the treat, but swallowed eagerly. His breast was littered with crumbs and dusted with sugar.

He touched the corner of his mouth with a napkin. Which was not immaculate.

"That's the thing about New Orleans, now. It's a *generous* city. Give you what you want before you hardly know to ask for it. Trouble is, acourse, that many a man wants a number of things that aren't particularly good for him. And those sorts of things are a New Orleans specialty." He lofted another ball of dough. Indeed, they were so light they almost floated. Only the snow of sugar weighed them down. "Like these *beignets* here. Delicious. And bad for you in just about every way there is. But New Orleans is going to give you all of them you want. Yes, sir. Unto a surfeit, Major Jones. Unto a surfeit . . ."

He ate and smiled. A dab of powdery sugar adhered to his nose. "Many's the man who leaves us sadder, but wiser." He dusted himself with his napkin again and added, "I'd say, you should be a happy man, *cher*. You're getting up from the table with all your winnings. Seems to me, our fair city's been good to you."

"Do you know what happened on the river today?"

"No. And I don't want to know. See, now. I collect facts. It's like collecting buttons. You don't have to do a thing with 'em, you don't want to. Facts are no bother. But too much outright knowledge makes a man uncomfortable. Simon-Peter, the major looks to me to want more coffee. And the truth is, I'm going to be cautious around you from now on. Careful as a poor relation in the visiting parlor. I didn't take you for a fool. I'm not this old for nothing. But I will admit to misapprehending the degree of your cleverness."

He smiled again, for that was his natural state, no matter the emotional climate. "Oh, it's another failing of ours, you won't have to draw a pistol to get me to admit it. No, sir. We all think we're just clever as old Talleyrand, Fouché and Marie the butcher's wife all balled up into one. Truth is that we're not so much clever as intricate. This is an *intricate* city. To the outsider, it passes for a clever one. But that's only because it has more layers than a twenty-dollar whore has petticoats. We make passing the time of day as slow and complicated as an audience with Louis XIV. Damnation, now, we were clever we never would have mixed ourselves up in this fool's war."

He would have talked all night, if I had let him. Talked, but said nothing. Along with food, talk was his remaining joy.

"And Miss Peabody? Can you say that you did not lie about her? With your suggestions that she . . . misbehaved?"

"Oh, now. I was only describing the possible avenues of behavior open to the ladies here in New Orleans. I spoke philosophically."

"You implied she was a . . . that she was given over to immorality."

"Did I? I don't recall exactly. Acourse, we may have different understandings of immorality. If you mean that I suspected her of a less than perfect decorum by *your* standards . . ."

"Admit that you blackened her name. By suggestion."

He began to find me tiresome. His smile failed. "Major Jones . . . has anybody ever told you that there are things in this life you really don't want to know? Has anyone ever whispered that in your ear? Have they, now? As for Miss Peabody, the truth is that none of us will ever know everything that happened—or that didn't happen—with the doors shut and the shutters closed up tight. But never underestimate the appetite of the female. Pretend she is a doll, and she'll devour you."

"That is no answer."

"See, now. You know what the difference is between a handsome woman and a plain one? Besides the obvious? It's just this, *cher*; the beauty gets to take her pick of follies. But the plain girl has to seize the folly that's offered her. She may never get another chance."

"Not all women choose folly. Do not judge the female race by Mrs. Aubrey."

His smile returned, but now it was a small thing. "I knew we were coming around to her."

"Was she the doll who devoured you?"

He laughed and slapped his girth. "Does it look like any woman on earth could swallow me up?"

His laughter had a brittle, desperate sound.

"You said yourself," I reminded him, "that the people of New Orleans are endlessly curious. But curiosity is not a local matter. I am curious, too. I like a story that has a proper ending. Tell me about Mrs. Aubrey and I will go."

He twisted his mouth like a rag that wanted wringing. But he did not answer.

"Why did you bring her down after all these years?" I demanded. "How many was it? Forty?"

"Forty-two."

"You waited forty-two years for a lover's revenge?"

His eyes hunted down the pink swells of his cheeks. "Nothing's ever quite that simple. Yes, I waited. But I didn't know exactly what I was waiting for. Until she began her business with the negroes. Selling them back into slavery. Yes, sir, I knew about that. Didn't take Descartes to figure it out. I knew that much, I admit it. And it offended me, *cher*. It offended me to a degree you will not credit. Because you know only a little of me." He smiled again, almost merrily. "And I'm a big man, as you can see. Based on size alone, I take some getting to know."

"She broke your heart?"

He let those words sink through the floor until their echo seemed dead and forgotten. Then he surprised me with the smallness of his new voice. "I broke my own heart. Fool that I was. God knows what she told you herself . . . Jane Aubrey does like to rearrange things. Fact is, yes, I loved that woman. But I *chose* to do so. At first. I loved the idea of loving a married woman—she was just a few years off the boat from England. Yes, sir. The much-heralded English rose. Her mother had married a New Orleans man—second marriage—and she brought Jane along. Married her off, quick as could be, to Gene Charboneaux. Not a bad man. And not a good man. Crooked as Satan in a poker game, but he had the gift of making himself good company. Even while he stole you blind. Told myself I would rescue that damsel from a thief and a liar. And I failed to understand that I was turning myself into a liar and a thief. I pursued her, Major Jones. I don't deny it. But, frankly, it wasn't much of a hunt."

He looked at me with flesh-smothered eyes. "Truth is, she *wasn't* a beauty. Though she had a little something. By God, I swear I didn't see it coming. Just thought I was in for a little dalliance, something out of a book. But once I got the ball in play, Jane took over the game. *She* fell in love with me. Like the lash of a whip and the burning of the flames So wild it frightened me. I'd just been playing, *cher.* But she raised the stakes higher than I knew they could go."

He scratched an ear with the quick strokes employed by a hound. "Oh, I'd filled her up with all sorts of crazy, romantic tales. I was in love with romance, *cher* . . . much more so than with any flesh-and-blood woman. Told her I was going to carry her off to South America, set up a kingdom amid the revolutions, make her a queen. Child's nonsense. Silliness, and nothing but. Just me talking for the sound of my own voice. But Jane hung on every word."

He twitched at a sharp-edged memory. "I got what I wanted, Major Jones. Yes, I did. That's the tragedy of it. I got what I wanted. Once in my life. And it ruined my life. Thing is, once . . . once she gave herself to me . . . once it wasn't a fine dream anymore, but something real and mean around the edges of all that glory . . . *then* she started closing herself off. She was the romantic one, see. I was play-acting, but she was the real article. The romantic kind that prefers a dream to imperfect flesh and blood, to sweat and bone. I didn't see it coming, not for an instant. Once she made me truly fall in love with her, so hard it was like being smashed on rocks every minute of the day . . . once that happened, she slammed her door in my face. Said she couldn't love me, after all. That what happened between us was only 'a little error of the heart,' as the French say. That she had a husband, responsibilities. All the things women say when the truth is impossible."

He twitched again. "Poor Gene Charboneaux had a miserable end. Miserable. I wasn't the only one, you see. Just the first. Far as I know. But, God almighty, I did love that woman. Ruined my life."

His eyes were no longer with me. "I have many failings, *cher*. Vices in the multitudes. But I never could quite destroy what I felt for that woman. Nothing like her. Nothing on earth, or in Heaven. Scorch you like the fires of Hell, then just get up and walk away."

He took up a ball of dough, then set it down again, untasted. "Talking immortal love, until she had you convinced, until you believed it yourself. Then, once she had you on your knees, she'd just walk away. Counting her money. Only thing she ever really loved, I do believe. Maybe it was the only thing she trusted." Muddling layers of chin, he shook his head. "Couldn't kill it, what I felt for her. Just couldn't kill it. So I never married. Just could not do a thing that cruel to another woman. Not that it doesn't happen all the time. But I claim my own peculiar sense of honor. Might even say I cling to it. Thought Jane might marry me after old Gene was gone, but I never even got to ask her. She married that poor fool Aubrey before Gene was half-way in the ground. Richest fool that ever sailed up this river. Killed him, too.

Acourse, he was a sailor and the Lord knows what he brought to the marriage bower. Besides his money. God knows, that woman loves money. I hope to God, I pray to God, she's found out just how much good it does a body."

Although it all sounded a terrible muck to me—and I could not think nice thoughts of Mrs. Aubrey—we are made to engage our fellow man, to offer comfort.

I said, "The queer thing, Mr. Champlain, is that she loves you. Even now. But you must know that."

I was not prepared for the outburst. Bricks shook and mortar crumbled.

"Then why didn't she come away with me, the damned whore?"

I had to let the air calm. Twas acrid as the smell of exploded gunpowder.

He wept before me, an old, misshapen man. Shedding tears in front of his servants, which I do not think is done.

"I would've taken her to the ends of the earth! To Heaven or Hell. Instead, she ruined our lives. It was stubbornness. Nothing but damned stubbornness. And fear. She was afraid of love, when it came back at her. Didn't trust it. That's the sin and the shame of it. She didn't trust love. Only money."

"This very night," I said, still hoping to soothe him, "I saw her cling to your portrait."

He looked at me as if I understood nothing, and never would.

"It's easier to love a portrait than a man," he said.

I COULD NOT sort it out and no longer wished to. I took me back to my hotel and slept. Doubtless snoring like Mr. Irving's Dutchman.

Is anything more tangled up than love? At times, I think it is our greatest blessing. Then I see it wielded as a curse.

We are strange beasts. After the day and night I had passed, you would have thought me fated for mad nightmares. Perhaps of my mother, or of my loss in India. Of burning men, of Hell, of spoiled lives. But after saying my prayers and giving my face a wash, I slept as soundly as a babe on laudanum.

A knock upon the door of my room awakened me. Twas a bell clerk, sent from below. He bore a silver platter, upon which lay a single visiting card.

"Waiting for you down to the lobby," the lad told me, before I even had time to read the name. "He says how I'm to ask if'n he can come up."

The card announced H. BEYLE.

Roused from a mighty slumber, I could not place the name. I stood there in my nightshirt, trying to gain some purchase on the world, and only woke up properly when a gentleman passed and deplored my impropriety.

The insult was just, but smarted. Then I remembered the person who was H. Beyle.

Twas that ancient Frenchman from the shop. Come to collect his payment for the stick. Like the Devil himself come round collecting souls.

My first impulse was childish. I wanted to hide the cane.

Of course, I did no such thing. I stepped back into my room and returned with a nickel for the bell-clerk. He did not seem as pleased as he should have been.

"Send a body to collect my night pot," I told him. "And ask Mr. Beyle to allow me fifteen minutes. Then he may come up, see."

The lad was just short of insolent. And no one appeared to take away my night pot, which I feared might leave the room seeming unpleasant. I barely had time to shave in cold water and pull on my shirt and trousers before the Frenchman rapped on my door.

I dreaded what was to come. For I did not want to give up the cane, but feared that he would ask an exhorbitant price. Through all the tumult of the past days, I had debated with myself how much I might pay without becoming a fool. For though we may be blessed with money now, we will not have it long if we are wasteful.

The only good fortune I saw in the situation was that I had less than fifty dollars in hand, the remnant of my borrowing from the Navy. Any sum agreed would need to be fetched, giving me time to amend impulsive behavior.

I told myself I might go as high as one hundred dollars in bargaining. Then I added another fifty. Although the sum was mindlessly extravagant for even the finest blade in a shaft of wood.

I wondered if Mr. Beyle would ask for more.

They are a nasty, greedy lot, the French.

The fellow was exactly as I remembered him, crooked over like a human question mark, with a narrow face deployed between permanently raised brows and a mouth that never quite closed. His white hair was too long for a proper gentleman.

He had got himself up dapper, though, for his visit. My Mary has always been a gifted seamstress and I learned enough of such matters from her to recognize that his clothing had been cut for his crippled form by a master's hand.

"Ah, *Monsieur le Major!*" he cried. "But have I come too early? It is ten."

Good Lord, it was. I *had* slept like Rip Van Winkle.

"Come you in, then, Mr. Beyle," I said, accepting his

hand. It slid in and out of mine as if he feared a hurt. "Sit you down. I think that chair is the pleasantest."

"*Merci, merci*. But your face is much improved, I think. You have not so much the toothache now, the damage? *Bon!* But then you will be in better spirits than you were upon our first *rencontre!*"

I wondered if that meant he would charge me more. Or try to. I put on a strict expression, almost dour.

"But you realize, of course, why I have come?"

"For payment."

"Yes, that is true. How I wish I could report to you that I am making a social call! But men must attend to their business. Only then can friendship . . . but what would you say? Blossom."

I wondered if the price would blossom, too.

"How much?" I asked.

"Ever so blunt! So much the Anglo-Saxon! But I think the Welsh are not Anglo-Saxon, yes? But you live side by side with them, of course, so you have become the same. I see that I have awakened you, you must pardon me. Perhaps you have not had your morning coffee? But I think the soldier always rises at dawn!"

Before dawn, if the soldier is a wise one.

"Well, I do not wish to detain you unnecessarily," I told him. Having slept late, I felt the press of the day. "Tell me your price, sir."

"I fear to tell it. It is very high, I think."

My heart sank. I really did want that cane.

"How much is 'high,' then?" My voice quivered as I spoke. And not only because I wanted coffee.

"It is high, but I think you can pay this price. Perhaps . . . as you are a man of honor . . . I think it is a price you will be glad to pay."

When those who wish to sell you a thing call you a man of honor, it is generally prelude to an attempted theft.

"Look you, Mr. Beyle. I am resolved to pay no more than . . . a hundred seventy-five dollars." I considered his face, then added, "That is, I meant to say one-hundred *eighty*-five dollars. I misspoke."

He whisked my offer away "But that is nothing, *monsieur*! I did not come to bargain."

Then what the bloody blue blazes *had* he come for? I nearly asked him in those very words.

"But I see that you still do not understand," he continued. "So I will explain. It is not the money of which I speak. I tell you already that the cane is yours. It has welcomed you into its history. It has chosen you. I could not take it back. It would be impossible!"

I did not trust a single word he said. Though even in that moment, I could not quite dislike him. Twas only that I could not make him out.

"The cane is yours," he repeated. "I do not ask a price, that is not the word. I ask a favor. That is better. A favor that I think will not bring harm to you."

I did not like the sound of that. Perhaps he wanted some sort of letter to help him pass his contraband through customs. I was about to set him straight about my code of morals and the difference between myself and the local citizens, when he leaned forward. Narrow he was as a child's cut-out toy

"*Entre nous, Monsieur le Major,* our mutual friend, *Monsieur le* Barnaby, is in danger. He has alarmed . . . certain elements . . . not only by his relationship with you, you understand, but through the matter upon which you have been engaged. I do not pretend to know every *détail* . . . but I have heard whispers. He has stepped on the toes, as you say. Toes he has not even seen. I think there is more to affairs than you understand. More than is meant to be understood. Once you are gone, he will not last the month. He has not been sensible. Always, he has known the *noir*. For so many years, he has made friends with the negroes. But always before he is discreet. Above all, that is what New Orleans asks! The discretion. In public, you must take the proper side. He has chosen the wrong one this time."

He gripped me with a gnarled, slow, tortured hand. "You must take him away! That is what I ask! You must make him believe that he must go. Please. This is the thing I ask of you. Not for the cane. For your friend—I think he is a friend to you, as well? As he has been to me?"

"But . . . this is his home."

The Frenchman made a pouty mouth, as if addressing a child. "*Monsieur le Major!* But I think you are a man of the world, *non*? As is Mr. Barnaby. As I once was myself. No, no! This is not his home. His home will be where he loves. Is it not so with you, *mon pauvre frère*?"

"My home is in Pottsville, Pennsylvania," I informed him.

My tone verged on the disdainful, but he surprised me with his reply. Old he was, but not entirely foolish.

"But is that not because your wife is there? Is there not a part of you that lingers elsewhere, perhaps? The cane . . . it chooses the wanderers, I think."

"Well, then, the cane is mistaken, sir. I intend to return to Pottsville and to stay there. I have had enough of the great, wide world."

"But, *monsieur*! Perhaps the world has not had enough of you? We cannot always choose such things for ourselves. But we will not argue. This is not the important thing. The cane . . . it is not impatient. It can wait in a chest for a generation, even longer. As you have seen. But will you take *Monsieur le* Barnaby with you? To your Pottsville?"

"You are not jesting? You believe he will be killed?"

The old Frenchman looked at me. "He has enemies you cannot imagine. Enemies *he* cannot imagine. He has crossed lines wiser men do not approach."

"But what if he won't go?"

"Then you and I will have done our parts, *Monsieur le Major*. As his friends. But he will go. You will persuade him. I know this."

He drew out his watch from his waistcoat, feigned shock at the hour, then said, in studied haste, "*D'accord?* We are agreed?"

"I will do what I can," I said honestly. In truth, I had already begun to shape my arguments to present to Mr. Barnaby. Nor were they weak ones, for he himself had given me the advantage.

"But you must not tell him we have spoken of this," Mr. Beyle added. "He is a proud man, *le* Barnaby. If told he is under threat of death, he would feel compelled to stay. As a matter of honor, of the courage."

"I shall not need to tell him."

He extended his frail hand again. "But this is very good of you! I think the cane has chosen wisely. You are a true *gentilhomme, Monsieur le Major*. Although I think you wear many disguises? To confuse the world?"

He made to leave, not having asked for a dollar. I wondered if he was really French at all.

"I would have helped Mr. Barnaby, anyway," I said belatedly. "I do not want payment for it." Then I said a thing hard on a Welshman. "I'd like to pay you, see. For the cane."

He turned again and smiled with amber teeth. "But, *monsieur,* I am old! What shall I buy with your money?"

"But you're a merchant!"

"I would say rather . . . that I engage in trade. If I may double the meaning, as we do in French. I give one thing, I ask another. It is not always money, you see. Sometimes I wish a little change in the world. At other times . . . I do a thing for my amusement."

"I tried to come round to your shop to pay you." I felt vaguely dishonest, recalling my parsimonious thoughts. "But I couldn't find it."

He whisked the world away again. "Ah, but it's a *very* hard shop to find . . . *très difficile.* I have a limited clientele these days, very exclusive, *monsieur. À bientôt!* "

"Wait!"

He turned from the door with a look more bemused than impatient. Although he made it clear he wished to leave.

"I must ask . . . surely, Mr. Beyle . . . that tale you told about the cane . . . about the canes, I mean . . . with the Italians and the old Arab and that young Frenchman . . . you don't really believe any of it, do you?"

His smile was not unfriendly, but neither was it for me. I could not figure it.

"You must let an old man have his stories," he said.

I WOULD HAVE liked to sit down to a proper breakfast, but the morning was already pressing noon and it seemed I would have to content myself with a later repast.

To my dismay, I did not enjoy that meal, either.

No sooner was I properly dressed—with the night pot still uncollected—than Mr. Barnaby come round, thumping on my door like a human battering ram.

He did not wait to step inside to share his news. Glancing up and down the hall to insure we were alone, he cried, "We got 'im, Major Jones! And he ain't pleased."

"Bolt, you mean?"

"None other, sir, none other!"

I drew him inside my room and shut the door.

"The negroes found 'im, they did, sir," he said breathlessly. "Cornered 'im like a rat in a leaded pantry. I think we ought to fetch 'im before they kills 'im."

twenty

$\mathcal{W}$E HAD BARELY locked away January, but you would have thought the day had been stolen from April. New Orleans had cast off the cold. Unmarred by clouds, a manly sun shone down on drowsy nature, impatient with her languor. Even the ramshackle dwellings by the roadside looked hospitable. When we paused at guardposts, the soldiers were alert and almost gay.

That handsome day was but a flirt. We knew it. But we were tired of the haggard winter and did not mind a tease, if prettily done.

Twas almost warm enough to summon flies.

We rode in an old-fashioned coach, not a hired cab. With the window leathers rolled up, the air caressed us. An old colored fellow drove steadily, as if he knew the measure of all things, and I did not ask Mr. Barnaby how he had commandeered our conveyance. I already knew enough to more than sate me. I wanted to make an end, even of knowledge.

I had jotted a note to General Banks before we left the city. Promising I would bring back Captain Bolt, if practicable. I gave no further details, for I wished no troublesome help.

Perhaps I already sensed what I would do.

Our destination was a ruined plantation, impoverished before the war began and then abandoned by some cavalier who rushed to battle instead of paying his debts. Mr. Barnaby told the story in all its tawdry details, the family ravished by pride and speculation, the mistress stunned by poverty and the daughters left unwed. Listening to his narration, I wondered if the family of that Rupert of the South had been much aggrieved to learn of the master's death in a cavalry spat.

But let that bide. I had another matter to resolve. Before we arrived at the scene of Bolt's captivity.

Mr. Barnaby overflowed with tales as we rattled along. Each shuttered dwelling seemed to have a name, in French or Spanish. Each name then had a reason. And each reason summed a long parade of foibles. Every family had a tangled history, whelping lions and alley cats in turn. Those who lacked a heritage invented one. It hardly mattered, as long as the fable pleased. Wealth and style could buy a past acceptable to the present. Just as poverty cancelled every glory.

When Mr. Barnaby paused at the sight of barren fields and brown water, I seized the opening.

"I have been thinking, Mr. Barnaby."

He looked my way with an almost-startled expression. Reality was humble cloth compared to the rich brocade of recollection.

"I should like you to come with me to Pennsylvania," I told him. "I have a business proposition for you, see. Pottsville lacks a proper outfitter for gentlemen. The rich go all the way to Philadelphia. Those who hope to become rich go to Reading. Pottsville is only good for woolen stockings and spare collars. I believe a well-run haberdasher's would return a handsome profit to all concerned."

Mr. Barnaby looked surprised. And doubtful.

I did not wish him to speak. Not yet. So I continued, "We would be partners, you and I. You would run the business, while I would supply the capital." I leaned toward him for emphasis. "New Orleans will not recover for years to come. If at all. The tales you tell yourself suggest the city has more past than it has future. But Pottsville is growing rich. Wise men will grow rich with it. The future of this country lies in the North, in coal and industry."

"That's very kind, sir, terrible kind. But I couldn't go."

"And why is that?"

"First off, sir, you understands that Magdalena wants looking after. I 'as 'er placed with a most respectable ladyfriend. For the period of 'er convalescence, as they say. Which I 'opes will not be long. And . . . and I know you 'as complicated feelings about such matters. But I intends to wed 'er, to make Miss Magdalena Mrs. Barnaby. If she'll 'ave me, sir."

I was not as shocked as the poor fellow expected. Indeed, I was hardly surprised. Still, I asked, as a friend must, "Won't that be risky?"

He all but exploded. With emotion, not with anger. "Oh, Major Jones! If any risk's worth taking, ain't it love? When a fellow's lucky enough to love a body what loves 'im back, shouldn't 'e plunge ahead? Shouldn't 'e dive off the cliff and take 'is chances?" He shook his head. "I should be an awful coward, if I didn't."

His eyes sought a connection beyond the ordinary. "I always says to myself, I does, that I'd rather love and end up broken-'earted, than never know the joys of love at all. Do I regret those sweet years with Marie? No, sir, not for a minute! Not for all the pain what come after she and our little babes met Yellow Jack. Sometimes I think love's all what keeps us going, begging your pardon. It's the only thing as makes this 'ard life soft for even a blink. No, sir, love ain't a risk. It's a necessity, it is. God would've made us different, if we was meant to be alone. But 'e made us so we're only 'appy together."

"Then . . . then you must bring your wife to Pottsville."

The words had escaped my lips before I could regulate them. I sat astonished at the thing I said.

Mr. Barnaby pondered. As if my offer might have some merit, after all.

"Well," he said, "I supposes that . . . given as 'ow certain aspects of 'er person is complicated—and I'll say no more, sir, I'll say no more—I suppose, speaking theoretical, that if a person 'ad traces of colored blood, as they say some does . . . said person would 'ave a better chance in the North. Are negroes and such welcome, Major Jones?"

That was a question greater than myself. The truth is that I did not like the answer I feared might be the honest one.

"Things are a bit confused," I allowed. "With the war, see. People . . . do not know their own minds. That is to say . . ." I reached inside and found a winning compromise. "Look you. We will give her out as a Spanish lady, your bride. It would not be a lie. Not exactly. For she is from the Spanish isles and speaks the tongue. Does she not? After a sort, I mean. And she is pale enough to pass for a Spaniard . . ."

He did not look convinced.

"Look you," I said, a bit irritably, "this is America. We can re-fashion ourselves according to circumstance. I have done it myself. In a manner of speaking. If we have the will, we can leave the past behind. And plenty of men have a past that is worth the leaving. Women, too. It would not be a lie, exactly, to claim your wife was Spanish in her origins. Who would know? Would you be more welcome in New Orleans?

A white man married to a woman seen to have negro blood?"

"I didn't mean to stay 'ere in New Orleans, sir. Not very long. Only until Lieutenant Raines comes back and I seen 'im established proper. I 'as a mind to go to Argentina. They wants people down there. And they speaks Spanish."

I played my trump. I will not beg your forgiveness for the gambling reference, for I was trying to save a good man's life.

"Lieutenant Raines will not be returning to the South," I told him. "Not until the war is over."

For the first time in our acquaintance, his rage rose up at me. He reared like a bull provoked, filling the carriage. I feared he would speak words he would regret.

"Hear me out!" I commanded. "You will listen until I am finished. If you wish my help at all with Lieutenant Raines. I intend to keep my promise, see. I shall do all in my power to see him released from his prison camp. But I will *not* have him paroled back to the South." I frowned to lend authority to my words. "Don't be a fool! You know the lad. Even with his parole signed, he would let himself be talked into serving again in some foolish manner. Lucky he was to be captured and not killed, as things stand now. He is the sort of lad whom war devours. The Confederacy would waste his life, while sparing men far worse. If I can gain his parole, Mr. Barnaby, I will insist that he remain in the North for the war's duration. It will be written into his papers, with his honor as his bond."

I tried to remain severe and avoid a smile, for I felt my argument closing like a trap. "Now, if you had a prosperous shop in Pottsville . . . perhaps I could find employment for young Raines. Nothing beneath his dignity. Or beneath the dignity he imagines for himself. We may see him safely through the war, you and I." With unnecessary meanness, I added, "If he is still alive, there in his prison camp."

"But—"

"There you have it, Mr. Barnaby. I will not be the instrument of the lad's death. And if he is returned southward, he will die. One way or the other. His father will not protect him. On the contrary, from what you yourself once told me of the father and his pride in his Richmond post, he would only plague the son. Listen, would you? Their cause is lost. Unless the North gives up, which is not likely. The blood already spilled has made men bitter. They will not shy from spilling oceans more. The Southrons have not discouraged the North. That is a bedtime tale for wounded pride. They have awakened the North to its power. And all the vanity of the Southron gentry will not stamp further armies from the earth, nor will it call factories for armaments from thin air. They cannot win, but can only delay defeat until they have ruined themselves and all they champion. You know it as well as I do. The North grows rich, the South grows poor, and the difference grows by the day. This war may drag on for another year. Mayhaps two. And the bitterness will haunt us long thereafter. But they've lost. The rest is spite. Accept my offer to bring your wife to Pottsville. And I will do what I can for Lieutenant Raines."

My companion removed a tear. Which disconcerted me.

I went on talking, although I might have stopped. "If you do not like Pottsville, which is a lovely town, you may do what you like once our business is established. You may take your share of the profits and carry yourself and your wife to Argentina. Or to anywhere else you have a mind to go. But come north with me now, Mr. Barnaby. It is for the best."

The big fellow had begun to weep abundantly, a response I had failed to foresee.

"Forgive me, Major Jones," he said, in a voice reduced and cracking. "I know you wants the best for all concerned. And I accepts, sir, I accepts. Speaking for myself and Magdalena. It's 'orrible kind of you."

"Nothing of the sort," I assured him. "I look upon it as a business venture. And expect a tidy profit, mind. As well as discounted goods."

Tears conquered his cheeks. I looked away. The sky outside the carriage was thrilling blue.

"It's just that I 'as grown unused to kindness," he told me.

HIS CAPTORS HAD not been gentle with Captain Bolt. His uniform was gone, replaced by rags, and his face looked as if he had gone some rounds with a pugilist. A nasty welt concealed one eye and I was not certain he retained all of his teeth. The negroes had bound his hands behind the slats of a ladderback chair, which stood in a derelict shanty under cypresses.

He was awfully pleased to see me.

"Thank God," he wailed through swollen lips. "Thank God!"

He seemed a sudden convert to the catechism.

"For the love of God, man," he begged. "Get me out of here, would you?"

"All in good time," I told him. "First, you and I must talk. And I mean plainly."

"Ask anything. Anything you want."

His guards moved closer to his chair, displaying iron muscles and broken smiles. I suspected they had enjoyed their term of authority and were not anxious to see it reach an end.

I looked about me. Besides my Christian self and Mr. Barnaby, a gamut of negroes had crowded into the cabin. The lot of them had followed our every step since our reception. Which had not been as warm as I expected. If anything, they seemed to resent my coming.

They looked to be runaway slaves and "free people of color" joined together in a common purpose, yet hesitant to mix among themselves. I suppose even negroes have their forms of snobbery.

The one thing they had in common was their temper, which was bad.

We might have been in Africa, in the twilight of that hut. Faces black and brown and beige surrounded us. Their persons did not smell of French perfume. Of course, young Bolt did not improve the aroma, since he had been left to wallow in his slops. Like the slaves upon that ship.

A beating knocks unexpected things out of a man.

"Who that, who that?" one fellow muttered anxiously. He bounced and bent, eyes jumping from place to place.

"That Gen'rul Banks, that who."

"Naw, that Gen'rul Butler, come back for his revengin'."

"Maybe it is, and maybe it ain't. But he sure one ugly white man. Little, too."

Others spoke French, I think, amid the hub-bub.

"You must all leave," I told them. "I wish to speak with the prisoner by myself."

They did not move at once. In fact, they did not move at all.

"Go on with you now. We need to speak in private."

They did not care for my request. Nor did they care for me.

Disconcerted, I turned to Mr. Barnaby, who sought to appease them in some odd vernacular. Grumbling, they took his direction and wandered outside.

At last, with great reluctance, the guards left, too. They looked me over as if they thought I deserved a chair of my own beside Captain Bolt.

Before he joined the coloreds, Mr. Barnaby took me aside for a whisper. He was not especially quiet and I suspected that he wanted Bolt to hear.

"They ain't in a trusting mood, begging your pardon. They ain't chock with good will, sir. They knows what the captain's done and they doesn't like it." He looked me up and down, more interested in my uniform than my person. "They're afraid you're going to take 'im off and free 'im, once you've got 'im in your power. He's been bragging about 'is father and 'ow important 'e is. When 'e wasn't trying to beg 'em with promises of bribes and all such like. 'E only made 'em angrier, with 'is chattering." He settled his hat farther back on his head. "They wants 'im brought to justice, Major Jones. And they ain't convinced that anybody wearing a blue coat is going to give it to 'im."

"Convince them," I said, a bit curtly.

He did not reply, but chewed his lip and left. Out in the yard, the negroes enjoyed their arguments.

"Don't waste any time, for God's sake," Bolt told me. "They're savages."

"Savages, is it?" I asked. "And are you civilized?"

"Oh, don't be an ass, Jones. Don't tease. My father's going to be unhappy enough with you as it is. Look at me. They've treated me disgracefully."

"They were only having a bit of their own back," I said mildly.

"Come on. Untie me, before they come back in. They're wild animals. Beasts."

"And what are you, Captain Bolt?" My tone grew stern. "Regard me, boy. Come down off your high horse. Or I will leave you here and walk away."

"You wouldn't do that. To a fellow white man."

"Would I not?"

"And to a brother officer."

"You are far from my brother, Captain Bolt. No matter what the Holy Bible says. Or the law of races, or military practice. Do you know what happened on the river yesterday?"

"I have no idea."

"One hundred and fifty negroes burned alive. Perhaps more. Men you meant to sell back into slavery."

To my astonishment, he looked relieved. As if he thought he and the world were well rid of the victims.

"They burned alive!" I repeated. "Can you imagine what that felt like, boy?"

"They don't feel pain the way we do."

"Do they not?"

"Jones, look. I'll see to it that my father rewards you handsomely. Forget what I said earlier. You'll be well taken care of. I promise you. Just—"

"Tell me, boy. Look at me and tell me it again. Say that they don't feel pain. That they don't hurt when they burn. Or when they are skinned alive and left for dead."

"Of course, they feel pain. So does a dog or a cat, for God's sake. But you can't seriously believe all that abolition nonsense, can you? Do you? You can't believe they're equal to a white man? That they have our faculties?"

"Perhaps it depends upon which white man we speak of. No, boy, I do not put the negro on a pedestal. But I am not certain that you belong on one, either."

"They sold out their own kind, for God's sake. That ridiculous voodoo priestess. The bucks we hired. They knew what they were doing. They enjoyed it. They took money for it."

"And does that make it right? What you have done?"

"It wasn't a question of right or wrong."

"If you are so superior, does that not give you a greater responsibility? To set them an example?"

"Jones . . . for God's sake. Don't be a self-righteous fool.
Spare me the cant. You know what we were doing? By rounding up stray niggers and getting rid of them? Do you know what
we were doing, if we could any of us be honest about it? We
were doing this country a favor. A *favor,* Jones. Good God.
What do you think's going to become of them after the war?
What's becoming of them now? They're lost. They're like little
children. Useless children. They'll never be a part of American
society. Now that they're free, they're worthless." He snorted.
" 'Free.' What does freedom mean to a coal-black savage? Tell
me what? The freedom to get drunk and sleep under a tree?"

"Yes," I said. "That, too. As well as the freedom to stand
up as a man."

"Jones, why don't you answer *my* question? What on
earth do you think's going to become of them? How could
they cope with the demands of civilization, for God's sake?
Do you think they'll be welcomed with open arms? Anywhere? South or North?"

"It will take time. I do not say it will be easy. It may take
twenty years. Or even thirty. But I believe the negro will find
his place. Along with the Irish and such."

"You're absolutely impossible! They won't be welcome
in a hundred years. Any man of sense would see it plainly."

"Why did you do it, boy?"

Outside the shack, in the handsome day, Mr. Barnaby's
voice opposed those of the darkies.

"Why did I do it?" Bolt repeated. "Why not? I told you.
We were performing a public service by getting rid of as
many as we could. Hell, why not sell them all? Officially?
Make it a government policy? Pay off the war debt and get
rid of the damned cause of the war at the same time?"

"Why did you do it? You did not need the money. Was it your idea? Mrs. Aubrey's? Your father's? Who put such a monstrous idea in your head."

"Susan Peabody."

I raised my hand to slap his vile face.

He recoiled, but smirked. "Oh, I don't mean she wanted to sell niggers to Brazil or Hispaniola. But she *did* want to ship them back to Africa, after all. Her and that fancy-boy coon who trailed her around." He smiled, revealing the loss of at least one tooth. "Jane Aubrey's no fool. She may be old as the hills, but she's no fool. She figured there was a way to make everybody happy. Susan Peabody could wave her handkerchief at her boats full of black-asses, 'Fare thee well, my noble savage' and all that holy horseshit. Then we could simply change the destination. With Miss Nigger-lover paying for the ships and the rest of it pure profit." He laughed. "They wouldn't know the difference, anyway. Cuba, Brazil, the North Pole . . . tell them it was Africa and they'd believe it."

"Who murdered Susan Peabody? You?"

"Don't be ridiculous. You know I'm smarter than that. Even now, you can't prove a thing against me. Not so that it would stick. Not with good lawyers. As for the money, I don't mind paying that back. I only took it for travelling expenses. And I didn't think they'd kill her, if you have to know."

"Who?"

"Her niggers. Her beloved niggers. Niggers, anyway."

"The 'pirates'? Your 'fishers of men'? Which was a blasphemy, boy, on top of your other sins. Was it Petit Jean and his brother thieves?"

"You've figured out a lot. Haven't you? I wonder how much, really."

"Was it them? Who killed her?"

He snickered. "Eventually. They kept her for a couple days. Before they finished with her. I expect she got to know her African pets a little better than she ever expected to."

"Because she figured out what you were doing? Is that why she was killed?"

"Sounds obvious. Doesn't it?"

"She learned of your scheme and—"

"I said it *sounded* obvious. I didn't say it was true."

I stared at him. Still bound, he sat there as if the tables were already turned. As if his father's influence had already set him free to pursue his fortune.

"Susan Peabody," he said, "wasn't the kind of person who ever figures out a damned thing. She was so wrapped up in her own ridiculous notions that she never stopped to think that anyone else might have ideas of their own. We could've shipped niggers to China for ten years and she wouldn't have noticed a thing. As long as she got to feel proud of herself and pet a wooly head every now and then."

"Then why was she killed? Her money?"

"I suppose money would've been the most sensible reason. But it wasn't that, either."

"Then why, man?"

"Her philanthropy."

"Do not you mock me, boy, or—"

"Pure philanthropy. In a sense. Look here, Jones. You've done an impressive job of following one line of yarn after another. I'd be glad to employ you myself, after the war. But you still don't think like an American. You're thinking in small, crabbed terms, as if you'd just crawled out of some dreary Welsh coal mine."

"Come to your point, boy."

"Susan Peabody was in love with her notion of sending

her black bastards back to Africa. But that's not why she came to New Orleans, you know. She just came with some vague notion of doing good. She wasn't here a month before the fanciest coon in town had talked her into supporting his scheme of sending them 'home' to Africa. Well, Jane Aubrey has more sense than any ten men of business I've ever met. Including my father. Didn't take her long to realize that Susan was flighty, that you couldn't count on her long. Last year, her zeal was devoted to shipping off negroes. Good business for all involved. Fine. But what about this year? Or the next? After she lost interest and moved on to table rapping or educating war orphans or, I don't know, Swedenborgianism? What then?"

I sat down in one of the feeble chairs vacated by the guards. I understood. The horrid genius of it made me sick to puking.

"You see it. Don't you?" Bolt asked eagerly, shamelessly, proudly. "A simple matter of business. Jane Aubrey knew enough about Old Man Peabody to know that he had one hell of a lot more stick-to-it in him than his daughter. Who might have joined a convent or taken to nursing lepers on her next crazy whim. No, Susan Peabody wasn't reliable. But her father was. It his beloved daughter was 'martyred' in pursuit of her dream of sending freed slaves back to Africa, he'd fund the business until there wasn't a pickaninny left south of the Ohio." Bolt smiled wistfully. "If you hadn't stuck your snout into things, we would've been in business for twenty years."

"You killed her. Because she wanted to do good."

"No, Jones. I didn't kill her. I told you that. And she was to blame for her own death, if you think about it in a practical way. She died because she didn't really mean it, all her meddling. She died because it couldn't hold her interest. Susan

Peabody was looking for a cause, all right. But she never would've found one that contented her. Because she didn't give a preacher's damn about people. Only about causes." I thought he would spit on the floor. Through his swollen lips. "She didn't care any more about niggers than I do."

"All right," I said, returning to my feet.

"Will you get me out of here now, damn it? Are you content?"

I nodded. "Wait here."

"Jones?"

I stepped into the late afternoon sunshine, which was so lovely it seemed to make evil impossible. As I emerged, the negroes fell silent in that ragged way a crowd has when some of the backs are turned. A lone bird called.

I strode up to Mr. Barnaby and said, "Come on with you. It will be dark when we return to town."

"But . . ."

"Come along, Mr. Barnaby. We both have much to do. And tell the negroes a thing, if you would be so kind."

He looked at me. In dread and fascination.

"Tell them," I said, "that we will not come again."

MR. BARNABY DID NOT speak as the carriage clattered along. I was not certain if he was disappointed in me or simply bewildered. The afternoon faltered. Twilight raced into night. Across black fields, lone lanterns gleamed. Watercourses shone faintly, longing for moonlight.

I had much on my conscience. And it would remain there.

At last, I said, "They mistook his identity. Their prisoner was not the man I knew. The Captain Bolt I knew has disappeared."

Mr. Barnaby thought upon the matter. Out in the darkness, the driver coaxed his horses. We had not paused to light the carriage lamps and rode in shadows as deep as any river.

Of a sudden, Mr. Barnaby said, "I expects the Bolt we knew must be in Texas by now."

"Or already in Mexico," I offered.

"Or half-way to Argentina," my friend added.

"Wherever he is," I said, "he may find justice. Although I suppose that we will never know."

"Right, sir. Right as rain. We'll never know."

I PICKED MY words when I spoke to General Banks. Condemn me for it, if you will, but I did what I thought best.

Still in uniform at the long day's end, he greeted me in his parlor with a grunt containing a multitude of questions.

"I have to disappoint you, sir," I said without delay. "I did not bring in Bolt."

He snorted. "Damn him to Hell. Just damn that boy. I hope he drowns himself out there in the swamps." And then he looked at me. With an eyebrow climbing. I was not yet accomplished as a liar and feared I had already been found out. "So you didn't find him? After all your fuss? Your note seemed pretty damned confident."

"I did not bring him back, sir."

"I *hate* to think of that bastard going unpunished."

"Perhaps," I observed, "he will find his proper punishment, one way or the other. There is a peculiar justice in the world."

"Well, you're feeling awfully philosophical. I'd expect you to be spluttering mad. That he still isn't caught. Just spitting hot, the way you usually are."

"I have done what lay in my power," I said.

He crossed his blue sleeves over his chest. "Sounds like you're giving up. Well, I'm not going to quit, Jones. All right, then. You've had your chance. Enough time's been wasted. Tomorrow morning, my troops start searching again."

"The thing is, sir . . . I believe he may already be out of our reach. If we consider—"

"We'll see about that. We'll just see about that." He unfolded his arms and began to pace. "I'm not a fool, Jones. Although you might well take me for one, given all that's happened right under my nose. I know his father's going to pull so many strings the little bastard won't get the punishment he deserves. But, in the meantime, I intend to make life as miserable for young Bolt as I can, if I get my hands on him. We'll see how he likes a military jail for a couple of months. Though the fact is that the bugger deserves to hang."

"I cannot say why," I told the general, who was digging his heels into the Turkey carpet, "but I believe he will have a nasty end. Pride comes before a fall, see. His pride will undo him. That is what I believe. His pride will prove his undoing. More surely than the worst military prison."

"I suppose we'll see," the general said idly.

"Or perhaps we won't see, sir. Perhaps we will need to take it on faith. War covers much."

"It just might cover Bolt's escape, that's the damnedest thing." Twas clear the general was a tormented man. He strode about, abusing the palm of his left hand with the fist of his right. I would have liked to tell him more, but there are times in this life of ours when a great deal is to be said for not saying a great deal.

"I have done what I could do," I repeated.

"And I suppose I should be grateful. Damn it, I *am* grateful. At least we've broken up that filthy trade of theirs. God knows, how long it might've gone on . . ."

I sensed he would soon dismiss me. For generals do not like to dwell on their failures. But the next turn of his remarks gave me a surprise.

"I suppose you'll be on the first ship back to Washington?"

"As soon as a berth is available, sir. After we have tidied things a bit. Mr. Seward will need time to fashion the matter so that it offers a comfort to Mr. Peabody. The sooner—"

"I don't suppose there's any way I could persuade you to stay on? As a member of my staff? With those new oak leaves on your shoulders, after all?"

I shook my head, though I was nicely flattered. Rare it is for a general to wish to retain a fellow who has embarrassed him. Of course, General Banks was still surrounded by Butler men and needed creatures he might consider his own.

I do not believe he liked me much. But he trusted me, more's the pity.

Well, we must have faith, and go through. Dwelling on our sins is a subtle vice.

epilogue

I HAD A DAUGHTER!

When I returned to my hotel, I found a letter waiting. One of our ships had put in with a pouch of mail, including the news that my Mary Myfanwy had given birth to a girl in January. Mother and child were healthy, for which I got down on my knees and thanked the Lord.

Twas heartening to be reminded that life goes on, despite the greed of death.

My darling and I had settled upon the names before I left. A son would have become James, but a lass was to be Angharad, a sweet Welsh name that summons lost, green hills. To our American neighbors, she might be simply Ann. But not at home, where memory warms the hearth.

Twas my mother's second name. Angharad. A name for gentle hands and gentler hearts.

And yet news of the birth brought new concerns. The autumn past I had encountered the pastor of our Methodist church under circumstances I could not approve. I would not sit again in a pew to listen to that hypocrite condemn poor folk whose sins were less than his own. That is not what good John Wesley intended.

The problem lay in the choice of a new church. My Mary and I disagreed. And though a husband must have the final word, faith should not be commanded. I had in mind a move to the Primitive Methodists, who enjoy simplicity and strictness. Mary would have none of it. She thought we should become Episcopalians. Her family were of the established church and her father, the Reverend Mr. Griffiths, had been a clergyman known throughout Glamorgan. He might have been a bishop, had his meanness been confined to those below him. My own father had been a Methodist parson, whose early death robbed hill and vale of kindness. I do not think he would have liked me deserting Christ for the English.

I would not be too hard on my beloved, but the truth is that the Episcopal Church is quite the social apogee in Pottsville. As it is elsewhere in America. I feared that, on top of our new-gained wealth, my beloved's head had been turned by aspirations. You will forgive my bluntness, but a painted church is like a painted harlot. Perhaps worse. For the Magdalene was dear to Christ, which I do not think the case with a wealthy clergyman.

Plain altars for plain hearts, say I. The highest temple will not reach to Heaven.

Well, time there would be to reconcile with my darling. Confident I was that I might reason her into agreement. Unless she sneaked about and had our daughter baptized high church in my absence. Which would have been a wicked thing to do.

How quickly we discover cracks in the bright façade of happiness.

Still, I had a daughter. And there was joy in it. Now we would be five, including Fanny.

I would have liked to leap aboard a ship that very instant. But matters wanted tidying. Nor was a vessel on orders for Philadelphia or Baltimore. It took me seven days to find a berth. Four more passed before we sailed.

There was a fuss about passages for Mr. Barnaby and his betrothed, as they were civilians. The Navy don't like giving rides for free. In the end, though, all come right. Captain Senkrecht intervened to help me, for which I am indebted to this day, and I made things nice by employing Mr. Barnaby officially. I was not certain I had that authority, but boldness favored David and the Israelites. We gentlemen chose to overlook the lass, who stayed belowdecks until we waved our farewells.

Mr. Barnaby sailed with a tear in his eye. New Orleans had been the scene of his greatest happiness and his greatest loss. And I do believe he was fond of the victuals.

We put in at Havana for the consul's mail. But there was more to our detour than diplomacy. I could smell it. Spies were everywhere about, including Europeans. The sort with flashy manners and frayed collars. Each one offered a visiting card that made him out a commercial representative. It seemed almost rude of them not to take more pains. But the Spaniard, by his nature, is not inquisitive, and the climate made even secret agents slothful.

We lingered nearly a week, feigning repairs as we kept an eye on a rumored blockade runner carrying quinine. And whispers there were in plenty of that cursed ship, the C.S.S. *Alabama*. She was spotted off Bermuda. No, she was last seen rounding Madeira. She was selling her loot in Vera Cruz. Or haunting the whaling routes between cliffs of ice.

Wherever she was, that ship was on my conscience.

But let that bide.

Havana is a pleasant town, although its energies seem much declined. Even the stevedores do not like to sweat. And the officials of Spain's empire much prefer fine uniforms to utility. They think themselves each one a maharajah. Still, it is a pretty place, although it wants a sweep and a daub of paint.

Magdalena was sufficiently well to be married. But, then, what woman is not?

She and Mr. Barnaby were joined in the eyes of God in a Roman cathedral. The decoration would have made all India blush. I stood their witness, girding my Christian loins in the face of Popery. But the thing that really put me off my ham was the Catholic priest. He made a fuss, declaiming a hundred reasons why a Protestant such as myself could not participate. I should have thought him honored that I showed.

All come right with a gold piece dropped in the poor box. The priest looked one way, I looked the other, and we may assume the Lord looked down on all.

I did not wish to stint such an occasion, so I invited the ship's officers to join myself and the couple for a supper at the finest hotel restaurant in Havana. We most of us got stomach sick, but I do not believe the Navy men held it against me. Or against Mr. and Mrs. Barnaby, who were spoony as young Romeo and his Juliet.

Two more Union vessels put into port, allowing us to sail on toward Baltimore. We had a run of wicked days on the waters, but I spent most of the voyage increasing my knowledge. Indeed, whenever I have a spare moment—and after I have spent an hour with the Bible—I believe it my Christian duty to pursue learning. We must make good use of the faculties God has given us and never forego a chance at self-improvement.

Even as a lad I liked to read. How sweet it must be to have an education! You will call me an ambitious man, but I hope my son will attend a university. It must be the finest thing in the world to spend one's youth surrounded by good books.

The officers loaned me what reading they had aboard. The choice was not especially elevated, but we must make do. So when I was not bundled in my greatcoat, staring at the pewter-colored sea and wondering if I had done more evil than good, I visited again with Lord Macaulay, who is ever of firm opinion. I let myself be reminded of the price of liberty by Mr. Motley—and of liberty's dangers by Mr. Carlyle, who is Scotch. The Navy men had no works complete, only random volumes. But I had read the missing bits before, as most men have.

I made it my purpose to read a book each day, no matter how late the lamp burned.

Mr. Prescott's works were a valued discovery. I always knew the Spaniards were a bad lot, but those Aztecs were as nasty a pack as ever turned up for their breakfast. Glad I was to learn they got what was coming to them. Grown men dancing around in feathers and cutting out living hearts. In broad daylight.

We steamed into the Chesapeake in the face of winter winds. Sleet lashed the decks as we entered Baltimore harbor. We were home. Or nearly so. And the weather almost made me miss New Orleans.

I CONFESSED WHAT I had done to Mr. Seward, our secretary of state and a fellow who knew how each dog and cat voted in New York State. I could not keep it in, see. All through the voyage, whenever I looked up from Mr. Carlyle or Mr. Motley, I saw the spectre of my rash injustice. It may seem to you too fine a point, but I did not much regret Captain Bolt's death. Yet, I rued the manner of it. I do believe the lad deserved to die. But his sentence of death had not been mine to pass. The law must be protected, obeyed and cherished. It is the noblest creation of sorry mankind.

I told Mr. Seward how I had left the lad, knowing the negroes would hang him from a tree. If not worse.

Mr. Seward, who was a banty bird no larger than myself

and a fellow of both vigor and impatience, fell into a stillness foreign to his manner. He sat behind his papersmothered desk in a morbid quiet. When he leaned back, the rasp of the springs in his chair come fierce as a gunshot.

He made a steeple of his fingertips, then touched the fleshy construction to his lips. I heard not only the bustle without his door but the slap of winter rain upon the window. Mr. Seward looked away for so long a time I felt myself forgotten.

Of a sudden, he snapped back to business, dropping his hands to the blotter on his desk.

"I swear to the Great God Almighty, Jones. If you ever go into politics, I'm getting the Hell out. Unless I'm damned sure I've got you on my side. Behind all that pious Christian blather, you're one nasty sonofabitch. I'd hate to be the man who got you riled."

He was never one for mildness of speech. Nor did I find him an accurate judge of character.

"Oh, Hell," he said, "done is done, I suppose." His face grew a look that might have been either a frown or a smile restrained. "I'm half inclined to think I would've done the same thing myself. Old Bolt was a Douglas man, anyway. Politically unreliable. No good to Lincoln, or to me. Mean, too. Cost poor Stephen plenty, with all his bullying out in Chicago back when. A man should never make an enemy he can avoid, unless he's damned sure he'll make a dozen friends in the process. Even then, he shouldn't burn his bridges."

He whacked his desk as though it wanted discipline. "Here's what we're going to do, Abel. You're going to forget you ever breathed a word to me about your last meeting with young Bolt. Far as I'm concerned, it never happened. You say it, I'll deny it. But you *won't* say it. Because you're going to forget about it yourself." He took my measure with one eye narrowed and the other opened wide. "Never spoil a victory with regrets. As long as you win, the campaign's been worthwhile. Remember that. It's as true in a man's life as it is in an election. Regrets are for people who can't make up their minds."

He drew a cigar from an inlaid box, but offered none to me. The fellow had known me long enough to recall that I shunned such vices. For his part, Mr. Seward was a chimney. His office was near as suffocating as that vault in which I had been sealed in New Orleans. He was so fond of his cigars I half expected our Navy to seize Havana.

That is a joke, of course. The United States will never seek an empire.

After lighting his roll of weeds, Mr. Seward sat back again and considered me. "I'll handle Peabody," he said. "Can't tell him half of what you've told me. Maybe none of it. I don't know. Shame you didn't at least get the money back. Would've softened the blow. But I suppose that's lost along with young Bolt." He snorted, which passed for a laugh. "Next time you go down there, I bet you'll hear all about the lost treasure of Do-Nothing Plantation. Doesn't matter. I'll figure something out, make old Peabody happy. As happy as he can be, under the circumstances. Want to make sure he's solidly behind us next year. He carries a lot of upstate voters with him. Can't have him jumping to some damned Copperhead for spite."

He stood up and began to reach across his desk to bid me farewell. Then he realized that our persons, when paired, were inadequate to bridge the expanse with dignity.

He stepped around the desk and thrust out his hand.

We clasped paws firmly. But he would not let me go when it seemed time.

"Now," he said, "what's all this foolery about you resigning your commission?"

"There is true," I told him. "I do not feel that I have more to give, sir."

He eyed me fiercely, gripping my hand with a strength you would not have credited in an older fellow.

"Suppose every damned officer felt that way? Suppose they all just up and went home? Where would we be then? You tell me that."

"I cannot speak for others, but for myself—"

"Not thinking about going into Pennsylvania politics, are you? Damned snake pit. I'd be glad to put in a word with Boss McClure and Andy Curtin."

"I do not believe that I am suited for politics."

"Horseshit! You're mean enough, that's for damned sure. And you're a grand master at convincing people you're something you're not. You even know when to wave the Bible and when to lay it aside. You're a *born* political man, Abel Jones."

"I do not mean to enter into politics."

"More's the pity." He released my hand, which smarted a bit. "Change your mind, you let me know. Andy Curtin needs all the help he can get. Damn it, go see Lincoln. He's got some news for you about that Reb lieutenant of yours. Get out of here. Or that damned Dutchman Nicolay'll be all over me again. One thing I've learned in this town—one of many, tell the truth—is that no man should keep his president waiting." He allowed himself a crafty little smile. "I wonder how long it's going to take Chase to figure that out? Tell Fred to come in, would you? Jesus Christ, I wish I was back in Albany."

Mr. Seward was right. Twas time for my appointment across the way. But just as I was about to let myself out of his office, Mr. Seward cleared his throat and called my attention back toward his person.

I saw him through a flannel veil of smoke.

"Damned lot of trouble about a couple of boatloads of negroes," he said. He sighed, although even his sighs come out like a bull's snorts. "Lincoln puts a good face on things. Hard to tell how much he really believes. Wouldn't want to sit down to a poker game with him. Myself, I'm not sure what the hell's going to come of the colored man, once he's well and truly free. You watch. Those Boston abolitionists are going to lose interest as soon as the mess is well and truly made."

It was a worrisome expression of doubt from a fellow placed so high. I might have left the office feeling glum. But Mr. Seward, bless him, lacked the mental repose for pessimism. He smiled with tobacco-ruined teeth.

"One thing's sure," he said with a spark of glee. "If the negroes ever get the vote, the sonsofbitches are going to vote Republican."

The Adventures of Abel Jones will continue!